'But why would you do this?'

'If, for no other reason, you might consider my position. It may surprise you to know that I do have some sense of honour. Well, Miss Hanwell?'

'Very well. I think I must accept your offer, my lord. I will try to be a comfortable wife.' Frances could hardly believe she was saying those words.

'You amaze me. So far all you have done is argue and refuse to listen to good sense!'

'But... I never meant...'

'There is no need to say any more. Come here.'

She stood and moved towards him. He turned her to face the light from the candles at his elbow and looked at her searchingly for perhaps the first time. Her remarkable violet eyes expressed every emotion she felt—at the moment uncertainty, and not a little shyness. It could turn out to be not the worst decision he had made in his life.

'Look at me,' Aldeborough demanded, and when she automatically obeyed he wound his hand into her hair and his lips sought hers.

* * *

The Runaway Heiress
Harlequin® Historical #811—August 2006

ANNE O'BRIEN

The Runaway Heiress

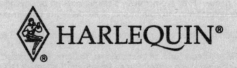

HARLEQUIN®

TORONTO • NEW YORK • LONDON
AMSTERDAM • PARIS • SYDNEY • HAMBURG
STOCKHOLM • ATHENS • TOKYO • MILAN • MADRID
PRAGUE • WARSAW • BUDAPEST • AUCKLAND

ISBN-13: 978-0-373-29411-4
ISBN-10:   0-373-29411-5

THE RUNAWAY HEIRESS

Copyright © 2004 by Anne O'Brien

First North American Publication 2006

All rights reserved. Except for use in any review, the reproduction or
utilization of this work in whole or in part in any form by any electronic,
mechanical or other means, now known or hereafter invented, including
xerography, photocopying and recording, or in any information storage
or retrieval system, is forbidden without the written permission of the
publisher, Harlequin Enterprises Limited, 225 Duncan Mill Road,
Don Mills, Ontario, Canada M3B 3K9.

All characters in this book have no existence outside the imagination of
the author and have no relation whatsoever to anyone bearing the same
name or names. They are not even distantly inspired by any individual
known or unknown to the author, and all incidents are pure invention.

This edition published by arrangement with Harlequin Books S.A.

® and TM are trademarks of the publisher. Trademarks indicated with
® are registered in the United States Patent and Trademark Office, the
Canadian Trade Marks Office and in other countries.

www.eHarlequin.com

Printed in U.S.A.

Please address questions and book requests to:
Harlequin Reader Service
U.S.: 3010 Walden Ave., P.O. Box 1325, Buffalo, NY 14269
Canadian: P.O. Box 609, Fort Erie, Ont. L2A 5X3

To George:
who encourages me with humour,
wit and understanding

Prologue

'Miss Hanwell, my lord.'

Akrill bowed stiffly and stood aside to allow the young woman to enter the room. She hesitated momentarily, aware of being the focus of attention from those awaiting her. In spite of her fiercely beating heart, she walked forward and willed herself to appear calm. From experience, she was too well aware of the many opportunities for humiliation in her uncle's house; she could not believe that she would escape unscathed from this situation, whatever the cause of the peremptory summons.

'Akrill said that you wished to see me, Uncle.' She kept her voice low and expressionless, proud of her skill in hiding the fear that had already begun to sink its sharp claws into her flesh.

'Come here, girl.' Viscount Torrington gestured impatiently. 'Come and stand here.' He pointed to the space before his desk.

She stood tall and straight before him, defiantly meeting his hard stare. She was unaccustomed to seeing him seated at his desk—he had neither liking nor aptitude for matters of business—and he appeared ill at ease as he shuffled the spread of papers before him. Aunt Cordelia sat in a straight-backed chair by the fireplace, her face stony, unsmiling, but with a glint in her eye of—what? Greed? Anticipated fulfilment? Frances could not tell. By the window, his back to her, stood Charles, her cousin. His rigid stance and deliberate distance from the proceedings promised her no comfort.

'You took your time, girl.'

'I came as soon as your message was delivered, my lord.'

'Then you should know,' Torrington continued without preamble, 'that it is all arranged.' He cast a quick glance towards his wife, who chose to remain aloof. 'In two days' time you will marry my son.'

To Frances the words seemed to reach her from a great distance. They made no sense at all. Her lips were dry and she found it difficult to form any words in reply.

'Marry Charles?' she managed eventually.

'It is a sensible and desirable family arrangement with financial advantages on both sides.' The Viscount frowned at the litter of bills and receipts. 'There will be no fuss. No guests. It will not be necessary. All the legal ends will be tied up within the week.'

'Charles?' Frances turned her eyes to her cousin in sheer disbelief. 'Do you want this?'

'Of course.' He turned from his contemplation of the bleak, unkempt gardens. His face was bland, his voice pleasing and unruffled. He allowed himself to meet her eyes fleetingly. 'It is a good settlement for all parties, you must realise. You must have expected it, Frances.' There was a hint of impatience as he registered the shock on her face.

'No. No, I did not... How could I?' A cold hand closed its fingers inexorably around her heart. 'I had thought that...' She clenched her fists in the folds of her skirts to prevent her hands trembling. 'When I reach my majority next month I will come into my inheritance—I can be independent. My mother's gift will allow me to—'

'Your inheritance is owed to your family,' the Viscount interrupted with an abrupt gesture towards one of the more official documents before him. 'Your marriage to Charles will benefit all of us.'

'No! I will not.'

Viscountess Torrington rose to her feet and approached her

niece with pitiless eyes. 'You should be on your knees in gratitude to us, Frances. We have given you a roof over your head, food, clothing for the whole of your life—and with no recompense. Your mother's high-and-mighty family wanted nothing to do with you.' She almost spat the words as she walked to stand behind her husband, in unity against Frances. 'You owe us everything. What right have you to refuse your uncle's bidding? Now it is time for you to repay us for our care.'

Care? Frances would have laughed aloud if the horror had not begun to creep through her bones, her sinews, to paralyse every reaction. All her hopes, all the plans that had helped to sustain her, had been destroyed by her uncle's words.

'But I shall be tied here for ever,' she whispered. 'I cannot bear it.'

'Nonsense, girl,' Torrington blustered and swept the papers together to signal the end of the discussion. 'The matter is now settled. You will not, of course, make any more ill-considered attempts to leave the Hall.' His fierce glance pierced Frances. 'You are well aware of the penalties for such disobedience.'

She closed her eyes briefly to shut out the brutal memories and her uncle's implacable face. 'Yes. I am aware.'

'Then get back to your work. Akrill will give you your tasks. We have guests tonight.'

Frances turned away, the nausea of panic lodged securely in her throat. In two days she would be trapped forever in this living hell.

Chapter One

Aldeborough lounged at his indolent ease in the corner of his travelling coach, braced effectively against the violent lurching with one foot on the opposite cushion, as he covered the short distance to Aldeborough Priory. He closed his eyes against the lurking headache.

A dense shadow, darker than its surroundings, stirred on the floor in the far corner of the coach. The moon fleetingly illuminated a flash of pale skin.

Was he asleep? Frances was pinning all her hopes on it. In spite of her impulsive flight from the Hall, without possessions except for the clothes she stood up in, and certainly without any forethought, she had chosen the coach with care. It had just been possible for her to make out the shield on the door panel in the glimmer from the flickering lamps—to distinguish a black falcon rising, wings outspread in flight, a glitter of golden eyes and talons on a vibrant azure field. It had to be Aldeborough—and he would be the means of her escape from Torrington Hall for ever. She shifted slightly to ease her cramped limbs, trying to breathe shallowly, to still the loud thudding of her heart that seemed to echo in her ears. If only she could remain undiscovered until they arrived at the Priory, she would have a chance to make her escape. And no one would be the wiser. No one would follow her and force her...

The Marquis moved restlessly. Frances shrank back into her corner, tensed, rigid, until his breathing relaxed again. She wriggled her spine against the edge of the hard cushion. It promised to be a long journey. She closed her eyes in the dark.

Suddenly a hand shot out with astonishing speed to grasp the folds of her cloak and pull her violently from floor to seat where the grip transferred itself like a band of steel to her arm. She gasped at the pain from that pressure on her previous injuries and failed to suppress a squeak of shock and outrage at such manhandling.

'What the hell…?' Aldeborough drew in his breath sharply, reining in his impulse to strike out at the intruder with vicious blows to head and body as he realised his initial mistake, and he tucked a pistol back into its pocket behind the cushions. He laughed softly. 'Well, now. Not an opportunist footpad after all. A lady, no less. I knew my luck was still in. What are you doing in my carriage at this time of night—or morning, as I suppose it now is?'

'Running away, sir.' It would be safer, Frances decided, to stick to the truth as much as she was able. Her voice held a touch of exhaustion, which she could not disguise, strained with other tensions that he could only guess at.

'Ah. From Torrington Hall, I presume. Do you work there?'

'Yes, sir. In the kitchens.'

'And do you suggest that I should turn the coach around and return you to your employers? Would they welcome such an open-handed gesture from me? I doubt it.' He mused on his reluctance to return to Torrington Hall, to put himself out for an errant kitchen wench.

'No, sir.' She tried to keep the fear that he would do exactly that from her voice. 'I doubt it would be worth your while. I…I am only a servant and will not be missed.'

'If not, why did you find it necessary to hide in my coach? There appears to be some logic here that escapes me. Do you suppose it is the brandy that is impairing my thought processes?' he enquired conversationally.

'Undoubtedly, sir.'

'So what do I do with you now?'

'You could take me to the Priory, sir.' She sank her teeth into her bottom lip as she awaited his answer.

'I could. That would be the easiest course of action. I could hand you over to Mrs— Devil take it! I have forgotten her name—my housekeeper. It would be far better to work for me at the Priory than for Torrington, I would wager.'

'It could not be worse, sir.' Her agreement was low, little more than a whisper. He almost missed her words.

There was silence for a short time as Aldeborough contemplated his unexpected travelling companion.

'Come and sit beside me.'

'I would rather remain here, sir.' I must remain calm, she told herself as panic began to build inside her. 'We seem to be travelling at great speed.' She was wedged into the opposite corner, hanging on to the straps and as far away from him as possible.

Without more ado and once more taking her completely by surprise, Aldeborough leaned forward, grasped her wrist and pulled her ungently on to the seat next to him. She pushed herself back against the cushions only just preventing herself from falling against him or on to the floor as the onside wheel of the coach fell into a pothole. A full moon illuminated the carriage interior, but it was sufficiently erratic to allow the lady to hide with some relief her flushed cheeks and lack of composure. And, even more importantly, her identity.

'So, we have established, to some extent at least, why you are here…so now—' his gaze fixed on her unwaveringly like that of a hunting falcon '—tell me your name.'

'Molly Bates, sir,' she replied instantly in flat tones, thinking furiously and casting truth to the winds, intensely aware that he still had possession of her wrist and his grasp was burning a bracelet into her flesh.

'Well, Molly Bates, I am afraid that I am drunk.'

'Yes, my lord.' Although there was no indication other than the reckless fire in his eyes and a slight slurring of his words. 'I believe you will have a fierce headache tomorrow.' She felt a certain malicious satisfaction in her prediction of his forthcoming discomfort.

'I wouldn't take your bet.' He grinned, showing a flash of white teeth. 'Let me look at you.'

He pulled her closer, then released her wrist to push her chin up with his free hand and smooth the dark curls that, with unconfined waywardness, tended to hide her features. She was unable to meet his eyes, which searched her face, but sat stiffly, willing herself not to pull away from him. It might be wise, she told herself, if she did nothing to provoke him. He was clearly capable of reckless and unpredictable behaviour. She could expect no pity here if he were to discover the truth. She trembled beneath his fingers.

'How old are you, Molly?' he asked abruptly.

'Almost one and twenty, my lord.'

With his thumb he traced her fine cheekbones and then along the line of her jaw. Instinctively, she pulled back with an intake of breath in protest.

'I won't hurt you, you know.' His voice was as smooth and rich as velvet. 'Not if you are obedient, of course. You must understand that there is a price to pay if a pretty girl takes refuge uninvited in the coach of a gentleman to whom she has not been introduced.'

She swallowed convulsively—she could not mistake his meaning. 'Yes, my lord.' In spite of her intentions to do nothing to antagonise him, she made no attempt to hide the wealth of bitterness and disgust in her reply.

Aldeborough laughed softly; it made Frances's blood run cold.

Suddenly his hand tightened in her hair and he drew her inexorably closer. 'You have spirit, Molly. I like that.'

Before she could respond he bent his head and crushed her mouth with his own. She struggled, her hands braced with all her strength against his chest, but to no avail against the power of his well-muscled body. His arm encircled her shoulders with uncompromising strength, his lips merciless, assaulting her senses, demanding a response. She was deter-

mined to make none, but the play of his tongue along her
bottom lip sent a shiver through her body. When he deepened
the kiss she fought to prevent her mouth from opening treach-
erously under his. She had never been kissed before and was
horrified at the turmoil of emotions that surged within her.

Then he released her as suddenly as he had pounced.

'How dare you!' Anger won when she had recovered
enough breath to speak, and decided, however waywardly,
that she did not care to be kissed in that manner.

'Dare?' He laughed. 'Since you were unwise enough to
accompany me, to throw yourself on my mercy, then I call
the tune. And you, darling Molly, must dance to it. You will
very soon discover that I *have* no mercy. Besides, why the
outrage? I am sure that you have been kissed before, as pretty
as you are. Surely you have a greasy-handed sweetheart in
the kitchens of Torrington Hall?'

'No. I do not. And I gave you no leave to call me by my
name.' As she could think of no other response, she took
refuge in formal dignity, however much it might sit at odds
with her role of the hapless Molly. 'You are no gentleman,
my lord!'

Again Aldeborough laughed, but with an edge of cynicism.
'Perhaps not, my dear, but I vow I shall be a good lover.' As
Frances gasped in renewed outrage, he tightened his hold and
his mouth claimed hers once more.

This time the movement of the carriage came to Frances's
rescue. As the violent lurching flung them apart Frances took
the opportunity to throw herself into the opposite corner
again, where he viewed her with some amusement.

'Perhaps this is not the most comfortable situation for a
seduction scene.' His mouth smiled, but she knew that she
could look for no sympathy from this man. 'We can wait
until we reach the Priory. Don't look so apprehensive, Mistress Molly. I will not touch you. Not until we get home,
anyway.'

He wedged himself into the corner of the coach again,
leaned his head back on the cushions and closed his eyes.
Within a few minutes his breathing had deepened and he

appeared to be asleep, leaving Frances the opportunity to review the traumatic events of the past hour. Her uncle's callous indifference. The decanter of port as spoilt and fractured as her dreams of love and happiness. She closed her fingers around the stained napkin on her wrist and fought back the tears that threatened to engulf her. You are just tired, she told herself. Tomorrow you will be free of all this. She turned her head and studied her heedless rescuer in the fitful moonlight. It was a handsome face, not classically fair like her cousin, but a face which compelled her attention. His skin was tanned from time spent outdoors in all weathers. He had a straight, masterful nose, a firm chin and hooded eyes, hidden now in sleep, but as uncompromisingly grey as a northern winter sea. Lines of cynicism were engraved between nose and mouth— that mouth, unsmiling now but with such beautifully sculpted lips. His hair was thick and dark with a tendency to wave, his brows equally dark and well marked. It was a face of flat planes, and strong angles, a face used to authority and command and to keeping its own secrets. It betrayed no softness—indeed, in repose his face was stern and austere. He would be a dangerous man to cross in spite of the indolent manner she had witnessed tonight.

Her eyes dropped to his hands and she shivered at the memory of his touch. She had never been touched like that by any man. They were elegantly long fingered, but they had left her in no doubt as to their strength. She shivered again and clasped her arms around her for comfort as her spine was touched by an icy finger of fear. What had she got herself in to? She had left without considering the wisdom of her actions—anything to escape from Torrington Hall, a callously contrived marriage and the never-ending authority of her uncle. A means of escape had been offered and she had leapt to grasp it with both hands. But at what cost? Frances found that her tired brain could come to no conclusion at all. She touched her cold fingers to her mouth, which still burned from a stranger's unwanted kisses.

Chapter Two

Aldeborough was woken by Webster, his valet, drawing back the heavy brocade curtains of his bedroom. The sun streamed in, indicating the hour to be well advanced, but the Marquis, in exquisite suffering, merely groaned and pulled the sheet over his head.

'It is almost noon, my lord. I have brought your hot water.' Webster ignored a second groan and set about collecting his lordship's clothes from where he had carelessly discarded them on the floor.

Aldeborough struggled back on to the pillows, clasping his hands to his skull. 'Oh, God! What time did I arrive home last night?'

'I couldn't say, my lord. Your instructions were, if you recall, that I should not wait up for you. I presume that Benson put you to bed, my lord.'

Aldeborough grimaced. 'Yes. I remember.' He winced at the memory of his coachman's less than gentle ministrations as he had manhandled him through the door and up the main staircase. He sat up, gasping at the instant throb of pain behind his eyes. 'What a terrible evening. What possessed me to spend it with Torrington's set? If it hadn't been for Ambrose's powers of persuasion, I would not have gone back there.'

'No, my lord. Very wise, if I might say so. Which clothes

shall I lay out for you today, my lord?' Webster had served Aldeborough for many years, since before his recent inheritance of the title when, as Captain Lord Hugh Lafford, he had fought with some distinction in the Peninsular Campaign, and thus his valet knew better than to indulge in trivial conversation after a night of hard drinking. Not that the Marquis had drunk quite so much or as often then, he mused. But things had changed, particularly since Lord Richard had died.

The Marquis took a cup of coffee from Webster and sipped cautiously as his brain began to function again amidst the lingering effects of brandy. 'I have appointments on the estate today with Kington. Buckskins, top boots and the dark blue coat, I think.'

'Yes, my lord.' Webster coughed discreetly. The Marquis, well used to his valet's mannerisms, raised an eyebrow enquiringly, wincing at the effort.

'Mrs Scott has instructed me to tell you that the young lady has breakfasted and is now waiting your lordship's convenience in the library.'

Webster enjoyed the resulting silence.

'Who?' Aldeborough's voice was ominously calm.

'The young lady, my lord. Who accompanied you home last night.' Webster carefully avoided looking in Aldeborough's direction.

'My God! I had forgotten. The kitchen wench. I remember remarkably little about the whole of last night!' he admitted ruefully, running his fingers through his dishevelled hair. But enough of his memory returned like the kick of a stallion to fill his mind with horror. 'Is she still here?'

'Yes and no, my lord, in a manner of speaking.' Webster kept the smile from his face.

Aldeborough frowned and then lifted a dark eloquent eyebrow.

'Yes, she is still here, my lord. But, no, she is not a kitchen wench. She is quite unquestionably a lady.'

'I see.' There was a long pause. 'I was drunk.'

'Yes, my lord. Mrs Scott thought it best that the lady remain until you had risen. She was most intent on leaving the Priory, but had not the means.'

Aldeborough flung back the bedclothes, ignoring the clutches of his towering headache.

'Thank you, Webster. I know I can always rely on you to impart bad news gently! Kindly tell—I can't remember her name!—the young lady that I will have the pleasure of waiting on her in half an hour.'

'Yes, my lord,' and Webster shut the door quietly behind him.

Only a little after thirty minutes later the Marquis quietly opened the door into his library. In spite of the speed, he was immaculately turned out, from his impeccable buckskins to his superbly cut coat of dark blue superfine. His top boots were polished to glossy perfection and the arrangement of his cravat reflected the hand of a master. His hair was now brushed into a fashionable windswept disarray *à la* Titus. He was perhaps a little pale with a distinct crease between his brows, the only indication of the excesses of the previous night. For a moment he stood motionless, perfectly in control, his cold grey gaze sweeping the room.

At first it appeared to be empty, but then he saw that the lady awaiting him was seated at his desk in the window embrasure. Her back was to the light, the sun creating a golden halo round her dark hair. It made a pleasing picture surrounded as she was by polished wood, richly tooled leather volumes filling the shelves, heavy velvet curtains and Turkey carpets in deep reds and blues covering the floors. The furniture was old, acquired by earlier generations of Laffords, heavily carved oak chairs and sidetables with no pretence to elegance or fashion. A fire crackled and spat in the vast fireplace to give an air of warmth and welcome. It was his preferred room at the Priory and he rarely shared it with anyone. But now he was faced with an uncomfortable interview with a lady who had somehow involved him in a scandalous escapade that was none of his making. The lady's face was in shadow, but he could see that she had borrowed a pen and was concentrating on a sheet of paper before her. As he watched, the lady, still unaware of his presence, and completely oblivious to the magnificence of her surroundings, threw the pen down with a despairing sigh and buried her face in her hands.

He closed the door quietly behind him and walked forward towards her. Hastily she raised her head and, with a guilty start, rose to her feet to stand slim and straight before him. Against his better judgement, he bowed slightly, and instantly regretted it.

'Good morning, ma'am. I trust you slept well.'

'Yes, my lord. Forgive me…' she indicated the pen and paper '…I was only—'

Aldeborough shook his head and drew in his breath sharply. 'My housekeeper has looked after you?'

'She has been very kind.'

'You have breakfasted, I trust?'

'Thank you, yes.'

Aldeborough abandoned the banal in exasperation and some self-disgust. 'Damnation, ma'am! This is a most unfortunate situation!' He swung round to pace over to the windows, which opened onto the stone-flagged terrace, and stared out over the park with a heavy frown between his eyes. The silence stretched between them, but he could think of no constructive comment. He turned his head to see that she was still standing in the same place, very pale with faint shadows beneath her eyes and tension in every line of her body. And on her cheekbone flared the vivid discoloration of a bruise.

'You are not Molly Bates,' he accused her, the frown still in place. 'My valet informed me that I had escorted a lady here last night and I see that he was quite correct. It is unfortunate that I did not come to the same conclusion before I allowed you to foist yourself on me! I confess that I remember little of what occurred last night with any clarity.'

'Indeed, you warned me of that, sir.'

'But…of course, I know who you are…' his gaze focusing on the ugly wound marring her fair skin '…you are the wretched girl who showered glass and inferior port over everyone within ten feet of you!'

She made no reply, simply waited with downcast eyes for his next reaction.

'So, if you are not Molly Bates, whoever she might be, who are you?' He failed to hide his impatience at her lack of response to a potentially explosive situation.

'I am Viscount Torrington's niece, my lord.'

'His niece? The heiress? I find that very difficult to believe.' His eyes surveyed her slowly from head to foot, taking in every imperfection in her appearance. They were, Frances decided, as cold and predatory as those of the hunting falcon on his coat of arms.

'It is true!' Frances clenched her teeth, lifting her chin against the arrogant scrutiny. 'Viscount Torrington is indeed my uncle. The fact that you thought I was one of the servants has nothing to do with it.'

'You clearly have an excellent memory, ma'am.'

'The entire episode is etched on my memory for ever, sir. I need hardly say I did not enjoy it.' Her flat tones did nothing to hide the barely controlled emotion as the horror of the previous night reasserted itself. The memories flooded back.

As they did for the Marquis, in terrible clarity.

It must have been very late. Certainly after midnight. The fire had long since disintegrated into remnants of charred wood and ash and no one had thought to resurrect it from the pile of logs on the hearth. Candles flickered in the draughts, casting the far corners of the dining room at Torrington Hall into deep shadow, but failing to hide threadbare carpets and curtains and a general air of neglect. That is, if any of those present had been interested in his surroundings. Half a dozen men in various stages of inebriation and dishevelment were seated round the central table where the covers had been removed some time ago and empty bottles littered the surface, testimony to a hard drinking session.

They had spent a bone-chilling but successful day, hunting across Torrington's acres, and had accepted an invitation from their host to eat at the Hall. They had dined meagrely—Torrington kept a poor table—but drunk deep so the company was past the stage of complaint. Lord Hay was asleep, his head slumped forward onto his folded arms. Sir John Masters studied his empty wine glass with the fixed intensity of a cat contemplating a tasty mouse. Sir Ambrose Dutton exchanged reminiscences of good runs over hard country with Torrington and his son, Charles Hanwell. The Marquis of Aldeborough, somewhat introspective, lounged completely at his ease in his chair, legs stretched out before him, booted ankles crossed. One hand was thrust deep into the pocket of his immaculate buckskin breeches, the other negligently twirled the stem of his wine glass, half-full of liquid that glinted ruby red in the guttering flames.

Burdened with a heavy tray of decanter and bottles, Frances entered the room in Akrill's wake. She had no interest in the proceedings, in the affairs of the men who completely ignored her presence. Exhaustion from her long hours in the kitchen imprinted her delicate skin with a grey wash and she was still frozen into her own world of hopeless misery, resulting from the shattering plans for her future.

Torrington, eyes glittering, the candlelight etching deep lines of thwarted ambition on his ageing face, raised his hand to indicate a refill of the empty glass at his elbow. Akrill nodded. Frances lifted the decanter to carry it from sideboard to table where her uncle waited, arm still outstretched in demand. She reached his chair and leaned to pour liquid into his glass. To her horror, without warning, the heavy decanter slipped from her tired fingers to explode in a shower of crystal shards and vintage port at her feet, splashing herself and Torrington indiscriminately with blood-red drops.

He turned on her with the venom of a snake. 'You clumsy fool, girl. Look what you've done. You'll pay for this!'

He lashed out in frustrated anger, the back of his hand making contact with her cheek in a sharp slap that brought the room to silence. Frances flinched, silently, swallowing the sudden flash of pain, and would have retreated, but caught her heel in the worn carpet and fell amidst the sparkling ruin at Aldeborough's feet. For a long moment, no one reacted, gripped by the exhibition of very public and casual cruelty, as Frances slowly pushed herself to her knees, hoping that the encroaching shadows would hide the worst of her embarrassment and humiliation. If she could only reach the door before her uncle drew any further attention to her…

A cool hand took hold of her arm and pulled her gently but firmly to her feet. 'Are you hurt?'

She shivered at his touch. 'No. I am quite unharmed, my lord.'

Aldeborough surveyed the girl before him with a faint stirring of pity as she tried ineffectually to brush the stains and slivers of glass from her skirts. Not a kitchen wench, he presumed from the gown she wore, despite its lack of style and elegance, but a poor relation, destined to a life of charitable poverty and dependence in the Torrington household. An unenviable destiny. His fleeting impression was of dark lashes, which veiled her eyes and cast shadows on her pale cheeks, and dark hair carelessly, hopelessly confined with a simple ribbon, falling lankly around her neck. Her fingers, he noted as he raised her to her feet, were ice cold and, although her voice was calm, carefully governed, her hand trembled in his and her cheek already bore the shadow of a bruise from Torrington's ill temper. Aldeborough became aware that he had been staring fixedly at the girl for some seconds when she pulled her hand free of his grasp to step backwards away from him. He continued to watch her, sufficiently sober to register that she appeared quite composed. Perhaps she was unaware that her fingers, now clasped so tightly together, gleamed white as ivory in the gloom.

'There is blood on your wrist and hand.' His eyes might be hard, grey as quartz, but his voice was gentle with a compassion that she had never experienced in her life and the firm touch of his fingers steadied her. 'I believe that you may have cut yourself on the glass. Akrill—' he gestured to the hovering butler '—perhaps you could help the girl. She appears to have injured herself.'

He thinks I am one of the servants! Frances fought back

the hysterical laughter that rose in her throat and threatened to choke her. *That is what I will be for the rest of my life. How can I escape it?* For the first time she raised her eyes to Aldeborough's, desperately, in a silent plea, for what she did not know, but he merely released her into Akrill's care before resuming his seat at the table and refilling his glass from a bottle of claret.

'Well, Aldeborough. What did you think of my grey hunter? A better animal than any in your stables, I wager.'

Torrington's words caught Frances's attention as she stood patiently for Akrill to wind and secure a napkin as a temporary bandage around her bleeding wrist. Aldeborough! Oh, yes! She had heard of him in spite of her seclusion in Torrington Hall away from fashionable society. Titled. Wealthy. Owner of magnificent Aldeborough Priory. A reputation for hard drinking and gambling and, with his title and fortune, one of the most eligible bachelors on the Matrimonial Mart. But a man at whom mothers of unmarried daughters looked askance, for he was not above breaking hearts with cruel carelessness.

'Most impressive, my lord. Excellent conformation. Good hocks. He took the hedges in style. I do not suppose you would be prepared to sell him?'

'At a price I might!' Torrington slumped back in his chair, fast sinking into morose despair as he faced his own private disaster. 'I am near ruin, cleaned out, everything gone except the entailed property. We shall have the local tradesmen knocking at the door, demanding payment before long.'

'Father!' Charles intervened, grasped Torrington's arm with a little shake as if to bring him to his senses and awareness of their guests. 'This is neither the time nor place to discuss such matters.' His attractive features carried lines of strain around eyes and mouth. His embarrassment was evident in his clipped tones.

'Everyone knows!' Torrington shook off the grasp impatiently. His clenched fist hammered on the table. 'Not a secret any longer. The horses are my only hope.' Then a sly smile curved his lips. 'But I shall come about. You'll see.' His words slurred as he slopped more wine into his glass and drank deeply.

'What's this, Torrington?' Sir Ambrose raised his eyebrows. 'Hopes of a fortune to rescue you from dun territory? Or is it the wine talking?' The mockery was evident in his smile.

'That's it. A fortune.' The Viscount rubbed his hands together in greedy anticipation. 'I have a niece—an heiress. She will restore our fortunes and then we shall come about. She will marry Charles—this very week. No one will look down on the Hanwell family then!'

'I congratulate you.' The sneer on Aldeborough's face was unmistakable. 'It must be a great comfort to you to see your restitution.'

'*You* would not understand—with your fortune!' Torrington's lips curled into an unpleasant snarl.

'Very true.'

'You were very fortunate in your inheritance, my lord.'

'Indeed.'

Tension vibrated in the room, raw emotion shimmering between the Marquis and his host. It could be tasted, like the bitter metallic tang of blood. Aldeborough appeared to be unaware of it. He searched in his pockets and drew out a pretty enamelled snuff box with gold filigree hinges and clasp, which he proceeded to open with elegant left-handed precision, apparently concentrating on the quality of the King's Martinique rather than Torrington's barbed words.

'Of course, we were devastated by your brother's death,' the Viscount continued in silky tones.

'Of course.' Aldeborough replaced the snuff box and picked up his wine glass. Sir Ambrose, watching the developing confrontation, found himself clenching his fists as he contemplated the possibility of the Marquis dashing the contents in Torrington's face and the ensuing scandal.

Instead the Marquis calmly raised the glass to his lips and turned his head, suddenly aware of the girl standing so still and silent by the door, her eyes fixed unwaveringly on him. He noted her extreme pallor, catching her gaze with his own, to be instantly struck and taken aback by the blaze of anger in her night-dark eyes. Was it directed at him? Unlikely—yet the tension between them was clear enough. Why should a dowdy servant or poor relation display such hostility, such bitter disdain, especially when he had been sufficiently concerned for her welfare to pick her up off the floor? But her hands had been so cold, her eyes filled with such intense emotion… Even now he caught a faint sparkle on her cheek. He shrugged. Perhaps he was mistaken. Perhaps he had drunk more than he thought—his imagination and the guttering candles were playing tricks. He had had enough of Torrington's company, his shabby hospitality and his scarcely veiled innuendo for one night. It would be wise to leave now, before he so far forgot himself as to insult his host beyond redemption. Although the temptation to do so was almost overpowering.

He abruptly pushed his chair back from the table and rose to his feet.

'Much as I have enjoyed your company, gentlemen, I believe that it is time I took my leave.' He moved with elegant grace, giving no hint of the alcohol he had consumed, unless it was the slight flush on his lean cheeks and his carefully controlled breathing.

Ambrose rose too to grasp Aldeborough's shoulder urgently before he could reach the door.

'You can not go like this, Hugh. It is the middle of the night, for God's sake. Are you driving your curricle? You will most likely end up in a ditch.'

'Do you think so?' For a moment Aldeborough froze, the expression on his face anything but pleasant. Memory of a curricle, overturned and broken, its driver sprawled lifeless beside it, lashed at him, the pain intense. And then, by sheer force of will as Ambrose winced at his own thoughtless and insensitive remark, the Marquis relaxed. 'No. I have the coach with me. And there is a full moon. I shall be at Aldeborough Priory in less than an hour.' He smiled cynically. 'Your concern for my safety does you credit, my dear Ambrose.'

'Hugh, you know I did not mean… I would never suggest…'

Aldeborough shook his head and managed a brief smile as he turned away.

He paused by the door to view the assembled company and bowed with a graceful mocking flourish. 'I wish you goodnight, gentlemen,' and then, with a sudden frown, 'I am heartily sorry for your niece, my lord Torrington. She deserves better.'

Without a further backward glance, and no thought at all to the unfortunate dark-haired girl who had incurred Torrington's wrath, he left Torrington Hall. Indeed, by the time he made his farewell, she had vanished from the room.

Frances Hanwell blinked, brought sharply back to her present surroundings by the sound of Aldeborough's harsh voice.

'But if you are Torrington's niece, his heiress, why in heaven's name were you playing the role of kitchen drudge?' In a flare of emotion, exacerbated by his throbbing head, the Marquis promptly abandoned the polite words of social usage and spoke from the heart to interrupt his own and Frances's bitter recollections. 'And why in hell's name did you need to hide yourself in my coach and take flight from your home?'

'I do not wish to discuss the matter, my lord, except to say that I believed that I had no option in the circumstances.'

'What circumstances?'

She merely shook her head.

'You are not making this easy! What is your name?'

'Frances Rosalind Hanwell, sir.'

He took a turn about the room and returned to confront her, so far forgetting himself as to run his fingers through his hair. 'I should have taken you back, Miss Hanwell. Returned you to your uncle.'

'I would not have gone. I will never go back. I would have thrown myself from the coach first.' The dramatic words were delivered with such calm certainty that for a moment he was robbed of a reply and simply stared at her in icy disapproval. In spite of her outward composure she had picked up the quill pen again, clasping it in a nervously rigid grip so that he saw there was ink on her fingers. She was taller than his recollection. And why had he not remembered her eyes? They were a deep violet and at present even darker in the depths of anger and despair.

'Have you no idea, Miss Hanwell, of the potential scandal you have caused? The obligation you have put me under? The harm you may have done to your own name?' The edge to his voice was unmistakable, but she did not flinch.

'Why, no. You are under no obligation, my lord. I merely used your coach—a heaven-sent opportunity—as a means to an end. No one will know that I am here.'

'I wager that your butler does! Akrill, isn't it? Don't tell me that you did not ask him to help you to leave the house undetected. I would not believe you.'

She bit her lip, her face even paler as she recognised the truth in the heavy irony.

'Servants gossip, Miss Hanwell. Everyone at Torrington Hall last night will know that you left with me and spent the night unchapearoned under my roof. What has that done for your reputation? Destroyed it, in all probability. And what sort of garbled nonsense Masters and Hay will spread around town I do not care to contemplate.'

'I did not think. It was just—' she sighed and dropped her gaze from the brutal accusation in his fierce stare '—it was simply imperative that I leave.'

'You have made me guilty of, at best, an elopement,' he continued in the same hard tone. 'At worst, an abduction! How could you do something so risky? Apart from that, you do not know me. You do not know what I might be capable of. I could have murdered you. Or ravished you and left you destitute in a ditch. You were totally irresponsible!'

'If I leave the Priory now, no one need ever know.' Anger spurted inside her to match his. 'I do not deserve your condemnation.'

'Yes, you do. And you cannot leave. Where would you go?'

'Why should you care? I am not your responsibility!'

'It may surprise you to know, Miss Hanwell, that I have no wish to be seen as a seducer of innocent virgins!' The muscles in his jaw clenched as he tried to hold his emotions in check.

'I am so sorry.' Frances turned her face away. 'I did not mean to make you so angry.'

Aldeborough poured a glass of brandy and tossed it off. His anger faded as quickly as it had risen. She needed his help and probably suffered from enough ill humour at Torrington Hall. The stark bruise and Torrington's obvious lack of restraint told its own story.

'Do not distress yourself.' He took a deep controlling breath and released it slowly in a sigh. 'Let us attempt to be practical.' And then, 'I remember the dress,' he remarked inconsequentially.

'I can understand that you would,' came a tart rejoinder. 'It is hideous and once belonged to my aunt—many years ago, as you can probably tell.' Her gaze was direct, daring him to make any further comment on the unattractive puce creation with its laced bodice and full skirts. 'And I believe it looks even worse on me than it did on her!'

'Quite. Never having had the honour of meeting Viscountess Torrington in that particular creation, I feel that I am unable to comment on the possibility.' He retraced his steps across the library to his desk and held out his hand towards her in a conciliatory gesture. 'Please sit down, Miss Hanwell. As you must realise, it is imperative that we broach the matter in hand and discuss your future.' She ignored his gesture and instead fixed him with a hostile glare; he leaned across the desk and took her hands to remove the pen from her. Her hands, he noted, apart from being ink splattered, were small and slender but rough and callused, her nails chipped and broken. Around her wrists—so delicate—were cuts and abrasions where she had fallen on the glass. He released them thoughtfully and flung himself into the chair on the opposite side of his desk.

'What were you writing?'

'A list of my options.'

He picked up the sheet of paper and perused it. It was depressingly blank. 'I see that you have not got very far.'

'If that is a criticism, I am afraid my thoughts were all negative rather than positive possibilities. But I will not return to Torrington Hall.'

'We have to consider your reputation, Miss Hanwell.' He looked down at the pen, a frown still marring his handsome features. 'You do not seem to understand that the scandal resulting from last night's events could be disastrous.' He abandoned the pen with an impatient gesture and leaned back to prop his chin on his clasped hands. 'I believe I can accept your reluctance to return to your uncle's house,' he continued, 'but have you no other relatives to turn to?'

'No.' She raised her chin in an unaccommodating manner. 'My parents are dead. Viscount Torrington is my legal guardian.'

'Then we must take the only recourse to protect your reputation.' His face was stern and a little pale. 'It is very simple.'

'And that is, my lord? I am afraid the simplicity has escaped me.'

'You must accept my hand in marriage, Miss Hanwell.'

'No!' Her reaction was immediate, if only more than a whisper.

He raised his eyebrows in surprise. Most young ladies of his acquaintance would have gone to any lengths to engage the interest of the Marquis of Aldeborough. But not, it seemed, Miss Hanwell.

'It is not necessary for you to sacrifice yourself, my lord,' she qualified her previously bald refusal. Paler than ever, there was only the faintest tremor in her voice. 'I am sure there must be other alternatives. After all, nothing untoward occurred last night, my lord.' She blotted out the memory of his drunken kisses. 'You were overcome by the effects of too much of my uncle's brandy.'

'Be that as it may, Miss Hanwell,' he replied with some asperity, 'I am afraid that my reputation is not such that polite society would give me the benefit of the doubt. And besides, as you have admitted, you have no other relatives who would give you shelter.'

She turned her head away. She would not let him see the tears that threatened to collect beneath her eyelids. 'I could be a governess, I suppose,' she managed with hardly a catch in her voice.

'Are you qualified to do that?' he asked gently, uncomfortably conscious of her unenviable position.

'I doubt it. I am simply trying to be practical.'

'But unrealistic, I fear. Can you play the pianoforte? Speak French or Italian? Paint in water colours? All the other talents young ladies are supposed to be proficient in? My sister frequently complains of the unnecessary trivia that appears to be essential for a well brought-up young lady.'

She could not respond to the hint of humour in his observation. Her situation was too desperate. She might, against her wishes, be forced by circumstances to return to Torrington Hall. It was too terrible to contemplate. 'No, I cannot. Or embroider. Or dance. Or…or anything really. My own education has been…somewhat lacking in such details.' The tears threatened to spill down her cheeks in spite of her resolution to deal with her predicament calmly and rationally. 'There is no need to be quite so discouraging, my lord.'

'I was trying to be helpful. What can you do?'

'Organise a household. Supervise a kitchen.' Frances sighed and wiped a finger over her cheek surreptitiously. 'How dreary it sounds. Do you think I should consider becoming a housekeeper?'

'Certainly not. You are far too young. And who would give you a reference?'

Frances sniffed and moved from the desk to sit disconsolately on the window seat. 'Now you understand why my list had not materialised.'

'Miss Hanwell.' Aldeborough came to stand before her. 'I hesitate to repeat myself or force myself upon you—something which you apparently find unacceptable—but there really is only one solution. Will you do me the honour of marrying me?'

She was surprised at the gentleness in his tone, but still shook her head. 'You are very considerate, but no.' She closed her mind to the despair that threatened to engulf her. 'I have an inheritance that will be mine in a month when I reach my majority. That will enable me to be independent so that my life need not be dictated by anyone.'

'How much? Enough to set yourself up in your own establishment?' Aldeborough's eyebrows rose and his tone was distinctly sceptical.

'I am not exactly sure, but it was left to me by my mother and I understand it will be sufficient. My uncle's man of business has the details. It was never discussed with me, you see.'

'But that still does not answer the problem of the scandalous gossip which will result. Your reputation will be destroyed. You will be ostracised by polite society. You *must* marry me.'

'No, my lord.' She pleated one of the worn ribbons on her gown with fingers that trembled slightly, but her voice was steady and determined. 'After all, what does it matter? I have never been presented, or had a Season, and it is not my intention to live in London society. How can gossip harm me?'

Aldeborough sighed heavily in exasperation, surveying her from under frowning black brows, allowing a silence charged with tension to develop between them. In truth, she was not the wife he would have chosen, brought up under Torrington's dubious influence, incarcerated in the depths of the country with no fashionable acquaintance or knowledge of how to go on in society. And yet, why not? Her birth was good enough in spite of her upbringing. Certainly she lacked the finer points of a lady's education, by her own admission, but did that really matter? She appeared to be quick and intelligent and had knowledge of the running of a gentleman's establishment, albeit threadbare and lacking both style and elegance. Aldeborough watched with reluctant admiration the tilt of her head, the sparkle in her eye as she awaited his decision, and fancied that she would soon acquire the confidence demanded by her position as Marchioness of Aldeborough. She had spirit and courage in abundance, as he had witnessed to his cost, along with a well-developed streak of determination. And, he had to admit, an elusive charm beneath the shabby exterior. The Polite World would gossip, of course, on hearing that a mere Miss Hanwell, a provincial unknown, was to wed the highly eligible Marquis of Aldeborough, but since when had *he* cared about gossip?

Besides, as his mother took every opportunity to remind him, perhaps it was time that he took a wife. As he knew only too well, life was cheap—he owed it to his family to secure the succession. If Richard had lived... He deliberately turned away from that line of thought. It did no good to dwell on it.

But far more importantly, he could not in honour abandon this innocent girl to the consequences of her ill-judged flight. He frowned at her, his expression severe. It was all very well for her to shrug off the social repercussions, but a young girl could be damaged beyond remedy by the cruel and malicious tongues of the *ton*. It was in his power to save her from social disaster, and duty dictated that he should. It was really as simple as that. Her vulnerability as she sat silently in his library, refusing his offer of marriage, contemplating the prospect of a bleak future alone, touched his heart and his conscience. He had made his decision and he would do all in his power to carry it out. But he feared that to convince the lady in question of the necessity of this marriage would prove a difficult task.

'I do not accept your argument.' He finally broke the silence, his voice clipped, his tone encouraging no further discussion. 'You have not thought of the implications and in my experience they could be, shall we say, distressing for you. But I have a meeting with my agent that I must go to—I have already kept him waiting. We will continue this conversation later, Miss Hanwell. Meanwhile, my servants will look after your every need. You have only to ask.' He lifted a hand to touch her cheek where the dark bruise bloomed against her pale skin, aware of a sudden urge to soothe, to comfort, to smooth away the pain. He drew back as she flinched and wished that she had not.

'No further discussion is necessary, I assure you, sir. I would not wish to keep you from your agent.' She tried for a smile without much success, hoping that her pleasure from his touch did not show itself on her face.

'You are very obstinate, Miss Hanwell. How can you make any plans when you have nothing but the clothes you stand up in?'

She could find no answer to this depressingly accurate statement, and merely shook her head.

'I must go.' Aldeborough possessed himself of her hand and raised it to his unsmiling lips. He left the library in a sombre mood. He did not expect gratitude from her, of course—after all, he had to admit, apparently, that he had some role in the disaster—but he did expect some co-operation. His sense of honour demanded that he put right the desperate situation that he had so unwittingly helped to create.

Chapter Three

'Lady Torrington has called, ma'am. I have explained to her that his lordship is unavailable, but she has insisted on seeing you. I have shown her into the drawing room.' Rivers, Aldeborough's butler, bowed, his face expressing fatherly concern. 'Do you wish to see her, ma'am?'

Frances felt her blood run cold in her veins and a familiar sense of panic fluttered in her stomach. Since Aldeborough's departure to keep his appointment with Kington she had enjoyed a number of solitary hours in which to contemplate her present situation. It had made depressing contemplation. Mrs Scott had provided her with a light luncheon, which she had no appetite to eat, and she was now taking advantage of his lordship's extensive library. Her education might have been limited, but she had been free to make use of her uncle's otherwise unused collection of books and normally Aldeborough's possessions would have been a delight. But not even a magnificently illustrated tome on plants and garden design, which should in other circumstances have enthralled her, had the power to deflect her mind from the present disaster.

'Will you see Lady Torrington, miss?' Rivers repeated as Frances hesitated.

'Yes. Of course,' she stammered. On one thing she was adamant. As she had informed Aldeborough, she would not go back to Torrington Hall. So the sooner she confronted her aunt, the better.

'And shall I bring tea, ma'am?' Rivers enquired. 'You might find it a useful distraction.' His smile held a depth of understanding.

'Yes, please.' She smiled shyly. 'You are very kind.'

Frances found Viscountess Torrington seated before the fire in the drawing room. Encouraged by Rivers's tacit support, she squared her shoulders, took a deep breath and advanced into the room. Its furnishings paid more attention to fashion than the library, with matching chairs and a sofa in straw-and-cream striped silk brocade, but it had the chilly atmosphere of a room not much used. It seemed to Frances an appropriate place for this unlooked-for confrontation with her formidable aunt.

'Aunt Cordelia.' She forced her lips into a smile. 'I did not expect to see you here.'

Her ladyship, she noticed immediately, had dressed carefully for this visit, no doubt intent on making an impression on Aldeborough. Her stout frame was draped in a green velvet three-quarter-length coat with silk braid trimming. A matching turban with its single ostrich plume, black kid half-boots and kid gloves completed an outfit more suitable for London society than country visiting. Her curled and tinted hair, glinting red in the sunlight, would have taken her unfortunate and long-suffering maid not a little time and effort to achieve the desired result, but nothing could disguise the lines of discontent and frustrated ambition round her cold blue eyes and narrow lips. If she was disappointed not to meet Aldeborough, she gave no sign as Frances entered the room.

'I dare say, but something has to be done to sort out this unfortunate situation. And I did not think it wise to leave so delicate a matter to Torrington. The outcome, if it became widely known, could be disastrous for all of us—' She broke off abruptly. Her words might be conciliatory towards

Frances, but her voice was harsh and peremptory, her gaze on her niece full of contempt.

'What is it you intend to do, Aunt?' Frances cautiously sat on the edge of a chair facing her.

'I have come to take you home. We can hush up the matter and continue as if nothing happened. Whatever might have happened here last night.'

'Nothing *happened*,' Frances answered calmly enough, but remembered Aldeborough's warning.

'I am afraid the world will not believe that. Aldeborough's reputation is too well known. There must be some plain speaking between us here, Frances. He might be rich, handsome and a prize in the matrimonial stakes—I cannot deny it—but it is also well known that no woman is safe from him, no matter what her class. And as for his brother's untimely death—the least said about that the better. But that is not our concern. Your reputation will be in shreds if we do not take immediate action, and that can only reflect badly on the whole family. What possessed you to run away and to throw yourself into Aldeborough's path? Of all men you could not have made a worse choice, you little fool. It is imperative that you come home with me now.'

'I am amazed at such concern, Aunt. I have to admit that I am unused to my feelings being shown such consideration.'

Her aunt ignored her sarcasm, fixing her with a stony stare as if she might will her into obedience. 'You will return with me to Torrington Hall. Charles has agreed to marry you at once as was planned. Nothing need change our arrangements.'

'Poor Charles! Should I be grateful for this, Aunt?'

'Of course. No one else will marry you after this escapade, that is certain. It will be impossible to keep it secret. All those so-called friends of your uncle, gossiping as soon as they are in their cups. It is too salacious a story to keep to themselves.'

'But I don't choose to marry. When I come into my inheritance I will be able to—'

'Your inheritance, indeed!' Lady Torrington broke in sharply. 'Don't deceive yourself, my dear. It is only a small annuity. Your mother's family cast her off when she married your father. There is not much money there, I am afraid. You have no choice but to come home with me.'

Frances held tight to her decision despite her body's reaction to her aunt's words. She wiped her damp palms surreptitiously on her skirts. She had, after all, never disobeyed her aunt so blatantly before.

'I am sorry to disappoint you, but no.' Frances was adamant.

'You foolish, stubborn girl.' Lady Torrington surged to her feet, to intimidate Frances as she remained seated. 'You have always been difficult and ungrateful. Are you really expecting that Aldeborough will marry you? A nobody when he can have the pick of the *ton*? Don't fool yourself. You will not trap him into marriage. You don't know the ways of the world. He will abandon you with a ruined name and no one to support you.'

'You appear, madam, to have remarkably detailed knowledge of my intentions.'

Neither lady had heard the door open. There stood Aldeborough, coldly arrogant, quickly assessing the situation, aware of the momentary shadow of relief that swept across Frances's face as she turned her head towards him. He executed a graceful bow and strolled over to stand beside Frances. As she rose nervously to her feet he took her hand, tucking it under his arm, and pressed it firmly when she made a move to pull away.

'Perhaps I should inform you that I have asked your niece to do me the honour of becoming my wife.' A smile touched his mouth momentarily, but his eyes remained cold and watchful.

Lady Torrington's eyes narrowed, lips thinned. 'You must know that she is not yet of age. You do not have Torrington's permission.'

'With respect, I do not give that for his permission.' He snapped his fingers. 'After her treatment at Torrington's hands, Miss Hanwell has expressed a preference that she should not return to Torrington Hall. It is my intention to fulfil that wish.'

'I do not know what you intend to imply about her up-bringing or what she has seen fit to tell you. I would not put too much weight on her honesty, my lord.' The Viscountess's eyes snapped with temper as she glanced at her niece. 'Frances must return home to her family. You will hear from my husband, sir.' She pulled on her gloves, clearly ruffled, but refusing to give way.

'Indeed, my lady. I am at his service. Perhaps you will stay for tea?'

'No, I thank you. I hope you know what you are doing, Frances. You would be wise to heed my warnings. I would be sorry if the story of your abduction of my niece was to become common knowledge, my lord.'

Aldeborough felt Frances's hand quiver in his grasp and try to pull free, but he merely tightened his hold and smiled reassuringly down at her.

'Abduction? I think not.' His smile, Frances decided, held all the sincerity of a cat releasing a mouse, only to pounce a second time. 'If it does, my lady, I might be compelled to enlighten our acquaintances about Torrington's role in the events. It is perhaps not good *ton* for a guardian to subject his ward to a lifestyle unfit for a servant, much less to make her the object of unseemly abuse. I would advise you of the foolishness of attempting to threaten me—or my future bride.'

'Then good day to you, my lord.' Viscountess Torrington inclined her head in false civility, bosom heaving in righteous indignation, an unattractive patch of colour high on her cheekbones. 'As for you, Frances, I hope that you do not live to regret this day. Unfortunately you were always headstrong and selfish, in spite of all the care we lavished on you!' In a swirl of outraged velvet and ostrich plumes, Lady Torrington left, sweeping past Rivers, who had materialised to bow her out of the room.

* * *

'So! You are headstrong and selfish, are you?' Aldeborough smiled as Frances grimaced. 'And what warnings were those? Or can I guess?'

'Only your dark and dreadful reputation, sir.'

He grinned, a sudden flash of immense charm that gave Frances insight into why so many misguided members of her sex were willing to be beguiled by the Marquis of Aldeborough. She chose to ignore the fact that it made her own heart beat just a little more quickly and put it down to the effects of her aunt's harsh destruction of her character.

'What I do not understand,' mused Frances, 'is why she was so determined to take me back. At best I was treated as a poor relation, at worst as the lowest of the servants. There was never any love in my upbringing. Only duty. And why should Charles consider marrying me if my reputation is so besmirched?' A slight frown marred the smoothness of her brow. Aldeborough was moved by a sudden inclination to smooth it away with his fingers. He resisted the temptation. Matters were difficult enough.

'That is not something for you to worry about. It is no longer necessary.'

'You are very kind. And, indeed, I am honoured, but you need not marry me. The mistakes of a night—my mistakes— should not be allowed to blight the rest of your life.'

'I was thinking of the rest of *your* life, Miss Hanwell.'

Frances raised her eyes to search his fine-featured face, touched by the compassion in his voice, but seeing little evidence of it in his expression. *No man had the right to have such splendid eyes*, she thought inconsequentially. Dark grey and thickly fringed with black lashes. But they held no emotion, certainly no warmth or sympathy, merely a cold, calculating strength of will.

She shook her head. Before she could reply, Rivers entered the drawing room again on silent feet and coughed gently.

'Sir Ambrose Dutton, my lord.'

Aldeborough turned to greet his friend, instantly recognised by Frances as one of her uncle's guests from the previous night. Her heart sank even further, if that were possible.

She could not face such an embarrassing encounter yet with someone who had witnessed her shame.

'Excuse me, my lord. Sir Ambrose.' She dropped a curtsy and followed Rivers from the room with as much dignity as she could muster, the enormity of her situation finally hitting home as she became uncomfortably aware of the cynical and knowing amusement curling Sir Ambrose's lips at the very moment he saw her unmistakably in deep and intimate conversation with his host.

'Well, Ambrose? Was I expecting you to drop by this morning?' Aldeborough's expression was a hard won study in guilelessness.

Ambrose's brows rose. So that was how he wished to play the scene. So be it. 'Yes, you were. How's your head, Hugh?' He cast his riding whip and gloves on to a side table. 'You don't deserve to be on your feet yet after Torrington's inferior claret.'

'If it's any consolation, my head is probably worse than yours.' He grimaced and threw himself down into one of the armchairs. 'I hope I don't look as destroyed as you do!'

'You do, Hugh, you do!' He paused for a moment—and then plunged. 'Forgive me for touching on a delicate subject. But why is Miss Hanwell apparently in residence at the Priory? It would appear that you had a more interesting night than I had appreciated.'

'You do not know the half of it!'

'So are you going to tell me?' Exasperation won. 'Or do I have to wring it out of you?'

'Why not?' Aldeborough took a deep breath, rubbed his hands over his face as if to erase the unwelcome images, and proceeded to enlighten Sir Ambrose on the events of the night.

'And so,' he finished, 'I brought her here, too drunk to think of the consequences. Although I am not sure of the alternatives since we were halfway to the Priory before I discovered her. I suppose I could have turned round and taken her straight back to Torrington. Still…' There was more than a little self-disgust in his voice as he glanced up and frowned at Ambrose. 'It was not well done, was it?'

'No.' Ambrose, as ever, was brutally frank. 'It is always the same—too much alcohol and you can be completely irrational. And as for the girl, throwing herself in your way so obviously. Was she worth it?'

'Show some respect, damn you!' Aldeborough surprised his friend by surging to his feet, rounding on him in a sudden whiplash of temper. 'Do you really think I would seduce an innocent young girl?'

'Probably not. Probably too drunk.'

Aldeborough relaxed a little, bared his teeth in the semblance of a grin, admitting the truth of it. 'You should know—I have asked Miss Hanwell to marry me.'

Ambrose paused as the significance of this statement sank in. 'Forgive me. I didn't realise. But, Hugh!' He rose to his feet, took a hasty turn about the room and returned to stand before the fireplace. 'Don't let them trap you into marriage. You wouldn't want to be connected with the Torrington set. And apart from that, she would not seem to have much to recommend her. She is no beauty.'

'No, she is not. But I believe that she needs a refuge. I can provide one.' Aldeborough turned away with weary resignation. 'What does it matter? As my loving mother would tell you, it is high time I took a wife and produced an heir to the Lafford estates. Any girl would marry me for my wealth and title. At least Miss Hanwell is not a fortune hunter.'

'What makes you so sure? Torrington would be more than happy to get his hands on your money through his niece. He probably put her up to it.'

Sardonic amusement flitted across Aldeborough's face. 'I am certain that Miss Hanwell is no fortune hunter, because so far she has refused my offer.'

'I don't believe it!' Ambrose stared in amazement.

'Oh, it is true. And, I might tell you, it has been quite a blow to my self-esteem to be turned down!'

* * *

The third stair from the bottom creaked loudly under her foot. Frances froze and held her breath, listening intently to the silent spaces around her. Nothing. Clutching her cloak about her with one hand and a bandbox containing her few borrowed possessions with the other, Frances continued her cautious descent. The splendidly panelled entrance hall, its polished oak floorboards stretching before her, was deserted—she had planned that it was late enough for all the servants to have retired. A branch of candles was still burning by the main door, presumably now locked and bolted, but it made little impression on the shadowy corners. If she could make her way through to the kitchens and servants' quarters, surely she could find an easier method of escape—an unlocked door or even a window if no other means of escape presented itself.

After her rapid exit from the drawing room earlier in the day, she had remained in her room, pleading a headache, and submitting to the kindly ministrations of Mrs Scott. It had become clear to her through much heartsearching that she must not only make some decisions, but act on them before she was drawn any further into the present train of events over which she appeared to have less and less control. She had allowed herself a few pleasant moments of daydreaming, imagining herself accepting Aldeborough's offer to allow her to live a life of luxury and comfort. She pictured herself taking the *ton* by storm, clad in a cloud of palest green gauze and silk. When she reached the point of waltzing round a glittering ballroom with diamond earrings and fashionably curled and ringletted hair, in the arms of a tall darkly handsome man, she rapidly pulled herself together and banished Aldeborough's austere features and elegant figure from her mind.

He has no wish to marry you, she told herself sternly. *He is only moved by honour and duty and pity.* She had had enough of that. And since when was it possible to rely on any man when his own selfish interests were involved? It would be far more sensible to find somewhere to take refuge for a few short months until she reached her twenty-first birthday and the promise of her inheritance.

There was only one avenue of escape open to her. She would make her way to London and throw herself on the mercy of her maternal relatives. Even though they had turned their concerted backs on her mother following what they perceived as a *mésalliance*, surely they would not be so coldhearted as to abandon her only daughter in her hour of need. Frances knew that it was a risk, but she would have to take it. London must be her first objective and here she saw the possibility of asking the help of the Rector of Torrington. If nothing else, he might, in Christian charity, be persuaded to lend her the money to buy a seat on the mailcoach.

So, having made her plan, determinedly closing her mind to all the possibilities for disaster, Frances continued to tread softly down the great staircase. She reached the foot, with its carved eagles on the newel posts, with a sigh of relief. All the doors were closed. There was an edge of light under the library door but there was no sound. Frances pulled up her hood, turned towards the door which led to the kitchens and sculleries and tiptoed silently across. Soon she would be free.

'Good evening, Miss Hanwell.'

Frances dropped her bandbox with a clatter and whirled round, her breath caught in her throat. Aldeborough was framed in silhouette, the light behind him, in the doorway of the library. In spite of the hour he was still elegantly dressed, although stripped of his coat, and held a glass of brandy in one hand. Her eyes widened with shock and she was conscious only of the blood racing through her veins, her heart pounding in her chest. Aldeborough placed his glass on a side table with a sharp click that echoed in the silence, then strolled across the expanse between them. He bent and with infinite grace picked up her bandbox.

'Perhaps I can be of assistance?' he asked smoothly.

Frances found her voice. 'You could let me go. You could forget you have seen me.' Her voice caught in her throat, betraying her fear. She tried not to shrink back from him against the banister, from the controlled power of his body and the dark frown on his face. Memories forced their ugly path into her mind, resisting her attempts to blot them out.

'I could, of course, but I think not.' Aldeborough held out his hand imperatively. She felt compelled by the look in his eyes to obey him and found herself led to the library, where he released her and closed the door behind her.

'You appear to be making a habit of running away. Might I ask where you were planning to go?' he enquired. 'Surely not back to Charles!'

'I will never go back to that house!' Frances replied with as much dignity as she could muster in the circumstances. 'I had decided to go to the Rector of Torrington for help.'

'And how were you intending to get there?' He allowed his eyebrows to rise.

'Walk.'

'For ten miles? In the pitch black along country roads?'

'If I have to.' She raised her head in defiance of his heavy sarcasm.

'I had not realised, Miss Hanwell, that marriage to me could be such a desperate option. Clearly I was wrong.'

Frances could think of no reply, intimidated by the ice in his voice.

He dropped her ill-used bandbox on to the floor and approached her, raising his hands to relieve her of her cloak. Her reaction was startling and immediate. She flinched from him, raising her arm to shield her face, retreating, stumbling against a small table so that a faceted glass vase fell to the floor with a crash, the debris spraying over the floor around her feet. She turned her head from him and buried her face in her hands, unable to stifle a cry of fear as the dark memories threatened to engulf her.

'What is it? What did I do?' Aldeborough's brows snapped together. Frances shook her head, unable to answer as she fought to quell the rising hysteria and calm her shattered breathing.

'Forgive me. I had no intention of frightening you.' He grasped her shoulders in a firm hold to steady her, aware that she was trembling uncontrollably, when an unpleasant thought struck him.

'You thought I was going to hit you, didn't you? What have I ever done to suggest that I would use violence against you?' There was anger as well as shock in his voice. 'Tell me.' He gave her shoulders a little squeeze in an effort to dislodge the blank fear in her eyes. It worked, for she swallowed convulsively and was able to focus on his concerned face.

'It's just that once I tried to run away,' she managed to explain. 'It was a silly childish dream that I might escape. But I was caught, you see...and...'

'And?'

'My uncle punished me—whipped me—for disobedience. He said I was ungrateful and I must be taught to appreciate what I had been given. I'm sorry, I didn't mean to...' Her voice trailed away into silence, her expression one of utmost desolation.

Aldeborough gently removed her cloak from her now-unresisting body. He steered her away from the shards of glass, scattered like crystal tears on the polished wood, and pushed her into a chair before the dying embers of the fire. He poured a little brandy into a glass and handed it to her.

'Here. Drink this. Don't argue, it will make you feel better—it's good for shock amongst other things. Although, from experience, I do not advise it as an aid to helping you forget.' The touch of sardonic humour at his own expense allowed Frances to relax a little and do as she was told. 'Now, tell me—what did you expect the Rector to be able to do for you that I couldn't?'

She sipped the brandy again, which made her eyes water, but at least it stilled the shivering. 'I thought that he would lend me some money to enable me to reach London where I could make contact with my relations,' she explained.

'But you told me you didn't have any.'

'It is my mother's family.' She was once more able to command her voice and her breathing. 'They disowned her, you understand, when she married my father. They thought he was a fortune hunter and too irresponsible, so they cut all contact.'

'Your father, I presume, was Torrington's younger brother. I never knew him.'

'Yes. Adam Hanwell. I remember nothing of him—he died when I was very young.'

'And your mother?'

'She was Cecilia Mortimer. She died just after I was born. That's why I was brought up at Torrington Hall and Viscount Torrington is my guardian.'

'As I understand it, the Mortimers are related to the Wigmore family.'

'Yes. My grandfather was the Earl of Wigmore. I hoped the present Earl would not abandon me entirely if he knew I was in trouble. I believe he is my cousin. Do you think he would?'

'I have no idea. And I cannot claim to be impressed by your plan.' Aldeborough ran his hand through his hair in exasperation. 'If they refuse to recognise you, you will be left standing outside their town house in Portland Square, with no money and no acquaintance in London. Or what if they are out of town and the house is shut up? Do you intend to bivouac on their doorstep until they return? It is a crazy scheme and you will do well to forget it.'

'It's no more crazy than you forcing me into a marriage I do not want!' Frances was stung into sharp reply. 'You have no right to be so superior!'

'I have every right. There is no point in making the situation worse than it is already.'

Frances sighed. 'It seemed a good idea at the time.' She raised her hands in hopeless entreaty and then let them fall back into her lap. 'Do you think I could be an actress?'

'Never!' Aldeborough laughed without humour. 'Every emotion is written clearly on your face. I cannot believe that you would actually consider such a harebrained scheme.'

'No. But desperation can lead to unlikely eventualities.' She tried to smile, but it was a poor attempt.

The Marquis noted the emotion that shimmered just below

the surface, prompting him to take the brandy glass from her. She did not resist. 'Let us be sensible.' He returned to lean his arm along the mantelpiece and stirred the smouldering logs with one booted foot. 'I think that we are agreed that you have very few realistic options. There is no guarantee of a favourable welcome from Wigmore. You have spent far too long unchaperoned in my house—don't say anything for a moment—so you *must* marry me as it is the only way to put things right.'

'But—'

'No. Think about it! Your reputation will be secure. We can call it a runaway match, if you wish. We saw each other at some unspecified event—unlikely, I know, but never mind that—and fell in love at first sight. With the protection of my name no one will dare to suggest that anything improper occurred. You will be able to escape from your uncle and a life that clearly has made you unhappy. And, until your own inheritance is yours, you can have the pleasure of spending some of my wealth and cutting a dash in society.'

It sounded an attractive proposition. For long moments, Frances considered the clear, coldly delivered facts, smoothing out a worn patch on her skirt between her fingers. She raised her eyes to his, trying to read the motive behind the unemotional delivery.

'But why would you do this? You don't want a wife. Or, certainly, not me.'

He laughed harshly. 'You are wrong. I do need to marry some time. It is, of course, my duty to my family and my name to produce an heir. So why not you?'

Frances blushed. 'I am not suitable. I am not talented or beautiful or fashionable… Your family would think you had run mad.'

He shrugged carelessly. 'You come from a good family and the rest can be put right. And it will stop my mother from nagging me. What do you say? Perhaps we should deal very well together. Your view of marriage seems to be even more cynical than mine! As a business arrangement it could be to the benefit of both of us.'

Frances still hesitated.

'If for no other reason, you might consider my position. It may surprise you to know that I do have some sense of honour.' His lips curled cynically. 'I would not wittingly seek to be accused of abducting and ruining an innocent girl. I do have some pride, you know.'

Frances took a deep breath. 'I had not thought of that.'

'Then do so. You are not likely to be the only sufferer here.'

'But you already have a reputation for—' She came to a sudden halt, embarrassed by her insensitive accusation.

'Ah. I see.' His voice was low and quiet. 'So my damnable reputation has reached even you, Miss Hanwell, shut away as you have been in Torrington Hall. Do you expect me to live up to it? One more victim from the fair sex will make no difference, I suppose. Perhaps I should seduce you and abandon you simply to give credence to the rumours spread by wagging tongues. I am clearly beyond redemption. Perhaps I should not insult you with an offer of marriage.'

Frances could not answer the bitter mockery or the banked anger in his eyes but simply sat, head bent against the wave of emotion. When he made no effort to break the silence that had fallen, she glanced up at him. The anger had faded from his face, to be replaced by something that she found difficult to interpret. If she did not know better, she might have thought it was a moment of vulnerability.

'Well, Miss Hanwell?'

'Very well. I think I must accept your offer, my lord. I will try to be a conformable wife.' She could hardly believe that she was saying those words.

'You amaze me. So far all you have done is argue and refuse to listen to good sense.'

'But…I never meant…'

'There is no need to say any more. Come here.' She stood and moved towards him. He turned her to face the light from the candles at his elbow and looked at her searchingly for perhaps the first time, turning her head gently with his hand beneath her jaw. Her skin, a trifle pale from the emotions of the past hour, had the smooth translucence of youth. Her eyebrows were well marked and as dark as her uncontrolled curls. Her remarkable violet eyes expressed every emotion she felt—at the moment uncertainty and not a little shyness. But equally he had seen them flash in anger and contempt. She had a straight nose, a most decided chin and softly curving lips. She was not a beauty, he thought, but a little town bronze would probably improve her. It could turn out to be not the worst decision he had made in his life. She dropped her eyes in some confusion under his considered scrutiny.

'Look at me,' he demanded and when she automatically obeyed he wound his hand into her hair and his lips sought hers. It was a brief, cool caress, but when Aldeborough lifted his head there was an arrested expression on his face. Frances had steeled herself against his kiss, but was now aware that his grasp showed no intention of loosening. She drew in a breath to object, but before she could do so Aldeborough placed his hand gently across her lips and shook his head.

'I must request your pardon if you are displeased. Are you displeased, Frances Rosalind? It seemed to me that we should seal our agreement in a more…ah…intimate manner, even if it is to be a marriage of convenience. What do you say?'

Frances was unable to say anything coherent or sensible and was overcome with a sudden anger both at Aldeborough's presumption and her own inability to respond with a satisfactory reply that would leave him in no doubt of her opinion of men who forced themselves on defenceless women, even if they had just agreed to marry them.

'Let me go!' was all that she could manage and thrust at his shoulders with her hands as she remembered the humiliation of his embrace in the coach. It was to no avail. Her confusion obviously amused Aldeborough for he laughed, tightened his hold further and bent his head to kiss her once more. But this was different. Aldeborough's mouth was demanding and urgent, melting the resistance in Frances's blood whether she wished it or not. It was as if he was determined to extract some reaction from her beyond her previous reluctant acceptance. And she was horrified at his success. Her instinct was to resist him with all her strength, but she was far too aware of the lean hardness of his body against hers beneath the thin lawn of his shirt. His hands caressed her hair, her shoulders, sweeping down her back to her waist. Her lips opened beneath the insistent pressure of his and she found herself responding to a surge of emotion, a lick of flame that warmed her skin and spread through every limb. Her hands seemed to move of their own accord, to grasp his shoulders more tightly rather than to push against them... when suddenly she was free. As quickly as Aldeborough had taken possession of her he released her and stepped away.

Frances was left standing alone in a space, feeling strangely bereft and unsure of what to say or do next. Her mind was overwhelmed by the enormity of what she had just done. Could she really have agreed to marry this man against all her previous intentions and heart searching? She felt a chill tremor touch her spine at the prospect. Of course there would be advantages—she knew that. It would remove her finally and irrevocably from her uncle's authority and without a stain on her reputation. Comfort and luxury would be hers for the asking with a guaranteed entrée into fashionable society. But Marchioness of Aldeborough? She pressed a hand to her lips to suppress a bubble of hysterical laughter that threatened to erupt at the unlikely prospect. And what on earth would his family think? It was all very well for him to deny any difficulty, with typical male arrogance, but she would have to face a mother-in-law who would doubtless see her as a common upstart who had wilfully trapped her son into a disastrous marriage.

A marriage of convenience, he had implied. Very well. He was driven by an impeccable impulse to protect her—as well as the desire for an heir. But she could not quite banish from her mind the leap of fire in her blood when he had kissed her, touched her. It might be a mere legal formality for him, but she was suddenly afraid of her own response. It would be better if she never allowed him to see the effect of his devastating smile on her heart or his elegant hands on her skin. She must never forget that it was duty and honour which drove him, whatever her own feelings might be.

She received no help as she stood, lost in her deliberations. Aldeborough merely stood and watched her quizzically, a faint smile on his lips.

'I think I should tell you that my uncle will not give his permission for our marriage,' she managed eventually in a surprisingly calm voice. 'Will that present us with a problem?'

'A special licence will solve the matter,' the Marquis stated, chillingly dismissive. 'We claim to have a bishop in the family so we may as well make use of him. It can all be arranged discreetly and quickly.'

'Thank you.' She swallowed at her presumption. 'There is just one thing.'

'What now, Miss Hanwell? You are very difficult to please, but I am sure it will not be an insurmountable problem.'

'You are laughing at me, my lord. I wish you would not,' Frances exclaimed crossly. 'It is just that I will not marry you in this dress.'

'Then I must do something about it, mustn't I?'

Frances blinked at the casual acceptance of her demand.

'I shall need to leave you for a few days to make arrangements,' he continued. 'I must ask you to promise that you will not try to run away again.'

'Or?' She could not resist the challenge to the implied threat.

'Or I might have to lock you in your room until I return.' Frances was left under no illusion that he would do exactly as he said.

'It is not necessary.' She sighed, with resignation to a stronger force. 'I will marry you. I will not run away.'

'Thank you.' He tossed off the rest of the brandy in his glass. 'I am relieved. Go to bed, Miss Hanwell. It has proved to be a long and tiring day, for both of us!'

Chapter Four

'Aldeborough! At last!' The voice was as smooth and cool as chilled cream. 'I have expected you home any time this past week. How could you have missed the Vowchurches' drum? I understand from Matthew that you have been at the Priory.'

Lady Beatrice, the Dowager Marchioness of Aldeborough, and despising every moment of her loss of influence in the Lafford household since the death of her husband, put aside a piece of embroidery and rose from her chair in her cream-and-gold sitting room. She waited with not even a hint of a smile for Aldeborough to approach, extending an elegant hand in greeting and allowing him to kiss her cheek. She was slim and dark and exquisitely dressed in a cream gown that perfectly complemented her surroundings. It was strikingly obvious from whom Aldeborough had inherited his features and colouring. She had the same cold grey eyes that at present were fixed on Frances, who had entered the room somewhat hesitantly in Aldeborough's wake.

Aldeborough saluted his mother's cheek with filial duty and grace, but the lack of affection between them was as clear as her neglect in returning the embrace.

'And who is this?'

'I have been at Aldeborough, ma'am, as you are well aware. There was some necessary estate business.' He turned back to Frances who had apprehensively come to a halt just inside the doorway. 'I wish to introduce you to Frances, Miss Hanwell.' He took her hand to draw her further forward into the room. 'Miss Hanwell, ma'am, is now my wife.'

The silence in the room was deafening. Frances continued to cling to Aldeborough's hand. She had rarely felt so alone as she did at that moment under the razor-sharp scrutiny. She made a polite curtsy and awaited events with trepidation as her ladyship's features froze into perplexed disbelief. The temperature dropped to glacial.

'Forgive me, Hugh.' Her ladyship ignored Frances. 'Perhaps I misunderstood? This is your *wife*?'

'Indeed, ma'am. We were married three days ago at Aldeborough.'

'But I had no idea. Who is she?' Her cold eyes raked Frances in an icy sweep from head to foot and apparently found nothing in the exercise to please her.

'Her guardian is Viscount Torrington. I met her at Torrington Hall.'

'Really?' Her lips thinned. 'I am afraid that I find this difficult to grasp, Aldeborough. How could you have conducted your marriage in such a clandestine fashion? You might have considered my position. Think of the scandal…the gossip. How will I face Lady Grosmont at her soirée this evening?' Her face paled with anger as she considered the repercussions. 'Surely as your mother I could expect a little consideration?'

'There will be no scandal, ma'am.' Aldeborough remained coldly aloof and unemotional. 'If anyone should comment, you will assure them that Frances and I had a…a long-term understanding and we were married quietly in the country for family reasons. The death of a distant relative, if you find the need to give a reason to anyone sufficiently ill mannered to comment.'

'*I* will assure them? I do not wish to lend my support in any way to this unfortunate liaison.'

'I had hoped for more of a welcome for my bride,' Aldeborough commented gently, with a hint of warning in his quiet voice that his mother chose to ignore.

'Richard, of course, would always have considered my opinion when making such an important decision in his life. He was always so thoughtful and conscious of his position as the heir. I might have hoped that *you*—'

'There is no advantage in pursuing that line of thought,' Aldeborough interrupted harshly. Frances saw a muscle in his jaw clench and his hold of her hand tightened convulsively, making her draw in her breath.

'And what of Penelope? What will she think?'

'What should Miss Vowchurch think? I cannot see what my marriage has to do with her.' He was once more in command, his fingers relaxing their grip.

'It has everything to do with her, of course. She has been expecting an offer from you. After Richard's death it was understood—'

'I am afraid that it was not understood by me. I have never given Miss Vowchurch any indication that I would make her an offer of marriage.'

'It has always been understood between our families. You must know that after Richard died you took no formal steps to end the connection.' Lady Aldeborough was implacable, refusing to let the matter rest. 'And now you have married this…this *person*. Who is she?'

Frances looked on as if she were watching a scene in a play at which she was a mere observer with no role for herself. There was clearly little love lost between Aldeborough and his mother and she herself was now provoking another issue between them. A bleak wave of despair swept over her to add to the weariness. After she had spent three days alone at Aldeborough Priory, the Marquis had returned and she had been thrown into a flurry of activity. First her marriage, followed immediately by three days of exhausting travel to reach London. And now this. How foolish she had been to hope that Lady Aldeborough might accept this sordid arrangement with equanimity. Indeed, it was even worse than she had anticipated. She wished Aldeborough had given her some warning. Obviously he had seen no need to do so, which depressed her even further.

'A penniless nobody who has trapped you into marriage.' Her ladyship was continuing her diatribe as if Frances was not present. 'How could you! Is there no way this marriage could be annulled? Or dissolved?' Lady Aldeborough's face was white with anger.

A delicate flush stained Frances's cheeks. With the haste and inconvenience of the journey following immediately after their marriage, there had been neither opportunity nor, it would appear, inclination for intimate relations between herself and the Marquis. For which, all things considered, she was heartily relieved. But would he betray her to his mother?

'No, Mother. It is not possible. Your suggestion is insulting in the extreme to both Frances and myself. I think you should consider what you're saying before you speak again.' Aldeborough turned towards Frances, his face a polite mask. 'Forgive me, Frances. I wish I could have spared you this, but it had to be faced.' He led her to a chair by the window looking over the square. 'Perhaps if you would sit here for a little while…'

As he returned to shield her from further recriminations, her mind was free to travel back over the previous days. She remembered as in a dream standing in Aldeborough Church in the grey light of early morning with a special licence and a flustered vicar and with Sir Ambrose and the vicar's wife as witnesses. No flowers. No music. Only the heavy starkness of Norman pillars and the air so cold that her breath had vaporised as she took her vows. She remembered the cold. No sooner had the vows been exchanged and her cheek dutifully kissed by Aldeborough than she had been installed in Aldeborough's coach and the long, tedious journey had begun. Sir Ambrose had thoughtfully presented her with a tasteful posy of yellow flowers and kissed her fingers and called her Lady Aldeborough, a situation that she still found difficult to believe, but it had helped to strengthen her courage.

And Aldeborough had been as good as his word. Her lips curled in memory of the beautiful dress that he had brought back with him to keep his promise. A dress of which dreams were made. In the height of fashion with a high waist and disconcertingly low neckline and tiny puff sleeves over long undersleeves, the jonquil taffeta was far more elegant than any gown she had ever seen. The tucked bodice was a little large, but nothing that a small alteration here and there could not remedy, and the silk ruching round the hem helped to disguise the fact that it was a little long. A simple satin straw bonnet with jonquil ribbons that set off her dark hair completed the ensemble. She had abandoned her puce disaster and travel-stained cloak without a qualm.

And not only the dress, but fine kid gloves and matching kid heelless slippers. Not to mention the delightful package of shifts and petticoats and silk stockings. She blushed faintly that he should have purchased such intimate garments for her. And who had chosen the dress for her? She had found it difficult to thank him. He had merely brushed it aside as a matter of no importance. But Frances was now more than grateful for his foresight. Under Lady Aldeborough's critical and unfriendly scrutiny, it was suddenly very important that she should be wearing a stylish blue velvet pelisse trimmed with grey fur and a pale blue silk bonnet, the brim fetchingly ornamented with one curling ostrich plume, both in the first stare of fashion.

She had thought herself fortunate in her new wardrobe but this house, now her own, threatened to take her breath away. Her first impression as they had arrived had been fleeting, but there was no doubting its style and magnificence. In Cavendish Square, one of the very best addresses, the brick and stone façade with its pedimented doorway, decorative columns and imposing flight of steps bordered with iron railings could not fail to impress. All was elegance and good taste. Aldeborough might take it for granted, but she could not.

She sighed as her attention returned to the heated words from the Marchioness and the cool rejoinders from Aldeborough.

'What your father would have said I hesitate to think. And Richard—'

Frances would never know what Richard would have thought or done for at this timely moment, the door burst open and a young man erupted with more energy than grace into the room.

'Matthew! Perhaps you might enter my drawing room in a more seemly fashion. Your brother and I were engaged in a private conversation.'

'Forgive me, Mother. I heard Hugh was back.' Matthew looked anything but sorry and shrugged off his parent's blighting words. 'Is it true?' He grinned as he embraced his brother in a friendly and vigorous greeting. 'I have just seen Masters in town and he has told me all.'

Aldeborough inhaled sharply in exasperation. 'So just what has Masters told you? Perhaps, brother mine, this is not the best of times to elaborate!' The warning was unfortunately lost in Matthew's exuberance to discover the truth of the matter.

'That you abducted Torrington's niece from under his nose and forced her into marriage to get your hands on her inheritance.'

Lady Aldeborough lowered herself carefully on to the chair behind her. 'This is even worse than I thought. What have you done, Aldeborough?' Her tone might be faint with shock, but her expression was steely.

'So, is it true?' Matthew insisted.

'Of course it is true. Would you not expect me to be capable of such dishonourable behaviour? Even you, it seems, Matthew.'

Matthew frowned at the bitter cynicism imprinted on his brother's face, echoing in his harsh tones. 'Well, no. I don't believe it, as it happens. Are you jesting? And if it *is* true—where is she?'

'Behind you. You will note her terrified appearance and the marks of coercion and cruelty about her person. I had to treat her most unkindly to persuade her that marriage with me would be an attractive proposition.'

Matthew grinned, shrugging with some relief as Aldeborough's expression relaxed and the tension slowly drained from his body, but he still had the grace to look more than a little embarrassed as he swung round towards the window embrasure. 'Exactly. You deserved that. You had better come and meet her. I dare not imagine what impression you have made on her,' Aldeborough added drily, but with a trace of humour at his brother's discomfort.

Aldeborough came to retrieve Frances from her seat by the window, taking her by the hand and leading her back into the centre of the room. 'This, my lady, is my graceless brother Matthew, who believes that I beat you into submission. You have my permission to snub him completely if you wish.'

'Please don't. I had no intention of making you uncomfortable. I am very pleased to meet you.' His engaging smile lit his youthful features.

Frances found herself smiling back at the genuine greeting from the young man who was very close to her own age. He was slim and athletic and looked to have just grown out of the ungainly lack of co-ordination of youth. He was fairer than his brother, with blue eyes and an open, laughing countenance that Frances instantly felt drawn to. His manner suggested that he stood in awe of neither his mother nor Aldeborough, and his clothing that he was experimenting with the more extremes of fashion. His cravat was a miracle of folds and creases and his striped waistcoat caused Aldeborough to raise his eyebrows in amused disbelief.

'And what have you been doing with yourself, apart from rigging yourself out like a dandy?' Aldeborough queried. 'Up to no good as usual, I expect.'

'Definitely not. No debts and definitely no scandals. I say, Hugh. You haven't changed your mind about buying me a commission, have you?'

'Certainly not!'

'But it looks as if we shall have to continue the war against Bonaparte.'

'Very true. But we shall have to continue it without you. At least until you are a little older.'

'But it will all be over by then. Do reconsider.'

'I will think about it. But don't raise your hopes.'

This was clearly a frequently held exchange of views. Nothing daunted, Matthew changed tack. 'By the by, the new horse you bought from Strefford was delivered yesterday. It is a splendid animal. Come and see it.'

'I think it an excellent idea for you to go off to the stables if you are going to talk horseflesh,' interposed Lady Aldeborough, determined to regain control of the situation. She rose to her feet again and disposed her shawl in elegant folds around her shoulders. 'It will give me the opportunity to get to know your new wife a little better. We can have a cosy chat over a dish of tea. Do you not think so, my dear?'

'Of course.' Frances's heart sank. She was not fooled by Lady Aldeborough's sudden change of demeanour. Her civility was knife-edged and threatened to be deadly. It promised to be a difficult interview.

'Will you be quite comfortable, my lady?' Aldeborough allowed her the opportunity to play the coward, but she would not.

'Certainly, my lord.'

'Very well, Matthew. Lead me to the horse. And no, you cannot ride him, before you ask. I will return very soon.' He gave Frances a brief smile of encouragement before following his brother through the door.

Frances was left alone with her mother-in-law. She could not allow herself to show any weakness or to be intimidated. Lady Aldeborough had the air of one who had spent a lifetime in achieving her own ends. And she would not be prepared to accept defeat on this occasion.

'Miss Hanwell. Oh, do forgive me—I still cannot believe that you have actually entered into this alliance with my son.' Her sugary tones set Frances's teeth on edge. 'Do come and sit here. I will ring for some tea. Perhaps you would like to tell me a little about yourself.' The Dowager smiled, but achieved it only through sheer effort of will. Frances responded with as much equanimity as she could muster. She had nothing to lose. She knew at once that she would never win the good will, much less the affection, of this dominant lady and she wished fervently that Aldeborough had not forsaken her to such an ordeal.

The arrival of the tea tray gave Frances a much-needed breathing space. When everything had been disposed to her liking, Lady Aldeborough handed Frances a fine bone-china tea cup.

'Now. Let us have a feminine gossip.'

Frances cringed inwardly, predicting accurately the direction it would take.

'Who are your family? Do I know them?'

'My uncle is Viscount Torrington—and he is also my guardian.'

'So, are your parents then dead?'

'Yes.'

'How unfortunate. I do not think I have ever seen you in London. Or at any country-house parties. Perhaps you have never been introduced into society?'

'I have always lived in the country on my uncle's estate.'

A pause developed as the Dowager considered the information. 'Perhaps you have other living relatives?' The catechism continued.

'The present Earl of Wigmore is my mother's nephew, my cousin.'

'Really?' Elegant eyebrows rose in apparent disbelief. 'I am somewhat acquainted with the family, of course, but I was not aware of your existence.'

'We have not kept close contact.' Frances was determined not to give any more cause for speculation.

'I see.' Lady Aldeborough placed her cup down with careful precision before fixing Frances with austere censure. 'Let us be clear about this, my dear. I am very disappointed in the turn of events. So shoddy, you understand. And as for what the world will make of the rumours of an abduction—'

'There was no abduction. I did nothing against my will.'

'Whatever the truth of it, it is quite shocking. As Marquis of Aldeborough, my son should have enjoyed a wedding at which all the members of the *ton* were present. An event of the Season, no less. Instead of which…' Her mother-in-law shrugged with elegant disdain.

There was no suitable response for Frances to make. She waited in silence for the next onslaught, raising her teacup to her lips.

'It makes me wish once again that Richard was still alive.'

'Richard?'

'My son. My *first-born* son.' The Dowager indicated with a melancholy sigh and a wave of her hand an impressive three-quarter-length portrait in pride of place above the mantelpiece. 'It is very like. It was completed a mere few months before his death.'

'I…I'm sorry. I did not know.'

'How should you? He was everything a mother could wish for. Duty and loyalty to the family came first with him. Not at all like Hugh. He should never have died.'

Frances studied the portrait with interest as her companion applied a fine lace handkerchief to her lashes. The young man before her was very like her husband. Indeed, the Laffords all had the same straight nose and dark brows and forthright gaze. Richard was dark too, like his brother, but the portrait highlighted a subtle difference between the two. The hint of mischief in Richard's hooded eyes and roguish smile were unmistakable. He sat at his ease in a rural setting with the Priory clearly depicted in the background, a shotgun tucked through his arm and a gun dog at his side. The artist was good, successfully catching the vivid personality and love of life—Frances had the impression that he could have stepped out of the frame at any moment. Even though she had never known him, it was difficult to believe that he was dead. What a terrible tragedy! No wonder his mother mourned him with such passionate intensity.

'Was…was it an accident?' Frances asked to break the painful silence.

'Some might try to imply that it was—to hide the truth from the world—but his death was to Hugh's advantage, a fact which must be obvious to all. It breaks my heart to think of it.'

Frances privately doubted that she had a heart to break.

Lady Aldeborough continued, long pent-up bitterness pouring out. 'And Penelope, his fiancée. So beautiful and elegant. So well connected—so *suitable*. She would have made an excellent Marchioness. As if she had been born to it.'

'I can see that she must have been greatly distressed.'

'Penelope has remarkable self-control. And of course she still hoped to become my daughter-in-law in the fullness of time. But now it has all changed. I do not know how I shall have the courage to break the news to her. But, of course, Hugh would never think of that. He has always been selfish and frippery. His taking a commission in the Army to fight in the Peninsula was the death of his father.'

As Lady Aldeborough appeared to be intent on holding her son to blame for everything, Frances felt moved to defend her absent husband.

'I have not found him to be selfish.'

'To be the object of an abduction or an elopement—or whatever the truth might be, for I do not think the episode has been explained at all clearly to my satisfaction—I can think of nothing more degrading.' Her eyebrows rose. 'That smacks of selfishness to me.'

'That was not his fault, in all fairness. My husband' —Lady Aldeborough winced at Frances's deliberate choice of words— 'has treated me with all care and consideration. He saw to my every comfort on our journey here. I accept that our marriage is not what you had hoped for, but Aldeborough has shown me every civility and courtesy. I cannot condone your criticism of him.'

'Be that as it may, there is much of my son that you do not know. But you have married him and will soon learn. I hope you do not live to regret it. Now, tell me. Have you a dowry? Have you brought any money into the union? At least that would be something good.'

Frances took a deep breath to try to explain her inheritance in the most favourable light when the door opened on the return of Aldeborough and Matthew. She grasped the opportunity to allow the question to remain unanswered and turned towards her husband with some relief.

They were obviously in the middle of some joke and Frances was arrested by the expression on Aldeborough's face. She had never seen him so approachable. His eyes alight with laughter and his quick grin at some comment were heartstoppingly and devastatingly attractive. She had much more to learn about her husband than she had realised. And the unknown Richard.

The smile stayed in Aldeborough's eyes as he approached across the room. 'I see you have survived,' he commented ironically, showing recognition of her predicament. 'I knew you would.'

'Of course.' Frances raised her chin and looked directly into his eyes. 'Your mother and I have enjoyed a...an exchange of views. I already feel that we understand each other very well.'

Aldeborough's raised eyebrows did not go unmarked.

He came to her that night.

Immediately upon a quiet knock, he entered the Blue Damask bedroom, where Frances had been temporarily accommodated until the suite next to the master bedroom could be cleaned and decorated to her taste. The door clicked shut behind him. He halted momentarily, his whole body tense, his senses on the alert, and then with a rueful shrug and a slight smile he advanced across the fine Aubusson carpet.

'Don't do it, Molly. I trust you are not contemplating escape yet again. It is a long way to the ground and I cannot vouch for your safety. Paving stones, I believe, can be very unforgiving.'

Frances stepped back from the open window where she had been leaning to cool her heated cheeks. The blood returned to her face in a rose wash, her throat dry and her heartbeat quickening. As ever, he dominated the room with his height, broad shoulders and excellent co-ordination. And, as always, he was impeccably dressed notwithstanding the late hour. He made her feel ruffled and hopelessly unsophisticated.

'No, but you could not blame me if I was! And I would be grateful if you did not call me Molly!'

He reached behind her to close the window and redraw the blinds, allowing her the space to regain her composure.

'Your maid did not come to help you undress? You should have rung for her.' He indicated the embroidered bell pull by the hearth.

'I sent her away.' Frances hesitated. 'I did not want her tonight. I have never had a maid, you see.'

She caught her reflection in the gilt-edged mirror of the dressing table. She looked exhausted. Beneath her eyes were smudges of violet, her pale skin almost transparent. And Aldeborough's unexpected presence made her edgy and nervous. She rubbed her hands over her face as if they could erase her anxiety. They failed miserably.

'I told you that it was a mistake for you to marry me.' Her voice expressed her weariness in spite of all her efforts to control it. 'Your mother hates me. And she will find great pleasure in telling all your family and friends that I am a fortune hunter with no countenance, style or talents to attract.'

He crossed the room deliberately to take her by the shoulders and turn her face towards the light from a branch of candles. He then startled her by lifting his hand to gently smooth the lines of tension between her eyebrows with his thumb. He frowned down at her as if his thoughts were anything but pleasant.

'I am sorry. It has been a very trying day for you. Perhaps in retrospect I should have seen my mother alone first, but I don't think it would have made much difference. I was proud of you. You were able to conduct yourself with assurance and composure in difficult circumstances. It cannot have been easy for you.'

Frances blinked at the unexpected compliment. 'If you are kind and sympathetic I shall cry.'

His stern features were lightened by an unexpectedly sweet smile. 'Thank you for the warning. I would not wish that on you. If it is any consolation to you, my mother doesn't like me much either.'

'No, it is no consolation,' she responded waspishly. 'I did not expect to be welcomed, but I did not think I would be patronised and condemned with every deficiency in my background and education laid bare in public over the dinner table. And if I have to listen once more to a catalogue of the skills and talents of Miss Penelope Vowchurch I shall not be responsible for my actions.' She proceeded to give a remarkably accurate parody of Lady Aldeborough. 'Can you sing, Frances? No? Of course, Penelope is *very* gifted musically. It is a pleasure to hear her sing—and play the pianoforte! Perhaps you paint instead? No? Penelope, of course... Does she have *any* failings?'

A shuttered look had crossed Aldeborough's face, but he was forced into a reluctant laugh. 'Don't let my mother disturb you. I don't believe that she means half of what she says.'

'I am delighted to hear it—but I don't believe you. You could have warned me.'

'Don't rip up at me.' His fingers tightened their grip.

She suddenly realised that he looked as tired as she felt, with fine lines of strain etched around his mouth, and his words were a plea rather than a command. For a second she felt a wave of sympathy for him—but quickly buried it. The situation, after all, was of his making.

'Why not?' She pulled away from his grasp, too aware of the strength of his fingers branding her flesh, but then regretted her brusque action. 'I... Forgive me, I am just a little overwrought. I shall be better tomorrow. I am really very grateful for all you have done,' she explained stiffly.

'I don't want your gratitude.' His voice was harsh.

She turned her back on him and stalked towards the mirror where she began to unfasten the satin ribbons with which she had inexpertly confined her hair. She was aware of his eyes on her every movement. A silence stretched between them until her nerves forced her to break it.

'It is difficult not to express my gratitude when you have given me everything that I have never had before.'

'I have given you nothing yet.'

'My clothes. All of this.' She indicated the tasteful silver and blue furnishings, the bed with its opulent hangings, the comforting fire still burning in the grate. 'Wealth. A title. Respectability. What more could I want?' Bitterness rose in her that he should take it all for granted.

'Next you will tell me that you would rather be back at Torrington Hall with Charles as your prospective husband.' Aldeborough's heavy irony was not lost on her.

'No.' She sighed, lowering her hands to her lap. 'In all honesty I cannot.'

'I like your honesty,' he commented gently. 'I would like you to have this. It is a personal gift.' From his pocket he withdrew a flat black velvet box. He handed it to her. It was much worn at the corners, and the clasp had broken loose. In the centre was a faded coat of arms stamped in gold. 'A bride gift, if you like. My mother still has all the family heirlooms and jewellery. I will arrange for you to have the ones that suit. There are some very pretty earrings, I believe, and a pearl set that you would like. But this belonged to my grandmother. She left it to me to give to my wife. It is a trifle old fashioned and not very valuable, but it has considerable charm and I hope you will wear it until I can give you something better.'

Frances opened the box to reveal a faded silk lining. On it rested an oval silver locket on a fine silver chain. The workmanship was old and intricate with a delicacy of touch. Its surface was engraved with scrolls and flowers, the centres of which were set with small sapphires. She opened the locket. Inside she found the empty mountings for a miniature with the words engraved on the opposite side *My Beloved is Mine*.

'It is beautiful,' she said softly, tracing the delicate scroll work with a finger, unable to meet his eyes. 'I have never been given jewellery before.'

He took the locket from her and moved to clasp it round her throat. 'The roses seemed appropriate, Fair Rosalind.'

The brief touch of his fingers on her neck as he fastened the clasp sent a shiver through her tense body. Her eyes, wide and dark, met his fleetingly in the mirror. He nodded.

'It suits you very well. There is a sapphire necklace the exact colour of your eyes.' He hesitated, lost in their depths for the length of a heartbeat. 'But I fear that my mother will refuse to part with it this side of the grave.'

The locket lay on her breast, the tiny sapphires catching the light like pinpointed stars with her heightened breathing.

She would have moved away from him, but he took hold of her wrist in a firm grasp, using his free hand to tilt her chin upwards. With one finger he traced the outline of her lips, his featherlight touch delicate and reflective. Her breath caught in her throat as she read the intention in his eyes. His arm slid around her waist, drawing her closer, and he bent his head to press his mouth to the pulse fluttering at the base of her neck, just above where the locket gleamed in the candlelight. Her immediate instinct was to raise her hands and push against his shoulders. Sudden fear engulfed her, surprising her in its intensity.

He raised his head. His eyes were devastatingly clear and possessive. 'Don't fight me, Frances.'

'I am not fighting,' she managed to gasp as he renewed his assault on her throat. 'I did not expect—'

'Of course. A business arrangement—that was what we agreed.' There was no mistaking the sneer in his voice. 'And it will be. You have my wealth and my name. And as long as you are discreet, I will not interfere with your… *amusements*. Neither will I impose myself on you overmuch.' Her heart sank at this cold assessment of their future. 'But I need an heir. And there must be no room for an annulment if your uncle decides to be uncooperative and you wish to escape from the clutches of Cousin Charles.'

'Yes, my lord. I know my duty.' Her reply was as cold as his, masking the misery in her heart.

'That sounds very cold comfort. I believe it is possible to derive some pleasure from a wifely duty.' A faint smile accompanied the mockery in the lines around his thinned lips. 'Am I so unpalatable to you as a husband?'

'No, my lord.'

He bent his head again to claim her lips with his own, at the same time releasing her hair from its ribbons in a perfumed cascade on to her shoulders. He wound his hand into the silken length of it to hold her in submission as he increased the pressure on her mouth. Against her will her lips opened tentatively under his. Shock swept through her as, withdrawing a little, his tongue traced the outline of her lips before invading again. He released her, but only so that his hands could deal with the fastenings of her gown.

'It seems that I must be servant as well as lover tonight,' he murmured against her throat.

He left a trail of feathery kisses from her jaw along the curve of her throat to her shoulder as his fingers expertly worked their way through the tiny buttons and laces. Frances was only aware of the heat spreading throughout her body from her toes to her hairline as the white sprigged muslin slipped into a pool at her feet. Her breathing was shallow and she gasped as his hard mouth returned to possess her lips once more. All she could hope for was that he would be understanding of her ignorance and lack of experience.

Aldeborough was acutely aware of her anxiety in the tension in every part of her body, in the rapid beat of her pulse beneath his lips. 'Do you trust me?'

She stood rigidly in his embrace.

'I don't know,' she replied honestly, her eyes wide with apprehension.

His answering touch was gentle, holding her captive, pressing her soft curves to the length of his body. He moved his hands to caress the sides of her ribs through her fine chemise and allowed his palms to brush the soft swell of her breasts. Then, as she heard his own breathing change, he let his hands fall and stepped back—but only to kneel at her feet with elegant grace to remove her garters. His fingers stroked the satin skin of her thigh, calf, ankle, as he smoothed her stockings down to her delicately arched feet.

At last he rose, pausing to snuff the branch of candles to allow her the anonymity of darkness.

He stood and looked at her in the flickering shadows cast by the one remaining candle. Her eyes were dark and fathomless like bottomless pools. Her skin ivory, flushed with rose, but icy, her whole body held in check as if her one desire was to flee from his touch.

'I am afraid,' she whispered.

'But there is no need.'

He stooped to lift her into his arms effortlessly, as if she weighed nothing, and then laid her on the high bed. He was touched by compassion. He would do his best for her, to make it an acceptable experience. He stayed only to divest himself of his clothing before stretching his body beside her and began to kiss her. Gently at first, them more urgently, her mouth, hair, face, then along her throat to her shoulders, his lips burning on her cool skin. She had never imagined that her cool self-possessed husband could generate such fire. She shivered as he pushed aside her chemise and allowed his hands to drift down her slender body, brushing her nipples and stroking her flat stomach. Frances felt a response awaken deep within her when she become acutely aware of his arousal, strong and hard against her thigh. He continued his exploration of her body, discovering tantalising curves and hollows that fit so naturally against his palms, teasing her nipples with his tongue until they became erect. She gasped at the electric effect, the heat in her blood, and hid her face against his shoulder, conscious of his own disciplined breathing as if holding his actions on a tight rein.

Then he changed his position so that he could part her thighs with his knee and stroke the impossibly soft flesh. For a long moment she held her breath, her whole body trembling at the touch of his fingers in such an intimate caress. Her brain refused to allow her to respond to the incredible sensation of his naked body pressed against hers, cool skin against cool skin. He lifted himself above her, taking as much of his weight as he could on his elbows.

'Trust me,' he repeated breathlessly. 'I will try to hurt you as little as I can. Now!'

With a firm thrust he penetrated her. She cried out against the unexpected invasion that filled her, stretched her, causing her to struggle for the first time against the intrusion.

'Lie still,' he ordered, but his voice was infinitely gentle. And he remained motionless himself except to brush his lips over her hair and eyes and then finally her mouth, parting her lips with his tongue as he had invaded her body. She allowed her taut muscles to relax again and as soon as he sensed it he began to move within her. Slowly at first. She tensed her muscles again momentarily against his total possession of her body, but his smooth controlled movements did not lessen. His thrusts became deeper and more urgent so that she clung to him, fingernails buried in his shoulders as there seemed to be no other alternative. Then, as desire finally overset his iron control, he shuddered into his climax, pinning her to the bed with the weight of his body. Frances lay in emotional and physical emptiness, sensation ebbing, leaving her devastated, drained of coherent thought. Why had she found it impossible to respond with any warmth—even the merest hint of pleasure? She knew in her heart that he had taken her with care and compassionate tenderness—so why did she feel that she had in some way failed him? And yet she had sensed something there for her in his touch far beyond her reach.

Aldeborough slowly withdrew to lie beside her, leaving one arm thrown possessively across her body. He had found her most appealing, slim and firm with small high breasts. Her skin was like water over silk. He smoothed his hand along the satin length of her back to her waist and over the curve of her hip. He had found no difficulty in becoming aroused and consummating their marriage. But in spite of physical satisfaction he was disturbed by a ripple of unease. True, she had not repulsed him, but he had been unable to break through her intense reserve. For the most part she had remained rigid and unresponsive.

He had not expected this, in spite of her ignorance. Aldeborough knew that she had a courageous, vital spirit beneath her quiet demeanour, and except for that one occasion in the library at the Priory, she had never flinched from him. Nor had she ever attacked him with tears or recriminations. He had thought that she would take some pleasure from their coupling, or at least accept it with equanimity. But not this withdrawal, rejection even. He was surprised by an unexpected twinge of failure for all his experience. He had not done his best for her. He could have taken more time to awaken her emotions and senses, but he had believed that it would merely have prolonged the agony of anticipation for her.

Aldeborough sighed and, drawing away from her, swung his legs over the edge of the bed, hunting in the dark to retrieve his discarded clothing. He was halted by the hesitant touch on his arm. He turned back to her where she lay, lost in shadows except for the gleam of the moonlight on her chemise.

'My lord...' her voice was barely a whisper '...did I displease you? I am sorry if you found me...unattractive. But I didn't know—'

'Frances.' It struck him like a physical blow that she believed he had abandoned her in disgust. And how hard it must have been for her to turn to him. 'You must never think that. I simply thought that you might like some privacy. That you might wish to sleep alone.'

'Of course. Forgive me.' The words tumbled out in an agony of embarrassment. 'I did not mean to imply... I did not intend to impose on you.' She turned away so that all he could see were her rigid shoulders.

He sighed. He should have been more careful with her. With all his experience he had frightened her and there was now little he could do to remedy it. His conscience pricked him with a full-blown blast of guilt. He rolled back on to the bed. 'Come here,' he said gently.

'Please don't be angry with me.'

Which was a strange thing for her to say. 'Why should I?'

He pulled the chemise modestly down around her ankles and rearranged the lace neckline so that it lay becomingly around her shoulders. He pushed her hair away from her face, running his fingers through the tangles until she cried out in protest. Her eyes were closed, but he was relieved that there were no tears. He drew her gently into his arms so that her head rested on his shoulder and tucked the sheet comfortingly around them both—as if she was a child in need of reassurance. She made no resistance.

'Are you comfortable?'

He felt the tiniest nod of her head against his chest.

'You must never think that you disgust me, Frances. Do you understand?'

'Yes, my lord.'

'You are allowed to call me Hugh.' She could hear the smile in his voice, but she had suffered enough intimacies for one night and simply turned her face into his shoulder.

Silence fell between them.

He felt no inclination to break it.

'Go to sleep, Frances Rosalind,' he murmured. Virgins were the very devil, he mused. Not that he had much knowledge of them. Letitia Winter's practised embraces were far more predictable and never disappointing. For a moment he enjoyed the image of Letitia's ample breasts and shapely hips, and remembered the touch of her clever fingers as she roused him to heights of mutual pleasure. And then he closed his mind to it. He stroked his wife's hair until she relaxed against him and her breathing deepened. She was warm and soft and pliable in his arms. He felt a surprising feeling of contentment steal through his limbs. Eventually he followed her into sleep.

She awoke as the first light of dawn crept into the room to find him gone. Her body felt sore as she turned over in bed and sat up, her muscles complaining. The imprint of his body and head were still clear beside her, but she had no memory of his leaving. Her gown and petticoats had been neatly folded on to a chair with her stockings on top and her shoes beneath, but his clothes were gone. She was not sorry. Shyness overcame her as she remembered the demands of his body on her own. And shame that she had been so frozen into unresponsive rigidity. But she also remembered his kindness and the gentle tenderness that she had not expected. She raised her hand to her mouth. She fancied that she could still taste his kisses and sense the imprint of his lips on her throat as if they had left actual marks on her fair skin. She swung her legs out of bed, hoping that she might regain her composure with her clothing before she had to confront him again.

Chapter Five

Frances need not have worried.

When she was ushered into the breakfast parlour by Watkins, the elderly butler, there was no Aldeborough for her to face, nor, to her intense relief, had Lady Aldeborough put in an appearance. Instead she was greeted by a friendly smile from Matthew and a direct and assessing gaze from a young lady whom she had not yet met but whom she immediately recognised. The lady had clearly just arrived, dressed in the sprigged muslin and blue sash of the débutante and dangling a straw bonnet by its ribbons in a cavalier fashion. She was sufficiently like Matthew to brand her as his sister, but her hair was much fairer with auburn tints. She was blessed with a youthful prettiness, a lively expression and a decided sparkle in her eyes. Frances found it an interesting experience to be under the shrewd scrutiny of a lady younger than herself. So this was Aldeborough's sister, who did not appreciate the benefits of education but was undoubtedly enjoying her first Season.

'Frances!' Matthew, with the familiarity of their previous acquaintance, sprang to his feet, abandoning a plate of eggs and creamed kidneys. His smile of welcome engulfed her and immediately helped her to control the nerves fluttering in her stomach. 'This is Juliet, my little sister. Last night she was chaperoned to a masquerade by Aunt Elizabeth, so you did not have the opportunity to meet.'

Frances met the considering gaze levelly.

'I heard the news on the family grapevine so I had to come home early to see you for myself.' Juliet was clearly a forthright young lady. 'Is it true? Did Hugh really elope with you and marry you out of hand without your guardian's permission?'

Frances flushed, silently cursing her fair skin that made her discomfiture very evident.

'Juliet! I must apologise for my mannerless sister, Frances. She is not known for her sensitivity. Come and sit and have coffee.' He pushed aside some of the debris of cups and plates on the breakfast table to make a space for her. 'Don't worry. Mama does not leave her room until after eleven o'clock.' Frances was mortified to feel her flush deepen further.

'I did not mean to embarrass you,' Juliet apologised with a gleam in her eye. She pulled up a chair to sit beside Frances and cast the ill-used bonnet on to the table. 'It all seems so romantic to me.'

'It was not at all romantic, I do assure you.'

'My sister reads improper romantic novels when Mama is not looking,' Matthew explained.

'Do be quiet, Matthew! To be carried off by a romantic hero into the night—it is far more exciting than anything I have read recently. Although I have to say that I can*not* see Hugh in the role of hero, but that is probably because he is my brother. He is very handsome, I suppose. And he rides a horse well. But I think I prefer fairer heroes with golden locks and blue eyes.'

Frances laughed at this ingenuous view of her rescuer and found it easy to respond in kind. 'Then I must try to live up to your expectations of a romantic heroine. Perhaps I should have a cup of coffee before I faint!'

When Frances was seated with coffee and bread and butter, Matthew explained the plan of action for her first morning in London.

'I have been given instructions from Aldeborough. He sends his apologies and says that he has a business appointment this morning from which he cannot renege, but he will be honoured to drive you round Hyde Park this afternoon at two o'clock. This morning I am to escort you on a shopping expedition.' Frances hid a smile as she recognised the grace with which Matthew had accepted his instructions. She was sure that he would prefer to spend his time elsewhere, but he accepted the delegation with good humour.

Juliet showed no such reluctance and clapped her hands in pleasurable anticipation. 'How delightful. I must come with you, of course.'

'This is not an excuse for you to run up bills,' Matthew warned her in an echo of his brother's strictures. 'Frances needs town clothes. We are to rig her out in prime style.'

'I'm so glad I came home when I did.' Juliet was not to be deterred.

'But I cannot impose on your time. You must have other plans,' Frances stammered.

'I have been given orders from on high. I dare not disobey!' Matthew exclaimed solemnly, but with a cheerful resignation.

Frances was secretly delighted to be taken in hand and offered no more resistance.

'When you have finished we will go. Where do you suggest first, Julie?'

'*Madame Francine*, without question. She has such wonderful creations. You are much darker than I am, Frances. And married, of course. What fun! Just think of the colours you will be able to wear!'

Frances's enjoyment of the morning was beyond her wildest dreams. She had never had fine clothes, and certainly not fashionable ones. At best she had had to accept Lady Torrington's cast-offs, which might be fashionable but not to Frances's taste or figure. Now, introduced as the Marchioness of Aldeborough, nothing was to be too much trouble. Madame Francine welcomed her personally, saw to her every comfort, offered her refreshment and expressed, in her suspect French accent, her desire to present the bride as the most stylishly dressed lady of the Season. And with such dark colouring, why, she would be a pleasure to dress.

'What do I do about money?' Frances queried discreetly and with some embarrassment of Juliet, who was in ecstasy over a magnificent but impractical opera cloak of rose satin with ruched edges. Matthew had opted, with some relief, to stay with their carriage, so delegating all responsibility to Juliet, who proved to have a very practical streak when it came to the necessities of life.

'Ignore it, of course,' she advised. 'Have all the bills sent to Aldeborough.'

'I cannot do that!'

'Why not? I could. Enjoy it. A rich husband is a great advantage to a lady. I shall certainly have to marry a gentleman who has sufficient money to keep me in the height of fashion.'

'That is not very romantic!'

'Perhaps not, but it is practical. Now, let us see what you will need for the beginning of the Season.'

The next hour flew by in a profusion of gowns and outfits for all occasions. Frances turned this way and that before the full-length mirrors. For walking, for morning calls, for afternoon visiting, for evening, for dress balls.

'But I shall never wear so many clothes.'

'Certainly you will. As Aldeborough's wife you will be expected to have dash and style. And you cannot under any circumstances wear the same evening gown too often!' With which piece of wordly wisdom Frances had to be content.

And then there were gloves and shoes and intimate items of underwear.

It was all too much. Frances was dazzled by it. But she was female enough to enjoy every moment, impressed by the way the new gowns flattered her slight figure and enhanced the rich colour of her hair and eyes. Even her skin glowed. Why, she almost looked pretty. Madame Francine and Juliet were both surprisingly complimentary. She found herself wondering what Aldeborough would say when he saw how she had spent his money and secretly hoped that he would not be displeased since she had found such pleasure in it. Perhaps he would not resent their marriage too much if she looked a little more attractive than the drab and impossibly dull Miss Hanwell. She smiled in the mirror at the almost unrecognisable Marchioness of Aldeborough and liked what she saw.

They rejoined Matthew some little time later at their carriage with the promise of delivery of some essential items later in the day. Some parcels came with them—Frances could not resist the prospect of wearing a new gown that very afternoon when Aldeborough showed her off in Hyde Park.

'And now, I think, *Josephine* for hats.'

Frances closed her eyes momentarily. Her cup was full.

After an exhausting morning spending Aldeborough's money, they headed home to partake of a light luncheon.

'Mama was planning to lunch with Lady Vowchurch and Penelope,' explained Juliet, 'so you won't have to suffer an inquisition today. She will have felt compelled to inform the Vowchurch ladies of the tragic events of your marriage!'

Matthew snorted, but wisely declined to become involved in malicious female gossip.

'Mama,' Juliet continued, 'sees Penelope as The Paragon. She is the ideal to which none of the rest of us measures up.' She giggled.

'I realised that last night. She appears to have a remarkable range of talents. I certainly could not compare. In fact, I failed miserably on all counts.'

'Neither could I.' Juliet was clearly pleased to have found a sympathetic ear. 'Penelope was forever questioning my governess about what I had been learning and blaming the poor lady when she discovered that I had learnt nothing. Poor Miss Dennison. I fear I was the worst of pupils. And Penelope was not even family, so she had no right to criticise her.'

'Tell me…' Here Frances saw an opportunity to elicit some

information without appearing overtly inquisitive. 'Do I understand that Miss Vowchurch was to have married your brother Richard?' she asked tentatively.

'Oh, yes.' Juliet proved more than willing to indulge in family gossip and fill in the gaps. 'And when he died it was Mama's plan that she should marry Hugh. Penelope did not seem at all reluctant. And Hugh never actually said he would not marry her. So we all expected it to happen, until you arrived.'

'Shut up, Julie. You gossip too much!'

'No I don't. And Frances ought to know what she has got herself into.'

Frances decided to pursue the subject. 'Lady Aldeborough told me that your brother Richard was killed, but that it might not have been an accident.'

'Of course, you would not know—'

Matthew interrupted and frowned in Juliet's direction to discourage her. For the first time a reserved expression appeared on his face and even Juliet looked a little downcast. 'Richard was thrown out of a curricle and broke his neck. Mama doted on Richard so it hit her hard and she has not got over it. But there is no doubt about it being an accident.'

Juliet opened her mouth to add to the story, but after another quelling stare from her brother she changed her mind.

So with that Frances had to be content.

Luncheon passed pleasantly enough, but Aldeborough failed to put in an appearance.

'He has probably forgotten all about you and gone to buy a horse,' commented Juliet with no respect for the Marquis. 'Or,' with maidenly disgust, 'he is at Gentlemen Jackson's Boxing Parlour!'

'Take no notice of her, Frances. It's more likely estate finance. Since he stepped into Richard's shoes he's been bedevilled by it. But Hugh's absence is my gain—I'll be honoured to drive you round the park this afternoon.'

'Can I come?' Juliet brightened. 'I have a particularly fetching bonnet I would like to wear.'

'Certainly not. I intend to drive the curricle so there is not enough room for three. And, before you ask, I have no intention of squeezing you in!'

'You could take the barouche,' she persisted in her most persuasive and sweetest tones. 'Everyone who is anyone will be in Hyde Park in the afternoon.'

'No.'

'I know. You only want to drive Aldebrough's horses.' Juliet flounced, her smile replaced by a petulant frown, and Matthew grinned in agreement.

Juliet waved them farewell. Frances, in a new fur-trimmed pelisse and silk-flowered bonnet, with a frivolous little feather muff, concentrated on wielding a delicious cream silk parasol with the style and dash advised by Juliet, under strict instructions from Matthew not to frighten the horses.

'I have never ridden in a curricle before.' Frances looked around with interest as they turned into the park.

It was a smart turn-out, if somewhat precarious to Frances's eyes, and, as Matthew informed her, all the crack. The matched bays, driven well up to their bits, were a splendid pair with glossy coats and mouths of silk.

'Will Aldeborough mind you driving his horses?' she asked, remembering Juliet's comment on Matthew's motives.

'No. Though I dare not take his new chestnuts. I would give my eye teeth to try them out, but it would be more than my life's worth to take them without permission.'

'And since you're hoping to persuade him to buy you a pair of colours?' she enquired with a hint of mischief.

Matthew laughed and had the grace to look a trifle sheepish. 'As you say, it behooves me to stay in his good books.'

'Is he persuadable, do you think?' she enquired with interest. The ease of relationship between the Marquis and his brother was clear to see.

'The horses or the commission? Usually he's very amenable, but I have my doubts about both.' Matthew shrugged and grimaced, but seemed unwilling to discuss the matter further. Frances smiled sympathetically before turning her attention back to the scene around her.

Matthew drove her sedately round Hyde Park. It was at its busiest with the members of the *ton* wishing to see and be seen. Gossip had obviously been busy, for Frances detected much interest in The Bride. Some of the glances were direct and overtly curious. Some were brief, followed by a whispered aside. She cringed inwardly from the content of the speculation and wished Aldeborough was with her. She felt her shoulders tensing and her fingers gripped the carved ivory handle of her parasol as if it would be torn from her grasp at any minute. What did she expect? Her marriage was obviously the *on-dit* of the moment. Matthew, aware of her growing silence, cast a glance in her direction, noting the set of her lips and the faint line between her brows, and proceeded to keep up a steady stream of trivial information about those who hailed them.

'You don't have to worry,' he ventured finally, as his comments elicited little response. 'No one will snub you, you know, no matter what the gossips say. As Marchioness of Aldeborough, you will have automatic entrée into the best circles. Unless you do something outrageous, of course, and that's unlikely.'

Frances smiled in gratitude. She was not convinced, but out of good manners she forced herself to relax and be entertained.

A dashing group on horseback overtook them and cantered sedately into the distance.

'Do you ride?'

'Oh, yes. Aldeborough and I decided that it is one of my few talents.'

Matthew looked at her with an interested enquiry.

Frances laughed at his expression. 'When I was deciding whether to become a governess or not,' she explained enigmatically. 'Aldeborough decided that, on reflection, it would not be a good idea.'

'I shouldn't think it would be. I remember Juliet treating

Miss Dennison very shabbily. I doubt if you would enjoy it
at all—marrying Hugh sounds a much better option to me.'

'Yes. I suppose it is.' Matthew's quizzical glance made
Frances change the subject rapidly. 'But I can ride. I occa-
sionally accompanied my uncle when he went hunting, to
exercise some of his horses. Would your mother approve, do
you think, if I rode in Hyde Park? It must have been the only
aspect of my upbringing not under discussion last night!'

'I doubt it.' They exchanged a smile in perfect understanding.

'Aldeborough brought home a little Spanish mare.' Matthew picked up the conversation again. 'She is at the Priory
for the present. She's not up to his weight—or mine, sadly—
but she would be perfect for you. Then you can cut a dash
with the best of them.'

'I would like that. Aldeborough was with the Army in the
Peninsula, I understand.'

'Yes. Forgive me. I forget how little you will know about
him—and I know he rarely talks about his army days. He
was a Captain in one of the Hussar regiments, but had to sell
out when Richard died. He didn't want to, but it left him little
alternative. I wish he would let me go.'

'He wasn't very encouraging, was he?'

'No. I could accept his decision with more forbearance,
but I know how much he enjoyed it. Not the carnage and the
loss of friends, and the horrors of the siege of Badajoz, of
course. But the strategy and the...well, you know. And he
was probably destined for great things. He was mentioned in
dispatches after the Battle of Salamanca.' Matthew sighed as
he manoeuvred his horses round a group of saunterers. 'I
wish he would talk about it more, but he just clams up. It is
one thing to read about it in *The Times*, but it is quite another
to hear it from someone who was in the thick of it. All I
know is, he would rather have stayed with his regiment—he
never wanted the title or the estate with all its duties. He must
find it very dull after the excitement of campaigning. Perhaps
that's why he is so rackety at present. I don't think I should
have said that to you, should I?'

'What? That my husband is rackety? Probably not.' Frances noted his consternation with some amusement.

'All I meant to say was—'

'I know what you meant to say,' she reassured him.

'That's all right, then. I would not want to upset you.' He then let the matter drop, with obvious relief, to introduce Frances to a passing acquaintance. But it left Frances with much to think about. Here were more facets to Aldeborough than were at first apparent and she discovered a sudden desire to know him better.

She was stirred from her reverie by Matthew.

'Just our luck,' he grinned ruefully. 'Here is The Iceberg. For once I wish Julie was with us. She is much better at social chit-chat.'

An ancient landaulet pulled up beside them as Matthew reined in the bays. So this was the much-admired Miss Penelope Vowchurch and, on first impressions, Frances felt her heart sink in her chest. She was a polished, handsome lady with glossy brown curls falling in ordered ringlets and clear, light blue eyes. Her skin was fair, flawless like the petals of a blush rose, her features regular in the classical mode. Her clothes were elegant and demure, nothing extreme, but with more than a brief nod towards fashion. Miss Vowchurch inclined her head graciously towards Frances, her social smile well in place. She was a talented water colourist, her singing voice was a delight to hear and she could speak French and Italian very prettily. She would never be ill mannered, never malicious. But there was a challenge in those clear eyes, which the smile did not warm. Frances experienced an urge to pick up the challenge rather than become a victim. She furled her parasol with determination. She had had enough set-downs from Lady Aldeborough to last a lifetime.

Matthew made the introductions, his tone carefully neutral.

'I am delighted to meet you.' Miss Vowchurch extended a slender gloved hand. 'Lady Aldeborough has lunched with my mama today and she has told us so much about you.' Her voice was as well modulated and as elegant as her appearance.

'Indeed? Lady Aldeborough spoke much of you at dinner last night. I feel that I know you already.'

Miss Vowchurch's eyebrows rose faintly. 'I believe that you are related to the Mortimers? We know them well socially. We are forever invited to their town house. But we were never, to my recollection, introduced to you there. I am sure I would have remembered.'

'I have not had the pleasure of making the acquaintance of the Earl of Wigmore, my cousin, but that will be remedied now that I am fixed in town for some time. Perhaps you are acquainted with my paternal relatives with whom I have been living, Lord and Lady Torrington?'

'We have been introduced.' Miss Vowchurch turned to Matthew, neatly shutting Frances out of the discussion of common acquaintance.

'I expect we shall meet at dear Phoebe's celebration party tonight. She is such a good friend of mine. Do you go there, Matthew?'

'Orders have been given. It will be a full family turn-out, I believe. And now that Frances is a member of the family, Aldeborough wishes to introduce her to as many of the relatives as possible.'

'It must be a little unnerving knowing no one.' Penelope favoured Frances with a pitying glance. 'I understand that you have not been in town before, that you did not have the benefit of a Season. It is invaluable in showing you how to go on in Society.'

'No. It was not possible—for family reasons. I am finding it a great pleasure.'

'It will soon become tedious when you know it well,' Miss Vowchurch replied with languid and fashionable boredom. 'I am sure Matthew will agree with me.'

'I am afraid I can not conceive of being bored.' Frances showed her teeth in a smile. 'After all, there is so much to see and occupy one's mind.'

'And where is Aldeborough this afternoon? I would have

expected him to drive you in the park—on your first day here. Perhaps he was too busy?'

So would I, thought Frances, but the light of battle was in her eyes and she was enjoying the polite parrying of swords.

'It was Aldeborough's intention to drive me here. He informed me of such at breakfast. But my husband is consulting his lawyer about some legal affairs of mine. My inheritance, you understand. It was most urgent and he wished to put my mind at ease about it. I find him most considerate in all things. It is such a relief to be able to leave such business affairs to the attention of one's husband. You cannot imagine.'

'It must be very comforting for you.' Frances was delighted to see the lady's lips set in a firm line and the smile disappear from her face as well as her eyes.

'Perhaps we should move on, Matthew. I believe we are blocking the drive. *Au revoir* until this evening, Miss Vowchurch.'

Frances bowed her head, intentionally copying Miss Vowchurch's graceful actions. She unfurled her parasol with a decided snap.

'Well done!' murmured Matthew with a straight face. 'Mama's Paragon has had her nose put just slightly out of joint! Juliet will be pleased.'

As they turned out of the park Frances returned to one aspect of the previous conversation. 'Tell me about the party tonight.'

'It's only a small gathering to celebrate the betrothal of our Cousin Phoebe to Viscount Petersfield.'

'Do I have to go?'

'But of course. As I said—you are part of the family now. Besides, it will be a good opportunity to meet people on a small scale—and many of the distant connections you will never have to see again. You will deal admirably. And you can get the worst over with all on one occasion.'

I suppose I will, thought Frances. Matthew understood how nervous she was feeling at the prospect of being abandoned in a sea of names and faces. She just hoped that Aldeborough would be as considerate.

Matthew turned the bays towards the park gates to return home to Cavendish Square. As he reined in to allow a wayward grey and its rider to edge round them, Frances became aware of a smart barouche approaching from the opposite direction. Its one occupant, a lady, smiled directly at Frances, and although she did not ask her coachman to stop, she lowered her parasol and raised her hand in friendly greeting.

'Who is the lady waving to us?' Frances asked.

'Oho! So Mrs Winters is back in Town, is she?' Matthew muttered, a cautious note entering his voice.

'Should we stop? She seems to know you well. She waved.'

'No. I do not think we should.' He shook the reins to encourage the bays to trot on. 'And it would be better if you did not acknowledge her.' But Frances had already smiled tentatively at the prospect of a new acquaintance.

'But why not? She looks charming. So open and friendly.'

'Yes. Well…she is.' For once, Matthew appeared rather uneasy. 'But not very respectable. She has a reputation, if you take my meaning. And we do not acknowledge her.'

'Oh. But she seemed to recognise me.'

'Yes.' Matthew turned his clear gaze on her. 'She knows Aldeborough,' was all he said.

Frances hesitated, her mind taking in Matthew's enigmatic reply. His meaning was clear. 'Oh. I believe I understand.'

'I am sure you do.'

The day left Frances filled with a curious blend of emotions. She had taken her first tentative steps as a member of London society. She had dreamed of such a fairy-tale enchantment all her life, but had accepted, bitterly, that unless she discovered a fairy godmother in an attic then it was not for her and she was destined to spend her existence cleaning out the grates of Torrington Hall. Yet, against all probability, she had been able to break the bonds of family and miserable dependence, to escape the life of drudgery and daily humil-

iations. And Aldeborough, although she had placed him unwittingly in an impossible situation, had married her, raised
her in status and acceptability, preserved her reputation from
scandal and gossip and launched her into polite society, all
within less than two weeks of becoming aware of her existence. And all, it appeared, without any inconvenience to
himself, as she had not set eyes on him all day. But, after all,
he had told her that they would live separate lives. And would
she really want to demand more from him than he had already
given? She could not think about that. After all, she could
not fault his strict code of honour and duty to protect her
from worldly condemnation.

Now she was dressed for the evening with the ordeal of a
family celebration to face. Nerves fluttered and swooped uncomfortably in her stomach at the prospect of so many unknown faces. They might have gathered for an important family event but the main topic of conversation would
undoubtedly be the remarkable *mésalliance* of the Marquis
of Aldeborough to an unknown from the depths of the country and the scandalous events that had precipitated it. She
paced the floor of her bedchamber, wishing that Juliet would
come and take pity on her and calm her anxieties with her
light-hearted chatter and irreverent comment.

There was a sharp knock on the door, causing Frances to
look up in anticipation. But it was not Juliet. Instead Aldeborough entered, dressed in formal evening attire for the first
time since Frances had met him. The black satin knee
breeches and swallow-tailed coat with white waistcoat embroidered in gold and with impeccable white linen gave him
an air of magnificence that took her breath away and robbed
her of words. How had she not realised that her husband was
so very handsome?

He advanced towards her with catlike grace, the candles
touching the tips of his black hair with gold and turning his
eyes to silver quartz. She found her hands taken in his cool
grasp and raised to his lips. The touch of his mouth on her
fingers sent rills of response along her skin.

'How can I expect you to forgive me, Frances Rosalind? I

have neglected you dreadfully today, in spite of all my good intentions and promises. You must have decided that I was a sad bargain in the marriage stakes.' His smile, which she was beginning to find irresistible, drew an answering one from her.

'I don't expect you to dance attendance on me, my lord,' she replied calmly, with as level a gaze as she could muster, their previous encounter forcefully in her mind.

'But your first day! It was unforgivable, even if unavoidable. I trust Matthew devoted himself to your entertainment and comfort?'

'Indeed he did. He told me he dare not disobey orders if he valued his life.'

Aldeborough laughed. 'I must remind him about that some time.'

'Juliet suggested that you were spending your day at Jackson's Saloon,' she informed him with the hint of a mischievous twinkle in her eye. 'Or buying a horse.'

'She would.' He grinned in appreciation. 'Nothing so pleasant, I do assure you. You were not abandoned for my own pleasure.' Frances felt a sudden warmth spread through her limbs at his words. 'All deeds and dusty lawyers—it seems to be never ending. But *you* seem to have spent your time most effectively. Let me look at you.'

He surveyed her critically and unsmilingly from her restrained curls to her new satin evening slippers. She immediately raised her chin, unsure whether she enjoyed that attention or resented the intense scrutiny.

Aldeborough circled her with a critical eye. She stood before him, outwardly calm and elegant in a simple column of palest *eau de nil* satin overlaid by delicate cream lace. The neck line was fashionably draped, allowing the swell of her slight bosom to peep above the low corsage. She wore long evening gloves in the finest kid and her only jewellery was his silver locket, which nestled between her breasts. The ensemble was completed by a painted ivory-and-lace fan with carved sticks. She looked lovely, he thought, as she spread the antique fan with innate grace and turned her head to fol-

low his progress. He was surprised by a surge of possessive-
ness and a quickened beat of his heart. Her skin glowed,
delicately tinted with rose and her eyes were the luminous
azure of dew-drenched delphiniums. For the first time since
he had set eyes on her, recoiling from the interested and salacious attentions of a group of drunken gamblers, she appeared relaxed and less haunted. There were no shadows beneath those glorious eyes tonight. He discovered that he was
holding his breath as he appreciated the depth of her charm.
No, he decided, she was not a beauty in the classical mould.
But, by God, he found her delightfully attractive. He stretched
out his hand to caress her cheek because he felt compelled
to do so. He was delighted to see the colour there deepen a
little.

'I like your hair,' he commented simply. Juliet's maid had
curbed its waywardness and dressed it in ringlets on the
crown of her head with one coaxed to fall becomingly on to
her shoulder. Tiny curls had been allowed to frame her face
and drift in wisps over her ears.

'Where is the country mouse I married?' He sounded satisfied with the transformation.

'Still here under this disguise!' Frances's voice expressed
all her feminine delight at the knowledge that she was turned
out in the height of present fashion and she loved it. 'If you
look very closely, you can still see the whiskers.'

'Well I must tell you that I like you very well, Madame
Mouse. You make a most acceptable Marchioness, in spite
of all your concerns.'

'Thank you, kind sir.' She dropped him a pert curtsy, to
hide her sudden discomfort at his compliments. 'But I must
tell you that I don't wish to go to this party. I'm terrified that
I shall freeze and be unable to say a sensible word to anyone.
And then what will your family think? Probably that you have
taken leave of your senses!'

'I guarantee that you will charm them all,' Aldeborough
encouraged gently. 'And it is important that we be seen together, that we find our marriage more than merely accept-

able. As I do.' He bowed formally. 'Then your reputation as my wife will be altogether without blemish.'

'Of course. I understand.'

He took her hand and placed it on his proffered satin sleeve. 'Then let us begin the campaign, my lady.'

Hours later Frances relaxed against her pillows. She felt tired and exhilarated, both at the same time, and could not contemplate sleep. She wielded her hairbrush, vigorously brushing her hair out of its ringlets in preparation for braiding it for the night. So many new faces, so many introductions, so many names and family connections. They blurred together. As good as his word, Aldeborough had kept close attendance, smoothing out the introductions, always solicitous and aware of the possibility of any discomfort, the epitome of a kind and considerate husband. There had been speculative glances, of course. It had to be expected. But no hint of gossip or unkind comment had been allowed to reach her ears. Aldeborough's coldly smiling assurance and, she had to admit, his sheer arrogance had made any unpleasantness unthinkable. As a result, her confidence had grown and she had found herself laughing, enjoying the conversation, playing her new role with surprising enjoyment.

Juliet and Matthew had been quietly supportive, instructed by Aldeborough, she believed, to divert any difficulties. Lady Aldeborough, forced by necessity into compliance and detesting every moment of it, had managed to ignore her beyond a supercilious stare. After all, there had been nothing in her appearance for that lady to carp at. Miss Vowchurch and her languid parent had been graciously condescending, promising an invitation to a small gathering of select people that they would be holding in the next week. They hoped that the new Marchioness, and Aldeborough of course, would grace them with their presence. Frances had smiled and equally feigned total delight at the prospect. But far more importantly, she had been introduced to the Countess of Lieven, one of the formidable Patronesses of Almack's, who had greeted her with chilling formality and little enthusiasm, but had promised admission vouchers. Frances knew that her acceptance into the *haute ton* was complete. Aldeborough had smiled cynically with a curled lip; it was amazing what a title and a fortune could achieve!

Her thoughts returned to Miss Vowchurch. Frances had had the leisure to observe the lady and had come to the conclusion that here lay a threat. Mrs Winters and her relationship with Aldeborough, revealed by Matthew as they drove in Hyde Park, was still an unknown quantity, but Miss Vowchurch had left Frances with a sense of disquiet. Aldeborough, of course, was no longer free and yet Miss Vowchurch had used every opportunity to catch his interest, even to flirt in a subtle, understated manner. Not with a fluttering of her lashes or the delicate use of her fan—that would be far too blatant for the proper Miss Vowchurch. But Frances had not mistaken the quiet conversation, the proprietorial hand on her husband's sleeve when she wished to attract his attention. And the Dowager actually seemed to encourage it, suggesting that Aldeborough should squire her to the supper table. Not that he had—he had ensured that his bride was comfortably settled—but it had given Frances pause for thought. The Paragon might be a Beauty, but she was no longer a young débutante. Why, she might be all of three and twenty. Perhaps there was an element of despair in her approach to Aldeborough. Pitying gossips would soon have her well and truly on the shelf and Penelope would not care for that humiliation.

And what of the Marquis? Frances's frown deepened. Well, he had not exactly encouraged Penelope, but nor had he put an end to her pretensions. Of course, he could hardly give her a public set-down, she mused, as she was such a close friend of the family, but did he really need to smile at her so charmingly or bend his head so intimately towards her to listen to her honeyed words? At least there had been no dancing so that Frances did not have to bear the mortification of seeing The Paragon in the arms of her husband in a waltz. It was amazing, Frances decided, how much she had come to dislike the lady on such a short acquaintance.

The door to her room opened.

Aldeborough!

She stiffened, her hand holding her hairbrush poised in mid-air. Her breath caught in her throat. 'I did not expect you to visit me, my lord.' She tried hard for composure and a smile and was relatively pleased with the result.

And she wishes I had not, thought the Marquis ruefully, as the confusion of doubt and anxiety flitted across her expressive features and the telltale blush stole up to her temples from the lace edging of her chemise.

'Shall I go away?' He sighed inwardly. Did he really want the burden of a reluctant wife tonight? He could have retreated, of course, with a polished excuse and found more congenial company elsewhere. But then he was taken aback by the sudden kick of lust in his gut at the sight of her sitting against the bank of pillows, eyes huge, hair unconfined.

'I did not know you were home,' she stammered, keeping the smile in place, realising that her initial comment had been less than welcoming. 'I thought that gentlemen went on to gaming clubs and…and such things.' Such as Letitia Winters; the insidious thought struck her, startling her by its aptness.

'It had crossed my mind,' he admitted with a serious expression. 'But, as I remember you once informed me, I am no gentleman.'

She felt herself flush vividly in consternation. 'I did not mean that. I was…' She floundered helplessly.

He laughed and moved to sit on the edge of the bed, trying not to notice that she imperceptibly drew away from him.

'You are forgiven. Besides, I thought I would like to spend some time with my new wife, who is looking so lovely.' He was surprised to hear himself say those words, but found it to be true. 'I hope you enjoyed all the compliments.'

He leaned forward to take the brush from her rigid fingers and lay it down on her nightstand. Then he framed her face with his hands, pushing her hair behind her ears, and applied his lips gently to her temples, her eyes and finally her mouth. Her perfume overwhelmed his senses, her lips were eminently kissable. Her skin was incredibly soft and smooth as wild silk, giving an impression of great fragility. Again he was struck by the growing urgency of his desire to take her. He released her to douse the candles, rapidly strip off his clothing and stretch himself beside her.

She was as warm and fragrant as he remembered, obedient to his commands, trembling as his hands touched her body. It was easier to enter her. She wound her arms around his neck, holding him closely, burying her face against his chest as he took his own pleasure. He took care not to frighten her, conscious of her inexperience, but although she did not resist him, as on the previous night she remained reticent and withdrawn, making no sound of either enjoyment or discomfort.

She was aware of his every touch. She knew what to expect, anticipated it, wanted it even, but for some unfathomable reason beyond her reach, her brain would not allow her body to accept or respond with pleasure. What was wrong with her? She could only cling to him, mould her body to his, accommodate him as he wished until it was over because she was afraid of so many things, afraid of rejection, of allowing him to become aware of her own growing feelings towards him, and of his retribution if she should displease him. She noted as from a distance the caress of his hands, his mouth, the whole long, hard length of his body, but it could not break through the barrier around her heart and her physical response. She found it was utterly impossible for her to show him anything of her own desire to touch him, to return his passion. And she could never explain to him—it would be too humiliating. She clung to him in a storm of desolation that threatened to drown her in its overwhelming torrent.

He sensed her relief when it was over and he withdrew from her. In spite of his physical satisfaction he felt piqued, hurt even, at her lack of response. It was no better than the first time he had come to her. And he had prided himself on his finesse in awakening feminine desires and responses in the hearts of those women who had shared his bed. He had never had any complaints. Letitia had always been more than co-operative in making herself available to his demands. He blocked out his wayward thoughts of that warm, inventive body and focused instead on the slight, unresponsive figure still cradled in his arms. Her eyes were closed as if to shut out the sight of him. He had thought he had detected a warmth in her, a spirit of generosity and courage, a need to give as well as to receive. Disappointment welled up within him as he was forced to accept that he had been mistaken. But what did he expect? Did he really want more from a wife as long as she was able to play the part assigned to her and produce the heir his duty to his family demanded? In the end, did it matter that she disliked the intimacies of the marriage bed and rewarded him with cold compliance? Yes, it did, and for perhaps the first time in his heedless life he did not know what to do about it. Without a word, he withdrew his sheltering arms and left her.

Tonight Frances made no effort to detain him. She buried her face in the pillows and wept all the tears that she had prevented him from seeing. And for what she wept she did not know. There was a great emptiness, a sense of abandonment within her, now made so much worse by Aldeborough's absence. And, she chided herself through her sobs, desperately aware of her rejection of him, she could hardly blame him if he never came to her bed again!

Chapter Six

At breakfast next morning Aldeborough noted Frances's pale features but without comment. She was quite composed and greeted the assembled family with a smile and a comment on how exhausting family gatherings were when faces and names were unknown. Matthew expressed the opinion that *all* family gatherings were a strain and to be avoided if possible. Frances laughed and agreed. She had spirit. But she found it impossible to lift her eyes to meet his direct gaze and answered briefly when he enquired whether she had slept well.

Aldeborough put down his copy of the *Morning Post* and addressed Frances directly. 'I thought, if you wish it, that we could perhaps see some of the sights since you have never been in town before. I'm sure it will amuse you. What do you think?'

Frances's face lit with pleasure. 'I would like that above all things. I have read about London, of course, my uncle's library was full of old history books and indeed some travel diaries, but I would dearly love to see the Tower and St Paul's and…and everything really.' She smiled, but without embarrassment at her lack of sophistication. 'I'm sorry if I seem such a country nobody, but you cannot imagine what it was like to be shut away at Torrington Hall all your life.'

Aldeborough laughed at her enthusiasm.

'Believe me, I can! So, since the sun is shining, we will gratify your wish. Are you busy this morning, Juliet?' He looked across to his sister who was sitting over a cup of coffee, leafing through the pages of *La Belle Assemblée*. 'Do you wish to accompany us? You notice that I don't bother to ask you, Matthew.'

'I'm engaged to meet some fellows at Tattersall's,' Matthew replied hastily, continuing to eat his way through a plate of cold beef and ham. 'History's not really my thing.'

'You surprise me. But it would do you good. Especially a tour of Westminster Abbey. Extending your education or something of that nature.'

'Hmm. I would rather look at horseflesh.'

'I'll come with you,' Juliet broke in, earning a quizzical look from Aldeborough. 'That is, if you can guarantee that our route will take in Bond Street.'

'I thought there might be an ulterior motive.' Aldeborough sighed. 'Let me see. Another hat? As long as it comes out of your allowance and I don't have to pay for it, I am sure it can be arranged.'

An hour later the expedition foregathered in the library, Frances deliciously turned out in a high-waisted morning gown of cream-and-white striped muslin and protected from the chill breeze by a cream silk spencer, frilled at wrist and neck. A matching reticule, French straw bonnet and cream kid gloves completed her toilette and she found that she was able to wield her parasol with more expertise and confidence than she had achieved the previous day. After some discussion, they had decided to take the barouche to the Tower of London when Watkins barred their exit.

'Forgive me, my lord. You have a visitor. I informed him that it was your intention to be away from home for the rest of the morning, but he insisted on seeing you.'

'Who is it, Watkins?'

'Viscount Torrington, my lord.'

Aldeborough felt Frances draw in her breath sharply and her apprehensive gaze fix on him. He remained impassive,

however, gave her a faint smile and responded calmly as if
a visit from Viscount Torrington so early in the day was the
most natural thing in the world.

'I suppose we had better see him. Will you remain here
with me, my lady? It might be for the best.'

Juliet made a diplomatic exit after casting a curious look
in their direction. 'I will go and see if Mama needs me to
run any errands while we are out. Unless you wish for me to
stay as well?'

'No. I think we can manage without you. Show the Viscount into the morning room, if you please, Watkins.'

'What does he want?' Frances was swept with a sudden
fear that her new life would all be snatched away from her.
She felt panic rise in her chest to catch her intake of breath.
She clutched her parasol and reticule with icy fingers.

'He can do nothing that can harm you,' Aldeborough replied soothingly, taking her hand. He was surprised at the
level of her consternation. He regarded her with narrowed
eyes when she clutched his hand fiercely as if she might be
physically torn away. He believed that, given the opportunity,
she would have fled rather than face Torrington. There was
far more involved here than he had realised. 'We will see
him together. There is no cause for such concern.'

'Yes, but...' She took a deep breath, forcing herself to be
calm. 'Of course. We must see my uncle.'

Aldeborough, deliberately formal, bowed Frances before
him into the morning room. Responding in kind to his
prompting, she advanced with an elegant inclination of her
head. It pleased him that she could play the role of Marchioness of Aldeborough with such grace and composure. He felt
a surprising glow of pride as she walked forward at his side.
Viscount Torrington was standing in the window embrasure,
looking down on to the square. He had ridden to Cavendish
Square from his town house in Grosvenor Square and looked
uneasy in the polished surroundings, slapping his riding
gauntlets against his dusty buckskins. His face was impassive,
but harsh grooves were evident across his forehead and

around his thin lips. He turned awkwardly at their entrance, tension in every line of his body, but his attempts at affability were quite deliberate. The two men bowed pleasantly and Frances made a slight curtsy.

'To what do we owe the pleasure of this visit, my lord? Perhaps I can offer you a glass of canary?' Aldeborough did not wait for a reply, but walked to the sideboard with its burden of bottles and glasses and poured out three glasses, one of which he handed to the Viscount.

'Thank you, Aldeborough,' he said genially. 'Forgive me. I realise it is somewhat early for morning visits, but I am rarely in town and I have to return to the country tomorrow. Business, you know.' Torrington's eyes flickered from Aldeborough to Frances and back again. He was clearly ill at ease.

'I am sure that Frances will always be pleased to welcome you to her home.' Aldeborough's tone was bland and non-committal. 'So what brings you to us so early?'

'I simply wanted to…that is…we need to straighten out the unfortunate events of nearly two weeks ago.'

Was it less than two weeks ago? To Frances, it seemed a lifetime.

'I regret… If you will forgive my plain speaking, I cannot have my niece living under your roof. I have her reputation to consider. There has never been any scandal in my family… I have come to take her home where she belongs.'

'Surely it is a little late for such solicitude, my lord?'

'I was not aware that you had left the Priory.'

Aldeborough remained silent, eyebrows raised, his calm gaze fixed on Torrington. Sweat broke out on the Viscount's brow and he allowed his eyes to fall. He coughed nervously and turned to Frances.

'If you would be so good as to pack your possessions, I will take you to Torrington Hall with me, Frances.'

Frances stood rigidly at her husband's side and made no move to obey. The Viscount looked helplessly from one to the other.

'I regret,' said the Marquis quietly, 'there has been some misunderstanding.'

'Oh?'

'I am, of course, relieved that you should be so concerned as to your niece's reputation. Unfortunately, your concern would seem to be a little late in the day. Indeed, if she had lived with me unchaperoned all this time, she would indeed be damned in the eyes of society.' His tone was bitter and his eyes bleak and cold like ice over granite. 'However...' his lips curved in the semblance of a smile '...I am enchanted to be able to inform you that the lady is now my wife.' He raised one hand to prevent Torrington's attempted interruption. 'This is now her home. There is no scandal attached to her name.'

'So soon? This cannot be! I have not given my permission.' Torrington shook his head in denial, unable to grasp the news. As it gradually sank in, he raised his head and glared at Aldeborough. 'I am her legal guardian,' he challenged. 'How dare you pre-empt my permission!'

'Oh, I dare, my lord. I believe you reneged on your guardianship when you subjected my wife to the humiliation of using her as a servant, without dignity and without the respect due to her,' Aldeborough replied harshly.

'But she is my ward.'

'No.' The Marquis turned to look at Frances and formally raised her hand to his lips. 'She is my wife. I would present to you the Marchioness of Aldeborough. She did me the great honour of marrying me at the Priory by special licence.'

'I will have the marriage annulled,' Torrington blustered.

'On what grounds?' Aldeborough kept a strong grip on her fingers. 'There are none,' he said firmly. Frances signalled her agreement, masking her eyes with downswept lashes.

'You will return with me, Frances. I insist.'

'No, my lord. You no longer have power over me to insist.' Frances's response was calm and matter of fact despite her inner turmoil. 'I will, of course, remain with my husband.'

'You will regret this, my lord. I'm sure you would dislike details of these vulgar events to escape—juicy morsels for men to gossip over in the clubs. I thought there had been enough gossip about your family of late.'

Aldeborough's face was pale with suppressed temper, but his voice remained even, untinged with emotion. 'Would you be considering blackmail, my lord? I would not advise it. It would do *you* far more harm if society was aware of your immoral actions towards your niece. If we are speaking of the improper, it is outrageous to use violence, in public, against a young woman of gentle breeding.'

Torrington drew himself up with as much dignity as was left to him. 'You have not heard the last of this.'

'Certainly. There are some loose ends to be tied up, I believe. My man of business will contact you about my wife's inheritance.' The Marquis had resumed his role of genial host. 'I would be grateful if you would instruct him as her ladyship will reach her majority in a few weeks. My wife is no longer your concern.'

'Damn you, Aldeborough. You will regret this, Frances. You may have to pay a heavy price for a title.'

'I think I will not regret it, Uncle.' Frances matched her demeanour to her husband's.

Torrington tossed off the forgotten drink of canary, set down the glass with unnecessary force, and stalked from the room in frustrated anger.

Frances turned to Aldeborough in bewilderment, her dark brows drawn together in a straight line. 'I simply do not understand why he is so anxious to return me to his guardianship. He never showed any concern for my welfare before. I was given to understand on so many occasions that I was an unwanted burden on the family. Quite frankly, I thought he would be glad to get me off his hands.'

'Apparently not. Were you tempted to go with him?' Aldeborough heard himself ask and awaited her answer with some interest.

He did not have to wait long.

'Never! I will never go back!'

'There is no question of it.' He paused. 'Can you tell me

why the prospect distresses you so much? I would not have you worry for no reason.'

She shook her head. Gathering the rags of her self-possession around her, she forced her face into a bright smile. 'No reason, my lord. Other than that I have no wish to be buried alive at Torrington Hall as I said at breakfast. Can we go now if we are to visit the Tower? Or do you think it is too late?'

'Not at all. The sights of London are at your feet and the barouche awaits.' He bowed her out of the Library, aware of a faint shadow of concern that would not go away. His wife could dissemble, he realised. He wondered why.

Frances settled into her life in Cavendish Square. To her relief, she had to suffer no more tête-à-tête with the Dowager, whose cold displeasure, cloaked in brittle good manners, continued to cast a shadow over the household. In Juliet she discovered a lively, sympathetic confidante with whom she could gossip and exchange ideas about fashions and other fripperies. She did not find it easy to open her heart to her new sister after her previous solitary existence, but Juliet was not discouraged by her reticence and entertained Frances with her chatter and enthusiasms. Matthew was invaluable. When he could be pinned down and distracted from any sporting activity on which he expended his energies, and be persuaded to squire the two ladies around town, he was the brother Frances never had. He was open and friendly to a fault, unfailingly good natured and willing to oblige, unlike his elder brother.

Frances saw little of Aldeborough. When she did, he was polite, courteous but invariably distant. He did not come to her at night, which left Frances disturbed by her conflicting emotions. She was not disappointed, she told herself, relieved even. Her inability to accept his touch, his caresses, without a frisson of fear troubled her, so surely it should be with a sense of relief that she accepted that he had no interest in her. Yet the memory of those fine-boned hands on her arms, her shoulders, her breasts, awoke in her a desire to repeat the experience. And her fingers curled into admirable talons when the image of Letitia Winters came into her mind and she imagined how Aldeborough might be enjoying such intimacies with her. Frances abandoned any attempt to understand the logic in her thoughts. But she missed him.

In the week following Torrington's unsettling visit, Frances was seated in the gold withdrawing room. She had abandoned Juliet, who for the past hour had failed to choose between a dozen hats for their afternoon promenade, and was passing the time perusing the pages of fashion plates in a new edition of *Le Beau Monde*. An evening creation in palest blue satin with a spangled gauze overskirt and deep ruching around the hem had just caught her attention when Watkins announced that, if her ladyship was at home to visitors, Mr Hanwell was awaiting her in the morning room. Her immediate response was to refuse. There was no one here to give her moral support—it would be so easy to have Watkins say that she was otherwise engaged. But that was cowardly and foolish, she told herself. Charles was her cousin and indeed had never shown her anything but kindness, even if it was of a superficial nature that would not bring him into conflict with his father. There was nothing here to disturb her.

Charles entered the room, ushered in by Watkins, and she rose to greet him. He was just as she remembered. Pleasing to look at, well groomed and dressed with propriety without being in the height of fashion, his fair hair fashionably cut, his hazel eyes warm and full of humour and with a smile of welcome on his face as he advanced towards her. He took her outstretched hand in his to draw her closer and took the liberty of close relationship to lean down to kiss her cheek. Frances found herself smiling with pleasure at seeing a familiar face in her new world.

'Frances. How well you look. Town life obviously suits you—why, you have grown quite beautiful in the weeks since I last saw you. Are you enjoying being in the first stare of fashion? And a title to give you consequence!'

Frances's unease quickly dissipated and she blushed at her

own foolishness at being afraid to receive Charles. He was not like his father. She laughed with him—receiving compliments, she had discovered, was most acceptable.

'Thank you, Charles. As you see, I am quite well. And I find that London is most entertaining—I had no idea.' Struck by a sudden thought, she asked, 'Did my uncle ask you to call?'

'No, indeed. Why should he? I hardly need instructions to visit my own pretty cousin. I am in town for a few days and what better way to spend some of my time. Would you be insulted if I said that I never realised how attractive you are?'

He kissed the hand which he still had in his possession.

'You flatter me, Charles. I am certain it has a lot to do with these new clothes.' She brushed a hand over her primrose muslin with pleasurable appreciation, enjoying the open admiration in Charles's face. 'Please sit down. Can I offer you a cup of tea?'

'Thank you, but no. I must not stay long.' He hesitated, as if making a difficult decision over his next words, then fixed her with a serious and concerned gaze.

'I don't find this easy to say—but I believe my father may have upset you on his last visit.' His eyes were full of sympathy. 'It was something he said when he returned home that made me think... It did not seem to me that he dealt with you with the respect and care that you merited. I thought I should come to apologise for him. He only has your best interests at heart, you know. We simply want you to be happy and not to have been forced into something that would give you distress.'

Frances was taken aback by such candour. 'Indeed, Charles, there is no need—'

'But there is,' he interrupted. 'Are you happy?' he asked brusquely.

'Well, I...' She pulled her hand from his clasp in some confusion. How should she answer?

'Forgive me if I seem too forward. But does Aldeborough treat you well? I know that he has a reputation—and his name has been linked with any number of ladies in the past. You do not deserve to be slighted or neglected by an inattentive husband.'

Frances stepped back from her cousin. She might appreciate his concern for her well being, but she would not discuss her husband with him. 'You must not say such things to me,' she responded, a cool note apparent in her voice. 'He is very kind and I can have no criticism of his behaviour towards me.'

'There, I have disturbed you, which is something I wished most to avoid.' Charles smiled ruefully, quickly attempting to heal the small rift that had appeared. 'I simply hoped that he does not neglect you. It can be very lonely in town if you do not have a wide acquaintance.'

'Indeed, I am not lonely.'

'Of course not. But I saw Aldeborough at Newmarket this week and noticed that you were not with him.'

'No. But he has his own life to lead. And I mine. There is no need for your concern.'

'And I am sure that you are finding much to entertain you. It would not be expected that you would live in each other's pockets. And I doubt you would approve of all of his interests.' He smiled to remove any hint of criticism. 'He lost a considerable amount of money at Newmarket—but I suppose that when you are in possession of such a vast fortune, losing so much is of little consequence.'

'No.' Frances frowned, uncertain of Charles's intentions.

'And with the problems in the Lafford family in the past, it really is a case of still waters. But as long as you are content, then I am satisfied.'

Frances felt a sudden urge to ask about these unspecified problems of the past, but a reluctance to encourage Charles kept her silent. And, after all, he would not be an impartial observer.

'Your solicitude is very touching.'

'But of course. You are my cousin.'

For a long moment Frances considered his words, studying his handsome face and compassionate eyes. Memories of her existence at Torrington Hall flooded back, forcing her to respond to the kind words with brutal honesty.

'Forgive me, Charles. I have to admit to some surprise. I do not remember you being quite so considerate of my feelings when I lived at Torrington Hall. You never enquired as to my happiness then.' She could not prevent the sting of censure as she tried to match Charles's present words with her past recollections of him. True, he had never shown the careless indifference, cruelty even, of her aunt and uncle, but neither had he shown her any affection, or championed her against the neglect. And he had not stayed his father's whip. For that she found it difficult to forgive him.

'Frances. That is untrue. You know how difficult it is to take a stand against my father. Even the slightest resistance or criticism pushed him to further excess. I always did what I could. But short of removing you from the household, I could not remove you from his jurisdiction. And, after all, he is your legal guardian. But perhaps I deserve your poor opinion.' A smile with a touch of sadness and regret lit his face and admiration gleamed once more in his eyes. 'I am pleased to see that things have worked out so well for you. I am only sad that we two could not have made a match of it as my father had planned. It was my dearest wish.'

Charles held her eyes with his own intense gaze for a long moment and then, as if embarrassed by this declaration and daunted by Frances's silence, he gathered up his hat and gloves and made to leave.

'I must go. Perhaps I have said too much, but my concern for you is immeasurable. Will you promise me one thing?' His face was set and serious. 'If you ever need help of any kind, please don't hesitate to ask me. I would count it a privilege to be at your service, my lady. And perhaps have the opportunity to put right some of the wrongs of the past. I am sure that you understand me.'

He raised her hand again to his lips and once more bent to salute her cheek, his eyes meeting hers with an intimate warmth that surprised her. She found herself returning the smile, relieved that she and her cousin should part on such good terms. Perhaps she had misjudged him in the past. She did not pull her hand away when he smiled so warmly at her.

Upon which the door opened to reveal the Marquis of Aldeborough on the threshold. With slow deliberation he took in the scene before him, eyes narrowed, expression enigmatic.

Frances looked at him in some consternation, angry at the sudden flush that stained her cheeks, but her gaze was steady and direct.

'Good afternoon, Aldeborough,' she said with calm composure. 'Here is Cousin Charles, who is in Town for a few days.'

'Of course. It appears to be becoming a habit of mine to interrupt meetings between your family and my wife, sir.' He executed an impeccable bow.

'I was about to take my leave, my lord,' Charles responded as affably as possible under that flintlike stare.

'Then do not let me detain you.'

Charles made an apologetic inclination of the head in Frances's direction. 'I trust that I will have the opportunity to see you again before I return to Torrington Hall, my lady. Perhaps at the Taverners' ball. My lord.' With a curt nod to Aldeborough, he left the room.

Frances turned to face her husband. 'You were not very friendly, my lord.'

'I do not feel very friendly. What was he doing here?'

'He only came to wish me well and hoped that I was happy.'

'I noticed.' His voice was cold with condemnation. 'He was kissing your hand. And your cheek. There is no knowing what liberties he would have taken if I had not come into the room at that moment.'

Frances was almost speechless at such an unwarranted accusation. 'Liberties?' she gasped. 'He is my cousin!'

'Be clear on this, Frances. I will not have you kissing other men, cousin or no.'

'Really!' A flash of anger lit her eyes as she rejected this high-handed attitude from her husband, who had absented himself at Newmarket for the past three days and left her to her own devices. And who, it seemed, not only had the reputation of being an accomplished flirt, but kept a very attractive mistress! 'How dare you dictate how I should respond to my cousin!'

'Very easily. And, let me remind you, you were very keen to escape from his presence some weeks ago. There seemed to be no warmth in your relationship then. Obviously I have missed something here.' His eyes were cold and searching.

'What are you suggesting? Besides, you said that we should live our own lives. As you are clearly doing!'

'With discretion!' he flung back. 'Kissing Charles in the withdrawing room is not discreet.'

'Are you really suggesting that *I* would do anything improper?'

'*You* might not, but I have little confidence in the rest of your family.'

'I really do not think that is fair when you—'

Frances bit back the words before she could say more, fortunately, she felt, as they were interrupted by the arrival of Juliet, who chose to be oblivious to the heated atmosphere in the room.

'Hello, Hugh. We've missed you. How was Newmarket?' He glared at her cheerful presence, but she ignored him. 'Was that your cousin I saw leaving just now, Frances?'

'Yes.'

'What a pity I did not join you earlier. I didn't realise that he was so attractive. You could have introduced me to him.'

Aldeborough looked from one to the other, his face suddenly expressionless, words beyond him.

'There really is no accounting for taste,' he snarled at last and with a gesture of disgust flung out of the room.

'What's happened to put him in such a bad humour?' Juliet stared after him in some surprise. 'His horse won at Newmarket so I thought he would be in a good mood. I don't suppose you asked him if he would accompany us to the Taverners' ball tonight?'

Frances sighed. A chill settled round her heart.

Chapter Seven

The Taverners' Ball was the event of the Season. Although early and London still shy of the *haute ton*, the crush in the flower-decked, silk-hung rooms of Viscount Taverner's magnificent town house testified to society's desire to put itself on show. And, of course, the Marquis of Aldeborough and the new Marchioness would be present.

For Frances, fashionably turned out in her favourite jonquil silk with cream and gold ribbons, decorated with knots of silk primroses, it was an occasion that combined pleasure, fear, satisfaction and jealousy in a subtle but complicated weave. Afterwards she was to remember it as a series of brilliant jewel-like cameos, one imposed on another, swamping her mind and senses with images that she would never forget—and one that troubled her heart and her dreams and allowed her no peace.

To her delight and intense relief, Frances found herself accepted and drawn into the Wigmore fold. Aldeborough took the opportunity of the Ball to introduce her to the Earl of Wigmore, a young, fair-haired man with an open smiling countenance. The Earl called on the help of his Countess who was, as he explained, a veritable expert on the ramifications of the family tree. Frances was soon identified as the daughter of Aunt Cecilia about whom No One Ever Spoke, not after she had been so misguided as to run off to marry such an

unsuitable young man and his grandfather had put his foot
down. The Earl, of course, had been far too young to remember the events in detail or to be involved in such undoubtedly
unfair banishment from the family's embrace. The old Earl
had been a stickler for family pride and advantageous marriages. And for Cecilia to flout his authority and deliberately
set herself against his dictates…

Well, that was all in the past now and should be forgotten:
and the Earl was sure that the Hanwells were most respectable—although they did not mix socially with Viscount and
Lady Torrington, you understand—and he was pleased to
make his unknown cousin's acquaintance, particularly since
she was now Marchioness of Aldeborough. He could not fail
to miss the cynical smile from Aldeborough as the Countess
invited Frances to take tea with her later in the week when
they might discuss their bloodlines at leisure. Cynical the
Marquis might be, but Frances could not deny her satisfaction
at their casual acceptance.

The country dancing presented Frances with a challenge
that she was able to meet without drawing too much attention
to her inadequacies, at least when her nerves allowed her
heart beat to quieten and her pulse rate to slow. Matthew,
beginning the initiation, proved to be as graceful on the dance
floor as he was on horseback, as well as an easy conversa-
tionalist, as he led her into a cotillion. She had some experience of the intricate changes and figures from her youthful
days of basic education with the daughters of the Rector of
Torrington.

'All you need is a little confidence,' Matthew encouraged
her, aware of her pallor and anxious glances at what her feet
might be doing. 'That wasn't too bad, was it?' as he led her
from the floor. 'Here.' He hailed Ambrose, unusually elegant
in dark coat and satin knee breeches. 'Let Ambrose lead you
through a quadrille. And remember, you are allowed to converse with him. Your feet can manage quite well without
being watched and you don't need to count so feverishly—
or aloud!'

Ambrose grinned; Frances smiled and relaxed, enjoying the
tempo of the music, the patterns of the measures, the butterfly
hues of the dancers around her. She glimpsed Aldeborough
further down the set, holding the hand of a vivacious brunette
as she twirled delightfully beneath his raised arm. Her dress
was the rose-embroidered white muslin of a débutante and
she was smiling shyly up into his face.

'Who is the lady dancing with Aldeborough?' Frances
asked as the movement of the dance brought them together.
Ambrose strained round the adjacent pair to look.

'Miss Ingram, one of this year's leading débutantes,' he
informed her. 'She is regarded as a diamond of the first water.'

'Yes, she is.' Frances managed to catch another glimpse
of the feminine figure, fair ringlets and large, deep brown
eyes.

'She has had a number of offers already,' Ambrose continued helpfully. 'Above my touch, of course, even if I was
considering getting shackled, which I am not. Her mama held
out high hopes of Hugh. So did a few others with eligible
daughters after he set up a flirtation. That is...until—' He
stopped, catching Frances's interested and faintly horrified
expression with some remorse. Then the demands of the quadrille parted them again. As it ended and he bowed over her
hand, leading her from the floor, he apologised.

'Forgive me, Frances. I should not have said what I did.
Not to you.'

Frances sighed, relieved that her relationship with Ambrose
was now sufficiently relaxed to allow her some honesty.

'Why not, if it is the truth?' She smiled reassuringly at
him, ignoring the ache in her heart. 'We both know I am not
the bride he would have chosen. I would rather know the
truth than live in a fantasy.'

'Yes, I suppose you would.' His face was grave, a frown
between his brows. 'Hugh does not realise how lucky he is!
And I suppose I should not have said that either.' He lifted
her hand to his lips again with more than a mere polite salute,
jolted by the depth of sadness in her eyes. As Frances turned

her head to hide her emotions from his sharp gaze, she was struck by the sensation of being under scrutiny. She looked up to see Aldeborough watching her from across the room. She held the gaze for a long moment, unable to interpret it, and then turned back to exchange a conversation with Juliet who had joined them, charming in maiden's blush pink, but not before she had noted the frown in Aldeborough's eyes and the tightening of his lips. She would not show that she cared.

Aldeborough detached himself from Miss Ingram to lead Frances into a waltz. His set expression and the cold quartz-like glint in his eyes did not auger well, but Frances set herself to ignore the drop in temperature. If he felt that duty forced him into soliciting a waltz from his wife, then she would oblige. And if he was still ruffled over Charles's visit, there was nothing she could do about it. She achieved a bright smile and swept a graceful curtsy.

'I think I should warn you that I have never waltzed before,' she informed him as his arm encircled her waist in what she could only describe as an intimate embrace. 'The Rector of Torrington did not consider it a proper dance for his daughters to participate in, so I have never learnt the steps.'

There was nothing intimate in his reply or his tone.

'I realise that. You have trodden on my feet at least three times since we began in spite of all my efforts to lead you. Perhaps your mind is on other things.' His expression and tone of voice gave her no encouragement.

'How unfair! I did tell you that I had no talents, if you remember,' she remarked, sounding, even to her own ears, waspish, but without remorse.

'I do remember. You were very accurate.'

'And you are in a very bad mood!' She jettisoned any attempts to be conciliatory and glared at him. 'You are spoiling my first ball.'

'Fortunately you are not short of partners who, it appears, are perfectly willing to be in a good mood.'

She could think of no way to answer this and finished her first waltz in glacial and dignified silence.

It was true that she did not lack for partners. Unfortunately, in the circumstances, Charles was one of them. As he put himself out to be charming, they encircled the floor with some grace, Frances's feet becoming more obedient to her will. He smiled and conversed like a man of sense, putting her at her ease, but all the time she was aware of Aldeborough's critical regard.

'Forgive me, Frances. I did not intend to give Aldeborough the wrong impression this afternoon or give him a weapon to use against you. I was only showing a cousinly concern.'

'There is no problem, Charles. Aldeborough and I understand each other very well.' She would not discuss her relationship with her husband, but she found it difficult not to respond to Charles's warm smile and expressions of concern, so different from the Marquis's chilly arrogance. She found herself returning his smile and laughing at his light conversational remarks. She would ignore the waves of disapproval from the man whom she was learning had the reputation of being nothing less than a rake.

The evening ended for Frances in an abyss. She furthered her acquaintance with Miss Vowchurch, but did not enjoy the experience or realise the repercussions that would spread like ripples from a pebble tossed carelessly into a pond. As that lady was chaperoned by the Dowager Lady Aldeborough, resplendent in maroon satin and nodding ostrich plumes, she had no choice but to exchange pleasantries between dances. Penelope looked enchanting in a white organdie gown with an overslip of spangled gauze and the cotillion which she had danced with Aldeborough made Frances very much aware of how well they were suited. She was all grace and elegance; she would have made an excellent Marchioness.

'How charming you look tonight.' Penelope could afford

to be gracious. 'I see that you have been improving your dancing skills.'

'Indeed. Matthew and Ambrose have kindly allowed me to practise on them. Their feet have suffered but they have been most complimentary.'

'Aldeborough dances so well. I saw him waltzing with Miss Charlesworth. How delightful they looked together. And at the moment—ah—I see he is waltzing with Mrs Winters. Have you been introduced? I admit to being surprised to see her here, but then she is received everywhere, although my mama would not consider inviting her to one of our select soirées. Aldeborough, of course, knows her very well. Perhaps he will introduce you.'

Penelope, demure expression intact, was invited to join a set with Lord Hay, a smile of satisfaction on her lips and the coldness of a serpent in her eyes, leaving Frances to assess the deliberate intent in that kind observation. Alone for a moment, she was able to take a closer look at the lady who had acknowledged her in Hyde Park. Mrs Winters's demeanour on the dance floor in the Marquis's arms proclaimed her experienced in the art of flirtation. The flame of desire in the lady's sparkling eyes could not be dismissed. Nor could the overt attraction of her voluptuous bosom and stylish figure, superbly enhanced by her low-cut gown. Her jewellery was tasteful, drawing attention to her long fingers and delicate wrists. Her golden curls, artfully arranged so that they fell from a high knot on to her pale shoulders, framed a charming face with much character. It was such a pity, Frances thought, that her green eyes were quite so predatory. Her own fingers curled into admirable catlike claws as she observed the lady casting flirtatious glances at Aldeborough, laughing at his comments. At the same time Aldeborough bent to catch something she had said, his cheek almost brushing her hair, an intensely intimate gesture. Frances's nails buried themselves painfully into her soft palms.

She raised her chin and turned away to find Ambrose, who had offered to procure for her a glass of wine, beside her. They stood in a window embrasure, Frances endeavouring to

cool her heated cheeks in relative privacy, sipping the bub-
bles. She looked at him and sighed a little. They were in
perfect accord and he did not pretend to misunderstand her.

'I suppose he has broken many hearts in the past.'

'Yes…' Ambrose smiled wryly '…but not intentionally, I
think. He would not be so cruel.'

'No.'

'Don't let him break yours.'

She tried to stem the rush of emotion that lodged in her
throat on being shown such unexpected sympathy.

'You are very understanding.'

She held out her hand after only the slightest hesitation
and Ambrose took it, holding it warmly between his own.

'He doesn't mean anything by it, you know. Don't judge
him before you know him better. He is the best friend a man
could have and the last months have not been easy for him.
He has lost much and gained little. He has not found it easy
to come to terms with Richard's death and he blames himself.'

'And, if the truth be told, I have not made the situation
any better for him, have I?' There was no self-pity in
Frances's eyes, merely acceptance. It touched Ambrose's
heart, so much so that for once it prompted him to take the
Marquis to task for being so blind to the feelings of those
around him. He pressed Frances's hand in sympathy.

At which unfortunate point, the friend under discussion
materialised at Frances's elbow, looking anything but ami-
cable.

'It is late. If I may interrupt your tête-à-tête, I will escort
you home, my lady.'

'Of course.' She withdrew her hand from Ambrose's light
clasp and made to follow, but Aldeborough stood back to
allow her to go ahead to join the Dowager and thus give him
the opportunity of a few words with Ambrose.

He was cold and dangerous, anger shimmering around him.
It drove him to utter the first thought that came into his head.

'If you were anyone else, I would call you out!'

'And I would refuse. Don't be ridiculous, man. There was

no impropriety in my conversation with Frances.' Ambrose's response was as deliberately casual as Aldeborough's was heated. He was more than a little interested to note Aldeborough's reaction.

'I do not expect to see you holding my wife's hand in the middle of a ballroom.'

'If you had not been encouraging your latest flirt, Hugh, *you* could have been holding her hand. And she would have enjoyed that much more.'

'I don't flirt!'

'And neither does Frances. If we were anywhere else, I would plant you a leveller.' Ambrose smiled, enjoying his success in provoking his friend. 'It is a pity you can't see what's under your nose.'

'And who gave you permission to call my wife Frances?'

'You did!'

Aldeborough's fury grew as he knew he was in the wrong. 'Go to the Devil.' He turned on his heel to stride after his wife.

Ambrose watched them leave the ballroom. Hugh was exhibiting all the symptoms of a jealous and possessive husband if he did but know it. Ambrose shrugged and went in search of some convivial company with whom he might play a hand of cards, a thoughtful expression in his eyes. He hoped Frances had the courage to stand up to the irate Marquis. The outcome might be interesting. Ambrose thought that Hugh might just have met his match.

She knew that it was not in his nature to allow the matter to rest or his anger to grow cold and she was afraid. She did not know what he and Ambrose had said to each other, but her husband had left the Taverners' town house in a towering fury. The atmosphere in the carriage was white hot with a tension that all but crackled in the air. The Dowager had appeared oblivious, filling the silence with inconsequential but often malicious comment on those present at the ball. Frances answered as required, all the time aware of Aldeborough's brooding presence. Juliet prattled about dresses and dancing.

Her maid removed her exquisite gown with care, unpinned her hair, replaced the pearl set in its velvet case and wished her mistress goodnight. Frances, troubled by all she had learned that night, paced the floor, the silken lace folds of her robe swishing round her feet. She kept her own anger stoked inside her, reliving her first sight of her husband pressing his lips to *that woman*'s jewelled fingers, refusing to acknowledge the underlying shimmer of nerves across her skin.

He entered with his usual feline grace, but without his usual courteous knock. He closed the door quietly, far more sinister than if he had slammed it, and turned the key in the lock. It spoke of an iron determination not to be gainsaid and made Frances catch her breath. He had taken time to divest himself of his evening finery and was now clad in a sumptuous blue satin dressing gown. The expression on his face was not a pleasant one.

She was left standing in the centre of the room in midpace, feeling foolish. This determined her not to be put at a disadvantage so she turned to face him, feigning a confidence which she did not feel.

'I see that you were expecting me, Madame Wife!'

'Yes.' She raised her chin higher.

'I did not expect to have to say this. I will not have you flirting with other men. Do you understand me?'

'I do not flirt with *other men*.' She was swept with a sense of outrage that she certainly did not have to pretend to. 'I have never flirted in my life. Your accusations are groundless.'

'So what exactly was Hanwell doing, holding your hands, kissing your fingers? And then I find you in a secluded conversation with Ambrose! It seems that I misjudged the woman I married.'

Her face paled at the injustice of it all. 'How dare you! Ambrose danced with me when *you* would not! You seemed to be far too involved admiring Miss Ingram—and I was only holding Ambrose's hand for…for comfort.'

'If it is comfort you want, try me.' He held out his hand imperiously, hiding the bitter jealously that lodged in his gut. It was riding him hard, to his disgust, but his control faltered as he remembered Frances, her eyes dark with pain that he had caused, offering her hand to his friend, who had had no compunction in taking it. The fact that he knew Frances to be totally innocent made not one bit of difference. She was his, and he would share her with no one.

'Give me your hands,' he repeated.

'No!' Frances hid her hands behind her back and shook her head. His arrogance spurred her on to the offensive.

'I am surprised that you had the time to notice what I was doing,' she reflected in a clear voice, shaking inside at her impetuosity. The result could be like rousing a sleeping tiger. 'How could you possibly drag your attention away from the charms of Mrs Winters?' Frances held her breath. What had possessed her to challenge him so openly?

Aldeborough stiffened as if she had struck him. 'I beg your pardon?'

'Mrs Winters was pointed out to me by any number of people,' she explained, with more intent than honesty, meeting his daggerlike gaze.

'What do you know of Letitia Winters?' His usual smooth tones had the edge of a blade to them.

'Very little,' she admitted. 'Is there more I should know? It appears to be common knowledge that you enjoy her company more than a little.' Frances turned her back on him and moved towards the fireplace, her shoulders tense as she awaited his reply, aware that she was playing with fire, but reckless enough not to care, carried along on a relentless wave of righteous indignation.

'She has nothing to do with our marriage. She is not your concern.'

'Then you have no right to question my behaviour, even if it was improper—which I do not to any degree admit! Charles and Ambrose have never treated me with anything but perfect propriety. You have no right to stand in judgement.'

'I have every right. You are my wife. And so you belong to me, body and soul.' He strode across the room, seized her shoulders and shook her with a barely suppressed anger and clenched teeth. 'If it is romantic dalliance you crave, then I will provide it. I have more expertise than Ambrose,' he added with an arrogance that took her breath away.

He tore at the ribbons on her wrapper, pushing the fragile material from her shoulders so that it fell with a whisper of silk to the floor. He felt her flinch, saw her eyes become flat and distant, and was instantly flooded with a terrible mingling of anger and desire. It swept away civilised behaviour and the manners of polite society and returned him to the basic primeval need of a man to possess the woman who was his.

'You seem unwilling to respond to my caresses with anything but tolerance. Perhaps I have not tried hard enough.'

She cried out involuntarily as the tangled emotions, kept at bay for so long, attacked her senses, but he silenced her by crushing her mouth under his, holding her lips captive with one hand twisted in her hair. He imprisoned her with his other arm, her body pressed firmly against his. He parted her lips, invading with his tongue, his mouth hot and hard. Here was no delicacy or gentle persuasion, no courtesy or consideration for an untutored bride, but intimate, demanding possession. The touch of his fingers burned through the fine lawn of her chemise and she was supremely conscious of the power of his body as he crushed her against him, breast to breast, thigh to thigh.

He unlaced her chemise and pushed it from her shoulders so that it caught at her elbows. His hot kisses blazed a molten trail, startling her in their intensity. She shivered. His hands ranged, carelessly, greedily, over her shoulders, her breasts, her back. He raised his head, eyes blinded with passion, to rake her pallor, and would have taken possession of her mouth once more when he caught a fleeting reflection of them in the mirror of her dressing table. He froze, eyes narrowed, fingers rigid. And then he startled Frances by abruptly releasing her, stepping back and away. Confusion swirled in her brain. Would he walk away and leave her in this tangle of emotion that she did not understand? She watched as Aldeborough walked to the side table and picked up a branch of candles.

'Turn round.' His voice was expressionless. He had his emotions well in hand, but it was still an order.

She backed away with a little shake of her head. She could not bear for him to see her shame and made to draw her chemise over her shoulders again.

He stretched out a hand to stop her. 'No. Turn round.' She could no longer disobey the stern command and turned, hesitantly, head bent, knowing what would be revealed by the unforgiving light from the candles.

He raised the light high, pushing the soft material down from her shoulders, exposing her back to the candles' flames. The soft light glimmered on the welter of pale silvery stripes across her ivory skin, from shoulder to waist. The scars were well healed but evidence, undoubtedly, of beatings that had broken the skin. And on more than one occasion.

For one long moment he said nothing, did nothing, unable to take in the enormity of it. Then he touched the marks with fingers suddenly exquisitely gentle, tracing the lines of the scars as they criss-crossed the skin, no longer satin smooth as it should have been. How could he have missed such brands before? Probably because you never looked, never expected anything so vile, he admonished himself in disgust. All anger, all unwarranted resentment against her drained out of him, to be replaced by infinite tenderness and compassion. On impulse, he bent his head and pressed his lips to the ugly traces of cruel treatment.

'Who did this to you?' he asked in a low voice. But he knew the answer.

She shrugged as if it were a matter of small consequence. 'My uncle.' But he was not fooled. He had heard the catch in her voice and he had felt the trembling beneath his lips.

Slowly, carefully, fighting to gain mastery over the fury that surged through his blood, he put down the candles on the dressing table, readjusted her chemise over her back and shoulders, refastened the ribbon ties with extreme precision and took her by the hand. He led her to the cushioned couch at the foot of the bed where he seated himself and pulled her to sit beside him. She followed him, biddable as a child.

'Can you tell me about it?'

She shook her head, biting her bottom lip, and pulled her hands away to clasp them tightly in her lap. For some reason that she could not analyse, the scars were degrading, as if the fault had been hers. She did not wish Aldeborough to know about them: she feared that he would feel less of her for causing them. It was bad enough that he should know, that whenever he touched her in future he would be aware of the ugly, disfiguring scars.

'Tell me!' he persisted, determined not to allow her to withdraw, shocked by the deep flash of fear in her eyes.

When she still remained silent he took possession of her hands again. 'Frances, not all men are like your uncle. I will not beat you. I will never wittingly hurt you. Tell me about the beatings.'

She found her voice, a little husky and uncertain, but firm enough. 'I did tell you, if you remember. My uncle...when I tried to run away. He tied me to the bed post and...well, as you can see.'

'But this is more than one beating, isn't it?'

'Yes.' She sighed.

'He hurt you.' He frowned as his mind failed to grasp the outrage of it.

She merely nodded, her teeth buried in her bottom lip.

'But why?'

'I don't think he needed a reason. But it is true that I was not always very co-operative. Probably I deserved it—I was always made to believe so. Once I was late home—my horse had gone lame, but he thought I had tried to escape again and... I don't want to talk about it.'

He was horrified at her calm acceptance of the punishments.

'Nothing you did could have made such treatment acceptable! Was there no one for you to turn to? Your aunt or your cousin?'

Her gaze lifted to his, filled with mockery. 'It was easier for them if they pretended it did not happen.'

He caressed her fingers, considering his next words.

'Did…did your uncle touch you in any other way?'

She shuddered under his hands as his meaning became clear. 'No,' she whispered.

Relief washed over him.

'Was there never anyone to show you any love, any affection, Frances?' He knew the answer and could not bear it.

She shook her head, hiding her face from him.

'You don't like men very much, do you? And, in God's name, who could blame you?'

'I have had no cause to.'

He released her to rub his hands over his face. 'I suppose I haven't helped any. What can I do?' He did not expect an answer, but her resilience surprised him.

'You have nothing to blame yourself for. How could you? You rescued me from a life worse than you can imagine, giving me a home of my own and all this.' She gestured to the room and her clothes. A delicate colour had returned to her face and sparkle to her eyes. 'I have a life of luxury. And I am no longer afraid. I do not wake up every morning, fearing that…that I might do something wrong which would merit punishment. How could you ever realise how important that is to me? How could I possibly have any recriminations against you?'

'But yet you still flinch from me. You accept my lovemaking, but without pleasure. I think that you still believe that I might beat you given any provocation. Do you find my touch so objectionable? Be honest with me, Frances.'

'No.' It was a mere whisper.

'Look at me, Frances.' She raised her eyes, dark with painful memories and suppressed tears that she would not allow to fall. 'I promise on my honour that I will never hurt you.' He smiled to try to lighten the tension. 'I will never beat you or strike you or any of the other dreadful things you might envisage. Do you believe me? Do you trust me?'

She looked into his eyes, compelled by the brilliance she saw there. 'Yes,' she answered simply.

'Probably you don't—but you will.' His tone was rueful. 'I'll make sure of it. No one will ever hurt you again.'

Frances responded instinctively by catching his hand and pressing it wordlessly against her cheek. It took him by surprise, amazing him, stirring within him a confusion of guilt and frustration. And also a violent leap of fury. His fingers clenched into a fist as he imagined them around Torrington's throat. That he should have damaged Frances, inflicted such cruelty on her, was not to be borne. He breathed deeply to rein in the anger that he could not express to Frances. And now he knew why she found it so difficult to respond to him physically. He sighed. He had a hard task ahead of him.

'Come here.' His voice and touch were gentle and brought the weight of tears into her throat. 'You are exhausted.' He lifted her in his arms, holding her close for a moment, then lowered her on to her bed. His intention was to leave her, but he could not, not when her fingers remained clasped to his. He felt a stirring in his heart that he could not name, but he knew that she deserved more from him at that moment than that he should walk away from her bed.

His eyes locked on hers. 'Not all men are cruel and thoughtless. Let me show you.'

Without hesitation, Frances opened her arms to him. This was the first time that any man had shown her such tangible kindness. He had by some chance unlocked a door and she had no desire to slam it in his face.

His hands were gentle, set to soothe and calm, in an urgent need to reassure and wipe away the ugly memories that must haunt her. Cool and immeasurably tender, his lips touched her hair, her eyes, the line of her cheekbones, and down to her throat where the pulse still raced. His hands skimmed her shoulders with featherlight movement before lingering on her back where he knew the cruel scars would always glimmer in the candlelight. She did not resist, but clung to him as he once again pushed away the ribbons and torn lace at her neck.

Her skin glowed pale as ivory and soft as gossamer to his fingertips as it warmed and relaxed under his touch.

He left her for a moment to remove his own clothing, but quickly, fearing a return of the fear that could turn her to ice in his hands. He searched her face, struck again by the brilliance of those sapphire eyes, now quite calm and full of trust. He realised what a heavy burden that could be, but he had made her a promise. Her dependence on him at that moment aroused him with a desire to possess her, but he kept a tight rein and set himself to pleasure her. He turned his attention to her breasts, so small and well formed as they fit perfectly into the palm of his hand. He caressed her nipples, and when he lowered his head to take one into his mouth she did not withdraw. Instead she surprised him by tightening her arms around him, pulling him close to her. She trembled when he allowed his hands to stroke down the length of her body, to part her thighs and touch the delicate skin, but she did not pull away, nor did she stiffen in rigid acceptance.

When he entered her with a single thrust, then held himself still to give her time to accept the intimate intrusion, she sighed and delighted him when she instinctively arched her body to meet his and allowed him to thrust more deeply. She was so soft. So tight. And this time she was ready for him. He was swept by a nameless emotion at his ability to make her respond. He whispered words of encouragement to her, foolish nothings, and she responded with little cries and whimpers. But not out of pain or fear. Her whole body was swamped with overpowering sensation. There was no room here for shyness or embarrassment. All she wanted was to feel the strength and power of his body against hers, the brush of his hands, the glory of him deep inside her. When he began to move, the thrusts more forceful, she moved to meet him, to answer the demands of his body and hers. Heat spread its fingers through her, to her very fingertips, which seemed to throb with the pressure of her beating heart, but it centred with fiery talons in her belly and thighs. It was unbearably intense, as close to pain as it was to pleasure, but yet it seemed to beckon her on with the promise of untold delight, although towards what she was still unsure.

He came to his climax, a final powerful thrust of his hips, a tensing of the muscles in back and thigh, lured on by the delicious warmth and softness of her body beneath him. He supported himself on his elbows to study her face in the light from the single remaining candle, his midnight-dark hair tousled, sweat still gleaming at his temples. Her mouth curved into a smile. The expression in his fierce eyes was incredibly tender. He smoothed her tangled hair from her face and pressed his lips to her forehead.

'Frances?'

'Yes, my lord?'

'Hugh!'

'Yes, Hugh.' She obeyed on a sigh of repletion. He would make do with that for the present.

'Did I hurt you?' It was suddenly important that he know.

'No. There was no hurt. I did not realise how…how…' He could see the flush on her pale skin even in the dim light.

'How enjoyable it could be?' There was a distinct smile in his voice.

'Yes, Hugh. That is what I meant to say.'

'You will find it even more enjoyable—when you are less tense and allow yourself to relax a little more.' He touched his lips to her temple, her eyes, her soft mouth in the lightest of kisses. 'I promise you.' He was acutely aware of her lack of true fulfilment—and contemplated rekindling the flames within her once more—but judged her too exhausted by the traumas of the night to pursue that end.

'I know,' she murmured against his chest. She felt warm and safe from the shadows of the past in his arms and at that moment could ask for nothing more. And yet there remained in her the memory of that elusive sensation of heat and excitement that had not quite overtaken her, an uncontrollable fire, ignited by his lips and his hands, which threatened to ripple through her and consume her very being. She shivered a little at the intimate prospect and then smiled and stretched against him in pure contentment. One day she knew she would find it with him.

That contentment shone in her eyes as she stretched up to press her lips to his with incredible sweetness. There was an arrested expression on his face, his heart beating forcefully in his chest, at her obvious trust as she lay in his arms and her unsolicited caress, but before he could think of anything to say, her eyes had fluttered closed and her breathing deepened into sleep. He smiled again, folding her more securely into his arms so that her head was pillowed on his shoulder, and allowed himself to sink into oblivion beside her.

Next morning Juliet persuaded Frances to accompany her to inspect, with the anticipation of buying, of course, the charming gowns produced by Madame Celeste, a new French modiste who had opened a shop in Bond Street and was fast becoming the height of fashion. Frances took little persuasion and the two ladies were about to leave on this pleasurable outing when Aldeborough waylaid them in the entrance hall.

He was dressed in a cut-away coat of dark blue superfine, of Weston's making, without doubt, which displayed his broad shoulders and narrow hips to excellent advantage. His pale pantaloons clung to his muscular thighs like a second skin, and his tasselled Hessians gleamed with a high polish. His cream satin waistcoat and tasteful fob watch completed his air of elegance and sophistication.

'Shopping again, I see. Don't let Juliet drag you round every dress shop in London, my dear. She will wear you out. Excess stamina in the pursuit of pleasure is a family failing.'

He looked directly at Frances, his eyes compelling her to meet his. She could not resist, wishing that the faint colour tinting her pale skin did not advertise so blatantly her beating heart and rapid pulse. She remembered all too clearly… Her blush deepened and she dropped her gaze so that she was unaware of his smile of satisfaction.

'And you would know all about that, dear Hugh.' Juliet rose to the occasion. 'How many miles was it that you were prepared to travel last week to watch a disgusting prize fight?'

'Ah! How indelicate of you, little sister! You should know nothing about such things. I suppose Matthew told you.'

'I shall not divulge my sources!'

'I see you are dressed to go out, my lord,' Frances interrupted the family repartee to which she was now becoming immune. 'Would you care to accompany us?'

'Never.' Aldeborough smiled. 'Have you tried Matthew? Well, of course you have. I knew I must be second choice.'

'Matthew had a pressing engagement.'

'Matthew always has pressing engagements. And on this occasion, fortunately, so do I. But before you go—it is my intention to go to the Priory at the end of the week. Some business needs to be completed before the month is out and it is easier if I am present. Ambrose is going to visit his uncle and Matthew will probably come with me—there may some rough shooting to tempt him. I wondered if I might persuade you to accompany us?'

His invitation was directed to both of them, but his eyes were fixed speculatively on Frances.

'I will understand if the pleasures and allure of town outweigh a few days in the country.'

Unexpectedly, he found that this was not true. He wanted Frances to accompany him. He felt a disconcerting need to spend some time with her, away from the formality of London, to get to know his elusive wife better. His wife! It still surprised him. And he was discovering depths in her that he could not have guessed at and which he found he wished to explore. When he looked at her delicately flushed face with its expressive eyes, determined chin and vulnerable mouth he could not erase the revelations of the previous night from his mind, nor the sight of those disfiguring scars on her fair skin. Anger and revulsion still simmered within him that she should have been handled with such deliberate cruelty. His powerful hands clenched into fists at the memory and a desire to seek revenge on her behalf tormented him.

And her response to his lovemaking had overwhelmed him. She was not shy at all. Nor was she cold to his advances as he had feared. However painful last night, it had breached the solid wall that had existed between them, created by her fear and his indifference. She had felt able to respond to his caresses and he had wanted to give her pleasure to erase the memories of fear and ill treatment. He had certainly given her pleasure. He felt a tightening in his loins at the memory of her body arching against his and the touch of her hands smoothing the skin down his back. And she had cried out and sighed his name as he had possessed her. He wanted her to come to the Priory.

Juliet responded as he knew she would.

'The Priory? Now that the Season is just under way? I could not possibly—just think of all the dances and parties I should miss. I could not think of going into rural seclusion.'

'Well, Mistress Molly? Do you wish to spend some time with me in rural seclusion?'

She hesitated for a second only, a small smile curving her lips deliciously and illuminating her eyes. 'Yes. I think I would. I would like it above all things.'

'Frances! How can you?' Juliet looked at her and her brother with utmost astonishment and no little degree of speculation in her lively expression. 'Do you want to be buried in the country when everyone who is anyone will be here in London?'

Frances laughed, suddenly feeling so much older than her new sister. 'But I enjoy life in the country. And I would like to go back to the Priory again.' It is my *home*, she thought. Far more so than Cavendish Square, however splendid, with its formal servants and rigid rules laid down by the Dowager. I want to go home. But she did not voice her preference, fearing to hurt Juliet's feelings. She need not have been concerned.

'I understand,' Juliet observed with more perception than her years would suggest, not at all insulted. 'I expect you will enjoy escaping from Mama's company.'

'It is a consideration,' Frances admitted with a little laugh.

'Then it will be my pleasure to take you to the Priory.' The Marquis took her hand: the surge of satisfaction within him was instantaneous.

Frances was delighted that he should invite her, that he should actively seek her company. And, as a voice whispered slyly in her heart, since the Priory was such a considerable distance from London, he would be well out of the orbit of Letitia Winters!

'Except that' —she raised her eyes to his again on a sudden thought— 'I will not visit Torrington Hall.'

'Of course not. I would never ask that of you.' His expression darkened, but his voice was full of understanding.

'I knew you would understand.'

'Not visit your aunt and uncle?' queried Juliet. 'Surely a morning call would be in order. Do you not wish to visit your previous home again?'

'There are reasons why Frances should not visit them,' explained Aldeborough simply, rescuing Frances from the need for explanation.

'Very well. If you are going to keep secrets from me!'

'If we told you, it wouldn't be a secret for five minutes. I will leave you to your shopping. We will set off on Friday morning.'

The shopping expedition was pronounced a great success by both ladies. With the prospect of time in the country to indulge her passion for riding, Frances was easily beguiled into the purchase of a delightful and extravagant riding habit in dark green velvet. The skirt with its heavy folds fitted her to perfection and the narrow jacket with a high neckline and frog fastenings in black silk braid carried the hint of the military. She knew that the rich colour set her dark hair and pale skin off to their best advantage. She was excited at the prospect of wearing it to investigate the estate and the surrounding countryside that was now her home. And in Aldeborough's company.

As they browsed their way homeward along Bond Street, they were hailed by a number of acquaintances, eager to further their contact with the new Marchioness of Aldeborough and to discuss the excellence of the Taverners' ball. One such was Miss Penelope Vowchurch, who had left her mother to exchange dull pleasantries with friends and was taking the air with a maid properly and discreetly in attendance. Her smile was cool and her demeanour a few degrees lower, but their proximity as she turned into Bond Street gave her no choice but to stop and converse with the Aldeborough ladies. Her smile was welcoming, as Frances had come to expect. Her eyes were not.

'Hello, Penelope.' Juliet smiled with gentle malice. 'How are you after such late hours?'

'We did not stay late,' Penelope explained calmly. 'My mama does not approve of excessive dancing or staying up beyond midnight. Did you enjoy the ball, Frances? I expect it must be one of the first you have attended, so unfamiliarity will give it a certain attraction. We, I'm afraid, find them sadly crowded and a little tedious.'

'I don't. I enjoyed it immeasurably.' Juliet was quick to pick up the nuances and took up the challenge with enthusiasm, to Frances's amusement. 'And I'm sure Frances did also.'

'Yes,' she agreed, 'it was most entertaining. So many people were very kind and welcoming.'

'Of course. They would be vastly interested in meeting you. After the news of your precipitate and unexpected marriage. I can understand their…curiosity. May I say what a charming dress you wore last night, dear Frances. Of course, that particular shade of yellow and gold are difficult colours to wear and can be most insipid. They do not suit everyone. I could not wear them.'

'Very true, but as a married lady, Frances is blessed with the freedom to choose her colours. I wish I could wear something other than white, but Mama insists. It is not always flattering, as I am sure you agree, Penelope?' Juliet knew that white flattered her very well but was not prepared to give quarter.

'Of course. I noticed that you achieved a partner for every dance. I don't suppose you had much opportunity to dance in Yorkshire.'

'I had none,' Frances agreed, refusing to be drawn into

making excuses. 'I fear my dancing will never be as elegant as I would wish.'

'I had the benefit of a dancing master, of course,' Penelope explained smoothly. 'A superior education is of greatest importance for those in the highest ranks of the *ton*. Mama thought that it was essential for me to be able to play my role in society. Aldeborough, of course, is an excellent dancer. All Wellington's officers are, I understand. Hugh and I have often waltzed together, at private parties, you understand. Mama does not approve of such informality in public. Such intimacy is most improper.'

'Surely you would have wished to waltz last night, Penelope. Everyone does so. You can hardly call it improper these days. Even *Wellington* approves of it, after all.'

'I expect you are right. But it does give pause for thought when you see such as Mrs Winters invited to the Taverners' ball. I thought they would have had more discrimination, but perhaps they merely wished to fill their rooms and be recognised as the squeeze of the Season. *She* was waltzing, I believe. And with Aldeborough on at least one occasion.'

'Aldeborough danced with any number of people. As did I.'

Miss Vowchurch deftly changed the direction of the conversation. 'I noticed that your cousin is in town. He was introduced to me at the ball. I found him to be most charming.'

'He can be very amenable,' Frances agreed, finding it difficult to believe that her cousin and Miss Vowchurch had anything in common or found anything to say beyond the most commonplace. 'I understand he will be here for a few days, but he usually spends his time at Torrington Hall.'

'He told me something of your background in Yorkshire. He was very informative.'

'Listening to gossip, Penelope?' Juliet chuckled. 'That does not sound like you. What would your mama say?'

'It was not gossip, I do assure you. It was simply family reminiscences. He told me that there had once been an understanding between himself and you, Frances, that you would marry.'

'There was such a proposal.' Frances was determined not to be drawn into such a discussion. 'But no formal plans were made.'

'He was most disturbed by the present situation. As I am. My marriage to Aldeborough was desired by both families, of course. It was no secret.'

'Sometimes, Penelope, we have to suffer disappointment in life.' The sparkle in Juliet's eyes showed no sympathy.

'Indeed. You would seem to have been well suited to your cousin, my lady. Perhaps you also enjoy life in the country, whereas it does not suit me at all. I am definitely a town mouse, as my mother always says.'

'Frances does like country life.' Juliet decided to cross swords on behalf of her sister. 'She intends to accompany Aldeborough to the Priory at the end of the week.'

'Oh?'

'It is an opportunity for her to see more of her new home,' Juliet added by way of unnecessary explanation.

'Have you ever been to the Priory?' Frances asked with an air of innocence.

'I have never had that pleasure.' The smile on Penelope's well-bred face became even more forced.

'I must persuade Aldeborough to hold a house party in the winter season, after I have had the opportunity to refurbish the public rooms. Perhaps you will accept an invitation to visit us.' The nice tone of condescension that she was able to achieve pleased Frances when she acknowledged Penelope's set expression and the glint of temper in her fine eyes.

'That will be delightful. When do you go?'

'Aldeborough said on Friday.'

Miss Vowchurch laughed with brittle humour, smoothing her kid gloves over her fingers.

'Take care if you are travelling with Aldeborough. History sometimes has a habit of repeating itself.'

'Forgive me.' A faint line appeared between Frances's dark brows. 'I do not take your meaning.'

'Why, nothing of consequence. Merely that travel is so dangerous these days. I travel as little as necessary outside

London. Ah! Look.' She raised her hand in greeting. 'Here is Lady Sefton. I must speak with her—a message from my mama. Enjoy your stay in rural tranquillity, my lady.' She extended an elegant hand in farewell. 'I look forward to hearing all about it when you return. And your plans for the Priory, of course.'

She turned to cross the street, the feathers on her satin straw bonnet nodding gracefully.

'And what do you suppose she meant by that cryptic comment?' Frances raised her eyebrows at Juliet's animated face.

'I have no idea.' Juliet shrugged with another crow of laughter. 'But I'm sure it was intended to cause trouble. I have never met anyone who can say so little and so pleasantly and intend so much harm. Do you think we managed to inflict on her as much discomfort as she intended for you?'

'I expect so. Juliet, you are incorrigible!'

'I know. But I could not allow her to patronise you so. Mama is bad enough.'

You showed a great gift for innuendo! I must remember not to cross you.'

'You must not mind her, you know, Frances.' Juliet took her arm in a warm embrace. 'It is simply a case of overwhelming jealousy. She had staked her future on being Marchioness, and now she is left in the unenviable position of having no suitor. And considering the family's financial situation, she is not likely to find another one very easily who will suit her mama. She has very high expectations. To give him his due, I don't believe that Hugh ever did intend to marry her and I think Richard only did so because Mama wanted it and he could not be bothered to obstruct her.'

'They are very alike, are they not? Your mama and Penelope.'

'Yes. What was it she called herself? A town mouse! A rat more like!'

The two ladies laughed in perfect understanding.

'I am truly grateful,' Juliet concluded as they turned back towards Cavendish Square, 'that you rescued us from the prospect of Penelope as a member of the family. I think we shall always be in your debt, my dear sister.'

Chapter Eight

Frances clung to the leather strap to prevent herself from being flung to the floor with every lurch and shudder of the coach. For the past several hours, since leaving York, they had bumped and swayed over the rutted track that provided the main road to Aldeborough Priory. This stretch was never easy, but inclement spring weather had churned it into a disaster of mud, mire and puddle. The coach was as comfortable as she had come to expect—her husband inevitably travelled in style—but its hard springing and the rigid cushions made such lengthy journeys exhausting. This did not depress Frances in any way. She smoothed her fingers over the soft fur rug tucked round her knees against the sharp draughts and rested her head as comfortably as possible against the padded squabs. Within two hours they would be at Aldeborough. Her spirits were high, buoyed up by the prospect of varied scenery, compensating for her physical discomfort.

And by the presence of Aldeborough. She had expected him to ride beside the coach as was his wont and as he had on their previous journey together to London. Instead he had opted to accompany her inside, his riding horse tied to the rear of the coach, while the rest of their luggage followed with Webster some distance behind at a more leisurely pace. Aldeborough travelled fast. If she had expected him to entertain her with conversation or comments on their surroundings, she had been wrong. Aldeborough was asleep, and had been for more than an hour, braced into the corner, one booted foot firmly planted on the seat opposite.

I don't know how you can possibly sleep through all this, she accused him silently, aggrieved, as they laboured out of yet another pothole. But she took the opportunity and indeed, pleasure to study his relaxed form at leisure. His strong hands lay at ease on his thigh. His figure was shrouded in a voluminous caped travelling coat, but by now she knew the set of his broad shoulders and well co-ordinated limbs. His expression in repose was stern, his mouth unsmiling with fine lines at the corner that gave him an air of worldly cynicism. It was a compelling face of flat planes and shadowy hollows with the faintest frown between his well-marked brows. His dark hair, thick and with a tendency to curl, gleaming like silk in a sudden intrusive shaft of sunlight, created in Frances the desire to run her fingers through it. She felt a warm flush invade her body at the train of her thoughts. She knew the intimate touch of those hands and lips, the virile strength of that well-muscled body. Her thoughts kept returning to that night after the Taverners' ball—and subsequent nights when he had come to her bed and welcoming arms. Her experiences had been in no way unpleasant, awakening even. She remembered the sensations with shocked pleasure as she had been persuaded to relax and respond to Aldeborough's expert attentions. So what were her feelings for him now? She bit her lip. She supposed she trusted him. And he had been so gentle and considerate. And he had turned her blood to molten gold with his caresses. She felt her blush deepen and was relieved that he could not read her thoughts. How could such an intimate act have given her so much pleasure rather than the fear and embarrassment of their previous encounters? But it had.

But what of him? She frowned at his oblivious figure. If rumour were true, with his wide experience of the female sex, he had probably not given her a second thought except what was demanded for duty and to achieve an heir to the title. And of course there was still the unresolved matter of

Mrs Letitia Winters with her golden curls and enticing figure. Aldeborough had not denied her angry accusations after all. And yet he had seemed to care when he smoothed her scars with such gentle fingers. And such scorching kisses.

Stop it! she chided herself as her thoughts went round in circles. He doesn't care for you. You are a burden and a means to an end, tied into a marriage of convenience in its truest sense. How could you possibly allow yourself to be won over by a handsome face and a wealth of worldly experience. You would be foolish to think in that direction. She deliberately turned her face away from her companion to stare blindly at the scenery that she had once thought so entertaining.

The coach began to climb steadily to the edge of the Wolds, after the drear expanse of the Vale of York, with even more jolting, forcing Frances to brace her aching muscles once more. Their speed dropped considerably, but the crest of the Wolds was in sight. They would soon be home. Suddenly her confused thoughts about Aldeborough were shattered by a loud oath from Benson on the box while the groom who rode beside him leaned down, at great risk to his own safety, to shout through the open window of the coach.

'Four riders ahead, Captain—m'lord. Been there some time an' all. By yonder copse on the brow, d'you see. Don't like the look of them m'self.'

Aldeborough was instantly awake, pushing his fingers through his hair and leaning to look out at the groom's direction.

'They're coming this way, Captain. What d'you want for us to do?'

'Keep driving.' Aldeborough's response was as calm as if engaged in a discussion of the weather. 'It is too dangerous to outrun them on this road anyway, even if we could. We would smash a wheel or injure one of the horses in these potholes. Let's see what they want. And, Jed…'

'Yes, m'lord?'

'Keep your pistols to hand!'

Frances leaned over to follow his gaze. The four riders

were unremarkable. Their clothing was plain and sombre with dark hats and coats. Nothing to attract attention except their presence on a lonely road and their watchful attitude. She felt an immediate flutter of apprehension, of fear, but remained silent, trying admirably to keep her composure and merely glancing enquiringly at Aldeborough.

His grey eyes were cold and sharply calculating. 'I don't like the look of this,' he admitted. 'Here!'

He rummaged behind one of the squabs and withdrew a brace of pistols from a hidden compartment, one of which he gave to Frances. 'It is primed and loaded. Use it if you have to. And with intent. You cannot afford to be squeamish. Can I trust you not to have a maidenly attack of the vapours?'

'I have never had an attack of the vapours in my life!'

He smiled at her indignation and proceeded to give her instructions, terse but calm, and Frances responded with a mute nod of understanding. The other pistol he wedged carefully on the floor beneath the seat, within reach from the door. Then he stretched across and took Frances by the arm, pulling her from the seat and on to the floor.

'Keep your head down. They may not see you to begin with and that could be to our advantage. Do you understand?' He scanned her face searchingly. She nodded again, ignoring her trembling hands, and tried to swallow the lump of terror that had lodged in her throat. 'Good. Don't worry. We will come out of this in one piece.' He touched her cheek fleetingly and returned to his own seat.

Immediately a shot rang out. The coachman began to pull his horses to a standstill, fighting to curb them as they plunged and reared in reaction to the loud retort. Muffled shouts were evident and then a clear voice issued orders.

'Be still! Don't move or we'll open fire. No tricks now—there's more of us than there are of you an' we're not averse to some target practice, are we, lads? Throw down your pistols. Gently now. That's right.'

The coach lumbered to a stop. Aldeborough still waited, making no move other than to signal to Frances to remain where she was at his feet. The voice rang out again.

'My lord Aldeborough!'

He smiled briefly and reassuringly at Frances, opened the coach door and leapt down into the road in one fluid movement. Before him were the four riders, blocking any further movement from the coach and all brandishing pistols.

'My lord Aldeborough?' their spokesman queried again, but he was clearly in no doubt. Aldeborough flourished an arrogant bow in his direction.

'At your service, sirs.'

'We've been expecting you, isn't that right, lads?'

'And how might I help? Jewels? Money? I fear that you are bound to be disappointed. I travel light.'

'Now what makes you so sure that we're common robbers, your honour?' The rider leaned forward on his horse's withers, waving the pistol and grinning at his companions. 'We'll be well paid for today's work. We don't need your money.'

'I am, you will notice, unarmed. Which should make your task so much easier.' Aldeborough spread his arms wide, displaying nothing but cold detachment, certainly not the fear that was paralysing Frances as she listened to the exchange.

'All to our advantage, then. And where's your pretty little wife? Not with you?'

'No. I travel alone.'

'Now that's a pity. We expected both of you.'

Frances was still half-lying in an uncomfortable huddle on the floor of the coach. She could hear the conversation clearly and, if she raised herself a little on her left elbow, could see the head and shoulders of the horseman through the coach window. He was as yet unaware of her presence, as Aldeborough had gambled, concentrating on his quarry. She was contemplating her best move, fighting down the surge of panic, when what she saw next made her blood run cold through her veins. The rider raised his pistol to shoulder height and aimed it deliberately at Aldeborough's heart.

'A pity you'll not live to enjoy your ungodly, ill-gotten gains,' he mocked with a sneer. 'You seem to have made one enemy too many, my lord.'

'Very probably. Perhaps I should have lived a more virtuous existence. As you obviously are.' Frances winced in some anxiety at Aldeborough's deliberate provocation. 'And which particular enemy did you have in mind? Who is paying you for this act of righteous revenge?'

'Not your concern,' he snarled. 'You'll soon have no interest in anything other than the fires of Hell, will he, lads?'

'Let's finish it.' One of the other riders, keeping the coachman and groom covered, shifted in his saddle uncomfortably. 'We've been here too long.'

The rider in Frances's sights grunted in agreement, checked his aim and cocked his pistol. She dared hesitate no longer. Without further thought she raised and cocked her own pistol, praying that the sharp click would not carry, took a minimum of aim through the coach window, held her breath and pulled the trigger. The shot reverberated deafeningly round her in the confines of the coach. She could not see the result of her action since the recoil threw her back on to the floor, but the result outside was instant pandemonium. The rider dropped his pistol with a sharp cry, clapping his hand to his chest and fighting to keep control of his horse, which shied violently. Aldeborough immediately launched himself towards the open coach door, leaning inside and snatching up the second pistol from where he had hidden it beneath the seat. All in one smooth movement he fell to his knees and aimed at the second rider who was approaching rapidly, pistol raised, to finish off the job where his compatriot had failed. At the crack of Aldeborough's own weapon he fell to the ground and lay motionless in the mud as his horse made its escape. Meanwhile, galvanised into action by the sudden turn of events, the coachman raised his long whip and brought it down again and again on the head and shoulders of the third rider.

There was still one armed rider who had them at his mercy. Aldeborough, with no firearm for his protection, remained on his knees beside the coach as the rider circled cautiously round to the opposite side, leaning from his horse to peer through the window and so catching sight of Frances cowering on the floor. She saw his face suddenly split by a grin

of malicious satisfaction as he realised that he still held a
trump card.

'Stand up, my lord,' he shouted. 'There's no hiding. Stand
up and be seen or I'll shoot your fair companion 'ere.'

There was a moment of terrible silence. There was no questioning his intention as he levelled his pistol into the interior
of the coach. He could not possibly miss Frances from this
range. She closed her eyes and waited, praying that Aldeborough would not expose himself to sure death, praying for
a miracle to save herself.

Then a maëlstrom of events erupted round her. Aldeborough rose to his feet and stepped from the shelter of the coach
to draw the rider's attention from Frances. The groom leapt
from the box and attacked the whip-beleaguered rider with
blows to legs and body. As the fourth assassin aimed his
pistol away from Frances towards the now vulnerable Aldeborough, there came the unmistakable sound of horses'
hooves, pounding the road surface in the distance but coming
rapidly closer. Frances rose to her knees, dragging her ham-
pering skirts around her, and launched herself to fall out of
the coach and land on the floor at her husband's feet. Without
thought for her own safety, her heart thudding loudly in her
chest, she steadied herself against the rear wheel and flung
her useless pistol with all her strength into the face of their
attacker. Her aim was not true, but it had the desired effect.
The marksman reacted automatically in surprise, dropping his
aim and pulling up his horse's head sharply. Aldeborough
saw his chance to grasp the horse's bridle and drag on the
rider's arm to spoil his aim and attempt to unseat him. In the
background the hoofbeats grew louder, three figures bearing
down on them, everything happening so quickly but to
Frances seemingly to stretch for a lifetime.

A distant shout from the rescuers carried on the air. The
two uninjured riders realised that escape was now in their
best interests. One untangled himself with a string of oaths
from the coachman's whip and the groom's blows, the other
pulled free from Aldeborough's grip by using the horse's
shoulder to pin him to the side of the coach. Aldeborough

had no option but to release him or be crushed by half a ton of horseflesh so that, by the time the newcomers arrived on the scene, the riders had made off to the crest of the Wolds, leaving two of their number lying in the mud.

'What kept you?' Aldeborough's smile relaxed the lines of tension around his mouth. 'We were in urgent need of you ten minutes ago.'

'My God, Hugh!' Ambrose assessed the dramatic tableau before him. 'I'm relieved to see that you're in such good spirits in the circumstances.' He and Matthew dismounted from their blowing horses, handing their reins to the accompanying groom, as Aldeborough stretched out his hand to help Frances climb somewhat shakily to her feet.

'What on earth…?' asked Matthew but Aldeborough shook his head slightly and his brother was quick to pick up the unspoken hint. 'You look as if you've been travelling on the floor,' he continued smoothly, addressing himself to Frances with a grin as he surveyed her dishevelled appearance. 'Did Hugh insist on such ill treatment? I'll knock him down for you if you wish. Just give the word.'

'I'm afraid he did.' She returned his smile, grateful for his deliberate lightening of the tension, as she attempted unsuccessfully to brush some of the mud from her skirts. She was not fooled. She was well aware of her husband's unwillingness to discuss the implications of the previous ten minutes in front of her.

'Of course I did. Didn't you know it's in the marriage contract? And Molly is an expert at travelling under coach seats.' Aldeborough turned to Ambrose. 'Would you cast an eye over our two dubious friends for a moment?' Then as Ambrose, followed by Matthew, moved to stoop over the two bodies, he turned to Frances. 'I trust you are unharmed, my lady,' he enquired gently. He might have been asking if she had slept well, but nothing could disguise the expression of concern in his eyes or the churning mass of fury in his gut at the prospect of what might have happened to her at the hands of the assassins.

'Yes,' she answered with clenched teeth in a forlorn attempt to stop the shivering that was taking over now that the danger had gone. 'But what about you?' She reached up to gently touch a graze on his right temple. He flinched.

'I was not aware of that.' He shrugged. 'A mere scratch.' He hesitated for a moment, weighing his words, undecided whether to say more, but then continued, 'I owe you my life, you know.'

'I thought he meant to shoot you,' Frances explained. 'Is he…is he dead?'

Aldeborough turned his head to where Ambrose and Matthew were finishing their inspection. 'I'm afraid they might both be.' He took her cold hands in his and saw the horror imprint itself on her face. 'You must not think about it. If you had not shot him, we would doubtless both be dead by now.'

'Dead!' Ambrose confirmed, his face grim. 'We shall not learn anything from them.'

'No. I expect they were thugs hired in York. If your groom could wait here for the coach containing our luggage, they could then arrange to take the bodies back to York. We might find out who they are or at least who paid them—but I am not too hopeful.'

'But they were not ordinary footpads, were they?' Frances broke in, voicing the thoughts that had been crowding into her brain for some time. 'They were not common highwaymen.'

'Perhaps not, but don't worry.' He squeezed her hands reassuringly. 'We'll be safe enough now with our gallant rescuers. Matthew's always good for seeing off any troublemakers.'

'But…' Frances persisted, unwilling to let the matter drop.

'Not now, Frances.' It was a command.

Aldeborough transferred his grasp to her arm to help her up into the coach again. When he became aware of the trembling that she could not control and so had failed to hide from him, he turned without a word and strode to his tethered horse, producing a small flask from his saddlebag.

'Drink this.' He unstoppered it and presented it to her. 'It will stop the shivering, so don't refuse.' Frances had the grace to look sheepish as this had been her intention. She took a gulp of the fiery liquid, making her gasp and her eyes water, but the warmth in her stomach was comforting and she drank again before returning it to Aldeborough.

'You were very brave, Frances Rosalind,' he said softly. 'I shall not forget this day.' He took a drink of the brandy himself, wiping his mouth with the back of his hand. 'Up with you. I'll ride a little way with Ambrose. Matthew will keep you company. You can tell him all about your adventure and the indignity of travelling on the floor of the coach. You'll be quite safe and we shall be at the Priory in no time.'

With Matthew and Frances comfortably ensconced, the coachman gave his horses the office to start. Aldeborough swung himself up on to his horse and he and Ambrose fell in at some little distance behind the coach.

'So, what's all this, Hugh?' Ambrose could barely contain his curiosity. 'A bit like the old times in the Peninsula, was it?'

Aldeborough laughed without humour. 'Yes, it was. But there you expect ambush and guerrilla tactics. You are prepared for it. I was not prepared today—too casual by half, it seems.'

'Hmm. It looked like a nasty incident and this is not known as a dangerous stretch of road that highwaymen frequent.'

'They were not footpads,' Aldeborough stated baldly, 'as my wife observed. And you are correct. It had the makings of a very nasty incident. With my blood on the road.'

'Hired assassins? It seems unlikely.'

'Very true, but they were. They knew who they were intending to waylay and had clear instructions as to the outcome. And it seems they were being paid handsomely.'

'Could they simply have recognised the black falcon on the coach panel and seen their eye to the main chance? It is fairly distinctive—you were hardly travelling incognito, were you?'

'They could, but I think they were well informed beforehand. The leader called out my name as they stopped the coach. And they were expecting Frances to be travelling with me. He asked me where she was.'

'So who knew you were travelling today?'

Aldeborough shrugged. 'Any number of people, I suppose.'

Ambrose was silent for a moment, frowning as he contemplated the possibilities.

'Been making any enemies lately?' he asked finally. 'Putting up the rent of your tenants or something of the sort?'

'No.' Aldeborough shook his head. 'I am seen as an improving landlord, I believe,' he stated cynically.

'Well, you couldn't be worse than your father. Or Richard. But that is not saying much.'

'Thank you,' Aldeborough commented drily. 'I am delighted that someone appreciates my achievements.'

'Your mother still giving you hell, is she?'

'Of course. Richard was the centre of her universe.' Aldeborough's set expression and icy tone did not encourage further discussion.

'So?' Ambrose took the hint. 'What of your footpads? Won a lot of money from anyone recently? Seduced someone's wife?' Impatiently the Marquis shook his head.

You have made one enemy too many, my lord.

Aldeborough remained silent for a moment. Then, 'I don't want this spread abroad, Ambrose. They were paid assassins and out for blood. Mine. They were not frightened of being recognised, their faces were not covered, so obviously they intended to allow no witnesses to remain alive. The fact that they failed was pure chance—and your timely arrival, of course.'

'Do I understand that it was in fact Lady Aldeborough who shot one of them?' As Aldeborough nodded, his friend continued, 'She has amazing spirit as well as a beautiful face. You're a lucky man, if you did but realise it,' he ended drily.

'Very true, as you have not hesitated to tell me before. I did not realise you were such an admirer.' There was a hint of warning, but lightly given. 'If it had not been for Frances, I would be lying dead in the road.'

'Be assured, Hugh, if your footpads or assassins had been successful, I would have been only too willing to come to Lady Aldeborough's aid!' Ambrose's lips twitched in dry amusement, claiming the familiarity of an old friend, and there was a glint in his eye. But then he stared straight ahead between his horse's ears, suddenly serious as a thought struck him and he refused to meet Aldeborough's enigmatic stare. 'But it gives you food for thought, does it not? That someone hates you sufficiently to be prepared to arrange your death.'

Aldeborough, for once, gave no reply.

'Good afternoon, my lord. My lady. We have been expecting you. I trust your journey was uneventful?'

'Yes. You're looking well, Rivers.' Aldeborough shrugged himself out of his caped greatcoat. 'Any problems?'

'No, my lord. I am sure you will find everything running smoothly and to your satisfaction. Kington expects to report to you tomorrow. He has left a letter for you in the library.'

'I will read it presently. Can we have tea in the library at once? I'm sure her ladyship will be grateful for some refreshment. Lord Matthew is with us. He's gone with the horses to the stables, but should be here presently.'

'Indeed, my lord. Everything is prepared. And perhaps I should inform you. Lady Cotherstone is in residence. She arrived last week. For a prolonged stay, I believe. She had considerable luggage.'

No expression crossed the butler's face, but Aldeborough caught the gleam in his eye and responded with a low laugh. 'Thank you, Rivers. It is as well to be warned. Where is she?'

'In the library, awaiting you, my lord. For some little time, I understand.'

'Then we had better go and announce our arrival.' He turned to Frances as Rivers retired to organise refreshments. 'Come and meet one of the skeletons in our family cupboard.'

'Who is she?' Frances's lingering unease over the violence of the attack was overlaid by a lively curiosity.

'Lady Mary Cotherstone. My grandfather's sister—my Great-aunt May. I've no idea how old she is—she will never admit her true age—she is eccentric, opinionated and outspoken to a fault. She married when she was very young—I am amazed that any man was willing to take her on—but she has been a widow as long as I have known her. She and my mother detest each other and spend as little time as possible under the same roof.' He grinned. 'You will like her extremely.'

Frances acknowledged this with a chuckle. 'Does she live here? Where was she when you first brought me here?' They made their way to the library, Frances divesting herself of coat and gloves to a waiting footman.

'She doesn't officially live anywhere. She does the rounds of her relatives and moves on only when their patience gives out or she loses her temper. I suppose she lives here more than anywhere. You will find her a most refreshing experience after the polite manners of town.' He opened the door into the library.

'Well, May. I hear you have taken up residence again. We are honoured. And I see that Wellington is still with us.'

'Aunt May to you, my boy. Show some respect to your elders and betters. Wellington is very well.'

Frances found herself in the company of a lady of extreme age and somewhat forbidding appearance. She was tall and thin to the point of emaciation. Her black hair, allowed to show no signs of natural ageing, was drawn back from her forehead to leave a row of girlish curls as a fringe. She was dressed remarkably in the fashion prevalent in the days of her youth with a tight buckram-lined bodice and a full, ruched overskirt caught up over a matching petticoat. The whole was trimmed with frivolous bows and flowers, which sat incongruously on her angular frame. Her face was heavily lined, but those around her eyes and mouth suggested that she smiled often—as indeed she did when she rose to meet Aldeborough. Wellington, an inappropriately named hound of mixed parentage but a quantity of long, tangled hair, growled and panted at her feet.'

'Well, Aldeborough. Let me look at you.'

She raised a bony, arthritic hand to turn his face to the

light, scanning his features with eyes uncannily similar to his own.

'You look well. Still missing the campaigning?'

'Perhaps.'

'You should not have let them bully you into selling out. I doubt your mother thanks you for it. I suppose you are still her least favourite son?'

Aldeborough, well used to his aunt's astringent style, shook his head and refused to rise to the bait. 'I had no choice but to sell out, you know that,' he said, ignoring one question and answering the other.

'Hmm. So you say.' She snorted in an unladylike manner and patted his cheek in dismissal. 'So.' She turned to Frances, who felt herself being raked from head to foot by the bright, inquisitive gaze. 'And this is The Bride. Are you going to introduce us?'

'This is Frances.' He drew her forward with a hand on her arm. 'My dear, this is my Great-aunt May.'

'You are not what I expected. I have had the dubious pleasure of making the acquaintance of Viscount Torrington and his wife.'

Frances was not sure how to take this, but decided that it was a compliment and dropped a small curtsy. 'I am pleased to meet you, my lady.'

'Don't stand on ceremony. Call me Aunt May like the rest of them. You're a pretty little thing. You're Cecilia Mortimer's daughter, are you not?'

'Yes,' Frances admitted in some surprise. 'Did you know my mother?'

'No. Although I probably met her. She was much younger—a different generation—but I remember the to-do when she ran off with your father. But I have to say that even that scandal pales into insignificance in comparison with your own marriage.' She turned her accusing stare on Aldeborough. 'What were you thinking of, Hugh? To abduct the girl from her uncle's house—is that the truth of it? It was not exactly good *ton*, was it? I though you had more style, boy.'

It gave Frances some cause for amusement to hear her self-assured husband addressed with such familiarity and in such an accusing tone. But if he was discomfited, he covered it well and responded to his aunt with good humour.

'Clearly I have spent an ungodly life, as I have already been accused once today.'

'Probably a surfeit of claret. And poor quality at that, if it was Torrington's.' She cackled with laughter. 'Have you forgiven him yet, my dear? It might be best if you do. And I never did like Torrington, even if he is your uncle.'

'Spare us all our blushes, Aunt May.' Aldeborough came to his wife's rescue, but to his surprise Frances chose to respond to this forthright lady.

'I have forgiven him. And I must tell you that my lord did not abduct me. He rescued me from an impossible situation— and it was of my making, not his. Indeed, I have no complaints.'

'Well, well, Aldeborough. You have a champion here. Very noble of you, my dear, I am sure.' Lady Cotherstone's eyes twinkled at the colour that had risen to tint Frances's pale skin. 'We must have a comfortable chat later when you can tell me all about it. I love gossip and don't get enough opportunities these days. I'll wager my pearl necklet that the Marchioness was up in arms. Let us have tea. Ring for Rivers. And here is Matthew—you didn't tell me he was joining us. Quite a family party, in fact. Perhaps we should have a bottle of port as well.'

There was no opportunity for the rest of that day for Frances to have any private conversation with Aldeborough. He did not come to her room that night and she found that she did not have the confidence to go to his. She spent a restless night, haunted by memories of violent death and the part she had played in it.

Next morning Frances made a point of accosting Aldeborough in the library before he left to meet Kington and to ride out to inspect a land-drainage project that had been put in hand along the flooded river meadows.

'Can I disturb you?'

He was leafing through a stack of papers on his desk with an air of resigned frustration. 'Of course. I am delighted to be disturbed by a lady as pretty as my own wife.' He stood and smiled in welcome. 'What are you planning to do today? Don't let Aunt May bully you into one of her schemes. She may be ancient, but she has more stamina than anyone I know unless it is Juliet. My sister is very like her.'

Frances smiled at his unexpected gallantry, but otherwise ignored it. 'About yesterday,' she began, without preamble, before she could have second thoughts. 'The highwaymen.'

Aldeborough continued to smile, but his eyes became hard and flat, discouraging discussion. 'They were just footpads. A normal hazard when travelling except that this time it was too close for comfort.'

Frances was determined not to be discouraged and met his eyes with her own direct gaze. 'I don't believe you. I am not a fool. They were not just footpads and it wasn't just chance, as you well know. They intended murder—they threatened to kill you.'

Aldeborough still refused to be drawn. 'Don't make too much of it. I have started enquiries in York; if there is anything to discover, it will be done.'

'So you think I should just forget about it?'

'Yes. What would be the point in worrying about it unduly?'

'But I killed a man! I have blood on my hands.' She heard a rising note of hysteria creep into her voice and fought hard to suppress it.

The expression on Aldeborough's face softened at her words and obvious distress. He immediately came round the desk to take her hand.

'Forgive me, Frances. I did not consider… Perhaps it is the effect of campaigning that makes a man accept death so cheaply. I have been thoughtless, not realising how you must react to such a horrifying incident.'

'I could not sleep for thinking about it. I kept seeing the pistol and the blood.'

He smoothed the frown from between her brows with a gentle finger. 'The only consolation I can give is that if you had not shot the rider, I would be dead, and you too. There is nothing more certain.'

'I suppose so.'

'So you must not let it prey on your mind. I order you to stop!' He replaced his finger with a gentle brush of his lips.

She laughed, if a little shakily, and, although her fears remained, had to admit the justice in what he said. 'Very well. I didn't mean to trouble you. Only…'

'I understand.'

'I expect you do. I will try not to let it worry me.'

'What an amenable wife you are this morning!' He stroked his hand over a ringlet, which had escaped from its pins, with a twitch of his lips.

'Yes, I am, aren't I?' she responded equally lightly. 'So you see, there is no need to resort to such extreme methods as highwaymen to rid yourself of a troublesome wife. Miss Vowchurch warned me that travelling to the Priory could be dangerous. She did not know the half of it.'

It was said as a joke, a light-hearted jest, laughter in her eyes, expecting a similar response from him. Instead his reaction was devastating. His hand fell from her hair, while the other one clenched into a fist on the papers he was holding. His eyes blazed in a face from which all blood had retreated, then went flat and cold. Fire and ice. He clasped her wrist in a grip that branded her with its heat.

'What can you possibly mean by that interesting statement?' he asked quietly and conversationally, his tone at variance with the controlled emotion in his face.

'What have I said?' she asked perplexed.

'I never believed that *you* would believe such slander.'

'I don't understand, Hugh. What should I not believe?'

'Richard's death will haunt me for ever. I don't need you to remind me of it or to repeat what the world chooses to believe.'

'Richard? What has he to do—'

'I will not discuss it. It is no concern of yours. My mother has clearly done an excellent job on you in the short time that you were under the same roof. I never realised that you were so much in agreement.'

'I understood that Richard fell from his curricle,' Frances answered carefully, wary of this sudden, unexpected explosion of anger.

'Oh yes! He fell. And broke his neck.' His face was a mask, his voice full of bitter self-mockery. 'And I inherited everything. So I must have been to blame, do you not think? It is all very logical. I must have hated my brother from the moment of my birth, for standing in the path of my ambition to possess the title and the fortune that goes with it. And how I must have rejoiced at his death. I must have offered up prayers of gratitude to God when I held his lifeless body in my arms and wiped the blood from his face.'

Frances flinched at the searing pain underlying the turbulence in his voice.

'Hugh—I never believed that. How could—?'

'And I do not want your pity!' He turned from her, releasing her wrist, and in a violent movement swept the papers from the desk in a maëlstrom of scattered sheets. 'I never wanted this. Neither his death nor his birthright.'

Instinctively Frances put out a hand to restrain him, to break the hold of the desire to destroy, but he stepped back from her, fighting to regain control and dispel the vicious mist that clouded his vision. She saw the effort it cost him in his clenched fists and the pulse beating rapidly in his throat.

'Forgive me. It was not my intention to inflict my family's private problems on you. I expect I should apologise for my unseemly behaviour.' His voice was flat and empty of emotion after the storm as he wilfully closed his mind to the flare of grief in her eyes at his deliberate distancing of her from his past. 'But not yet!'

He flung down the forgotten papers, still grasped in one hand and now hopelessly mangled, and strode to the door, wrenching it open, but not before she had seen the anguish beneath the anger in his eyes.

'Where are you going?' She followed him to the door, hand outstretched to detain him.

'Out!'

He slammed out of the library, his footsteps echoing down the corridor, leaving her bereft and bewildered. What had she said? She had never even mentioned Richard. And what had his mother to do with it? Penelope's flippant comment edged back into her mind.

Take care if you are travelling with Aldeborough. History has a habit of repeating itself.

But what had she meant about history repeating itself? Frances's mind flew back to the conversation with Matthew in Hyde Park, when she had asked him about the fate of his eldest brother. He had been very non-committal about Richard, reluctant to go into any detail, leaving her dangerously ignorant of an event that clearly had torn the family apart— and still had a desperate effect on Hugh. She smoothed her fingers gently over her wrist, which he had clasped so passionately. It was time that she found out the answers to a few pertinent questions.

Ambrose arrived unannounced in the library as Frances lingered, picking up the ill-used documents, undecided on her next move.

'Good morning, Frances. Where's Hugh? I agreed to ride out with him to inspect some project or other on the estate.' He smiled and kissed her hand with easy familiarity.

'You've just missed him. I expect he has gone to the stables to meet Kington. Matthew is there as well, I think.'

'Right. I'll catch up with them.' He turned to go.

'Ambrose. Before you go, I need…' She hesitated, unsure what to say next.

Ambrose turned back, surprised at the tension in her voice, and noticed her anxious expression for the first time.

'Are you quite well? You look a little pale.'

'I am perfectly well. Only… Ambrose, can I ask you to tell me about Richard—how did he die?'

A wary expression crossed Ambrose's face. 'Why? What has Hugh said?'

'Nothing. That is the whole problem. No one will talk to me about it, other than in vague hints and innuendo about *gossip* and *scandal* that leave me in the dark. And I think I've just said something terrible.'

'Well, I would tell you, but I think it would be better coming from someone in the family. I know Hugh would not want me to gossip about it and as a friend I should respect his wishes.' Ambrose considered the matter for a moment. 'But I agree that you should know. Why don't you ask Lady Cotherstone? She will be a fount of all knowledge.'

'Yes. I will. I think I have hurt him very badly, Ambrose. I've never seen him so angry.'

He took her hand and gave it a reassuring squeeze. 'I will go after him. Don't worry over it. You did not know, so how can you blame yourself?'

'Ambrose…' Frances hesitated and then continued. 'I would rather you did not tell him that I spoke to you. I would not wish him to think that I was gossiping behind his back.'

'Of course. If that is your wish.'

Frances was waiting impatiently for Aunt May when she eventually emerged from her bedchamber, Wellington puffing at her heels.

'Good morning, my dear. Where is everyone?' Her toilette was even more bizarre, a stiff creation with a demi-train in figured puce damask, her hair secured under a tiny lace cap. A powdered wig, thought Frances, would not have been out of place. But she was far too anxious to be diverted by Aunt May's antique outfit.

'Out. But never mind that.' She raised her hands in exasperated frustration. 'Forgive me, Aunt May. You have got to tell me the truth about Richard—what happened to him? Was it an accident? Where does Hugh fit into it? No one will tell me the truth. I asked Ambrose, but he said I should ask you.'

'What a sensible young man. Still letting it fester, are they? And I don't suppose Hugh will talk about it at all. What has happened to put you in such a state?'

'I suggested, in a jest, you understand, that the highwaymen's attack on us yesterday could have been an attempt by him to get rid of a troublesome wife.'

'Which attack? You had better tell me from the beginning. Let us go into the morning room and fortify ourselves with a glass of port. Don't be so unhappy—it can all be straightened out. You learn that when you have lived as long as I have. Now, my dear. From the beginning.'

'I killed a man.' Frances looked anxiously at Aunt May, expecting to read condemnation in her face.

'Did you, my dear? I am sure you had your reasons. You must tell me all about it. Drink this and relax a little.' Soothed by Aunt May's calm acceptance, she sipped a little port and calmly told all.

Frances described the events of the previous day, including Aldeborough's reluctance to discuss the danger and finally her own inappropriate words, in jest but inflicting so much harm. And she told her about Penelope's mischief-making words, although at the time she had not realised their significance. 'So I need to know,' she finished.

'Of course you do, my dear. Where shall I start? With Richard, I suppose. I never knew him as well as I know Hugh. He was a bright, lively boy, always bursting with energy and the apple of his mother's eye. He was quick to realise this, of course, and was clever enough to use it to his own advantage. He did everything to keep his mother sweet and she would hear no wrong of him. Not that there was any wrong to tell—unless he was a little too selfish and careless of others. Reckless, too, I dare say. He was always into scrapes. But then, young men often are.' She sighed, her eyes unfocused as her mind travelled back over the years. 'He was very much like my brother, their grandfather. They say it runs in families. Well, Richard was the reckless one. I don't know if he would have made a good Marquis. He had only just inherited the title and he was very young. I don't really think he cared enough for the duties and responsibilities involved, only for the consequence and the money, of course. There was plenty of that.'

'So how did he die? It must have been quite recently.'

'Less than a year ago. Richard and Hugh were very close. There was only a year between them in age so they grew up together. It was a curricle race. Hugh was on furlough and, as I understand, Richard challenged him to a race. There was an accident. Richard's curricle was attempting to overtake Hugh's on a bend. The wheel went into a ditch at the side of the road and the curricle overturned. It was as simple as that and pure chance that Richard hit his head when he was flung out on to the verge. He struck a tree root or a hidden boulder—I don't know the detail—but he never recovered consciousness. I always thought curricles were too dangerous by half, but you cannot stop young men from indulging in risky sports.'

'But if it was an accident as you describe, I don't understand the problem.'

'There was none. But the Marchioness, God rot her soul, was beside herself with some extreme emotion—anguish, she claimed, but I thought it more likely to be frustrated ambition. She had always been able to influence Richard far more easily than Hugh, which was useful since she had no intention of giving up her guiding hands on the reins of the family. But now she was about to be thwarted with Hugh in the saddle. Anyway, she uttered some very unwise observations, loudly and publicly. She never did have any integrity. She hinted that the race was all Hugh's idea in the first place and that Richard had been forced off the road. That he was too good a driver to have made such a mistake. And Hugh had benefited, of course, inheriting the title and the fortune on his brother's untimely death. If you say things like that often enough, people begin to gossip and put two and two together, even if the sum does not add up. It was the *on-dit* of the Season.'

'But what a terrible thing to do!' Frances's eyes widened in horror as she now realised the pain her words would have unwittingly inflicted. 'Did she not realise the damage it would cause?'

'Of course she did. She blames Hugh and has left him in no doubt of it. She resents that he has inherited everything when her favourite boy is dead. And he has gone his own way, making changes without consulting her. There is no wonder he has become cynical and as reckless as Richard. If people believe ill of him, he'll give them something to blame him for. It is natural enough.'

'I suppose so. And I accused him of trying to kill me. I am not surprised he stormed out. And I am not sure how I can put it right.'

'Difficult, I agree. And with a mischief making little cat like Penelope Vowchurch stirring the waters with her pretty paws…well. She wanted the marriage with Hugh so she will be driven by envy. Women with so much self-control are always trouble. But as for Hugh—if you take my advice, I would leave him to simmer a little before I prostrated myself in abject mortification! He can be an uncomfortable opponent when he is feeling aggrieved.'

Frances laughed ruefully. 'I know. I am hoping that a ride round the estate will help. And I think I am a coward on this occasion.'

'I don't believe that for a moment.' Aunt May leaned across to pat her hand bracingly. 'You strike me as a very resourceful young lady. Come on.' She surged to her feet, dislodging Wellington, who had been snoring fitfully on the flounces of her dress. 'Since the sun is shining, let us go and inspect the formal flower beds. They are sadly neglected, you know, but the snowdrops should give a good show. There is nothing like fresh air to lift your spirits. Are you interested in restoring the gardens? They used to be beautiful in my younger days.'

Ambrose caught up with Aldeborough in the stables where he and Matthew were inspecting the hooves of one of his hunters. His greeting was perfectly civil, but his expression was shuttered and Matthew's silence and raised eyebrows said it all.

After five minutes of monosyllabic conversation, Ambrose had had enough, and decided to break his promise to Frances.

'She did not know, Hugh. You can hardly blame her.'

'Ah. I see you have had communication with my wife this morning. And I suppose she told you all about our exchange of views.'

'No, she did not. You have to give her credit for more loyalty than that. But she knew she had said the wrong thing and stirred you up. What she did not know was why. She was very upset, so I sent her to talk to Lady Cotherstone.'

'What's the problem?' asked Matthew, coming into the conversation halfway through, as he returned from the saddle room with a hoof pick and proceeded to inspect the problem foot.

'Richard's accident,' stated Ambrose baldly when Hugh chose not to reply.

'What about it?'

'Not a thing,' interjected Aldeborough with self-mockery. 'Except that my wife seems to believe that I might have murdered my brother.'

'Oh, is that all! She asked me about it weeks ago. I gather Mama had been giving her the family history and dropping her usual vague hints. I did not tell her very much. We should have told her the truth, Hugh. It would have prevented this.'

'It seems that everyone has been conversing with my wife except me.' Hugh's lips thinned with barely contained temper.

'And look what happened when you did!' Ambrose's reply was brutal. 'Look, Hugh, nobody believes that old scandal.'

'Only Mama. And nobody listens to her anyway.' Matthew stood up and shrugged.

'And Penelope Vowchurch! Who had the kindness to warn my wife of the dangers of travelling in my company.' Aldeborough's bitter anger was hard held.

'I don't believe it!'

'No? Well, perhaps Frances was making it up. Why not

ask her? I'm sure she will confide in you. Now, if we have finished discussing the legs of this misbegotten animal I am going to meet Kington at Malton's Cross. And before you ask,' he snarled, 'I don't want your company. You wouldn't want to ride with me today.'

He swung on to his bay gelding and rode out of the stableyard at a rigidly controlled canter.

'We dealt with that well between us, didn't we?' Ambrose grimaced at Matthew.

Matthew sighed and began to lead the lame hunter back to its stable. 'There is no reasoning with him and he will not talk about it.'

'He was very close to Richard, wasn't he?'

'Yes. He loved him.'

'Is it not surprising when you consider that they were not very alike?'

'No, they were not,' Matthew agreed. 'Richard was the wild one. Always up for some adventure, some wager, whereas Hugh was steadier, more considerate. But Mama never saw that. The first born was the sun in her firmament. I did not really know Richard very well. He never had much time for me. I suppose I was too young and too much of a nuisance. I had a tendency to hero worship in those days but he soon cured me of that—his boredom made me see the light. So I transferred it to Hugh, especially when I saw him in his regimentals. It was enough to awaken envy in the heart of any boy.' Matthew grinned. 'Hugh always had *time*—he was amazingly tolerant of a brat who wanted to ride his horse across the formal lawns or try out his dress sword on the chickens at Home Farm. You know the sort of thing.' He laughed at the memory.

'I can imagine. I am surprised he didn't bury you!'

Matthew laughed aloud, but quickly sobered again. 'It is all still very recent, of course, and I suppose the wound is still raw. And to have Mama express her preference so cruelly, and accuse him of wanting the title and being responsible for the accident. He doesn't care for the consequence at all. What he really wants is to take up his commission again.

He does not exactly enjoy estate matters. It must all seem very tame after Salamanca.'

'But he does it well. Look at the improvements he has made in such a short time, and the new ideas and the repairs that had been neglected for years.' Ambrose swept his gaze round the stable block, which looked the epitome of good management in the morning sun. 'I remember when the roof here was almost in a state of total collapse. And the stable doors were rotting on their hinges.'

'That's Hugh.' Matthew nodded. 'He'll be a better Marquis than Richard. Or our father, for that matter. At bottom, he cares more.'

Ambrose picked up the reins of his horse and prepared to mount. 'You know that, I know that, but it does not make the situation any better for Hugh.'

Frances heard Aldeborough return in the early evening. She was in her bedroom when she heard his door open and close. She waited, but he made no attempt to communicate with her.

Now or never. She swallowed her nerves and walked through the adjoining dressing room, knocked firmly on his door and entered without waiting for a reply.

Things did not look promising. Aldeborough was standing with his back to the room looking out over the formal gardens. He did not turn round when she entered. Despite the early hour, he held a glass of brandy in one hand. He looked windswept and mud splattered, but had made no attempt to change his clothes. She could not see his expression.

'I have come to ask your forgiveness. I did not know about Richard.' Her voice was soft but firm.

Still he did not turn to face her. 'I believe that I should be the one apologising to you.' His tone was bleak and insufferably polite. 'Ambrose told me that it was an innocent comment. Indeed, I am sure it was.'

'Oh.'

'Did you talk to Aunt May?'

'Yes.'

'So now you know the whole sorry story.'

'Yes. I could wish that you had told me.'

'I did not see the need.'

'No. You told me, as I remember, that it was none of my affair.' Frances found it hard to contain her growing frustration.

He turned at that, his face pale, his expression stark.

'And I would rather, in future, that you did not discuss my personal affairs with Ambrose.'

She drew in her breath before she could make a sharp reply. Now was not the time for temper.

'Very well.'

Silence stretched between them.

'Why will you not talk to me about your brother?' She tried again. 'You made me tell you about the marks on my back, the beatings. You gave me comfort.'

'It is not the same.'

'Why not?' she persisted, hoping to break through the barrier that he had so effectively built around the painful wounds. 'Scars are the same whether on the body or soul. Talk to me about Richard, Hugh.' He noted her use of his given name, still something rare, but he still rejected her attempts at reconciliation.

'You know all there is to know from Aunt May. I can tell you nothing more.'

'But I care that you have been maligned. How could anyone possibly believe that you would harm your brother?'

'You do not know me,' he said bitterly. 'How do you know what I am capable of?'

She put out a hand as if to touch him, to offer comfort. He drew back, imperceptibly, but she sensed his reaction. It hurt.

'I don't need your pity.'

'I was not offering any.'

'Then, if there is nothing else you wish to say... I have to dress for dinner.'

'No. I have nothing more to say. You have made the matter very clear.' Pride came to her rescue. 'I will not impose on you further. I clearly misinterpreted our relationship.' She could not resist it. 'Perhaps you should inform me of the subjects that I am allowed to discuss in future!'

She turned on her heel and made a dignified exit, head high. She closed the door quietly; she may as well have slammed it.

Aldeborough groaned and thrust a hand through his hair. He poured another glass of brandy to give his hands something to do and considered flinging his glass to shatter against the panels of the closed door. He put it down carefully before he did just that. He had dealt with her abominably. All he could see was the utter desolation in her beautiful eyes. Perhaps after all he was no better than Torrington. He would never scar her body, but without doubt he had hurt her by destroying the bond of understanding that had begun to grow between them. He deserved more than her censure, he deserved that she should hate and fear him—and she most certainly did not deserve his rejection. He must put things right. And he would have to apologise to Ambrose and Matthew, of course. He rubbed his hands over his face in disgust and self-loathing as the events of the day replayed through his mind in mind-searing detail. And, apart from that, there was the question of who hated him enough to pay armed thugs to shoot him down in cold blood.

You have made one enemy too many.

The implication was not clear, but all he could think of was the confrontation with Torrington. And his liaison with Frances. But how that would lead to a vicious and well-organised ambush by paid assassins he could not envisage.

He fervently wished he was back with his regiment in the Peninsula.

Chapter Nine

Aldeborough mended his relationship with Matthew and Ambrose with ease: they simply ignored his previous edgy temper and continued as if nothing had happened. When he attempted an apology, Ambrose threatened to floor him with a straight left if he couldn't keep a civil tongue in his head in future, so the matter was settled. They rode the estate, enjoying the onset of a period of fine weather. They fished the trout stream, unsuccessfully, but with damp enthusiasm. They enjoyed some rough shooting at the Priory and on the neighbouring land owned by Ambrose's uncle. A local race at Kiplingcoates, over a four-mile course of lanes and bridleways, gave them the opportunity to assess local horseflesh and lose a considerable amount of money. The evenings were spent in playing cards for small sums in the library at the Priory. If a deal of alcohol was consumed, it was not sufficient to impair their enjoyment of country pursuits. Aldeborough was able to throw off his unusual depression although the purpose of the assault on the York road remained an irritant. But, as there was no repetition, the incident receded into the background. Enquiries in York, as might have been expected, revealed nothing.

For her part, Frances spent most of her time becoming reacquainted with the Priory. She remembered it, of course, from the days when Aldeborough had first brought her here, but now she had the time and inclination to explore it fully. Originally, as its name indicated, it had been the settlement of Augustinian monks, but with its dissolution under Henry VIII it had come into the hands of the Lafford family. There were still remnants of the magnificent monastic buildings, neglected now and robbed of their stone—ruined arches, crumbling pillars, outlines of cloister and refectory, which Frances investigated with dreams of incorporating them into a pleasure garden. The main house was of Tudor design with gables and buttresses in golden local stone but with traces of old brickwork. More recent Laffords had added wings and fanciful towers so that to the eye it presented an impossible fusion of style and taste. Frances loved it. Its rambling lack of uniformity appealed to her and she felt at home here far more than she ever had in the magnificent town house in Cavendish Square. But, she was honest enough to admit to Aunt May, perhaps that had much to do with the absence of the Dowager. Here she was the unquestioned mistress of her own home and enjoyed the freedom.

But she was equally aware that the house needed much love and care. It had a chill, neglected air where dust and mice reigned supreme and so did damp and mildew. The structure was sound enough, but the Priory needed to be lived in. Aldeborough's parents had spent little time here, preferring life in Cavendish Square, the country merely providing the opportunity for hunting and winter house parties.

The spring weather tempted Frances into the estate. The formal gardens swept from the balustraded stone terraces to a ha-ha from where the parkland stretched to the horizon. Tastefully positioned clumps of trees in spring foliage beckoned the onlooker to ride and explore. The flower beds had been long neglected, the skeleton staff making little impact on the encroachments of nature, and the kitchen gardens no longer produced for the needs of the household. Frances could imagine the old brick walls once more glowing with roses and espaliered fruit trees, the walks vibrant with flowers.

She toured the rooms, cellars, attics and cupboards with an

enthusiastic Mrs Scott, who was delighted to have a mistress interested in day-to-day household activity. She talked herbs and gardening with Aunt May as well as the gossip about their neighbours and London society. She was content to leave kitchen matters to the competent cook who had ruled the roost since Aldeborough's childhood, which earned her the immediate support and co-operation from that testy individual. Her days were full and filled with small pleasures as she considered refurbishing some of the holland cover-shrouded rooms and restocking the walled herb and vegetable garden. To be mistress of her own home gave her consider-able delight and fulfilment. Whatever was lacking in her ed-ucation at Torrington Hall, she had acquired the knack of communication with the servants and knew how to run an efficient establishment. At her direction, Rivers marshalled indoor and outdoor servants for an assault on the neglect so that the oak floors and linenfold panelling began once more to glow in the candlelight at the end of a series of exhausting days. Cobwebs and spiders were swept ruthlessly from the plaster ceilings. The mice went into hiding.

Sheer curiosity drove Frances to investigate her husband's bedchamber, which opened through a connecting dressing room from her own. If she had needed an excuse, she would have claimed that it was her duty to ensure that it was clean and in good order, but in truth she was drawn by a need to learn more about the man who now had control of her life and, if she would admit it, of her heart. It was a beautiful room, like her own in the old part of the house, with oak-panelled walls and intricate plaster ceiling. It was a very mas-culine room, sparsely furnished from the previous century with a carved chest, a chair with a tapestry seat, a livery cupboard, the only modern addition to the old furniture being a dressing table and mirror. Frances smiled: such necessary additions for a man whose appearance was rarely less than suave and elegant. But it was the magnificent bedstead that dominated the room. It was hung with dark blue velvet cur-tains and valance, rather dusty but sumptuously lined with grey silk and ornamented with gold cord and fringing. She ran a hand gently along the nap of the rich material, realising that whatever she had hoped to discover in this room, she was doomed to failure. Apart from a pair of silver-backed brushes and a snuff box on the dressing table, there was little to indicate her husband's taste or character. Except perhaps for the neatness, no doubt a consequence of a military life of campaigning and the influence of Webster, the most efficient of valets. No portraits on the walls, no personal possessions. Without compunction Frances lifted the lid of the chest to investigate the contents. Nothing. The only life in the stillness was the dust motes glimmering gold in the sun's rays through the leaded windows. It was as if the Marquis was merely a temporary visitor, passing through, rather than the master of the estate.

Leaving Aldeborough's room to some competent cleaning under Rivers's watchful eye, Frances took herself eventually to the attics. For the most part they were empty except for a number of chests that yielded unexpected treasures, packed away long ago. She mentally consigned the boxes of official-looking paper with ribbons and seals to a later date and re-fastened the chests containing worn and stained household linen, but instructed Rivers to have a number of items conveyed to a small drawing room that she and Aunt May had taken to using in the evenings.

'I think you should read this, Aunt May,' exclaimed Frances with a mischievous smile. She was seated on the floor at Lady Cotherstone's feet, her dusty skirts and the contents of various boxes spread around her.

'What is it? I cannot believe that anything in a book will be of benefit to me at my time of life.'

Frances turned over a few more pages with care, peering at the faded, uneven writing. 'It has no name in it, but it is a collection of recipes and housewifely advice,' she explained.

Aunt May pushed aside a piece of embroidery from her lap. 'I believe that I will leave the cooking to Mrs Scott and whoever reigns in the kitchens. I was never interested in such things. Now, herbs and medicines are a different matter. Anything of interest about that?'

'Not that I can see. Here is Eel Pie with Oysters. A Pie with Pippins. Marrow Pie…Scotch Collops…Barley Broth…'

'It seems to be very plain and frugal fare. Perhaps you should put it back in the attic for fear that it gives Mrs Scott ideas. And perhaps you would care to pour me a glass of wine.'

Frances laughed and did as instructed before returning to her rummaging. 'It is mostly trinkets and ribbons—look at this fine pair of gloves—and…what do you suppose this is?' She held up a small bunch of fragile dried leaves tied up with a tarnished silver ribbon and with a yellowing label attached.

'Well, now. It looks very much like a love token. They were very fashionable when I was a young girl.'

Frances raised her brows and sniffed the greying twigs which had begun to disintegrate over her skirt. 'It smells like Rosemary. And listen to this.' She read out the accompanying sentiments.

Rosemary is for Remembrance
Between us day and night,
Wishing that I might always have
You present in my sight.
And when I cannot have
As I have said before,
Then Cupid with his deadly dart
Doth wound my heart full sore.

Frances held the token carefully, a wistful smile on her lips. 'Did you ever receive one of these, Aunt May?' she asked, her voice betraying more than she was aware.

'Yes, I did. I was not a handsome girl, but I did not lack for suitors. But what about a pretty child like you?'

Frances shook her head, bending over the poem so that her curls hid her face.

'I do not suppose such frivolous sentiments would be encouraged at Torrington Hall,' Aunt May probed gently.

'Certainly not. My aunt and uncle were never motivated by any feelings other than duty.'

'And Hugh?' The enquiry was deceptively casual.

Frances laughed, but Lady Cotherstone's ears were quick to detect the sadness, the longing.

'He is very kind—but there is no romance. How could there be? It was all a terrible mistake. And now I have made him so angry. He would not—write me a verse like that.' She stroked the yellow paper with gentle fingers, thinking of the long-dead lady who had been honoured with such tender sentiments.

Lady Cotherstone pursed her lips thoughtfully and wisely said nothing.

Aldeborough registered his wife's efforts in the Priory, her growing confidence and authority, with some pride and amusement, but made no comment. His relations with Frances were not mended. When she met with Aldeborough she was pleasant, smiled at the tales of the fish they might have caught and was willing to outline her suggestions for the new pottager, but he could not mistake the constraint in her voice or the reserve in her eyes. The hurt and rejection were still very strong and as time passed he became less sure how to put it right. It surprised him that he cared so much to put it right. But he hated the wary reserve in her dark eyes and the lack of animation in her face when she thought she was unobserved. Her smiles were fleeting and lacked any real warmth or enjoyment. He found increasingly that he needed to see her smile with unreserved pleasure, to smile at him. He spent the nights alone because he doubted that he would be welcome in his wife's bed and he was unwilling to force himself on her—but he did not enjoy them.

As for Frances, she vowed to abide by her husband's expectations. She would be an amenable and conformable wife and nothing more. If he wished to shut her out of parts of his life, then so be it. And she would never show him how unhappy it made her. Or how a sudden desire to feel the caress of his hand or the touch of his lips could awaken an intense ache around her heart. She rubbed her hand between her breasts as if she might erase the pain. To no avail. She shrugged and retreated inside a brittle shell where nothing could hurt her. She had had a lifetime of practice and she could live without Aldeborough's attentions. And if she envied the lady with the keepsake, then no one but herself need know.

Aunt May, well aware of the cold atmosphere, for once chose to be diplomatic and make no comment, although she frequently wondered how such a handsome man of the world as her great-nephew could be so blind in the ways of women.

To give him his due, Aldeborough tried to reduce the distance between himself and his bride.

'I understand you ride, my lady.'

'Yes. One of my few talents, if you remember.' He winced at the barbed comment.

'Come with me.' To prevent any refusal, he took her hand and tucked it cosily under his arm. He felt her body stiffen at the unexpected gesture, but ignored it. He also felt the shiver that ran through her and saw the uncertainty in her face as she lifted her eyes to his. It pleased him.

'Where are we going?'

He led her out on to the terrace and round to the stableyard where Selby, the head groom, awaited them with a grin on his weathered features.

'A surprise,' he said, smiling down at her. 'Selby has something to show you.'

'Morning, Captain. My lady.' Selby, who had served as Aldeborough's groom in Spain, disappeared into the stables at a gesture from the Marquis and returned a moment later leading out a bay mare, already saddled and bridled.

'She is yours, if it would please you to ride her,' Aldeborough explained, deliberately casual, but watching her reaction with far more than his apparent dispassionate interest. 'She is not up to my weight, but she should suit you perfectly. She is keen and lively, but has no vices.'

Frances opened her mouth but no words came out, merely a little cry of delight. She remembered that Matthew had once spoken about this mare.

'I bought her in Spain.'

Frances approached the mare and rubbed her hand over the glossy coat, threading her fingers through the dark mane. She was a dark bay with a hint of Arab in her small head and arched neck. She turned dark liquid eyes on Frances and snuffled at her fingers as she snatched at the bit, ready to run.

'She is beautiful,' Frances whispered. 'Has she a name?' She continued to caress the satin neck.

'She does not have one, unless it is Spanish. She is for you to name.'

'I have never owned anything so perfect.' She could not take her eyes from her unexpected gift. The mare tossed her head and danced on the spot, eager to show her paces. Frances felt the suspicion of tears behind her eyelids and blinked rapidly, feeling foolish. She could not look at Aldeborough, but leaned her forehead against the mare's silken shoulder. She wanted to fling her arms around her husband's neck, to press her cheek against his heart, but she could not fight past the barrier between them.

'How can I thank you?' Her lips felt stiff and the words sounded cold and formal to her own ears.

'You don't have to. I thought you might find these useful as well.'

Aldeborough held out a flat packet wrapped in soft leather. She turned from the mare to take it from him hesitantly.

'Open it,' he encouraged.

'Yes. Of course. It's just that…' She tried to explain the swell of emotion in her breast. 'I am not used to receiving presents, you see.'

Frances opened the packet. 'They are lovely.' She held the soft leather riding gloves, fashioned in a masculine style with a gold fringe and embroidered gauntlet.

'Perhaps you will ride out with me,' Aldeborough prompted, 'and let the mare show you her paces.'

'Perhaps… But I must…I can't…' How could he be so

kind, so generous, when she had been so unforgiving! It was so unfair of him!

Before she dissolved into tears that she could no longer contain, Frances picked up her skirts and fled into the house, leaving Aldeborough and Selby to raise their eyebrows at the unpredictability of women.

Frances encountered Aunt May on the stairs.

'But what's wrong? What's happened?' Lady Cotherstone put out a hand to detain the distraught lady.

'Aldeborough has given me the Spanish mare. She is the most beautiful thing I have ever seen.'

'Well, of course. Now that is something to cry about!'

Frances flushed in exasperation and fled to the privacy of her bed chamber.

A visit from Viscount and Lady Torrington and Charles did little to ease the tensions that continued to simmer below the surface. They drove to the Priory in a dusty landaulet, which had certainly seen better days, to make a formal morning call, the last thing Frances expected, but her aunt and uncle had clearly put themselves out to please. As the assembled company sipped tea in the morning room, Frances was aware only of the clash of tension behind the pleasant façade.

'Dear Frances,' exclaimed her Aunt Cordelia, 'we simply had to come to give out felicitations to the bride. And you, my lord Aldeborough. We are very sorry to lose our niece from our home, but we are delighted that she has made such an excellent alliance. And we are sure that you are highly satisfied with your choice!'

Aldeborough bowed his agreement, a bland smile bracketing his mouth. It would have served no purpose to shatter the deliberate attempts at amiability, even though Frances felt an urge to fling her teacup at her aunt's nodding ostrich plumes.

If Viscount Torrington remembered the content of his previous conversation with Aldeborough, he showed no sign of it. He conversed equably with the Marquis on such matters as horse breeding and the need for local road improvements.

Aldeborough was his usual urbane self, handling the whole event with cool politeness and a smile that held neither warmth nor affability. Frances could almost see the barely contained anger shimmering around him. It took all of his self-control not to take a riding crop to Torrington and whip him from the door. He tried to block out the memory of the cruelty and humiliation inflicted on Frances and the permanent scarring that would be a constant reminder of her devastated childhood. His fingers clenched to the imminent danger of the fragile china in his hand. Now was not the time, but one day Torrington would pay for his betrayal of the trust of guardianship.

Meanwhile Frances came to the conclusion that the visit had been engineered by Charles. He made an excellent impression with his polished manners, impeccably turned out in a well-cut coat of dark green superfine and spotless white buckskins. His fair hair gleamed and his regular features could not be anything but pleasing. His smile was open and genuine as he lavished his attention on Aunt May. He flirted with her a little, encouraging her to gossip and laughing at her fine-drawn descriptions of their London acquaintance. Frances looked on in fascination.

It was all very pleasant. As Frances measured out the tea from the caddy into the silver teapot she found herself wondering if her memory served her well. Life at Torrington Hall had been one of neglect and hard work—cruelty, even. She remembered the cold bareness of her room, the long hours of household drudgery, the crippling indifference without care or love and the agony of her uncle's whip. The blood drained from her cheeks at the intensity of her memories and her heart increased its rhythm, but she followed her husband's lead and smiled as she answered some trivial query of her aunt's.

They took their leave after the requisite period of time and Frances walked with her guests to the door.

'Perhaps you will find time to visit us at the Hall,' Lady Torrington suggested.

'How kind. When estate duties permit, I will bring my wife to visit you.' Aldeborough's urbanity knew no bounds.

'I can understand your wish not to allow Frances to make the journey alone. The highwaymen—the news of that was quite shocking.' Charles's tone was solemn as he expressed his concern.

'I was not aware that it was common knowledge.' Aldeborough's eyes narrowed.

'News like that spreads. Footpads are a threat to us all.'

'And you did begin enquiries in York,' Aunt May reminded her nephew. 'Rumours are sure to spread. I expect that is how you came by your knowledge, Mr Hanwell.'

'Why, yes, Lady Cotherstone. Akrill, our butler, had all the details. You know how it is.'

Aldeborough accepted the explanation with a smile that showed his teeth. 'Of course. Your solicitude, Charles, is most gratifying.'

Aldeborough's eyes met Lady Cotherstone's fleetingly, but with a hint of warning. She merely smiled serenely and engaged Lady Torrington in a surprisingly detailed discussion of the best ways to preserve plums for winter consumption, which lasted until they were all standing on the gravelled drive beside Torrington's landaulet.

Charles managed a few moments of private conversation with Frances as his mother was handed up into their carriage.

'I would hate to think that you were in any danger. You know that you can rely on me for help if you need it. You have only to send word.' He paused to select his words carefully. 'Whatever the problem.'

'You are very kind. But I don't anticipate any further danger.' His persistence surprised her, but all she could read in his eyes was thoughtful attentiveness.

'How should you? But don't forget.'

He kissed her hand, holding it a little too long before he turned to follow his father.

Aunt May loomed behind her. 'Now there is an interesting young man.' A heavy frown marked her forehead. 'Very presentable. I wonder why it is that I don't take to him.'

'Why on earth not?' Frances looked at her in surprise. 'You seemed to find him very pleasant company.'

'True. But I don't know. Perhaps he was a little too pleasant. He is most gallant with a manner that can only please. He seemed very anxious about you.'

'Yes. He was. He is my cousin, after all.'

'Hmm.' Aunt May was not to be put down. 'What a dreadfully common woman your aunt is. I am amazed that she did not ask to look through your linen cupboards.'

Frances raised her eyebrows. 'Were you possibly listening in to our conversation, Aunt May?'

'I tried, but not very successfully. Did she ask you if you were breeding yet?'

Frances could not control the colour that flooded her face to the roots of her hair.

'Yes, she did, if you must know.' Embarrassment clashed with indignation.

'And are you?' She had not heard Aldeborough's approach until his gentle enquiry caused her heart to jolt. His grey eyes were suddenly intent, holding her own startled gaze.

Frances recovered quickly. 'You will be the first to know, my lord, when I am!' she snapped and turned on her heel. She had had enough of family for once and it was not even midday.

The week ended in true March fashion with high winds and violent storms. The Priory was lashed by driving rain with standing water on the lawns and broken branches everywhere. Confined to the house, Frances investigated the contents of a much-neglected still room, throwing out the noxious substances that had been decomposing in their jars for years. Aldeborough got down to some tenancy agreements while Matthew prowled about and got under everyone's feet. Aunt May took to her bed as the only sensible place for someone of her advanced years—with Wellington and a bottle of claret for company.

Eventually nature relented, producing a fine morning with scudding clouds and sunshine, to the relief of everyone. Kington arrived, wet and mud splattered, to report to Aldeborough who was cleaning guns in the gunroom with the renewed prospect of some shooting.

'Nothing to worry you, my lord, but I thought I should report. There's been some damage with the high winds.'

'I expected as much. Anything immediate?' Aldeborough put down the gun and started to clean the oil from his fingers. 'The house seems watertight and we did not lose any of the roof. I have not been down to the stables yet, but Selby hasn't reported anything amiss.'

'No, that's fine, my lord. I don't know about the tenants yet—I'm sure I will by the end of the day. Old Huckerby's cottage will need re-roofing again for sure. But there are some trees down in Home Wood that we need to clear and the ditches need unblocking along the West Road. The other thing is the Chinese Bridge, where Tippet's Brook comes out of the West Lake. Some hefty branches have smashed against the supports in the wind and become wedged underneath so the bridge is unstable. It is still in one piece, but not to be trusted. I thought I should tell you in case you or Lord Matthew rode out that way.'

'Thank you, Kington. I will warn everyone. It is not a priority—it is only ornamental, so no one else from the village will use it. We can put it low on the list after old Huckerby! You would do well to keep him sweet if you want him to layer your hedges—he is still the best hedger I have ever seen, in spite of his rheumatics.'

Kington grinned. 'I am on my way to see him now. I will leave the matter of the bridge to you then, my lord. I will go and warn Selby.'

'And I will inform Lord Matthew.'

The house seemed to be empty. Eventually Aldeborough ran Aunt May to earth.

'At last. Someone alive in this place. Where is Frances?'

'I will still be alive when you are dead and gone, my boy.' She frowned at him in mock disapproval. 'As for Frances, when I last saw her she was planning a ride to blow away some cobwebs. If you had been at breakfast with us, you would not have to ask!'

He ignored her sharp comments, well used to her lethal sniping. 'Do you know if she has gone alone?'

'How should I know?' A spirit of mischief encouraged May to do a little none-too-gentle stirring. 'Why did you not go with her?'

'It may have escaped your notice, but I have been busy.'

'Hmm! Too busy to ride out with your wife? It would not surprise me if she had gone to meet Cousin Charles. Now, there is a fine upstanding man. He was very solicitous when he called last week, or did you not notice? He has a very flattering way with him and could be counted quite attractive. She might like a little masculine attention.'

Aldebrough chose to ignore the malicious sparkle in Lady Cotherstone's eyes, but could not quite deny the sharp tug of jealousy. His lips tightened into a straight line that May recognised with a surge of unholy glee.

'Since you do not know who she might be riding with, perhaps you could tell me where she was intending to go?' His tone was clipped on the verge of impatience.

'No. *You* should know. You are a fool, Hugh!'

'Thank you. I know I can always depend on you for a useful comment!'

He turned towards the door and then swung back, a frown beginning to gather between his bows. 'Do you think she might have gone with Matthew?'

'Did I hear my name mentioned?' Matthew came in, dressed for riding.

'Well, that answers my question.' Aldeborough's frown developed, his eyebrows settling into a black bar.

'Which one?'

'I was hoping that Frances might have gone for a ride with you.'

'No. I have not seen her since breakfast. I know she was keen to take the Spanish mare out, but she did not say where she intended to ride. What's wrong?'

'Kington says the Chinese bridge is in a dangerous state

so don't use it. I think I had better go and look, just in case
Frances decides to return by that route. It is probably nothing,
but…' He shrugged, but could not dislodge the sense of unease.

'I will come with you.'

They set off across the open parkland to the south. The
wind was still blustery with banks of cloud looming on the
horizon, but the fitful sun made it a good day for a ride. As
expected, Selby had reported that her ladyship had taken the
Spanish mare, now christened Beeswing, about an hour ago
and had headed across the open pasture to the far belt of trees.
And no, she hadn't taken a groom with her.

'She said she was going to try the mare's paces. They
looked right good together, my lord. A pleasure to see. She
had her on an easy rein and they cantered off all right and
tight. I don't reckon you need to worry any.'

And although Aldeborough agreed, the kernel of doubt still
churned in his gut. He and Matthew skirted the formal lawns
and rode out of the dip to canter up to the top of the rise
from where they would be able to see the gleaming expanse
of the West Lake with the Chinese Bridge at its eastern end.

They heard the approach of hoofbeats even before they
reached the crest.

'That will be Frances now.' Aldeborough acknowledged
the relief in Matthew's voice, pulling his horse to a walk, but
then hesitated, listening intently.

'If it is, she is out of control. Listen! That is a flat-out
gallop.' Apprehension tightened its grip in his chest. They
reined in and waited.

His worst fears were realised. The mare came over the rise,
riderless, at full gallop. She had been heading for the Priory,
for the warmth of her stable, but veered towards the presence
of the two riders and familiar horses and allowed Matthew
to catch her bridle without too much difficulty. They did a
rapid inventory. She was wet from head to foot, her saddle
covered with mud, and there was a deep graze, oozing blood,

on her off fore. Otherwise she was unharmed, merely frightened, with laid-back ears and panic in her eyes.

Aldeborough issued rapid, clipped orders to Matthew, his habitual drawl replaced by a rasp of steel. 'Take the mare back to the stables. Bring the curricle back with you along the track to the spinney in case we need it. Spring the horses if you have to. I hope she just took a toss in the dead ground and will be none the worse for it. But hurry, man.' Matthew needed no urging.

Aldeborough pushed his horse into a gallop towards the crest of the rise, emotions held firmly in check. He refused to think, to imagine the possibilities of what he might find by the Chinese Bridge. Could he have done anything to prevent it? That fact that he could not made no difference. He would not allow the panic that gripped his chest and hampered his breathing to claim mastery over him.

On reaching the crest he pulled up his labouring horse to scan the distant prospect of lake, stream and bridge. The lake had overflowed its banks, inundating the flat pasture, turning the well-mannered stream of Tippet's Brook into a miniature torrent. The bridge was still standing and indeed appeared to be secure, but the trapped boughs were clearly visible against and under the supports. There was no sign of Frances. Aldeborough gathered up his reins and galloped on down the hill, but with some caution given the muddy descent. He continued to scan the water meadows with anxious eyes. As the angle of the bridge changed at his approach, he became aware that one side of the balustrade, made of interlocking spars in a rustic oriental pattern, had collapsed into the lake. Then his eyes locked on to a splash of vibrant green, which could not be mistaken for reeds or sedge, at the side of the bridge. Without compunction he applied spurs to his horse.

She was lying in the water beside the bridge. Her body was partially out of the lake as if she had attempted to drag herself on to the bank, but she must have been weighed down by the heavy velvet of her habit, now completely waterlogged. The torrent was again threatening to submerge her and she did not move at his approach. Aldeborough threw himself from his mount and waded into the water, oblivious of the fast currents and the dangerous debris that threatened to drag his feet from under him. First he had to disentangle her skirts from the branches, but it proved to be an impossible and far too lengthy task with the water swirling ominously around them. Abandoning finesse and resorting to brute force, he tore the heavy material to release her body. Then he grasped her shoulders, fighting to drag her inch by inch from the mud and rushing current on to the safety of the bank. It took all his strength but he dare not relax, dare not stop to regain his breath. The only thought that filled his mind and blotted out all else was that she had been in the water some time, that her body was inert, that she might be dead.

The events seemed to run in slow motion, to stretch for ever, but within minutes, Aldeborough had dragged them both to the sodden grass and reeds of the bank. He dropped to his knees, gasping, drawing breath painfully into his lungs, but could not rest until he had turned her unresponsive body so that he could see her face. She was soaked from head to foot and covered with mud from the stream bed. There were streaks of it on her ashen face and in her hair, which had tumbled down around her shoulders. Her eyes were closed.

'Frances. Frances.'

He gathered her into his arms, pushing the wet strands of hair back from her face, searching for any sign of injury or broken bones. She was deathly pale. For one heartstopping moment her face was replaced by that of Richard, her inert body as lifeless as Richard's in a terrible repetition of the curricle race. He found he could not breathe. Could not think. He turned his face into her hair, murmuring her name, holding her tightly as a nightmare of memory swept through him to carry him back into the past.

'Don't leave me. Don't die, Frances.' He was unaware of his words, the promises he made, rocked by a torrent of despair. He cradled her against his heart.

Gradually, through the mists, reality broke through, sense returned. There was no blood. No obvious wound. No terrible repetition of the nightmare. He forced himself to focus on the faint but steady pulse in her neck where he had pressed his lips. She gasped, began to cough and struggle against his confining arms. He lifted her a little, allowed her to sit up, but kept a supporting arm about her shoulders, taking a few deep breaths to steady himself as the immediate panic receded.

'Frances?'

Her eyes opened slowly and focused on him, confused and blurred, but cleared as memory returned. 'What happened?' she gasped, pushing against his arm.

'Be still a moment.' There was no hint of the ravages of emotion that had threatened to unman him in his reply. 'You took a fall.'

'Yes, I fell. I remember now. The lake.' She grasped his arm, fear leaping into her eyes. 'Beeswing? Is Beeswing unharmed?'

'Like all sensible mares, she's back in her comfortable stable by now.' He worked hard to keep his tone light, an undercurrent of humour, and to still the trembling of his hands in the aftermath. 'Can you tell me what happened?'

'I was coming home. It was very windy. The water was fast, but the bridge seemed secure.' She wiped a hand across her face to push back her hair. 'We stepped on to the bridge. And I remember—there was a noise. A sharp crack. It must have been one of the supports. Beeswing shied and before I could do anything she seemed to lose her footing and fell through the balustrade into the lake. I remember the water rushing over me—the cold—and I couldn't get out—and then nothing. I think I must have hit my head.' Her eyes were blank with shock and her pupils dilated at the memory of her helplessness. She tightened her hold on Aldeborough's arm where she still grasped it. 'Are you sure she's not harmed? It was a terrible fall.'

Aldeborough got to his feet and reached down to help her to stand. She was beginning to shiver violently from cold and reaction. He must get her home, out of the cold whip of the wind.

'She's fine,' he reassured her, keeping an arm around her.

'At least she didn't fall on you. And look, here comes Matthew to the rescue.'

'But how did you know where to find me? I don't understand.'

'It's not important now.' He was very aware of her confusion as reaction began to set in. 'Let me get you home.'

'But what of my beautiful riding habit?' She was suddenly conscious of the sodden cloth of her underclothes clinging uncomfortably to her body and its liberal smearing of mud and slime. 'The velvet will be ruined. It was so beautiful.'

'I will buy you a new one.' He was even able to smile at her disordered priorities. 'I will buy you a dozen!'

He stripped off his coat to wrap it around her trembling shoulders, hoping to transfer some of the vestigial warmth from his body to hers. Then he swept her into his arms, in spite of her instant assertion that she was perfectly capable of walking, and carried her towards the curricle and Matthew.

At the Priory Aldeborough carried her into the house and up the stairs, fending off explanations and expressions of concern, issuing orders for hot water, towels, and her ladyship's maid. Only when he had shouldered his way into her room did he lower her to the ground. He turned her to the light to scan her face intently. There were faint shadows under her eyes, a pale shade round her mouth, and a bruise was beginning to develop on her hair line. Her hair hanging limply on to her shoulders was an impossible damp tangle of curls. The sodden cloth clung to every curve and swell of her body. Beneath his concern Aldeborough was shocked by the sudden tightening in his loins and an unexpected wave of desire that all but swamped his senses. He forced it under control as, with trembling fingers, he began to deal with the buttons and strip off her close-fitting jacket and then her skirt. She simply stood unresisting, arms at her side, following his orders, too stunned to respond, tremors still racking her body. By the time she was standing in her petticoats, her maid arrived with footmen carrying a bath into her dressing room, followed by more with buckets of steaming hot water.

'I will leave you in competent hands. Take care of her,' he instructed the maid, his mouth grim.

'Of course, m'lord. Her ladyship will soon feel more the thing.'

He beat a grateful retreat to his own dressing room. He was almost as wet as Frances and needed time to regain his composure.

An hour later he re-entered her dressing room. It was empty apart from the debris of water, towels and ruined velvet, so he continued on into her bedchamber. Frances was alone, seated before a fire that had been hastily lit, looking pretty and fragile in a lace and satin robe as her hair dried into unruly curls. Her colour had returned. She looked pink and relaxed from the hot water and, to his relief, immeasurably recovered from her ordeal.

She looked up at the opening of the door and smiled shyly. 'I am sorry I caused you so much trouble. Riding was my only talent, if you remember. I can not even lay claim to that now.' Her smile took on a wry tinge.

He smiled sympathetically, but shook his head. 'The bridge was damaged. You could not have prevented it. Kington reported the damage caused by the storm this morning so that is why we had come to find you, in case you chose to ride in that direction. Your talent still stands.'

'That is a relief. It does my self-esteem good.'

'You will need it. I am reluctant to mention it, but by tomorrow you will have a magnificent black eye to explain away.' He resisted the temptation to run his fingers over the injury, to soothe the hurt. He thrust his hands into his pockets.

Silence fell between them.

He too had stripped off his wet clothes and was clad in a magnificent dark-grey dressing-gown with black frogging and velvet revers. She had never seen him in it before. His face was stern, his mouth unsmiling, but she thought he looked magnificent. She could think of nothing to say.

He walked towards her, placing his hands on her shoulders to pull her from her chair, feeling her shiver, her breath catch at his touch. Without a word, without thought, he allowed instinct to dictate and dragged her to him, holding her against his chest, and crushed her mouth beneath his in urgent need. He was already hard for her and his emotions were running high.

'My lord, it is broad daylight,' she stammered when he at last raised his head to scan her face with a fierce stare.

'So it is.' He released her for one moment and strode across the room to lock the doors.

'Now, my lady. I want you. I will try to be gentle, but God help me, I want you now.'

He stripped the cover from the bed and lifted her there with consummate ease. His hands made short work of her robe, in spite of her inarticulate protests, leaving her exposed to the bright rays of the sun that gilded her curves and cast entrancing shadows, enough to heat a man's blood if he were not already aroused. She had no idea, he thought, how alluring she looked at that moment. He shrugged out of his dressing gown and came to kneel beside her.

'Let me look at you. You are so beautiful.'

His eyes swept her body, so finely boned, so delicate, the curve of her ribs and the swell of her hips enticing him to run his fingers along the length of curves, dips and hollows from throat to knee. He needed to touch her, to reassure himself that she was alive and unharmed. And that she was his. The blood pumped through his veins, hammering in his loins. He fought hard to keep control but was, for once, not confident.

'Do you realise how beautiful you are?' Her skin was tinted palest rose at his intimate appraisal, but she had recovered from her initial shock and responded, to his delight, without shyness.

'You are beautiful too,' she said. His laugh became a groan as she raised her hands to spread her fingers over his chest and move them slowly down over his flat stomach to his hips, not in denial but in blatant invitation. Nor was there any mistaking the anticipation in her eyes.

For good or ill, his restraint was at an end. He took her

wrists to pinion them above her head and launched an assault on her mouth with his own. His kiss was hot and urgent, seducing her lips apart so that his tongue might invade and possess. She responded willingly, her blood heated by his words, the passion in his eyes, the hard-held control in his sinews and muscles as he held himself in check. He used his tongue and teeth on her nipples, first one and then the other, until they became erect peaks of desire and she cried out in shocked pleasure, astounded by the depth of need and delicious sensation that he could ignite in her, arching her body against him, wanting to give more, wanting him to take more.

When he sensed her readiness he stretched over her to spread her thighs with the weight of his body, releasing her wrists and tightening his hold on her hips so that he might lift her and allow him to enter. It moved him beyond words that she needed no persuasion, but opened herself willingly. One strong thrust was all it needed for him to bury himself in that incredible hot, tight, velvet glove.

'Look at me. I want you to look at me when I take you.'

He all but drowned in her beautiful eyes. He could not hold back. His thrusts became harder, deeper, his breathing heavy, sweat glimmering on his face and shoulders. She clung to him through the onslaught, her nails inflicting crescent wounds into the slick skin of his shoulders until with a final surge, a tightening of muscle in arms and thighs, a hoarse groan of satisfaction, he emptied himself into her.

They lay still, the room silent except for their heightened breathing as it returned to normal. He pushed himself up on one elbow and thigh to look at her. She returned his gaze with a steady acceptance and then smiled, the sun striking sapphires from her eyes. He lifted a hand to stroke her hair but for a moment hesitated as a blinding thought pierced his brain, sharp and devastating as a lightning strike—and just as unnerving. No! He pushed the idea away. It was a normal reaction, merely of the moment and the circumstances because he had feared that he had lost her. But he could not quite rid himself of it.

'What are you thinking?'

'I was thinking…' He shook his head as if to clear his mind and continued smoothly, 'I was thinking that I have been a very selfish lover. I wanted you too much.'

She shook her head in denial, letting her fingers drift over his shoulders and then along an old sabre wound that marked his ribs in a long slash from breast bone to hip.

'You are scarred too. I did not know.'

'Yes.'

She lifted herself to press her lips to the raised welt. He drew in a breath at the impossible tenderness of the gesture and was surprised to feel an immediate tightening in his belly although he had thought himself sated. But it would please him to use it to her advantage.

'This is for you, Frances.'

He leaned across and lowered his mouth to her in the gentlest, most tender of caresses. Where he had been dominant and demanding, now he awoke her body with slow caresses, of lips and tongue. When he parted the soft flesh between her thighs with experienced fingers, stroking, pushing into the warm, clinging wetness, she sighed and abandoned herself to his will. He awakened in her such feelings as she had never experienced, never dreamed of. Her skin was so sensitive, his touch so glorious, that she hovered on the edge of exquisite agony. Her only awareness was the intensity of the heat in her belly and thighs that seemed to be slipping out of her control—and for a moment she knew fear.

'No,' she gasped. 'I cannot…' She resisted, trying to turn from his impossible demands on her body, only to whimper in rapture as his teeth closed over a nipple, torturing it into life.

He raised his head. 'Yes. Yes, you can. Let me give you the pleasure you gave me.'

He slipped effortlessly inside her, filling her with a need she did not understand. He set the pace slowly now, thoroughly, allowing her time to absorb every sensation, withdrawing and then reclaiming her with long firm strokes. He watched her reaction as the heat built. And when it burst through her whole body in a shower of gold, imprisoning her in long shudders that were completely beyond her control, she cried out. And it was his name she cried. Only then did he complete his own pleasure, control once more in place, until he lay spent beside her. He was as breathless and dazed as she was. She turned and hid her face against his shoulder, her hair spread over his chest.

Aldeborough was descending the stairs in mid-afternoon when a visit from Selby swept his intense sense of well-being away. He was waiting for him in the entrance hall.

'I think you should come down to the stables, Captain.'

'What is it, Selby? A problem?'

'I believe so, Captain.' His face was set in lines of concern. 'I need you to take a look at the mare.'

Beeswing was placidly eating oats in her stable and whickered softly on Selby's return. Aldeborough was surprised to see Kington already there.

'What's wrong? She seems to have recovered well enough.' He ran his hands over her shoulder.

'What do you make of this, my lord?'

Aldeborough bent and ran an expert hand down the mare's off fore to where he knew the would find a deep graze across the shin. It was quite deep and very even. The bleeding had stopped and Selby had been mixing a concoction to apply as a poultice to the swollen flesh.

Aldeborough looked up sharply at Selby, a faint chill creeping insidiously through his veins.

'A bullet?' He had seen enough wounds on men and animals in Spain to recognise it immediately.

'Aye, Captain. And look at this. Kington here found this buried in one of the uprights of the bridge balustrade which had fallen in the water.'

On the palm of his broad, callused hand was a familiar object. A lead shot from a pistol. Aldeborough picked it up, rubbed his fingers over it consideringly, making sense of Frances's recollections.

'So that was the sharp crack Frances heard. A bullet. Not

the wood. The supports held but the mare was struck, panicked and fell through the balustrade.'

'Most likely, my lord,' Kington added his corroboration. 'It came from the direction of the spinney, it looks like. It would have been easy to use it as cover.'

Aldeborough's lips thinned, his eyes becoming glacial. 'I don't want this to go any further. Don't talk about it to anyone. Do you understand me?'

'Yes, my lord. There's no point in worrying her ladyship.'

No, there was no point in worrying Frances, agreed Aldeborough silently as he returned to the house. But this put an entirely different complexion on the attack by the highwaymen. Just who was the target?

Chapter Ten

Aldeborough was careful to allow no reference to the incident at the Chinese Bridge to cloud Frances's enjoyment in the following days. As far as he was aware, only Kington and Selby knew of the discovery of the evidence and they could be trusted to keep silent. Although she could not be ridden, Beeswing continued to make a good recovery and the wound knit well. It would leave hardly a scar. Meanwhile the Marquis devoted some of his time to introducing his wife to the more far-flung reaches of the estate and the tenants who lived in the village beyond the church. He put her up on one of his hunters and rode the estate with her. And he found himself appreciative of her company. She had charm and a ready wit as her confidence increased and she relaxed in his presence. She was also interested in his schemes and plans and was willing to explain her own ideas.

It was not all estate work. They galloped across the park, head to head, revelling in the wild glory of speed and sensation. Her eyes sparkled and she smiled. When she beat him in a race to the stables she laughed aloud with the joy of it. It pleased him to see the shadow of old fears fade from her eyes and the lines of ever-present watchfulness smooth from her face. The contentment suited her, giving her a youthful bloom and a beauty of which he had not been aware. It pleased him that he could do that for her and he would pre-

serve that contentment with whatever means at his disposal.
And it delighted him to see the colour steal into her cheeks
when a new green velvet riding habit—and such a perfect
fit!—arrived mysteriously from town.

At night he lost himself in the soft curves and enticing
secrets of her receptive body, so slim and apparently delicate,
but so firm and smooth to the caress of his hands. She was
his and he felt the power of ownership when her skin warmed
to his touch and her body moved beneath his, and when she
sighed in his arms and curled against him as she fell exhausted into sleep. It was a novel experience to have his eyes
and thoughts drawn to her when she turned her head in a
particular way or lifted a hand in a graceful gesture to tuck
in a stray curl. He wanted to let his fingers stroke down her
cheek, her throat, all the elegant length of it, and press his
mouth to where the pulse beat beneath the fair skin. Indeed,
he could not get her out of his mind.

Her bruises might have faded to mere shadows, but his
increasing desire for her staggered him with its intensity.

For Frances the days were in the nature of a revelation.
She had never experienced companionship before and here
there was friendship and perhaps even affection freely offered. Her growing love for him she firmly smothered beneath
a friendly exterior. He did not want her love and she was
relieved that he did not look for it. It made it easier for her
to dissemble. If it hurt her heart, then so be it. She would
accept what he was prepared to offer. Perhaps it was her own
love that made her receptive to the affection and respect from
those around her for the new Marquis, from Rivers and Webster and the house servants to Selby, Kington and those involved in the running of the estate. And the tenants in the
village. As an onlooker, perhaps she saw more than Aldeborough did. There was never any overt criticism of Aldeborough's father or of Richard, owner of the title for such a
short time, but Frances got the strong impression that her
husband was regarded as an enlightened man who would
remedy the neglect of past years.

Even with her ignorance of the details of estate management, it was easy for her to see the signs of neglect and lack of investment. Poor road surfaces, dilapidated cottages, no evidence of any development of the resources of the estate, basic and outdated farming techniques. The tenants and local community looked to Aldeborough for a commitment and he was strongly aware of it. Huckerby was not the only one to complain about his leaking roof.

So Frances found herself discussing schemes for quarrying on the eastern boundary of the estate and the merits of crop rotation or the wool production of different breeds of sheep. And the possibility of developing some selective horse breeding if the stables were to be extended and further improved. But he would not talk about Spain, apart from the odd casual reference. And he would never mention Richard's name. She shrugged and wisely left both topics alone.

Of her uncle and cousin at Torrington Hall, there was no word. Frances heaved a sigh of relief. There were enough potential tensions without further contact from that quarter.

'You asked me to meet you here, my lord.'

The library was flooded with bright sunshine, dust motes dancing in the unseasonably warm air and a faint perfume pervading from the vase of early daffodils. It was now near noon and the business between Aldeborough and Hedges was almost at an end. They sat on either side of the magnificent desk, a welter of papers spread over its surface between them. Frances detected an air of restlessness, of dissatisfaction even, about her husband, but that hardly surprised her as she now knew his tolerance of paper work to be low. As she entered he looked up, a shadow of concern crossing his features, but it was quickly gone—indeed, perhaps she had imagined it— and he rose to greet her with a smile that made her pulses leap. The fingers which she placed in his outstretched hand trembled at his touch. Would she ever learn to control her responses to him? She had no hope of it.

'My lady. I am delighted to see you. You are an excellent excuse to abandon all this for half an hour.' He indicated the official documents and estate maps on the desk. 'Hedges will tell you that I will accept anything as an excuse, but then he has not had the pleasure of meeting you before. Let me introduce you.'

Hedges, Aldeborough's man of business from York, an elderly lawyer with receding hair and heavily lined features, rose stiffly to his feet and acknowledged Frances with a bow and a few words of congratulation on her recent marriage. His sombre face relaxed into a smile as he agreed that a break from boundary disputes was always welcome and especially when the interruption was so pretty. Frances laughed at his unexpected gallantry and offered to ring for the refreshment that Aldeborough, in the throws of legal complications, had clearly forgotten.

'I asked you to join us because Hedges has some information that is most pertinent to you. Come and sit here and he will explain all.' Although his words were light, Frances thought his face was surprisingly stern as he moved from his seat at the desk to allow Frances to take his place.

'Is it the inheritance?'

'Yes, my lady.' Hedges nodded in acknowledgement and began to shuffle a stack of papers before him.

'So you managed to squeeze the details out of my uncle at last.'

'It has taken no little time, but the whole transfer of business is now complete. Here are the terms of your mother's will.' His tone was grave and he glanced briefly at Aldeborough before he began, spreading out the documents before him. 'I won't trouble you with all the finer points...' he hesitated '...much of it is in legal terms, which you do not need, but the main gist is very straightforward. On your twenty-first birthday, you will inherit the sum of £30,000. It is invested in bonds and shares and the interest will come directly to you, payable half-yearly, if that is acceptable. It is to be in your ladyship's gift entirely to settle as you should wish for the future. It has been the tradition for it to be settled on the female line of the family, to allow the daughters of the family considerable independence in their own right, as you will be aware since your mother, Lady Cecilia Mortimer, settled it on you, her only daughter.'

For a moment there was silence in the library. Then, 'So much money?' whispered Frances, hardly able to comprehend Hedges's clear statement of the facts. 'I can hardly believe it. My uncle gave me to understand that the sum was very little, nothing more than pin money—I am sure they were his exact words. Why would he do that?'

'I cannot answer for your uncle,' replied Hedges placidly, well used to irrational behaviour from his clients when large sums of money were involved. 'Whatever was said, my lady, it is a vast sum. You are a wealthy woman in your own right and it gives me great pleasure to inform you of it.'

She looked across at Aldeborough. He had remained silent as Hedges told her of the inheritance, leaning with one arm along the mantelpiece, looking down into the cold fireplace. Now he raised his head. She had been right about the frown, the unease. But again it was quickly banished.

'You have little to say, my lady.' Hedges's smile held a hint of amusement. 'I find that even more amazing than the amount of pin money which is now yours to spend on whatever fripperies you desire.'

'Forgive me.' She laughed. 'I cannot think at all rationally at the moment. Thank you for the information, Mr Hedges. I did not mean to seem discourteous.'

He smiled. 'I quite understand, my lady. It is not an uncommon response.'

Aldeborough, realising that something was expected of him, walked across the room to raise her hand to his lips. 'I am delighted for you, my dear.'

Then why did she get the impression that he was not? That there was some problem of which she was not aware? She rose to her feet, chiding herself for her suspicions. Aldeborough's preoccupation was far more likely to be tied up with his own inheritance, not hers. She banished her anxiety with a smile at Hedges and her husband.

'If you will excuse me, I'll leave you to your dusty documents. I need a little time to…to think about all this. I shall take a walk in the garden to collect my thoughts a little!'

'Of course.'

'I am pleased to have met you, Mr Hedges.' She walked from the library as if in a dream.

Aldeborough seated himself once again in his chair, facing Hedges across the desk, a thoughtful expression returning to his face.

'I should express my thanks that you were willing to keep silent about the specific clause. I do not know if you consider it unethical, but I believe that it might be in my wife's best interests in the short term.'

'Have you some concern about it?'

'Yes, I have. I would rather not discuss it with my wife until a few matters have been clarified. I would prefer it to remain between ourselves.'

'It is certainly a most unusual clause,' Hedges agreed.

'Can I challenge it through the courts?'

'I doubt you would have much success. It has now stood for a number of generations.'

'I am afraid I have to agree with you.' Aldeborough picked up a quill pen and idly twirled it in his fingers. 'And there is certainly no ambiguity in the clause.'

'True. It is very clear in its implications. If your wife dies, or if she is childless by the time she reaches the age of twenty-five, thus leaving no issue to whom her inheritance can be willed, the money will revert to the care and jurisdiction of her father. And since Adam Hanwell is deceased, to her father's family, the Hanwells. And thus to Viscount Torrington, your wife's uncle and erstwhile guardian. To be used as he sees fit.'

'But why not to her husband? Surely that would be far more usual.'

'It is unclear. I believe it must have stemmed from the personal circumstances of a Mortimer bride in the sixteenth century—the Welsh Marches bred them, I believe, a troubled place with the need for advantageous marriages in border disputes with Welsh raiders. I presume that marriages were made purely for their financial and military advantage and if an unfortunate bride mysteriously disappeared or was even murdered by a reluctant husband, once he had his hands on her dowry, then such a clause would safeguard her life or at least the chance of issue from her. On the face of it, it seems very simple: no wife—no children—no money. But whatever the reason, that is how it stands. It is, indeed, a vast sum of money. Can I presume that you will inform your wife at a suitable time, my lord?'

'Of course.'

'If I may be so bold, my lord, I do not foresee a problem,' Hedges stated in a matter-of-fact tone. 'Her ladyship looks to be in excellent health. And I am sure that your own wish will be to produce an heir to your own estates and title as soon as may be. In that circumstance, this clause will be completely null and void.'

'Indeed.' Aldeborough agreed yet still seemed preoccupied.

'You can be sure of my discretion in these matters,' Hedges assured him.

'I know.' Aldeborough roused himself from his distraction and smiled ruefully at Hedges. 'Forgive me. It has given me much to think about. I would thank you for your efforts on behalf of my wife. I can guess that working with Torrington was not easy.'

'I am always pleased to be of service, as I was to your brother and father. If I might say, my lord, it is a pleasure to do business with one so concerned for the future of the estate. And now, if that is all, my lord, I will take my leave of you.'

Hedges's departure left Aldeborough with considerable food for thought, none of it palatable. Whose life was being put into danger? Was it his, as he had first thought? Or was it Frances? The accident—or more accurately the murder attempt—at the Chinese Bridge began to take on an even more sinister quality. For now, it was his choice not to tell Frances but he must, at all costs, keep a close watch on her movements. She must certainly not be allowed to ride about the estate unaccompanied. And when they returned to London… Well, he would meet that problem when it arose. It was outrageous that Torrington should continue to have such a long reach to affect Frances even after her marriage and her escape from his grasping clutches. Aldeborough shrugged off the sense of helplessness that threatened to darken his mood. They would have to live with the terms of the will, but he would ensure that she remained in ignorance of the potential danger and so continue to enjoy her new-found peace of mind.

Deep in thought, Frances found her inclination leading her into the herb garden. The warm sunshine was beginning to stir the fragrances that would fill the intimate walled area with heady pleasure in summer. She had much to think about, so the peaceful seclusion suited her mood and she knew she was unlikely to be disturbed. She was an heiress! Her inheritance was not merely an easy competence, but a fortune beyond her dreams. And hers to settle in the future as she wished. She had much for which to thank her unknown mother and previous strong-minded Mortimer ladies. She sat and watched the first bees begin to investigate the growing lavender spikes, unable to quite accept the facts of her new wealth. But one fact was startlingly clear. Viscount Torrington had lied and deceived her, giving her to understand that she would always be dependent on him for her welfare. And that, she concluded with simple and unassailable logic, was the reason why he had been so assiduous in planning a marriage between herself and his heir Charles. Many things began to fall into place for her as surely as the pieces in a mosaic.

It explained, she realised, why her uncle had been so angry over her marriage, sending Aunt Cordelia to fetch her back to Torrington Hall, determined to take her home from London, angry enough to threaten Aldeborough. Her fortune would have solved all Torrington's financial difficulties overnight. Paid off the mortgages, the gambling debts, put money back into the failing estate land. What a valuable asset she had been without even knowing it. And now it was lost to him and Charles. She had been used and manipulated by the only family she had known—and they had lost everything on the night Torrington's vicious conduct had finally driven her to escape in Aldeborough's coach.

And she had Aldeborough to thank for her rescue. A sensation of warmth and gratitude spread round her heart, her lips curving into a smile—to be instantly checked as if a door had slammed in her mind. An icy hand gripped her throat, her blood running cold. Aldeborough had taken her and married her, but at what cost? She forced herself to sit, gripping the edge of the stone seat with rigid fingers, and think calmly. Was this the explanation for the highwaymen? To kill Aldeborough and leave her a vulnerable widow? Surely it was too cold blooded, even for Torrington. But if Aldeborough had died, then she would be freed from this marriage, and what would be more natural than for a young widow to return to the protection of her family? And that would put her back into their control. And her money. It could not be! But why not? What would be better, after a suitable period of mourning, of course, than a second advantageous marriage to her cousin, who would be delighted to manage her affairs for her. The pieces fitted seamlessly together. The highwaymen had been paid off to kill Aldeborough, and Viscount Torrington would reap the benefits.

She sprang to her feet. Hugh! She must tell him. Warn him. She could not grasp the enormity of it that her marriage should have put his life in danger. And she was the cause. She had reached the wrought-iron gate in the wall when she heard footsteps approaching through the laurel shrubbery. Her heart lifted. It would be Hugh coming to find her. She could explain her fears to him.

It was not Aldeborough. Charles emerged from the laurels, treading purposefully towards the house, approaching from the stables. He saw her immediately, lifted a hand in greeting and changed his direction. Frances retreated back into the herb garden as Charles joined her, gathering her composure round her like a cloak, banking down the sudden spurt of anger that leapt through her blood.

'Good morning, Charles. I am surprised to see you here again so soon. Morning visits seem to be becoming a habit. I do not think that Aldeborough would encourage too close an acquaintance, all things considered.' She was coolly polite, successfully masking her anger and resentment, even though her fingers shredded a tuft of lavender stalks as she spoke.

Charles was unaware. His face lit with pleasure at the sight of her and his smile held great charm. 'But Aldeborough does not know that I am here. And besides, I came to see you. I was sure that *you* would not object. You look well.' He bowed over her hand with a graceful flourish.

'Why are you here, Charles?'

'To enquire after your well being, of course.' A shadow of concern crossed his face and he increased the pressure on the hand that he had kept under his control. 'We heard about your accident at the bridge. But I see that you have recovered, so I have no need to be concerned for your health on this occasion.' He paused and allowed Frances to snatch her hand away. 'If I might presume…it could have been far more serious, as I'm sure you realise. I am surprised that Aldeborough did not warn you of the storm damage. Did he not know?'

'Yes, he knew. But only after I had taken Beeswing to ride across the estate. And he was not to know where I would ride. What are you suggesting, Charles?' Her chilly tones were at variance with the spring warmth of the garden around them.

'Why, nothing, dear Frances. You are very trusting.'

'Why should I not be?'

'Why not, indeed? Of course, your relationship with your husband is your own affair. But my advice would be to take care. You are, after all, an heiress to a considerable fortune.'

'As I am sure you are aware. And have been for ever. It surprises me that I was the last person to know that I am worth something in excess of £30,000 a year. Why do you think that was, Charles?'

His expression took on a hint of wariness, but he continued to smile and answered easily with a shake of his head, 'I am delighted for you, Frances. I felt that I had to come to congratulate you.'

'Why did my uncle lie to me?' Frances persisted. 'Why did he lead me to believe that I would come into a small competence that would never be enough to give me independence or attract an advantageous marriage?'

'I was not conversant with my father's business dealings with you,' he answered with an expression of relaxed confidence on his face. 'Perhaps you misunderstood him. Why should you have worried about financial matters? As your guardian, my father would have seen it as his duty to take all such burdens from you. You cannot blame him for that.'

'I was not treated as an heiress.' Anger licked at her skin as the memories surfaced. 'I was not presented, I was not given a Season in London, I was not allowed to take my rightful place in society. I was treated as a poor relation— indeed, no better than a servant in my aunt's kitchen—with no consideration for my wishes or my happiness. And as for—' She pressed a hand to her lips and strove for control. She would not say more.

'Frances, I am so sorry that you should feel this way.'

'And could my inheritance have had anything to do with the proposed marriage between you and me?'

'How can you value yourself so little? I have always admired you.'

'I find it difficult to believe. I find it easier to believe that I and my inheritance would have been safely and quietly married off to you, with no one the wiser. It is well known that my uncle's finances are in dire straits.'

'Would you believe me if I told you I love you? You have become so beautiful, so elegant. How could I not love you?'

'No!'

'But I do. I always have.'

'So why have you never spoken of it before now? Why did you never show me any such affection? Why did you never snatch the whip from your father's hand? How dare you talk to me of love?'

'I thought you knew of my regard. It was always understood that we would marry when you had reached your majority. It is entirely my own fault if I did not make my feelings clear. All I can ask is that you will forgive me.' It was so smooth, so reasonable, and yet Frances knew in her heart that his words were empty and insincere.

'It no longer matters, does it?'

'Come away with me.' Lines of frustration were etched around his mouth and he attempted to seize her hands, but once more she thwarted him and stepped back. 'I will always love you.'

'No. I don't believe you. What nonsense is this? I am married—what can you possibly be suggesting?'

'Are you hoping to find love in your marriage?' Charles saw his chance, an opportunity to take advantage of her insecurity. He continued, his tone persuasive, sowing seeds of a bitter harvest. 'Aldeborough does not care for you. He never wanted it. He only married you to stop the scandal that he had ruined you after all—for himself, not for you. It is well known that he keeps a mistress in London. And he would marry Penelope Vowchurch if he had his way. He always intended to. He will never give you the love and admiration that I feel for you. Come away with me.' There was more than a hint of desperation in his voice. An urgency. 'Aldeborough will agree to a divorce quickly enough if you threaten to cause a scandal and drag their family name through the mire. And I will marry you.'

'Thank you, dear Charles.' Frances faced him with deliberate and heavy sarcasm. 'You will be kind enough to rescue me from a scandal of my own making. You cannot imagine my gratitude. And Aldeborough is to be sufficiently co-operative to divorce me. I see you have it all planned. And you, of course, will be richer than you could ever have dreamed.'

The smile disappeared from Charles's face and a harsh note of injustice crept into his smooth voice. 'My father was stupid beyond belief to allow you to escape his authority. It has ruined the family.' He fought for control, turning away from Frances to pace the path between the scented rosemary and sage. He succeeded in calming his breathing and returned to her, his face smoothed of his anger and frustration. His words were calm, reasonable even. 'But you could redeem it. You owe us at least that.'

'I owe you nothing. I think you should leave. There is nothing for you here.'

She made to turn away, not wanting to hear more of his smooth excuses or empty declarations of love, but his reaction to her words held no hint of the lover. His lips curved unpleasantly into a sneer and his eyes narrowed. He caught her wrist in a rough grasp, ignoring her cry of discomfort, refusing to release her.

'I see. I should have realised. The lure of status and a fortune even larger than your own is very strong. I had not thought it of you, Frances. Presumably you are not willing to forfeit your title—it means far more to you than the gift of genuine love.'

'You do not love me, Charles.' Frances met his eyes with dignity. She would not be intimidated. 'You never have. If you had, you would have done all in your power to ensure that your father treated me with care and consideration, not the cruelty and degradation which was my portion—and of which you must have been aware.

'Perhaps I should warn you,' she lashed out. 'The highwaymen on our journey here have troubled my thoughts a great deal of late. You knew about them, did you not, Charles? And it was *not* common knowledge. They were hired murderers, not interested in theft, but in blood. I find it very interesting that you should be so well informed.'

'What are you insinuating? What lies have you been listening to? Is it Aldeborough who has poisoned your mind against me?'

'Are they lies, Charles? Who would have most to gain if I were widowed?'

A trace of unease flashed in his eyes for an instant.

'You have no proof!'

'Of course not. But if Aldeborough is harmed in any way I will think that you or my uncle would be more than a little involved. Do you deny it?'

'Of course I do. This is mere fantasy, Frances.'

'Possibly. Just like the depth of love that you have declared for me. I think you should leave. You are not welcome at Aldeborough Priory, Charles. Now, if you will release my wrist.'

She faced him, eyes blazing. His hand fell away.

'Very well. Since you reject my offer so cruelly, I will bid you farewell, Frances. I hope you enjoy your new wealth. But before I leave, I would still wish to fulfil my other objective in coming here this morning. Despite your accusations and suspicions, it would be very wrong—petty, even—if I failed in completing my family's obligation to you.'

He searched in his pocket and removed a small object. 'This belonged to your mother. I brought it to give to you. It is yours by right. If you will permit me.'

He stepped forward to pin, with carefully impersonal fingers, a little brooch to the bodice of her gown. It was a simple ring brooch fashioned of amethysts and seed pearls.

'There.' He stepped back. 'It becomes you. I wish I could have given it on a happier occasion.'

He turned on his heel without another word and left the garden to the heedless bees and Frances, who covered her face with her hands in a storm of emotion. She would have been surprised if she had been aware of the satisfaction in her cousin's eyes.

Following a short period of reflection, which did nothing to calm her state of mind, Frances returned to the house. Uppermost in her thoughts was Charles: how dare he offer her marriage, how dare he pretend to an attachment that quite clearly had never existed until the prospect of a fortune had been snatched from before his eyes? As if she would believe his protestations of love and admiration. But her indignation soon vanished as her thoughts progressed to more serious issues. Was Torrington truly behind the ambush on the road from York? Of course Charles had denied it. What would she expect? But she thought that he had been less than comfortable with her accusation. And what terrible seeds of doubt Charles had sown. Deliberately, of course, but none the less successfully with such an unwarranted insight into her hopes and fears. After all, she knew that Aldeborough did not love her. He had never pretended otherwise. Letitia Winters was no secret. And her mother-in-law certainly had dreamed and planned for an alliance with Penelope Vowchurch. But had Aldeborough known about the bridge? Could he have stopped her? No, of course not. She could not believe such ill of him, would not believe it, but Charles had done his worst and the faint wisp of doubt remained to curl in her brain. It was no secret that he had married her out of honour and duty, destroying forever the possibility of a loving relationship. All her new-found confidence and delight in Aldeborough's presence had been undermined, leaving her uncertain and ill at ease.

Knowing that Charles had manipulated her and angry at his success, she decided that she needed some sensible company to give her thoughts a calming direction. She crossed the entrance hall with the intention of finding Lady Cotherstone, who usually spent her mornings in the small winter parlour, when she heard voices from the library. The door was partially open. It seemed that Hedges had finished his business with Aldeborough and was gone. The voices she heard were those of her husband and Aunt May, so she changed direction, intending to join them. On some impulse she hesitated outside the door to hear Aunt May in mid-conversation.

'So she is an heiress?'

'So it seems. It explains a number of things that I did not understand.' Aldeborough's voice was thoughtful and she heard the rustle of papers as he cleared away the aftermath of Hedges's visit.

'Some interesting clauses there,' Aunt May continued.

'Mischief making, I would say, although I can appreciate the original purpose behind them.'

'I think you may be right. I think it will pay me to take more care than has been my wont. There is a danger here that I do not like.'

'You should never have done it as you did, Hugh. To assist her to run away and then marry her without Torrington's permission or even knowledge.'

'I know. I do not need you to remind me.' Frances heard a note of resignation. 'It was despicable and I deserve to be horsewhipped. But it is done and we have to live with the consequences.'

Before she could hear any more damaging comments, Frances pushed the door further open and made an entrance.

Lady Cotherstone sat by the fireplace, Wellington at her feet, a glass of claret in her hand. Her wrinkled face lit in welcome.

'Frances! Come here, my dear, and let me kiss you. I understand that you have received some excellent news.'

'Yes. I still find it difficult to take in.' Frances obeyed, if distractedly, allowing the old lady to pat her hand and kiss her cheek with the casual affection that her own family had never shown her.

'So you are an heiress. And you, my dear boy—' she raised her eyebrows at Aldeborough '—could be accused of being a fortune hunter. If, of course, you needed the money. As I am sure you don't.'

'Only if I have to pay for your upkeep much longer, Aunt May. Look at the way you're making inroads into my claret, not to mention the port my father laid down.'

He turned to Frances with an easy smile, completely unaware of her present distress. 'I hope the news made you happy.'

She looked at him, unsmiling, considering her response. Could she tell him of her anxieties? She could not find the words—but neither could she remain silent. 'I overheard your conversation. I didn't intend to,' she explained stiffly. 'I am sorry that our marriage has put your life in danger.'

'My life?' His reply was careful, his expression bland. 'What did I say that made you think that?'

'About taking care—about danger. My uncle obviously blames you for removing the possibility of a fortune from his grasp. It explains the highwaymen, does it not?'

'It is possible,' he agreed, treading carefully, 'but there is no proof. It is certainly not your fault. There is no blame whatsoever attached to you.'

'But if you had not married me, you would be in no danger. And, you see, there was never any need for you to burden yourself with me.' She fought to control her distress. 'I had the money to be independent and set up my own household after all.'

'I see.' Any warmth in his face was gone. His eyes were cold. 'How unfortunate for you that you did not know about your inheritance sooner.'

'And for you. Then you could have married someone of your own choosing who would have been acceptable to your family.'

You should never have done it as you did…

I know.

The words, confirming all her fears, echoed again and again in her mind.

Tension, bitter and bleak, stretched between them.

He saw the desolation in her eyes, terribly aware that he had forced her into marriage against her wishes. And that the marriage had put *her* life in danger rather than his. He could not warn her. Could not tell her about the pistol shot at the bridge, or explain the clauses in the will, which would once again implant fear in the very core of her existence. He felt paralysed by lack of choice and retreated behind a stony façade.

She returned his gaze. Suddenly all she could focus on was Charles's poisonous words. And she knew the truth of them. That Aldeborough loved Letitia Winters and would, without doubt, have chosen to marry Penelope. His caresses had meant nothing. His love and the delights of his body were given elsewhere. She must never allow him to know that he had captured her heart on the night when he had pressed his lips to the scars on her back and shown her how to enjoy the exquisite pleasure of his lovemaking. She had too much pride. He must never be burdened by the knowledge of her love, which he had not sought. He must never know. She had done enough damage.

Lady Cotherstone, looking from one to the other, decided for her own reasons to intervene. 'What nonsense! You are very acceptable to me, my dear, and I am the only family that matters. In my opinion, Aldeborough could not have done any better for himself when he married you. You appear to me to be the ideal wife.'

Frances continued to look at him, a clear question in her eyes.

'My aunt is always perceptive.' His reply rejected her silent query and was particularly enigmatic to Frances's intense disappointment and frustration. The pain around her heart increased to invade her whole body. 'I hope that you are able to live with the situation,' he added.

'And you, too, my lord.' Her voice was flat and without hope.

Aldeborough's gaze suddenly sharpened as he surveyed his bride and his hands stilled on the papers before him.

'Is something amiss, my lord?' There was a distinct and deliberate challenge in Frances's response to the scrutiny.

He walked around the desk to stand before her and raised his hand to touch the pretty jewel pinned to her bodice.

'An attractive brooch.' There was a question in his voice. 'Have I seen it before?'

'No, my lord. It belonged to my mother, so I believe.'

'Indeed. And how did it come into your possession?'

'Charles gave it to me.'

'And when might that happy event have taken place?'

'About an hour ago. In the herb garden.' She lifted her chin and met his eyes. She would not explain further.

'Would it make any difference if I expressed a dislike of my wife accepting jewellery from another man?'

'No, my lord. If it belonged to my mother, it is rightfully

mine. I have nothing else of hers. Would you wish me to refuse it?'

Lady Cotherstone sighed and again broke the tension. 'I have decided that I would like to spend some of the Season in town. If you have finished estate business, Hugh, I would return with you.' It was an imperious command. 'A few weeks of entertainment and the opportunity to visit friends is just what I need. And Wellington would enjoy a change of scene. When shall we go?'

'My lady?' Aldeborough asked Frances.

'Whenever you wish, my lord.' She took refuge in formality.

'Then as soon as may be. My immediate business here is complete.'

'Then I will go and talk to Mrs Scott and tell her of our impending departure.' Frances turned and walked out without a backward glance.

'Take care with her, Hugh.' Aunt May rose from her seat and shook out her voluminous brocade skirts.

'It is my intention.'

'She loves you, you know.'

'No. I do not believe she does.' Aldeborough went to stare out of the window, not seeing the promise of spring in the blossoming flower beds or the rooks flirting on the breeze. 'Her experiences at Torrington Hall were hideous beyond belief. Now she feels comfortable and safe. And for that she is grateful, that is all. But the safety may be becoming an issue and I don't want her to be aware of it. She once told me inadvertently that one of the main advantages of this marriage for her is that she is no longer afraid. I would not have that peace of mind destroyed for anything. And I think I may have already jeopardised it unwittingly.'

'I cannot think how. And you said I was perceptive. But I will wager my pearl necklet that girl loves you. All you have to do is give her some way of showing it. Unless you don't wish to, of course. Relationships can be far easier without the burden of love, as I am sure you are aware. All I would say is—don't make the same mistake that your parents did, living in isolation from each other, both of them becoming bitter and uncaring.'

'And Charles?' he asked, discovering a sudden desire to seek reassurance against the jealousy that burned with a bright flame in his gut on seeing Frances wearing the amethysts and pearls. 'Perhaps she has more affection for him than she has for me after all.'

'Of course she does not! She cares nothing for Charles. But you are hardly in a good position to object to her wearing her mother's brooch when Letitia Winters has been seen wearing a very fine emerald necklace recently.'

Lady Cotherstone was rewarded by a sharp intake of breath from her nephew and hid a smile of satisfaction. To her delight, he flushed and refused to meet her wickedly glinting eyes.

'This is all far too deep for me!' The Marquis grimaced as he tried to escape from his aunt's deliberate probing. 'Aunt May, I could wish you would not find so much enjoyment in stirring up the mud at the bottom of the pond. You are an interfering old woman, but I have to admit that you are one in a million.' He came round the desk to kiss her cheek. 'There are developments here of which you are perhaps unaware. I would be grateful if you would leave it for now.' He looked tired, strain around his eyes.

'Such as the accident on the bridge?' She held up her hand as Aldeborough failed to control his surprise at her insight. 'I will resist asking you what really happened. But I was not born yesterday, Hugh, and I have ears. You cannot expect people not to talk. I have seen Frances riding your chestnut hunter and I do not believe for a moment that she simply fell in the water. And the bridge did not collapse under the mare, did it? All I will say is that you need to take care for her…and yourself. Now—' she made her way to the door '—tell me when I must be ready to travel. I have a lot of luggage to organise.'

As she reached the doorway, Lady Cotherstone paused to survey her nephew, struck by a sudden thought.

'Well, Aunt May? What now?'

'I was just thinking, Hugh. Have you ever considered writing poetry?'

'Poetry? What bee have you got in your bonnet now? No, I have not!'

'A pity!' She walked out, leaving Aldeborough lost for words.

Chapter Eleven

'I cannot understand why anyone would choose to spend a dull evening at Almack's! And as for the inflated conse-quence of the Patronesses—it sets my teeth on edge to have to be polite to them. I hope you don't expect me to undertake the role of chaperon.' Aunt May's notion of a round of pleas-ure in London did not include an evening at—as she put it—the stultifyingly rigid, dowdy assembly rooms, where nothing mattered but consequence and formality and where all she would be allowed to drink was tepid lemonade or tea.

'Because we have received admission vouchers,' explained Frances, not for the first time. 'And, as you are very well aware, if I am to complete my début into London society, it is important that I appear at Almack's! You are just being difficult.'

'Hmm! I dare say.'

'Besides, we do not need you,' she added wickedly. 'Al-deborough has agreed to accompany Juliet and myself, so you can stay at home and converse with the Dowager!'

'More fool he!'

Their return to London had been slow, exhausting, blighted by constant carping from Lady Cotherstone about the state of the road, the inns, the beds and anything else that took her fancy, but otherwise had been blessedly uneventful. Alde-borough had escaped the worst of the complaints by choosing to ride with Matthew, leaving the carriage to the two ladies and Wellington. Frances found herself out of all patience with him, at the same time experiencing some relief that she was free to pursue her own thoughts without Aldeborough's unsettling presence.

In Cavendish Square Juliet welcomed them with undisguised enthusiasm, pleased at the prospect of Frances's company once again. The Dowager sniffed and hoped that Lady Cotherstone had had a comfortable journey, but voiced the opinion that she would find town life far too strenuous at her time of life and would soon long for the tranquillity of the country. Hopefully before the end of the week. Aunt May's eyes twinkled as she declared that she was not nearly too old and would enjoy renewing old friendships. And as for Wellington! Lady Aldeborough hoped that accommodation could be found for That Animal in the stables. Aunt May, pretending deafness, ignored this suggestion and Wellington was soon under everyone's feet. It promised to be a friction-filled household.

Between Frances and Aldeborough there was a coldness. The relaxed, harmonious days when they had just begun to discover such pleasure in each other's company had been eroded, those revealing words spoken by Aldeborough etched diamond bright in Frances's memory. Now they kept their distance, stepped carefully around each other, unwilling to unearth more damaging influences on their marriage. Frances discovered a desire to wear her mother's brooch with surprising frequency. Aldeborough chose to ignore it. Charles would have been delighted with the results of his meddling.

Almack's was everything that Frances had been led to believe by Aunt May, but it was undoubtedly the key to her full acceptance into polite society and so she was determined to enjoy the occasion. She chose to wear the jonquil gown that she had worn on her wedding day and smiled at the memories it resurrected. She sighed with a mixture of pleasure and ruffled pride as she remembered Aldeborough's high-handed actions, his refusal to allow her to refuse his offer, his determination that she should be restored to society with a spotless reputation. But perhaps Charles's bitter attack held more truth than she wished to accept. He would not wish to be denounced as a seducer of innocent virgins, however much he might appear to be unconcerned with his reputation as a rake. But there was no point in allowing her mind to circle again and again. She would hold the knowledge of her love close in her own heart, despite the pain, and concentrate on making a suitably demure impression on the exacting Patronesses of Almack's.

Aldeborough, unaware of his wife's troubled mind, was formal and elegant in black satin knee breeches and swallow-tailed coat as demanded by Brummel's stringent rules and was surprisingly amenable when chivvied by Juliet at his willingness to squire them rather than spend an evening with his cronies. It suited him to keep Frances under his eye. He could not envisage any harm coming to her here in London, surrounded by his family, but he was not prepared to take the risk. Besides, he had some delicate unfinished business to complete, and he believed that Almack's would provide him with the opportunity.

It gave Frances the chance to renew acquaintances. It was all most satisfying. The Countess of Wigmore invited her to take tea one afternoon in the coming week. Lady Vowchurch and Penelope smiled condescendingly and Miss Vowchurch, after stating how much they had been missed, expressed her relief that Frances and Aldeborough had escaped the frightening attack by common footpads. And was it true that Frances had been thrown from her horse when at the Priory? How terrifying for her! It all went to show that life was far safer in town, as her mother always insisted.

Frances accepted the expressions of concern with grace, brushing off any suggestion that she had been in great danger and making light of the whole affair. But she had to admit that she was quite touched by such solicitude and consideration for her safety.

She was surprised to see Charles in evidence. He had expressed no intention of being in town and she had not thought that Almack's would have held any attraction for him. He acknowledged her presence with a curt bow, unsmiling face and as brief a greeting as family connection could allow without comment. Gone was the easy smile, the professed concern, to be replaced by a hard-edged stare and stony face. He clearly considered her accusations as an insult, she thought, but her suspicions remained as strong as ever. Charles did not ask her to dance, for which she felt considerable relief. She saw nothing of his tall figure after the first hour and presumed that he had taken himself off to more congenial haunts.

Aldeborough danced with Penelope, smiling down into her lovely face. Frances averted her eyes and concentrated on some trivial conversation with her own partner in the country dance.

During the evening, after a particularly energetic quadrille and a less than skilful partner, it became necessary for Juliet to repair some damage to one of her flounces. Frances agreed to accompany her, to catch her breath and to help in the pinning of the torn material in one of the small anterooms that provided some degree of privacy. On their return to join a country dance set, which was just forming, Frances heard a voice that she had no difficulty in recognising and had her instantly rooted to the spot.

'How can I possibly thank you, Letitia. It was an imposition that you could easily have refused. I would not have blamed you in the circumstances.'

The answering feminine laugh was low and seductive. 'I am sure I will think of something in recompense. It is not often that I receive such requests, as you might imagine.'

Frances turned to the open doorway of a similar antechamber to the one she and Juliet had just made use of. She felt the blood drain from her face and her fingers clutched her fan to the imminent danger of the ivory carving. There, as she knew she would, she saw Letitia Winters, seated on a silk brocade sofa, the Marquis seated beside her, the palm of her hand pressed to his lips. As she continued to stand, silently, rigidly, Juliet equally motionless at her side, Aldeborough raised his head and took a small package from his pocket which he pressed into Letitia's hand where his kiss had been.

'I certainly owe you this,' she heard him say in a low voice, a familiar heartstopping smile lighting his face.

'I am always pleased to be of service, my lord.' Letitia, laughing up at him, tucked the package into her reticule and tapped his cheek playfully with her fan.

Frances discovered that she could not breathe and then realised that it was because she was holding her breath. She made a small involuntary movement that caught the attention of the intimate couple and they looked up towards the open door. Frances read guilt into their frozen silence. It was her worst nightmare. No sooner were they back in town, regardless of what had occurred between them at the Priory, than Aldeborough had to make contact with That Woman at his first opportunity. No wonder he had been so willing to attend them that night. She would have stepped forward, with what purpose in mind she was not sure, but she became aware of Juliet's hand descending with a firm hold on her arm.

'Let us return to the ballroom, dear Frances,' Juliet murmured in a calm voice. 'We are promised for this dance and will be missed.'

Frances turned her head to see a mixture of shock and sympathy in her friend's eyes and felt the tightening of her fingers around her wrist as she made to resist. 'Indeed, it would be better if we left now.'

Compulsively, even knowing that it would increase the pain in her heart, Frances turned back to the scene before her. Aldeborough had released Letitia's hand and risen to his feet. He took two steps towards her, a frown between his brows, his eyes unfathomable. She could not look away. The tension arcing between them, holding them in thrall, was so intense that Frances could almost taste it, bitter and sharp. Juliet and Letitia were silent and motionless. She and Aldeborough might have been alone in the room.

Again and again in her mind was replayed the scene of

him, his head bent over Letitia's hand, his lips pressed to her palm in an intimate caress, his eyes smiling down into hers. The hurt stabbed at her heart with the terrible accuracy of a rapier. Had all his tenderness at the Priory, all his care, been a lie? Had he been thinking of Letitia Winters all the time, even when he caressed her and caused her body to tremble in uncontrolled response against him, when his mouth and hands had roused such glorious sensations that she had forgotten all else and surrendered to him? She could not bear it. She had begun to trust him and he had broken that trust—and with it her heart. Why had she ever thought that he was a man on whom she could lean, a man who would accept all the love and adoration she was capable of, and perhaps even return it? Charles had been so right. How foolish she had been. A wave of humiliation crept over her and she felt the telltale colour stain her cheeks.

All Aldeborough could see was the depth of hurt and misery in her eyes, on her face, before she hid it with a downsweep of her lashes and a tightening of her lips. What impossible timing! He knew what Frances must think, but here was no time or place to explain. Yet all he wished to do was to take her into his arms, hold her close and soothe away the sorrow, the terrible emptiness. The problem was, he realised, they had too much power to hurt one another. He had not realised it, but would have to consider it carefully in his dealings with her.

He moved towards her, hand outstretched. 'Frances?'

She deliberately turned on her heel without a word. What more did he expect? She walked back towards the dancing, spine rigid, head held high, pride pinning a smile to her lips to hide her grief-torn heart.

Frances passed a wakeful night, only falling into a restless sleep as the sky brightened before dawn. She awoke with a headache, low spirits and a strong desire to hide under the bedclothes. She resisted such a cowardly retreat and sat before her mirror at her dressing table, too aware of her pale complexion and the violet shadows beneath her eyes. How dare Aldeborough consort so openly with Letitia Winters, when all the *haute ton* at Almack's would be watching and speculating, eager for gossip to enliven their shallow existence? Dancing with her in public was one thing, but an intimate conversation in a private room, which involved him kissing her hand and presenting her with a gift! She flung her hairbrush crossly on to the floor and rose to pace the room. But Mrs Winters was so beautiful, so alluring. Of course Aldeborough would prefer her vibrant, golden-haired company to that of his countrified, undistinguished wife—wouldn't he? Hadn't he agreed with her that she had no talents to excite interest? She wasn't even fit to be a governess, let alone Marchioness of Aldeborough! Frances sniffed in a deluge of unusual self-pity.

And yet, she mused, Aldeborough had not seemed to be totally indifferent to her. She remembered the caress of his mouth on hers, the drift of his hands over her skin. She shivered and longed to be held in his arms again, to feel his lips ignite fire in her blood so that she forgot everything but his touch.

I love him, she acknowledged. She shrugged hopelessly. She couldn't deny it any longer. But she also had to accept that he did not love her. Sometimes he wanted her. But he did not love her. What a fool she had been to hope for more. And how could she have had so little pride. She had surrendered to his demands, had sighed beneath him, smoothing the flat planes of his back and shoulders, allowing him such intimacies that she blushed at the memory. And he had betrayed her with Letitia Winters. And not only that, he had danced with Penelope Vowchurch, and they both had appeared to enjoy it immensely! For once Penelope's lovely face had glowed with genuine happiness as she had smiled up into Aldeborough's eyes. Fury warred with desolation within her. She had not heard him return home last night, even though she had lain awake listening for the click of his door. It must have been very late—if at all! Tears began to slide down her cheeks. She would not let him see that his rejection reduced her to such straits. She brushed them away, but they were quickly replaced by others. She would show him that she did not care where he spent his time—or with whom he spent his nights.

Aldeborough groaned inwardly when he came face to face with Frances in the library around midday. He had had far too little sleep. It had been a mistake to go on to White's after Almack's, even though the night had been relatively young. He had drunk too much brandy, lost too much money and his head ached abominably. He knew he deserved it. He had hoped, in a cowardly fashion, as he was the first to admit, that he would not meet Frances until she had had a chance to cool down. It was his own fault. But he had needed to speak to Letitia and it was remiss of him not to have done so previously. He was in her debt. How was he to know that Frances would walk in on them at just that moment in a secluded alcove when, to all intents and purposes, he was indulging in intense communication with his mistress. The fact that he was no longer her lover and had not been since his marriage would make no difference. Frances would have been well informed by gossip and could not be expected to believe otherwise. Aldeborough felt ill used but resigned.

He could not forget the expression on Frances's face. Horror at first, disbelief even, and then contempt and a terrible hurt. He felt wretched at having been the cause. He should have come home with her, talked to her, tried to put it right. And he had not. He had retreated from the prospect of an emotionally charged conversation with a tired and incredulous wife. Nor, he had to admit to himself, had he enjoyed the open disapproval in his sister's face when she accompanied Frances back to the dancing. He would rather lead an attack in the siege of Badajoz. He despised himself as much as Frances probably did.

In the library he was left in no doubt of her mood.

'Good morning, my lord. I trust you slept well.' The formality chilled his blood.

His worst fears were realised. She had taken considerable care with her morning toilette. Her curls had been artfully arranged to fall in casual, shining ringlets on to her shoulders, tempting a man to release them into wild profusion. Her morning dress, which might have been deliberately chosen to enhance the sapphire of her eyes, was a creation in pale blue muslin. It was cut fashionably low across the bosom and, although it had demure long sleeves and a frilled neckline, its fragile fabric clung to her body and revealed her feminine curves. She might look exceptionally fragile and feminine, but the bright, brittle edge in her voice and in her smile cut him like a knife and he recognised the light of battle in those sapphire eyes. How on earth was he to explain his mistress to his wife? If Frances was more sophisticated she would merely pretend the situation did not exist. Or that it did not matter. But Aldeborough had to accept that, increasingly, anything that made Frances unhappy did matter deeply to his own state of mind. He was finding it increasingly difficult to keep her out of his thoughts.

'Thank you. Yes,' he lied. 'And you?'

'Perfectly well. I was looking for the *Morning Post*. I thought it would be in here. Have you seen it?' She was cool and composed, with the aura of an iceberg. She deliberately avoided any eye contact, rather focused on a point just above his head.

'No.'

'Then I will go and ask Aunt May. Wellington has probably chewed it up by now. I am sorry to have disturbed you.' She moved purposefully round him to the door, her back straight, her chin high.

He had to stop her. 'Frances!'

'Yes, my lord?'

He gritted his teeth at her deliberate and distant formality. 'I plan to go to Newmarket—I have a horse running that is well fancied. Will you come with me? Colbourne is organising a house party on his estate in Suffolk. You will know many people there and you might enjoy it.'

Her eyes met his at last. He wished they had not, then he would not have seen the contempt in them. There was a tiny pause as she contemplated her reply.

'How kind of you to invite me. I think I prefer to stay in town.' She would not even make an excuse of previous engagements. He could make of it what he wished.

'I see.' His mouth hardened into a straight line. 'Can I say nothing to persuade you?'

'I doubt it.' Her chin rose higher in direct challenge.

He chose not to rise to it, but regarded her through narrowed eyes. 'I shall be gone a few days, possibly until the end of the week. I could wish that you would come with me.'

'Really, my lord? You must do as you see fit, of course.' And probably spend the time with Letitia Winters, she thought. 'I have no demands on your time. We both have our own lives to lead.'

So it was war.

'Come here, Frances Rosalind.' Aldeborough belatedly took up the challenge: it was clear in his eyes and in his stance as he held out his hand, palm up, in command.

Frances approached him. Outwardly her self-assurance held. Inwardly she quaked. She must not give way now! She put her hand in his and allowed him to draw her inexorably towards him. Her eyes were trapped by the unassailable force in his and she was unable to look away.

He encircled her waist with one arm, releasing her hand to wind his fingers into her hair to hold her imprisoned. His touch was not particularly gentle. With deliberate intent he covered her mouth with his, lightly at first and then with increasing pressure as he felt her resistance. He angled his head to capture her lips completely, no tenderness here but deliberate possession. She stood stiffly in his embrace, determined not to give him the satisfaction of a response, but she failed miserably. His kiss was thorough, demanding, scalding. He forced her lips apart so that his tongue could invade, creating impossible sensations of heat and need. She could not suppress a sigh as delicious tremors flooded through her and she clung to him for support.

He retreated and raised his head once more to challenge her. His eyes were still calculating, but with a fire in their depths that seared her. 'If it was a declaration of war, Frances Rosalind, then you should be prepared for battle.'

'I thought I was,' she managed to gasp.

'Then show me,' he demanded before he renewed his assault. She could not deny him, indeed, she did not wish to do so. His teeth scraped her lower lip and his tongue once again plundered her mouth with an arrogant assurance that she would respond with equal fervour. And she did. For as her mind resisted, her body betrayed her. He tightened his arms around her, crushing her breasts against him, holding her thighs immobile against his. She was intensely aware of the power of his hard, muscular body against hers and trembled in longing.

'Hugh!' she whispered his name against his mouth. He merely changed his assault to her throat, her shoulders, her breast where the frail muslin revealed her soft skin, covering them with burning kisses that sent thrills of anticipation through her veins. She tightened her fingers in his hair, eyes closed, surrendering to his demands.

Suddenly she was free.

She opened her eyes, disorientated. He had released her and stepped back. The expression on his handsome face was enigmatic, his mouth set in a firm line as if he might be displeased with her.

'Come with me to Newmarket.'

'No.'

'I am sorry I cannot persuade you, Frances Rosalind. It seems that we must exist for a few days without each other. As you so correctly observed, we have our own lives to lead.' He inclined his head curtly. 'Forgive me. I appear to have disordered your hair. I am sure you can remedy it. Goodbye, my lady.'

He left, closing the door quietly behind him. He would like to have slammed it, but refused to give himself the satisfaction.

Frances stood where he had left her, one hand pressed to her tender lips, the other to her heart, whose rapid beating was threatening to choke her. The tears that she had refused to shed in his presence threatened to spill from her eyelashes. She wanted him. Oh, how she wanted him. And he could never be hers.

Outside the door, Aldeborough cursed himself silently, his hands clenched into fists. All he had done was make a bad situation worse. And he was left with the memory of the softness of her lips as they opened beneath his, the perfume of her hair filling his senses and the way her body, every curve and hollow, fitted perfectly against his. What the hell had been his motive? To punish her? To satisfy his own need for her? What an abject failure that had been! All he had done was rouse his body to a raging hunger to possess her, when what he truly desired was for her to look at him with love and trust in those glorious eyes, to turn into the shelter of his arms and rest there against his heart. Anything but the terrible desolation he had left her with.

Guilt smote him afresh. What on earth was he thinking, to go to Newmarket and leave Frances alone in London when he knew that her life might be at risk? Was he out of his mind? But the last thing he wanted was to remain to be rebuffed and sniped at by a frigid and unco-operative wife. No! To hell with it. He would go to Newmarket—and to the devil, if that is what she believed. The only action he could take, for his own peace of mind, was to ensure that, in his absence, his wife did not venture out unaccompanied. That much he could do. He went in search of Watkins to leave some crisp and efficient instructions.

On the following morning Frances was cajoled—or bullied, as she personally considered—into accompanying Aunt May on an apparently urgent appointment. Juliet was still abed after a week of parties, breakfasts and routs, claiming that she was worn to the bone, and for once could not be persuaded to join them.

The main objective of their outing was to visit the establishment of Rundell and Bridge. 'For,' as Aunt May explained, 'if my diamond necklace needs cleaning and perhaps resetting, then I will go to the best. Lord Cotherstone always swore by Rundell and Bridge for quality when buying jewels.'

'But do you need it today?' Frances would rather have stayed at home. A nagging headache and a desolate emptiness in the region of her heart made the expedition—any expedition—unattractive. 'When did you last wear it?'

'Oh, not for years. In fact, probably not since Juliet was born. But if I am to stay in London for any length of time, think of the opportunities. Besides, a woman should never be without a diamond necklace. And mine is distinctly dingy.' Aunt May cast Frances a keen glance. 'Come along. An outing in the fresh air will do you good. And it will stop you thinking about Aldeborough and what he might be getting up to.' Juliet had thoughtfully brought her up to date on the interesting events at Almack's, not failing to include Aldeborough's perfidy in detail. 'It is not fashionable to miss him, you know. You could try flirting with someone else to pass the time—a little flirtation is always good for the spirits.'

Frances was horrified that her thoughts could be so easily read. Pride rose to her rescue. 'There is nothing wrong with my spirits. And I assure you, Aunt May, I have no desire to know what Aldeborough is doing. I am certainly not missing him. What a foolish suggestion!'

'Glad to hear it. Go and fetch your bonnet.'

There was nothing more to be said. As the morning promised the possibility of showers, it was decided to order up the barouche rather than walk. This would also allow Lady Cotherstone to take Wellington with her. He could not cope with a long walk these days, and neither, she announced, could she.

It surprised Frances that Aunt May was greeted as an old and much-valued customer, ushered into an inner sanctum with many bows and expressions of concern for her health, by Mr Bridge himself. To Frances's amusement, Lady Cotherstone flirted like a young girl, remembering the days when her late and rarely lamented husband had bought her stones of considerable excellence from that very shop. The business was concluded to the satisfaction of all, the necklace handed over for refurbishment and Mr Bridge expressing the hope that the new Marchioness of Aldeborough would perhaps patronise his establishment in the near future. Having admired a very pretty gold bracelet, Frances expressed positive intentions to return when, she told herself, her heart was less sore.

She saw the lady, standing beside their barouche, as they were bowed out of the shop by Mr Bridge. She wore a fur-trimmed pelisse against the cold in a rich peat brown that enhanced her golden curls. Her pale straw bonnet was silk edged, decorated with matching silk flowers, its brim framing her lovely face. Her skin was translucent in the grey morning light and her eyes were of a particularly soft blue, but on inspection Frances saw that she was not in her first youth. She had a maid to carry her gloves and reticule, standing at a discreet distance. She gave the impression that she had been awaiting them, by design rather than chance, for some little time. Frances recognised her immediately and froze in indecision as a sudden wave of anger, not unmixed with jealousy, swept through her.

The lady, not unaware of her effect on Frances, walked gracefully forward. 'Good morning, Lady Aldeborough. We have not been introduced, but I believe that you are aware of who I am.' Her voice was pleasantly low and musical. Frances could imagine Aldeborough being unable to resist anything she demanded from him in those persuasive tones and she burned with envy.

'Mrs Winters. Yes, of course. You have been pointed out to me.' Frances took a deep breath to compose herself in this unlooked-for situation. Good manners overcame personal inclination, but that did not mean that she had to be anything other than coldly civil. 'May I introduce Lady Cotherstone, my husband's great-aunt. Aunt May, this is Mrs Winters, an...an acquaintance of my husband.'

'I know who she is.' Aunt May held out her gnarled hand to greet the lady and smiled with relish. 'I am very pleased to meet you.'

Mrs Winter smiled wryly, showing a glimpse of perfect teeth. 'I would value a conversation with you, Lady Aldeborough—and with Lady Cotherstone, of course, if it is convenient.'

For a moment Frances was speechless. Into her mind leapt her last memory of Mrs Winter in vivid detail: Aldeborough bowing gracefully over this woman's hand as she smiled and tossed her golden curls provocatively. And she had had the audacity to encourage him, one hand resting intimately on his arm in the privacy of a curtained alcove. And now she was requesting a conversation! Frances contemplated turning on her heel and snubbing Letitia Winters in public, no matter what the social repercussions. But not so Aunt May, who read the sparks in Frances's eyes correctly and took control of the situation with masterly decision.

'Mrs Winters. Letitia, is it not? Let us not stand upon ceremony. I suggest we get into the barouche and stop blocking the pavement and attracting attention which none of us wants. And since the sun has decided to shine on us, we could take a turn round Hyde Park.'

The ladies bowed to such superior management and settled themselves into the barouche with fur rugs tucked round them by an attentive footman. Unless she was prepared to walk home alone, Frances had no choice in the matter. Mrs Winters, leaving her maid with strict instructions to await her at the entrance to the Park, was able to express some relief to herself. She had not been convinced that she was taking the wisest course of action, but she had watched events at Almack's with interest and concern. Far more amusing, she acknowledged, than the social occasion itself, which was invariably dull with its rigid rules and eagle-eyed Patronesses. And as for the refreshments, Mrs Winters had felt that a few of those present could have benefited from a glass of good port before the evening was over. But she had seen Frances's unhappiness and her cold response to Aldeborough and had been sorry for it. She suspected that her own very public conversation with him had been partially, if not wholly, responsible. A pity. She sighed as she pulled her pelisse more closely round her shoulders. She liked Aldeborough—more than a little, if the truth were told—and was sorry that their

liaison had come to an end. If all gentlemen were like him…
But she felt that she must do her best for his wife. A taking
little thing. Very young, of course, but with some style and
countenance and a forthright way with her that Mrs Winters
admired. And it would be a pleasure to upset the Dowager
and Penelope Vowchurch. Now Lady Cotherstone was a wily
old bird. Her presence here this morning might just be what
was needed, especially if The Bride was a little shy—or
downright reluctant—at taking advice from Aldeborough's
mistress.

Until they reached the ornamental gates their progress was
slow and they talked stiltedly about the weather and the present fashion for fur cloaks in the unseasonably cool weather.
Lady Cotherstone carried the burden of the conversation,
amused by the reticence of her two companions. But once
into the quieter drives of Hyde Park, sparsely populated at
this time in the morning, silence fell. What a bizarre situation,
thought Frances. What would Aldeborough say if he heard
that she was associating in public with his mistress. And as
for the Dowager! Her immediate anger had subsided a little
and a bubble of hysterical laughter rose in her chest. She was
intent on suppressing it when she caught the lady's eye, noting the gleam and the quick smile of mischief. She could not
help but respond, at the same time wishing with all her heart
that Mrs Winters did not exist.

'I know what you are thinking.' Mrs Winters broke the
silence. 'What would Aldeborough say if he saw us riding
together round the Park?'

Aunt May cackled inelegantly before Frances could think
of a suitable reply. 'I could tell you, but perhaps it would not
be polite in this mealy-mouthed society. Well, Mrs Winters.
Is this not cosy? I had no idea my morning was going to be
so interesting.' She sat back with her hands folded around
the plump and somnolent body of Wellington, ready to be
entertained.

'You said that you wished to have conversation with me,'
said Frances stiffly. 'I do not believe that we have anything
to say to each other. How can I possibly help you?'

'I hope that *I* might be able to help *you*, my lady. I believe that I need to speak. Forgive me if my observations seem very personal but, you see, I saw the distance between you and Aldeborough last night at Almack's.'

'You are mistaken. And what possible concern is that of yours?' Frances's reply was icy.

'Why, none. And normally I would not presume—unless I helped to cause that dissension. My dear…' she leaned forward to place her hand gently on Frances's, trying to ignore the resulting flinch as Frances tried to pull away '…let me speak plainly. Aldeborough has no relationship with me other than friendship. And he has had none since your marriage.'

Frances found herself engulfed by embarrassment, her cheeks flushed with sudden heat despite the chill wind. She cast an anguished look at Aunt May, who merely shrugged her shoulders with a speculative gleam in her eye.

'I have a great affection for him and I wish him well,' Mrs Winters continued. 'But you have to believe me—I mean nothing to him. I envy you.'

Frances decided that it was a time for honesty rather than false modesty, so she swallowed her self-consciousness. 'How can I believe you? At Almack's my husband singled you out. And you appeared to have a prolonged and intimate conversation. It seemed to me that you were very well acquainted in spite of your protestations of innocence.'

'It was merely a matter of completion of business. Of a financial nature, you understand.' Mrs Winters smiled rather sadly. 'Who do you think ordered the beautiful dress that you wore for your marriage and wore again at Almack's? He could hardly ask his mother to arrange it, could he? And I arranged the purchase and dispatch of a particular riding habit—I understand the original was damaged.'

May muffled another crack of laughter. Frances had to smile at the prospect. 'Aldeborough told me what to buy and I arranged it. And very beautiful you looked too. The pale satin was perfect for your colouring. He described you exactly.'

'Then I have to thank you. I have never owned anything

so fine.' Frances still found it difficult to unbend, but had to acknowledge her debt. 'And all the accessories, of course.'

'And you were thinking that Aldeborough had bought the underwear!' Aunt May patted her knee understandingly.

'Aunt May, you are incorrigible.'

'Can I say something?' Mrs Winters studied her gloved hands for a moment as if considering her next statement. 'Aldeborough does not deserve his reputation. Yes, it is self-inflicted, but chiefly to spite his mother and those who would accept her slanderous comments rather than the evidence of their own eyes and their knowledge of the man. His closeness to his brother could not—should not—be questioned. It hurt him beyond belief and he chose to defend himself by becoming the reckless heedless creature that gossip had created. We became…acquainted at a time when he had first returned to London from the Peninsula. His brother had died and he had just sold out. He was not very happy, you understand?'

Frances nodded. She understood the damage brought about by Richard's death and the Dowager's bitter reaction only too well.

'He cares more for you than you might believe.'

'No.' Frances's reply was dogmatic. 'He would have been better off without me.'

'I cannot agree.'

'You do not know.' It was little more than a whisper. Frances studied her clasped hands, knuckles white, in her lap.

'Very well. I must accept your knowledge of the situation, but may I be blunt? If you will take my advice, you will not allow yourself to become too intimate with Penelope Vowchurch. She has a cold ambition that bears watching and she had high hopes of marriage with Aldeborough. She also has developed a surprising liaison with Charles Hanwell, your cousin. They are not to be trusted.'

'Charles? And Penelope?'

Frances became aware that Aunt May beside her was nodding in agreement. She looked at her with raised brows.

'Don't look at me like that, my dear. I know he is your

cousin. But I think there is truth in Mrs Winter's observation. And, if you are honest, *you* think so too.'

Frances sighed. 'Forgive me. You have given me much to think about this morning. I suppose I should be grateful.'

'Then I have fulfilled my obligation to you and your husband. If you would let me down at the gate, my maid will be waiting for me there. I am pleased to have been of service to you, my lady.'

'Thank you, Mrs Winters.'

'Please call me Letitia. Although I doubt if our paths will cross with any frequency in the future. I find that I am sorry for that.'

'So am I.' In spite of everything, Frances found herself able to give the lady a smile of genuine warmth. 'In other circumstances, perhaps we might have been friends.'

'One more thing—' Mrs Winters prepared to alight '—make him talk to you about Richard.'

'I have tried, but he will not.'

'Don't give up. It is important that he does.' She raised her hand in farewell as she alighted gracefully from the carriage and turned away.

They were silent for much of the way back to Cavendish Square.

'I think you need to talk to Hugh,' was Aunt May's final comment on the morning's revelations.

'Yes. I have not always been sympathetic.'

'That is not at all what I meant. You have had your reasons and my nephew is not the easiest man to read. Don't be too ready to take the blame. But you both need to be more honest with each other and not so bound up in the aftermath of past events. It will not be easy.'

'No. It will not be easy—but I must agree with you.' Frances's tone was bleak. 'I will talk to him. When he returns home from Newmarket…whenever that might be!'

Chapter Twelve

The three days that followed in Cavendish Square had a deceptively peaceful quality. On the surface the Aldeborough household enjoyed its varied and disparate existence. The Marquis remained in Newmarket and it was uncertain when he would return. Ambrose, whose visits to Cavendish Square were sufficiently frequent to make him one of the family, was still in Yorkshire, shooting rabbits on his uncle's estate, but with imminent plans to return to town. Matthew, always attracted by the promise of horseflesh and gambling, had accompanied Aldeborough. Frances and Juliet were thrown into each other's company and enjoyed the experience. They walked in Hyde Park. They shopped in the most stylish streets and frittered money on whatever took their fancy— for, as Juliet observed, what is the use of an inheritance if it is not to be used for pleasurable purposes? They watched a balloon ascension and attended a soirée and a small private party. Aunt May was selective in her participation, but could be relied upon to chaperon them when the Dowager refused or pleaded a headache. It came to much the same thing. That lady's attitude towards Frances remained frosty with a politeness as keen as a drawn sword, but as her daughter-in-law was now on visiting terms with the Earl and Countess of Wigmore, and a substantial heiress, there was little room for censorious comment. Frances found the disapproving glances tiring but no longer distressing and accepted it with cheerful resignation.

But she missed Aldeborough deeply. She expected—and longed—to hear his footstep in the hall at any time. She missed the easy companionship that they had begun to enjoy at the Priory and had been so wilfully destroyed by his confession to Aunt May. And she missed his charming smile, which made her catch her breath, and the nerve-tingling touch of his hands and his lips on her skin. She found it difficult to sleep. She could no longer pretend that she felt nothing but gratitude towards him. She had fallen in love with him...and was overcome with grief that he did not love her. She must be content with his need for her body. It was better than nothing. But in the privacy of her bedchamber she shed the tears that she would never permit him to see.

At breakfast on the fourth morning, with only Frances and Juliet lingering over the teacups, trying to decide on the respective merits of a visit to the lending library or a drive in the barouche, Watkins interrupted them.

'A letter for you, my lady.' He offered it on a silver salver. 'It was delivered personally for you a moment ago.'

'Thank you, Watkins.' She smiled as she tore it open in eager anticipation. Letters and invitations were still a new experience for her.

'I expect it is another invitation.' Juliet stifled a yawn. 'I declare that we could be out every night of the week. Perhaps it will be something different—a breakfast or a poetry reading.'

'You don't like poetry readings! No. No it isn't.' Frances concentrated on the single sheet in her hand, her eyebrows raised in surprise. 'Listen to this.' Her relationship with Juliet was now such that she had no hesitation in reading the missive aloud.

> *My dear niece,*
> *It has grieved me that a rift has opened between myself and the daughter of my only and much-loved*

*brother. I understand your feelings and can only offer
my apologies for any misunderstandings in the past. I
have always had your care as my first priority as your
guardian and I wish to fulfil that role to the end.*

'Well!' Juliet interrupted, a gleam in her eye. 'I must
say, that does not sound like your version of events!'
Frances shook her head in disbelief and continued.

*I know that you have been informed of the extent of
your inheritance and I wish you well for the future now
that you have almost reached your majority. I have in
my possession some keepsakes, letters and items of jewellery that belonged to your poor mother, which were
entrusted to me until you came of age. They are of no
great monetary value, but I am sure that for sentimental
reasons you would wish to possess them. I would like
you to have them now. I shall be in town tomorrow and
I would like to discharge this obligation as soon as possible. I do not think that it would be wise for me to visit
you as Aldeborough has made his censure clear. There-
fore might I be permitted to suggest that you visit Torrington House yourself so that the matter can be settled
quietly and without fuss. I am sure that you will see the
necessity for acting with discretion.*

*I will put at your disposal my coach, which will await
you at the entrance to Cavendish Square at two o'clock
this afternoon. I trust this will be convenient for you.
Your obedient servant,
Torrington*

'Well! What are you going to do? From what you have
told me, I would not wish to visit him. And certainly not
alone. Perhaps you should wait for Hugh to return.' Juliet

rested her chin on her clasped hands and awaited Frances's decision.

'But if he has some of my mother's possessions! I have nothing of hers except this brooch—' she touched the amethysts at her breast '—indeed, I was not even aware that any mementoes or keepsakes existed. And letters! I cannot forgo them, Juliet, indeed, I cannot. And I would hate him to return to Yorkshire with them still in his possession. I have to accept his offer.'

A decided sparkle illuminated Juliet's eyes. 'I could come with you, of course. Would that still count as discretion?'

'I doubt my uncle would think so, not if he knew you!' Frances laughed but the idea attracted her. 'Would you come with me? He does not exactly say I have to be alone. And I would dearly love your company.'

'It would be exciting. An adventure. And, as long as Aldeborough does not get to know, there will be no harm done. And I may get to see your fascinating Cousin Charles!'

'He is not fascinating and I am sure I should not encourage you. Besides, I do not think he is in town any longer—he said at Almack's that he intended to return to the country almost immediately.' After a moment's reflection she asked, with a studied casualness that she hoped would hide her interest, 'What do you think your brother would do if he found out?'

'Hugh? I am not sure. But he can be very severe if he thinks I have done anything immodest or dangerous. But I do not think *you* have to be concerned, dear Frances.' A sly little smile touched Juliet's lips.

'I wish I had your confidence. Aldeborough and I had an…an argument before he left for Newmarket.'

'I know. It was about Mrs Winters.'

'Juliet! How did you know that?'

'Aunt May, of course. There is not much that goes on in this family without her knowing. But don't worry. Hugh will never be severe with you. I have seen him smile at you.' With which enigmatic comment Juliet left Frances to contemplate the wisdom of a visit that might drive her absent husband to extreme measures. It was an interesting prospect. It was a pity that he would never know of it.

The two ladies, suitably garbed for their afternoon visit, were waiting at the entrance to the Square at the appointed hour when a plain, unmarked coach pulled up. A footman jumped down and helped the ladies to ascend the steps. They were driven off at a smart trot the short distance to the Torringtons' town house.

'The knocker is off the door,' said Frances with more than a hint of disappointment in her voice as she leaned forward to see their destination, an undistinguished town house, rather narrow and in need of new paint. 'I hope he has not left already, but then, since he has sent the coach...' Her fears were clearly ill founded, for as they pulled up the front door was opened and a liveried servant ushered them into the house. He preceded them quickly up the staircase, giving them little time to note the shabby furnishings, meagre furniture and the general air of neglect, and opened the door into one of the large reception rooms on the first floor overlooking the small unkempt garden at the rear.

'If you would make yourself comfortable, my lady. You are expected. I will arrange for tea to be brought.'

They were left alone to wait for Torrington.

The room was as dingy and badly furnished as Torrington Hall. Frances could only remember one visit here when she had been a child and so had little recollection of the house. She traced her finger through the dust on one of the walnut side tables while Juliet adjusted her flower-trimmed straw bonnet in the badly foxed mirror over the mantelpiece. She wrinkled her nose with displeasure.

'It does not have an air of being lived in, does it? I cannot imagine when a fire was last lit in this grate.'

'Not for many weeks. I wonder why—'

She was interrupted, the door opening to reveal, together with the expected tea tray, not Viscount Torrington, but a smiling Charles Hanwell, as urbane and self-possessed as usual and certainly more approachable than on their previous meeting at Almack's.

'Charles. I did not realise you were still in town.' Frances allowed him to take her hand in a cousinly salute as the footman left the tray and closed the door. 'Didn't you say that you were leaving when I saw you at Almack's?'

'Yes. That is what I said.' He continued to smile at her, but she detected an edge to his voice as he inclined his head towards Juliet. His words startled her. 'I did not expect you to be accompanied. I fear that I cannot say that I am pleased to see you, Lady Juliet.' His elegant bow held more than a touch of irony.

'I had a letter from my uncle,' Frances stated, unease touching her nerve endings with its icy fingers.

'No, you did not. I sent the letter. My father is in the country.'

'Forgive me, Charles. I do not quite understand. Are *you* offering to give me my mother's possessions?'

'There are none, to my knowledge. That, my dear cousin, was merely a lure to bring you here. I knew you would not be able to resist. Such sentimentality, Frances, can be dangerous.'

'What do you want of me?' Those icy fingers spread to her heart.

'I am sure that you are intelligent enough to work it out for yourself.'

'Do I presume it is money?'

'Of course.' Charles's lips continued to curve in the semblance of a smile, but Frances saw no humour in his face. 'I had no choice but to bring you here. My other plans failed, so I am left with one final option.'

'Other plans? I thought you wanted to marry me.'

'Past history, my dear Frances. My intentions have changed. I had not bargained on your presence, Lady Juliet, but it need not intrinsically alter my design.'

'But what do you want? What do you intend to do with us?'

'You will remain here for a little while—I assure you, you

will be quite comfortable. I have some arrangements to finalise. You will not expect any attempt to rescue you, of course.'

Frances curved her lips into what she hoped was a smile filled with total disbelief and disdain for her cousin's plan. 'Of course there will be an attempt to rescue us! How could you doubt it? As soon as we are missed—'

'Come now, Frances,' Charles interrupted with a careless shrug. 'Do not play the fool with me. I would wager any money that you told no one of your intentions this afternoon. After all, who would you tell? Your resourceful husband is in Newmarket. The Dowager? I doubt it. Your inimitable aunt? Perhaps. But you did not, did you?' He caught the telltale flush that stained her cheeks and smiled. 'Of course you did not. We both know that no one will come here to search for you.'

'I don't believe that you could contemplate keeping us prisoner!' Juliet looked at him in disbelief.

'Oh, yes, he would.' Frances was now convinced of her cousin's guilt. 'I believe he has tried to cause harm before. Isn't that right, Charles? On the road to York? You tried to kill Aldeborough, didn't you, so that you could marry me and take the money for yourself. What are you trying to do now? Do you intend to blackmail Aldeborough? My inheritance in return for my life?'

An amused smile crossed Charles's face. 'The thought had crossed my mind. But you need not trouble yourself about the means, dear cousin. Last time, purely by chance, I failed. I shall not do so again. I am truly sorry that you would not accept my offer of marriage, Frances. It would have saved us both so much pain and heartache. But now it is irrelevant.'

He opened the door and stood, confident and amused at the inevitable success of his plan, his hand on the latch. Frances felt her fingers curl into claws and an overwhelming desire to mar his handsome face with feline scratches.

'You cannot escape through the windows—they are all securely locked. And there is no one to hear you if you call

out for help. My servants can be remarkably hard of hearing.
I will leave you to your reflections. Good afternoon, ladies.'

'Can he really keep us here?' Juliet enquired with remarkable composure in the circumstances.

'I suppose he can. After all, who can stop him?'

'When does Aldeborough return?'

'I don't know. We could be here for days. What an awful
prospect.' Frances surveyed the room bleakly. 'One thing is
certain. We have to escape.'

'Charles was right, I am afraid. The windows are not an
option.' Juliet tried unsuccessfully to push one open. 'And
even if we smashed one, it is a long way to the ground. I
don't relish a broken leg.'

'And no one knows we are here because we deliberately
did not tell anyone.'

'And I suppose you have the letter with you? You didn't
by some chance leave it in the breakfast parlour for someone
to find?'

'I am afraid it is in my reticule.' Frances sighed. 'We have
put ourselves in a very difficult position.'

'We need a strategy. What would Hugh do?' Juliet seated
herself and clasped her hands.

'Get over rough ground as lightly as possible. Is that not
a favourite military objective with Wellington? But I am not
sure that it helps us now.'

'Somehow we have to get Charles out of the way and the
door open.'

Silence hung in the room as they assessed the hopelessness
of their situation.

Juliet, idly pulling at her gloves, suddenly turned her head
with an arrested expression. 'Do you remember the novel we
read that Mama was so sniffy about when she discovered it
behind the cushions in the morning room? The one with the
castle in the Alps and beautiful Marianne. And the Wicked
Baron Oliver who wanted to force his attentions on her.'

'Yes. *Raven's Castle*. What on earth has that to do with
anything? Honestly, Juliet, here we are imprisoned in this—'

'But do you remember how Marianne escaped from him?' Juliet interrupted.

Frances thought for a moment. 'She pretended she was ill and took to her bed where she groaned a good deal, then she hid behind the door when the Wicked Baron came to offer her help and hit him with a candlestick, which laid him out on the floor. That was more or less the story as I remember it. I thought it was a bit far-fetched at the time.'

'Could we do that?'

Frances met Juliet's quizzical expression and a smile began to curve her lips as the image developed in her mind. She crossed to a sidetable, picked up an elegant bronze figurine of a hunting dog and weighed it, somewhat thoughtfully, in her hand. If she was to prevent Charles from blackmailing Aldeborough out of an extortionate amount of money, she and Juliet must win their freedom. It seemed it would call for some forceful and imaginative action.

'I cannot think of a better idea. Which part would you like to play? The languishing invalid or the intrepid attacker?'

Juliet giggled. 'Oh, the invalid. I am sure I could do that. After all…' she suddenly became serious '…we have nothing to lose, have we? I have decided that I do not care for your Cousin Charles at all.'

'Neither do I! Let us discuss tactics.'

They set the scene with great care and dramatic intent. The dust-laden curtains were loosened from their ties to cast the room into suitable gloom, apart from one branch of candles that Frances arranged on the small table beside the silk-covered sofa on which Juliet would play out her major role. Meanwhile, that enthusiastic young lady removed her bonnet and unpinned her hair so that it lay romantically on her shoulders.

'What do I do with this statue?' Frances lifted the bronze again. 'If I were Aunt May, I could hide it in my skirts. There's not much hope with this dress, is there?' She eyed her light muslins critically.

'Just put it behind the door until you need it,' Juliet advised. 'It looks very heavy. Don't kill him, will you?'

'I will try not to!'

'What a pity we have no *blood*. That would look most realistic—and suitably shocking! Charles would *have* to come to my aid.' Juliet eyed with interested speculation the knives that had come with the cakes on the tea tray.

'I am not cutting my wrists—or yours, for that matter—for you!' Frances was quick to see the direction of her thoughts.

'But think of the effect on Charles—he could not possibly think it was a trick, that I was merely feigning illness if I was covered with blood!'

Frances picked up a knife. 'It is not very sharp,' she observed dubiously.

'We don't need much. Just a little cut and you could dabble the blood on my bodice. It will not hurt. Just think of it as part of the adventure.'

'Why are *you* not volunteering?'

'I need all my strength and concentration to act.'

'And I suppose I don't to hit him on the head.'

'He is your cousin. Come here and I will do it for you.'

'I cannot argue against that.' Frances held out the knife reluctantly.

Frances closed her eyes as Juliet applied the knife as gently but effectively as possible to her bared forearm. There was a sharp stinging pain, which made her draw in her breath on a gasp, and she tried not to look at the blood that immediately seeped from her torn flesh.

'There. That wasn't too bad, was it? Now, if you let the blood drip on to my dress. Yes. That's very good. I never liked this pale green anyway—far too insipid. Are you feeling quite well, Frances? You do look a little pale. It is amazing how much such a little cut will bleed.'

Frances, swallowing hard, tried not to think of her blood being smeared over Juliet's bodice and skirt and was relieved when Juliet, satisfied at last, tied her handkerchief around the wound to staunch any further bleeding.

'Are we ready? Let us start before my nerves fail me.' Frances rubbed her arms to dispel the shivering and positioned herself between the sofa and the door. Juliet stood beside the sofa, hands already clutching her throat in dramatic mode. She grinned encouragingly at Frances and the play began.

Juliet began to cough. She bent over, choking and retching, one hand pressed to her stomach, the other clawing at her throat. Her eyes were closed, her face contorted into a mask, her clothing spattered artistically with Frances's blood. The coughs were punctuated with cries of anguish. Nodding in satisfaction, Frances turned and hammered on the door for attention.

The door opened precipitately to admit the footman. His eyes grew round in shock and his face visibly paled as he took in the horrific picture, Juliet gasping and choking with blood on her gown, Frances in hysterics.

'My lady! What's happened? What can…?' he gabbled, falling into silence.

'My sister,' shrieked Frances. 'She is in such distress. What can I do to help her?' She ran to the footman to clutch his arm convulsively. 'Please! You must tell Mr Hanwell. We need his help.'

'Mr Hanwell is about to go out.' The footman could not take his eyes off Juliet, who continued to cough and moan.

'Fetch him.' Frances shook his arm violently. 'It is a matter of life and death.'

The footman turned on his heel and all but ran from the room. Juliet raised her head to grin at Frances. 'Well done!' she whispered.

'Don't stop now,' Frances murmured back. 'Charles must be in no doubt that this is genuine if I am to take him by surprise.'

Charles arrived in the doorway, taking in the scene at once. 'What's wrong with her?' he demanded in a voice harsh with latent panic. Frances simply stood, wringing her hands and sobbing loudly. 'She seemed perfectly well an hour ago.' His tone was cold, but even he appeared shaken by the tragic figure before him.

Juliet collapsed limply on to the sofa, head flung back, gasping for breath. Then once more she doubled up in painful retching, which soon developed into harsh coughing. One trembling hand was stretched out blindly for help. Only the most heartless creature could ignore such suffering.

'She needs help!' Frances managed to cry. 'She had eaten one of the cakes—and then she began to choke. All this blood! And she can hardly breathe. Please help her.' She looked at Charles with piteous, tear-filled eyes. 'I do not know what to do for her.'

Charles considered the heartfelt appeal for a moment and then approached the sofa, kneeling to take a closer look at the sufferer, thus turning his back on Frances. *Now*, she told herself, *do it now*! She pushed the door gently closed, picked up the bronze hunting dog and advanced silently to where he knelt. Charles moved as if to rise to his feet. *Don't move*, she prayed. *Just stay there for one more minute!* Juliet's coughing reached a violent paroxysm that caused Charles to bend over her once more.

'She is choking. She simply needs to—'

As he took hold of Juliet's hand to pull her to her feet, Frances lifted her arm and struck her cousin a firm blow on his head.

He crumpled soundlessly to the floor.

Juliet sat up and applauded. 'I never thought that I should be so grateful for cake crumbs!'

'Don't rejoice yet!' Frances warned her, eyeing the inert figure before her with some trepidation. 'We still have to escape from this house!'

Chapter Thirteen

After an uncomfortable, but rapid, journey from Newmarket, Aldeborough and Matthew arrived in Cavendish Square in the late afternoon. Aldeborough had deliberately cut short his stay, waiting only to see one of his promising young horses win a valuable race. He found, to his discomfort, that his thoughts returned again and again to Frances: the exploits of his horses came a far distant second. He remembered her distress when he left her, her pride when she had witnessed him in what appeared to be an intimate discussion with his mistress, her stubborn but intrinsically loving spirit. He longed to feel her body shiver under the touch of his hands. He longed to press his lips to her silken skin, to that exact place at the base of her throat where her pulse quickened when he excited her. He longed to possess her and feel her body, soft and responsive to his every move, under his. And beneath it all ran the faint undercurrent of unease that he should not have left her alone. If she had suffered any harm… He would never forgive himself, and rightly so. Knowing the dangers, he had been selfish enough to deliberately leave her for his own pleasure. As Matthew observed, he was anything but a sociable companion on the journey home—he wished he had stayed in Newmarket for the rest of the racing.

'Good afternoon, my lord. We did not expect you back quite so soon.' For once, Watkins appeared more than a little ruffled. 'I think your presence is required in the withdrawing room. At once, my lord.'

Aldeborough, abandoning his enticing daydreams and self-flagellation and shrugging off Matthew's uncomfortable comments on his character, entered to find Aunt May, Miss Vowchurch and the Dowager Lady Aldeborough in various stages of complaint and unease.

'Aldeborough! At last!' Aunt May accosted him immediately. 'There isn't the faintest chance that Frances returned with you, is there? And Juliet?'

'Why, no. We have just this moment arrived back from Newmarket.'

'They should have been back by now. I am most concerned.' Even the Dowager showed less than her usual icy composure.

'I agreed to meet them this afternoon,' added Miss Vowchurch gently, 'but they did not keep our engagement.'

Aldeborough stiffened. 'Tell me what you know,' he demanded of Lady Cotherstone. 'Why was she allowed to go out unaccompanied?'

'She received a letter this morning delivered by a man in livery. But Watkins can tell us no more.' Aunt May handed Aldeborough the empty cover on which was inscribed Frances's name and title in firm black strokes. It told them nothing.

'Frances and Juliet went out together just before two o'clock,' she continued. 'They did not take a carriage and they did not say where they were going. It seems that there was an element of secrecy in their departure.'

'And it is now—almost six o'clock.' Aldeborough consulted his fob watch with fingers that were not quite steady.

'Did she have any invitations for this afternoon?' he asked, holding his emotions on a firm rein. 'A balloon ascension or something as nonsensical, which could have gone on later than expected?'

'She did not say so.' Aunt May shook her head. 'I thought they had gone for a turn round the gardens here in the square. Nothing other than that.'

'Who would write her a personal letter? Viscount Torrington? Wigmore? Does she know anyone else?'

'Perhaps you should consider that she has gone to see her cousin, Mr Hanwell.' Miss Vowchurch dropped her observation into the strained conversation with deliberate calm. 'They have always seemed very close. And I know they had some communication at Almack's. Perhaps they arranged to meet.'

'Are you suggesting an assignation?' Lady Cotherstone asked.

'Of course not! That would be most improper of me! You know Lady Aldeborough far better than I do. I am sure it is something quite innocent. I do not think Frances would consider an elopement, do you?'

'Well, she would not take Juliet with her if she was. A ridiculous suggestion!' Aunt May's acerbic comment put paid to that direction of speculation.

'How do you know what she was thinking, Lady Cotherstone?' Penelope looked round at her audience. 'I understand that she has also had a long conversation with Mrs Winters. Perhaps that has something to do with her disappearance.'

'What?' Aldeborough had difficulty in preserving a calm exterior.

'They drove round Hyde Park together, so I am told.'

'Your suggestion is most indelicate, Miss Vowchurch. Presumably you were not told that I was present with Frances on that occasion. It was an unexceptionable conversation. There is nothing to be concerned about there, Hugh.' Lady Cotherstone frowned at Miss Vowchurch, who ignored the displeasure but gazed at Aldeborough with innocently open eyes.

'Of course not. I am sure there is a perfectly innocent explanation and they will soon return home.' She smiled at the Dowager. 'I am sure that dear Frances would never do anything detrimental to the family name, would she, Lady Aldeborough?

Aunt May caught up with Aldeborough in the hall where he retrieved his greatcoat and pulled on his gloves once more.

She clasped his arm with surprising strength despite her arthritic fingers, fixing him with an unblinking stare.

'I should never have left her here alone.' Tension was clear in the lines of strain around his mouth, but he had himself well in control. 'I knew of the dangers and chose to ignore them. I must find her.'

'Of course you must. Bring her back safely, Hugh. Do not blame yourself too much.'

'Has she left me, Aunt May? Does Charles Hanwell still hold a place in her heart after all?' The words were wrung out of him. 'I did not think so, but perhaps I was wrong.'

'Of course not. What can you be thinking of! Where is your good sense? I do assure you she has not left you. You would do well not to listen to anything that scheming little hussy in there has to say. I have never heard such trouble-making. She's like a vixen in a chicken run.' She gave his arm a final shake. 'Bring them both home.'

'Where do we go first?' Matthew asked as they descended the steps.

'Wigmore first—Portland Place. I suppose it is just possible that she went to see the Earl and Countess. I know she spoke to them at Almack's.'

They had no luck there. The Countess had not seen Frances since Almack's, although they had made an arrangement to take tea together.

'Torrington?' They stood on the steps of the Wigmore town house.

'It is the only other possibility I can think of. But I cannot for the life of me think why she would go there.'

St James's Square was already steeped in deep shadow by the time they arrived. Some of the houses showed lights burning in the windows of the first floor, but Torrington's address appeared to be in darkness and the knocker was off the door.

'It looks as if they are all out of town. What we need is a little local information.' With calm efficiency, his anxieties buried deep under the need for instant action, Aldeborough retraced his steps to the entrance to the Square where he accosted a scruffy urchin who was loitering in the gutter. 'Here, lad. Has there been any activity around here recently? Is the gentleman who lives there—' he pointed at Torrington's house '—at home?' In one hand he tossed a coin that gleamed persuasively in the remaining light.

The lad eyed Aldeborough speculatively and wiped his grimy face on his sleeve. 'Yes, yer honour. There's been comings and goings all day. The old geezer ain't 'ere. But the young 'un is.' He kept his eyes on the glint of gold as if it might disappear at any moment. A second coin joined the first. 'Saw a carriage at the door earlier today. Don't know if there's anyone here now, though.' He snatched and ran as the coins were tossed in his direction with a grin of thanks. Aldeborough returned to where Matthew's dark figure was partially hidden by the shrubbery in the Square's central garden.

'What are you thinking, Hugh? Kidnap? Abduction? But why?'

'It is a long story, Matthew, and there is no time to tell it now. Just trust me. It is imperative that we get in there.' He studied the house with care from their leafy refuge, eyes narrowed, assessing the possibilities for forcing an entry if it became necessary. 'The blinds are drawn upstairs. I think I would like a closer look. Let's try round the back. The kitchen or a cellar might allow us a safer opportunity.'

'No! Wait!' Matthew grabbed his arm, pulling him urgently back behind the iron railings. 'The front door is opening. It could be Torrington now.'

They stepped back silently to merge with the shadows. There was no light cast on the doorway and as the door opened, no light shone from the hall inside. All was cast in deepest shadow.

'What's happening?' Matthew whispered. 'Is there someone in the doorway?'

'No one that I can see. Let us just—'

Two shadowy figures detached themselves from the gloom and appeared on the top step, moving nervously, cautiously, as if conscious of surrounding danger in every sound, in every shadow. Then hand in hand, they scurried down the steps and hurried along the pavement as fast as their little kid shoes could carry them.

'Frances!' Aldeborough, closely followed by Matthew, leapt from their concealment and raced across the street towards them. A shriek from Juliet startled everyone as Aldeborough's hand closed round her wrist and Frances turned, her hands curling amazingly into fists to face their attackers.

'Hugh! Thank God!' Frances could find no other words to express her relief, but buried her face in her husband's shoulder as his arms clasped round her. She could feel his heart beating as rapidly as her own and simply held on to his sheltering arms.

'Are you hurt? Where's Torrington?' His keen eyes swept over them, searching for signs of harm, fortunately unable to make out the bloodstains on Juliet's gown in the darkness.

'It is not Torrington. It is Charles.' Juliet supplied the information as she recovered from her fright in Matthew's brotherly embrace. 'He...he is on the floor in the upstairs drawing room.'

'Matthew. Take the girls home and get Aunt May to look after them. Say as little as possible about tonight's events.' Aldeborough issued rapid orders. 'Don't stop for anything. I'll join you as quickly as I can.'

With a fleeting kiss against Frances's temple and a quick hug for his sister, Aldeborough turned and swiftly merged with the shadows in the direction of Torrington's house.

By the time Aldeborough arrived back at Cavendish Square, Matthew had turned the girls over to Aunt May with sufficient explanation to satisfy her momentarily, and was about to return to his brother's aid in St James's Square. Aldeborough shook his head to deflect any questions, merely informing Matthew that Hanwell was unable to shed any light on the events of the night, but would surely do so at some future occasion. Looking at Aldeborough's face, Matthew had no doubts and was glad that he was not in Hanwell's shoes. He had rarely seen his brother look so grim.

Earlier Aunt May had swept the ladies upstairs before the Dowager could emerge from her room to investigate, leaving Frances to the care of her maid until Aldeborough returned. It would be good to leave them alone together, she surmised. Meanwhile she discarded Juliet's bloodstained apparel and encouraged the child to chatter on, marvelling at the fortitude of youth.

Thus Aldeborough discovered his wife sitting comfortably before the fire in her bedchamber, a cup of hot chocolate in her hands and her maid hovering solicitously round her. She appeared, to Aldeborough's careful scrutiny, quite relaxed. She had come a long way from the tense, anxious girl whom he had rescued from Torrington Hall.

She turned her head as he entered, a smile illuminating her features, her eyes glowing with gold reflection from the candles. All the anger and hurt of their previous meeting appeared to have been swept away and he was content to let it be so. He walked towards her, signalling for the maid to leave, and skimmed his fingers down her cheek. She put up her hand to imprison his, pressing it against her, her eyes locked on his. He felt the beat of his heart falter and then restart, slow and sure and it struck him how much she meant to him. If she had been killed… He could not think of it.

He sat beside her, lifting her fingers to his lips, unable to take his eyes from her expressive face. She smiled at him and his mouth went dry.

'Well, Madame Wife, what adventures have you been having when I have not been here to keep my eye on you?' His tone was deliberately light and he linked his fingers gently with hers.

'He kidnapped us,' she explained simply.

'Charles, I presume?'

'Yes. I can not believe that he would go to such lengths. I know that he needs money and hoped that he would get it by marrying me. And I know that he feels a grudge against you for taking me away from him. But I actually thought, for a moment, he meant to kill us,' she admitted. 'He might simply have been trying to frighten us, of course. Perhaps I was just being silly. It would have been so easy to blackmail you, would it not, to release Juliet and myself? I am so thankful you came to rescue us—and that it is all over.'

The grim expression around Aldeborough's mouth did not lighten as he decided to say nothing about Charles's motives. If she was thinking blackmail, then so be it. It was far better than her knowing murder. Or that for him the affair was anything but over.

'Tell me how you escaped. How did Charles come to be lying on the floor of his drawing room with blood in his hair! You obviously managed quite well without Matthew and myself—you did not seem to need any help to escape.'

Frances laughed, although her voice still trembled a little in reaction. 'I think Juliet enjoyed it and will probably talk about nothing else for days. I should warn you that she has now decided that she would like to be an actress! She played the role of languishing invalid with tremendous vivacity—I could even have believed in her performance myself. Poor Charles had no chance.'

'Poor Charles, indeed. How did he come by the large lump on the head?'

'I hit him. With a bronze statue of a hunting dog.'

'Frances! Where is the gentle, retiring wife I married?' His lips twitched in suppressed amusement.

'What choice did I have? We thought you were still away and no one knew where to find us. In *Raven's Castle*—one of Juliet's favourite novels, you know—Marianne rendered the villain unconscious with a candlestick. So we decided to try the same strategy.'

'What is this?' He took hold of her wrist, lifting her arm to investigate the inexpert bandaging on her forearm.

'Well…' Frances blushed. 'We decided—that is, Juliet decided that we needed blood in the interests of dramatic realism, so that Charles would see the blood and believe that it was a genuine emergency and she was truly ill. We had to get him into the room so that I could creep up behind him. Juliet used a cake knife.'

Aldeborough felt the blood drain from his face. 'I don't know what to say,' he admitted, when his heart returned to its normal beat. 'It certainly proves that a forlorn hope can pay off. I am all admiration.' He bent his head to press his lips to her wrist above the lawn handkerchief.

'You are quite sure he was not dead?' He could not mistake the flash of fear in her eyes.

'No. A severe headache and a blow to his self-esteem, but he will live to tell the tale. But why did you go there? How could you both be so foolish as to put yourselves into that position?' His voice was gentle but he needed to know. 'Knowing what I do about your uncle's past treatment of you, I cannot believe that you would willingly visit his house.'

'It was a letter. An offer from my uncle to give me some possessions of my mother. I could not resist it. He said that he had some jewellery and other keepsakes, even letters. I would dearly have loved to have them, only I don't believe they really exist—it was merely a ruse by Charles to get us to the house. But he didn't expect Juliet, of course. Please don't be too angry.' She studied her linked fingers, unwilling to raise her eyes to his, afraid of what she might see there. 'Juliet said you might be if you found out. She said you could be very severe!'

'Did she, now? She has cause to know. A more headstrong girl I have yet to meet—unless it is my wife, of course.' He drew her into the circle of his arms to reassure her. 'I can almost find it in me to feel sorry for Charles.' But only if he could overcome the fury that bubbled under the surface of this calm conversation with his wife. 'I don't suppose he thought he would have to face two such resourceful females.'

Aldeborough suddenly remembered one of the more damaging comments made by Miss Vowchurch in an undoubted attempt to create a rift between them.

'Speaking of headstrong, is it true that you talked to Letitia Winters?' he asked conversationally.

'Who told you?' Frances looked up, her eyes watchful.

'Penelope. She also suggested that perhaps you had run to Charles and left me.'

'Did she really?' He was delighted to see those glorious eyes flash with sudden anger. 'She seems to have been remarkably busy in giving information, much of it false. But, yes, I did speak with Mrs Winters. She deliberately waited for me when I was returning from Rundell and Bridge with Aunt May.' Her steady gaze was forthright, challenging Aldeborough to disapprove. He found that he did not dare.

'I would give anything to know what you discussed.' He could not disguise his discomfort, to Frances's enjoyment, which she proceeded to hide.

'I won't tell you. It was between the two of us. And Aunt May, of course.'

'Lord. There's never a dull moment. And you drove round the Park?'

'Yes.'

'That would set the tongues wagging! Would it upset you if I said that I would rather Mrs Winter did not become a particular acquaintance of yours?'

'No. I can understand how uncomfortable it would be,' she agreed drily. He could not mistake the mischievous gleam in her eye. 'Letitia said exactly the same thing. I suppose it would be quite improper.'

'Not prudent, certainly.'

'And you would not want me to discuss you with your mistress.'

'No, I would not. And she is not my mistress!'

'No. Letitia said that as well.'

'Damnation, Frances! We should not be having this conversation. Come here.'

He had one intention. He was already hard for her and he would assuage his need and his guilt by making love to her with all the tenderness he could aspire to. He would make it beautiful for her, wipe away the memory of Charles and the ugly fears of that dark room in St James's Square. He drew back the heavy curtains to allow the moonlight to flood the room and gild their naked bodies. His touch feathered, lingered, enticed, no pressure of time or fulfilment. He would take all the time she needed to feel beautiful and loved. He pleasured her with lips, teeth, tongue, teasing her nipples into hard peaks of desire. When he lifted her above him, easily, effortlessly, the sight of her took his breath away. Shoulders, breasts, the curve of her hips all highlighted in soft moonlight, her hollows and secret places shadowed and mysterious. He lowered her on to him, slowly, filling her with his desire and power.

He let her set the pace and depth, glorying in her lack of self-consciousness. She was quick to learn, arching her body back with innate grace and elegance, no shyness, no need to hide herself from his deliberate gaze. Her mouth, when she leaned down to take his, was soft and seductive, the swollen lips parting to allow him to plunder her sweet mouth. In that moment she was totally alluring and he shuddered with suppressed desire, determined to rule his emotions until her satisfaction was complete. When he was unable to guarantee his control any longer, he reversed their positions, pinning her to the bed, still deep inside her. She moved fluidly to echo his every move, his every thrust. She was perfection. When he could withstand her enchantment no longer, he shuddered to his own climax, her name on his lips.

For Frances it was a moment of pure revelation. She felt that her whole body throbbed with love for him and for the gift that he gave her that night. His hands and body wove a mystery for her, layer upon layer of delicious sensation. The beauty of it moved her to tears, which spangled on her lashes and cheeks in the moonlight. She surrendered totally to his caresses, to his movements, no reticence, no withdrawal. Even when he lifted her to straddle him so that he could fill her deeply, she drew in her breath, shocked at first, and then began to move to give him pleasure as well as herself. She leaned forward to cover his face with kisses. His throat, the knotted muscles of his shoulders, the broad planes of his chest.

The shimmering light granted her the freedom to express her love for him in the unspoken language of languorous caresses, delicate touches. She clung to him, moved with him, opened her thighs and arched her hips for him. Her lips were tender from his kisses, her eyes dark as midnight and luminous as the stars, her breasts sensitive to his every touch. When he finally thrust hard and deep she absorbed the shocks, revelling in the slide of sweat-slicked skin on skin. Her own release, an explosion of the heat that had gathered in her belly to flash through her blood with all the power and brilliance of a shooting star, shook her to the core so that she cried out before she lay in his arms and trembled in the aftermath of sensation.

She fell into exhausted sleep, leaving him to look at her serene face with an emotion approaching incredulity. The wide generous mouth, the straight nose. Eyebrows dark and a little heavy. She looked very young and vulnerable and enchantingly beautiful. Against all intentions he had fallen in love. He swallowed the sudden obstruction in his throat as the realisation struck him with the physical force of a blow to the stomach. When on earth had this happened? And yet it seemed to him that he had been waiting to love her all his life. He would give her everything in his power. Protection, security, comfort.

His conscience battered him with the memory of her abduction and the bullet embedded in the Chinese Bridge. But he would do better. Without disturbing her he stroked her hair where it curled down on to her breast. And the burden of his love need not be too great for her. She need never know. Except through his actions, which would probably be clear to anyone who cared to look closely enough, or believe it possible. Which she never would. But whatever happened in the future, whatever the outcome between himself and Charles, he would remember this night for ever. It would have to be enough.

'It is not possible for me to simply close the door and turn the key on these events, Frances.'

Aldeborough prowled across the library, resolution governing every line of his body. 'I know he is your cousin and I know you would rather forget about the whole affair and believe that it is over and he will never trouble you again. But it is not finished. You have to accept that he is dangerous—a real threat—and the only way to stop him is to make his crimes public and so discredit him. I will not have him intimidate you again. I could not live with that fear overshadowing us.'

Frances studied her hands, her dark brows drawn together as she considered his words. 'Very well.' She raised her eyes to his, a troubled frown still marring her smooth forehead. 'But what about you? Will it put you in danger?' She rose from her seat in the window embrasure to lay her hand on his arm. 'I couldn't bear it, Hugh.'

'I will be in no danger. You will have to trust me.' He covered her hand with his own and smiled down at her with a tenderness that made her heart race and the blood rush to stain her cheeks with delicate colour.

'What will you do?' She strove for calm and normality in her tone.

'My first task is to make contact with Charles. It should not be too difficult.'

'Will he have gone back to Yorkshire, do you think?'

'I do not think so and I am prepared to gamble on that. I think he will be waiting to see what my next move will be. He has too much to lose if he gives up now and buries himself at Torrington Hall. There is nothing there for him—except poverty and isolation from polite society. I am confident that he will stay in town.' He clasped her hands tightly. 'You must stay here with Juliet and Aunt May. You must not go out alone. Do you understand?'

'But I do not see how I can be in any danger!'

'Give me your word, Frances!'

'I suppose I must.' There was no arguing against the firm command.

'I know how hard it is for you to do so. But I have to know that you are safe.' His grim expression relaxed to be replaced by a reminiscent smile. 'You were able to give me your word once before.'

'Yes. But only because you threatened to lock me in my bedchamber for a week. I did not feel that you had given me any choice!' Frances smiled at the memory. 'But, yes, I promise. I will not go anywhere alone.'

Aldeborough bent his head to brush her mouth gently with his own. He raised his head to search her face, his eyes fiercely possessive. Then he lifted her hand and pressed his lips against her soft palm, closing her fingers over the caress.

'God keep you.'

He strode out of the room, leaving Frances to press her palm with its searing imprint against her heart.

Aldeborough left the house dressed for an evening at his club. First he called at Torrington's address in St James's Square, to be informed by a disinterested but informative footman that Mr Hanwell was not at home, but was expected back later that evening. No, he thought that Mr Hanwell had no specific invitation for that evening. Perhaps he intended to dine and then visit his club?

Aldeborough stopped off first at White's, his own club. He was hailed by a number of acquaintances, but refused an invitation to join in a hand of whist when he saw that Charles was not present. Ambrose was, having lately returned from his uncle's estate, and he elected to accompany Aldeborough. He received no satisfactory explanation as to why Hugh needed to find Charles Hanwell so urgently, knowing nothing of the events of the previous day, but he was not deterred. He was struck by the controlled passion in Aldeborough's eyes and decided that it did not bode well for Hanwell. On the off chance that he might have put in an appearance at Brooks's, they strolled across St James's Street, but again with no success. They tried Boodle's, where Charles might have decided to dine, but again they drew a blank. This left a number of gaming establishments, notorious for their high stakes and wild play. Aldeborough sighed and began what looked like an exhausting and frustrating night.

At Storridge's in Pall Mall, one of the first people he saw at the faro table was Matthew. Aldeborough raised an eyebrow in some surprise, moving quietly to stand behind him, and placed a hand on his shoulder.

'I will not ask what you are doing here,' he murmured in his ear and stayed to watch as his brother finished the hand somewhat self-consciously and promptly lost.

'I was winning until you arrived,' Matthew retorted as he threw down the cards in disgust, but had the grace to look a little sheepish.

'How much have you lost? No, don't tell me. Perhaps I should let you go to Spain. I would worry about you less. Have you seen Charles Hanwell tonight?'

'No. I suppose you have tried all the usual places? I will not ask why you want him, although I think I can guess.' He thought for a moment. 'Have you tried the new establishment a few doors along? Very discreet. And expensive, I am told. Too rich for me.'

'Despite his lack of funds, it sounds the sort of place Hanwell would frequent. Will you come?'

The hour was late when they were shown in to the discreet establishment by a black-clad footman. The club was still quiet, but there were sufficient gamblers to allow games of Macao and faro to be under way.

There, involved in a game of whist, was Charles Hanwell. He looked pale and hollow-eyed, but otherwise none the worse for wear considering his injury of the previous night. Any bruising from Frances's well-aimed statuette was hidden by his hair. He was laughing, indulging in some light witticisms with his partner, Lord Belmont, a glass of port at his side. Sir John Masters, always a keen gambler, threw down his hand of cards in disgust, and on seeing Aldeborough approach, raised his hand in greeting.

'Come and join us, Aldeborough. You might change my run of bad luck.'

'I doubt it.' Aldeborough picked up the discarded cards and grimaced at the poor hand. 'I would call it a night if I were you.'

Charles Hanwell raised his eyes to fix them on Aldeborough standing before him, flanked by Matthew and Ambrose.

Perhaps he grew a little paler, but he clearly decided to brazen out the situation. He greeted Aldeborough with false conviviality.

'Good evening, Aldeborough. Come to play a hand of cards?' His lips twisted in sardonic malice. 'Or perhaps you prefer dice?'

'I have no preference.' Aldeborough replied lightly but his eyes were bleak and icy as they rested on his wife's abductor. 'Other than who I play with, of course.'

'I cannot pretend to understand you, my lord.' Hanwell looked at Aldeborough speculatively, considering the direction of the conversation. Aldeborough was obviously here for a purpose but he would be prepared to gamble on the fact that the Marquis was unlikely to do or say anything to harm his wife's reputation.

'I am sure you do. Unless you have a very short memory for events of last night?'

Charles inhaled sharply. So. He had been wrong. This was to be a confrontation. On the attack, he took up the challenge with his next words.

'I am surprised that I am worthy of your interest, Aldeborough. I have little money. You saw to that when you abducted my cousin, who should have been my wife, and so ruined myself and my father.' The deliberate venom behind the words had the other gamblers around the table shifting uncomfortably in their seats. Aldeborough circled the table to take a vacant seat opposite Hanwell as if his intention were indeed to play.

'I have reason to believe that your cousin is more than satisfied with the outcome of that night.' His tone was still light, conciliatory. 'Your father was certainly not wise in his gambling on her inheritance to put your estate to rights. Perhaps you will be more successful.' Aldeborough shrugged. 'But perhaps I should warn you. My luck is in at present.'

'I know. I backed against your horse at Newmarket!' Sir John Masters added with a grimace. 'And lost.'

'You have the devil's own luck, haven't you?' Hanwell sneered.

'Yes. I believe I do.'

'Perhaps it is time it ran out.' Hanwell lifted the wine glass to his lips, his expression set as he determined to push events to a definite conclusion one way or the other. He disliked the impression of cat and mouse, with himself as the tormented rodent.

'Why would you think that? Are you ill wishing me? We are family, after all. Are we not, Charles?'

Aldeborough raised his hand to summon a passing footman with a tray of claret, all the while keeping his gaze fixed on Hanwell.

'I think you are the one out of luck,' he continued. 'I spoiled your plan for keeping the heiress for yourself, for marrying her against her wishes and against her best interests. And, as I understand, she played her own imaginative role— only last night—in escaping from your clutches.'

A fascinated audience now concentrated on every word, watching the faces of both men.

'But does your wife realise,' Hanwell took a rapid decision in an attempt to deflect any further detrimental revelations, 'that since her marriage to you her life has been put at risk? There have been too many incidents, haven't there, Aldeborough? Is it your intention to get rid of her? After all, your brother met an untimely death too, didn't he? And that was an accident. Or was it? We are all aware that the unfortunate occurrence was very much to your advantage.'

Silence fell on the room, all ears tuned to the outcome of such provocation, horror registering on many faces. But a sense of relief flashed momentarily into Aldeborough's eyes. Charles had taken the bait.

'No…look, man…you can't say things like that!…Richard Lafford's death was an accident… He broke his neck… There is no blame…' A dozen voices broke the lull.

'Well, Charles?' The smile on Aldeborough's face was not pleasant.

'It is common knowledge that Richard Lafford's death handed a title and a fortune to Aldeborough, isn't it?' Hanwell looked round the circle of incredulous faces for support.

'I would suggest that an accident would seem far too coincidental.'

'No! You will withdraw such slander.' Matthew, previously a silent spectator of his brother's campaign, leaned across to grasp Hanwell by his cravat and almost drag him from his seat.

Aldeborough stretched out a hand to restrain Matthew. 'Leave it, Matthew,' he ordered gently. 'Let me finish this.' He turned back to Charles with deliberate intent, and lowered his voice.

'It is true. I certainly gained financially from my brother's death. But I would find no advantage in my wife's death, would I? I trust you know the terms of her mother's will—of her inheritance? Of course you do! There is only one person here who would gain if my wife died now. And that is *you* in the long term. Her fortune would go by default to your father, and thus to you. I think the *incidents*, as you term them, have more to do with you than with me.'

'How dare you! How dare you try to blacken my reputation with ill-founded accusations?' Charles's voice rose as panic crept in, but he kept his eyes fixed on Aldeborough like a rabbit on a hunting eagle.

'It was your choice to discuss this unsavoury affair in public.'

'Pushed into it by you!'

'Then let me push a little harder, *Cousin Charles*.'

Aldeborough picked up his untouched glass of claret as if to raise it to his lips—and flung the contents in Hanwell's face. As the blood-red liquid dripped from Charles's furious and shocked features on to his coat and shirt, he leapt to his feet, prepared to fling himself at his tormentor, only to be restrained by those who stood nearest.

'You will meet me for this, my lord Aldeborough,' he snarled.

'Do you think so?'

Matthew put a restraining hand on his brother's shoulder. 'No. Don't take the challenge. He's too drunk to know what he's saying.'

'Are you too drunk, Hanwell?' Aldeborough enquired gently. 'I don't think so.'

'No. You know I am not. Do you accept the charge of cowardice and murder? Or do you accept my challenge?'

'Of course I take your challenge.' Aldeborough's lips curved to show his teeth in a smile, all the more deadly because of its complete absence of humour and the satisfaction that his plan had worked. 'You know I never refuse a challenge. I will meet you with utmost satisfaction. Perhaps your seconds would care to discuss arrangements with mine. Matthew? Ambrose? If I might suggest, Hanwell, it would be wise to choose your seconds from the gentlemen present.' He looked round the expectant faces, anticipating the nods of acceptance. 'It would not be politic to broadcast the content of our...disagreement.'

'It shall all be arranged.' Ambrose shook off his astonishment at the rapid turn of events—he must discover from Matthew what exactly had occurred in his absence—and found his voice again. 'With all speed. This affair should be settled quickly to prevent further gossip.' He had never known his friend to act with such deliberate provocation.

Aldeborough nodded in agreement. 'Until tomorrow, then. Seven o'clock. The Archer's Field.'

He inclined his head abruptly to Hanwell and the assembled company and left, well satisfied with the events of the night, oblivious to the reaction that immediately erupted behind him.

By the time Aldeborough returned to Cavendish Square, the hour was far advanced.

He undressed, shrugged into his dressing gown and, without knocking, let himself in to his wife's room. She was asleep, but with a candle still burning on the nightstand as if she had been awaiting his return. He sat beside her on the bed, gently so that he would not disturb her. Her hair was severely confined into a plait for the night, but curls had escaped around her face, which was faintly flushed in sleep. The fingers of her right hand curled on the lace bedspread.

She looked very young and vulnerable. He would, he thought, give his life to ensure that she remain safe. The thought did not surprise him at all, even though he had known her for such a little time. He decided, against the prompting of his body, to retire and leave her undisturbed, but she stirred and opened her eyes. She smiled at him in complete trust. His heart quickened its beat at the knowledge that he had achieved this response in her. He could not leave her.

'I worried about you,' she whispered sleepily.

He caressed her cheek with fingers that trembled from the powerful and instant surge of emotion through his veins.

'Sleep with me, Frances Rosalind. I need to be with you tonight.'

'Of course. You need not ask.' Her eyelids were already closing again.

He cast aside the dressing gown and stretched beside her, drawing her close, her head on his shoulder. She sighed and let herself sink once again towards sleep.

'Frances?'

'Yes, my lord?'

'Nothing, really.' He smiled. 'Just that I thought I should tell you that I love you. Tell you how much you have come to mean to me.'

'Hmm?'

Not the reaction that he would have hoped for, but he was not to be deterred. A deep-seated need drove him on. It was suddenly imperative that he tell her. That he explain. That she should know the longings and desires which he had kept hidden in the depths of his heart.

'I love you so much. I cannot understand why it has taken me so long to discover it, to accept it.' He turned his cheek against her hair, marvelling at its softness against his skin. His voice low, an edge of weariness in it, he hesitated a little as he let his mind drift back over the weeks, intent on putting into words his overwhelming emotions towards the woman in his arms. 'God knows, I did not want to marry you,' he admitted. 'You knew that. And I did not love you—I hardly knew you. You were an unnecessary complication that I neither needed nor looked for in my life. Our marriage was simply a way out of a difficult situation, for both of us. And I expected nothing more.' His smile held a degree of bitterness as he remembered his careless acceptance of responsibility towards a wife, his determination that she should make no demands on him or bring any significant change to the pattern of his life. 'I wanted you, without doubt. You are very lovely and it pleased me to kiss you, to touch you and take you to my bed. But love…that was something I did not look for. But then I simply fell in love with you. Slowly. Imperceptibly. Until I found that I could not get you out of my mind, what you were doing, what you were thinking… You mattered to me. It was as simple as that.

'Do you know what I remember? I can still see you standing in your bedchamber in Cavendish Square, fear in your eyes—which I had put there—the scars of your uncle's whip on your back and all you could say was that you were grateful to me for rescuing you. It makes my blood run cold. You deserve a better husband than I have been, darling Frances. I am not proud of the way I have acted towards you. I have no excuses.'

She moved a little against him, curling more securely into the warmth of his body. He tightened his embrace.

'But I would give my life's blood to wipe the memory of that fear away and restore to you everything that you were denied by your family. Security. Happiness. Serenity, knowing that no one will ever hurt you again. For understand this, Frances, I will never do anything to bring you harm. Or allow anyone else to do so. I swear it.

'I need you, Frances. To smile at me. To wake beside me so that I can hold you in my arms. Because I love you. You are my heart and soul, my whole life. Do you believe that?' It was suddenly so urgent that she should.

She made no reply. He turned his head to glance down. 'Frances?'

He smiled wistfully, a little sadly, now aware of her deep breathing. Her warm breath whispered against his shoulder, her hand relaxed with fingers curled against his chest. He doubted that she would remember any of his words in the morning when she awoke. When he would be gone from her side.

'Sleep well, dearest Molly,' he murmured. 'Tomorrow it will all be over, one way or the other.'

Smoothing her hair from her face, he pressed his lips to the faint pulse beating at her temple. He remained wakeful, content simply to hold her in his safekeeping until the false dawn lightened the sky.

Frances woke very early, alone, with a terrible sense of doom. She flung back the covers and crossed with hurried steps to Aldeborough's room. It was empty and somehow desolate. She could only guess that he was engaged in something dangerous and that she could do no more than wait until he returned. She walked over to his dressing table and touched his silver brushes, tracing the engraved pattern with her fingers. She remembered the highwaymen on the road to the Priory, their violence and intent to kill, and refused to contemplate the possibility that he might be harmed. But she could not check the tears that rolled slowly down her cheeks on to her lace chemise.

Chapter Fourteen

The sky brightened imperceptibly round the huddle of dark figures.

'I cannot believe we are doing this, Hugh.' Matthew ran his fingers nervously through his hair.

Aldeborough buttoned up his coat of dark superfine with supreme indifference to his brother's concerns.

'I never thought I should be supporting *you* in a duel! Richard possibly, you never. I don't suppose you would consider withdrawing?' Matthew's tone reflected that he knew it was a hope not worth voicing.

'How good a shot is he?' asked Ambrose with a frown of some concern.

'I have no idea.' Aldeborough's cold reply cast the threesome into silence.

'You might delope,' suggested Matthew finally.

'I think not. That would, after all, suggest that the blame is mine.'

'But he might kill you! I have to say that you seem remarkably unconcerned about it!'

'Unconcerned?' Aldeborough's eyes blazed into fury as he turned on his brother. 'You have no idea—' He stopped to re-establish control over the anger that leapt through his veins like molten lava as he remembered the fear in Frances's eyes. He continued in a quiet voice, the flames once more banked but the anger no less intense, 'This confrontation between Hanwell and myself has become inevitable. Since the day of my marriage, my life has been in danger. And more recently Frances has become the target of her loving cousin.'

'But, Hugh! Surely—'

'Why are you so shocked? You knew of the ambush on the road to York. It was the first attempt—but certainly not the last. And they could all have so nearly succeeded. I did not realise how far Hanwell was prepared to go to achieve his ends. So, yes—I am *concerned*! Such a mild word. The threats have to stop. And this is the perfect opportunity to expose his sins before witnesses. To threaten him with public dishonour. My wife's safety and peace of mind are in the balance and I find that I will do anything in my power, go to any extremes, to keep her safe. So, against all common sense, I am prepared to risk Hanwell's skill with a pistol. I have no little aptitude and will gamble on it.' His brows snapped together, the planes of his face harsh in the early light. 'And that will be an end to it.'

At seven o'clock promptly, a professional gentleman in black frockcoat, who had been standing divorced from the proceedings, walked briskly forward to take control of the events, fluttering handkerchief in hand.

The scrap of cloth dropped to the floor.

Aldeborough aimed at Charles Hanwell's heart. But then, with deliberately controlled intent, he aimed wide to the right and fired his pistol. His aim was excellent. He missed.

Hanwell lifted his weapon and fired with deliberate intent to wound, to maim, to kill.

'Honour is satisfied, gentlemen.' Ambrose strode forward, relief written clearly in his movements.

'No, by God, it isn't.'

Hard-held temper snapped. Aldeborough strode the length of the field towards Charles, pushing Ambrose aside, right arm held stiffly but with no sign of pain or discomfort and choosing to ignore the steady trickle of blood that had begun to stain his cuff and drip from his fingers. Hanwell could do nothing but stand. He did not have long to wait.

'Is honour satisfied, Hanwell?'

'You have no proof,' muttered Hanwell hoarsely, face pale, fists clenched at his side.

'I do not need proof to do this.' Aldeborough strode on to reach his quarry and without hesitation drove a punishing left fist into Charles's face, catching him expertly on the point of his chin, laying him out on the floor at his feet. 'I should warn you, if you get up, I will knock you down again,' he snarled through clenched teeth.

Charles wiped his sleeve over his bloody nose. 'You can prove nothing.'

'I have not actually accused you of anything.'

Hanwell saw murder in Aldeborough's eyes despite his carefully chosen words.

'They were accidents. I had nothing to do with them.'

'Which accidents were those?' Aldeborough snarled. 'We would all be interested to hear.'

Hanwell felt the eyes of his seconds focus on him as they waited with unabashed interest for his reply. He closed his lips in a straight line, shook his head.

'The highwaymen on the York Road? The assassination attempt at the Priory?' Aldeborough prompted. 'My wife's abduction? What was your intention then?'

Hanwell shook his head once more as if to clear his brain. 'I have never wished your wife ill.' He could not meet Aldeborough's eyes. 'But it should have been mine—the inheritance. That was always the plan. She would have married me.'

'So you decided to take matters into your own hands. I should have killed you for the pain you put my wife through. And my sister.'

'That was a mistake.' Panic bloomed. 'It should never have happened.'

'At least you paid the penalty.' Aldeborough's lips curled with what might have been the ghost of a smile. 'My wife has a sure aim, it seems. You would not want *that* story to become common knowledge, would you? It would not enhance your reputation to any degree.' He leaned down to grasp Charles by his shirt front and half-drag him from the floor. 'I would have no qualms about leaking the story, you know. And the reasons behind it. And listen well, Hanwell. If any harm, however small, comes to my wife in future, I will kill you.'

Hanwell cowered before the magnificent blaze of uncontrolled anger in those predatory eyes.

'Come away, Hugh.' Ambrose approached and caught Aldeborough's shoulder, tugging gently. 'You have proved your point. And before witnesses.' He looked down at Hanwell in disgust.

In that one glance Hanwell saw the future for him: his reputation in ruins, his position in society destroyed and with it his hopes of financial restitution. He cringed as Aldeborough flung him back to the floor and turned away. 'I was not the only one to blame, my lord.'

'No?' Aldeborough looked back with a cynical lift of his eyebrows. Only he had heard him. 'Not trying to shift the blame, are you?'

'You might look closer to home,' Hanwell managed a sneer.

'Who are you suggesting? Unless Matthew has decided to rid himself of all opposition to the title?'

'Who do you think might have an interest in your being free to remarry, my Lord Aldeborough?'

Aldeborough halted with an arrested expression on his face. He turned to Hanwell again, giving him his full attention. 'Of course. I never thought...'

'Mine is not the only interest in your family affairs, my lord. And it has made my task so much easier to be fed details of your movements from someone so well informed. You thought you had been clever enough to work it all out. You do not know that half of it.'

'Yes. I see. I think that perhaps you have said enough.' Aldeborough stepped back. 'The matter is finished, gentlemen.' He addressed the seconds, his voice again raised, and then spoke once more to Hanwell, bowing ironically and whispering, 'Permit me to tell you, sir, you are despicable.'

Frances stood by the window in the breakfast parlour, nerves stretched to snapping point.

'I do not understand why you are so anxious,' Juliet complained. 'Since you do not know for certain where they have gone, why worry about it? Do come and sit, Frances. I am sure they will return at any moment and wonder what all the fuss is about.'

'I simply know there is something wrong.' Frances continued to scan the empty square, picking at the lace edge of a lawn handkerchief with nervous fingers. 'Hugh left before dawn and so did Matthew.'

'Probably gone for an early-morning ride,' observed Aunt May complacently. 'It is not unknown.' Not a frequent member of the breakfast parlour and still garbed in an eye-catching wrapper of vivid puce and cream stripes, she continued to feed Wellington with pieces of bread dipped in tea, placidly ignoring the evident disgust on Juliet's face. 'Do sit down, my dear. You are giving me the headache. Listen!' She raised one bony hand as distant sounds emanated from the vicinity of the front door. 'That is probably Aldeborough now, so we can all be at ease again. Thank God.'

Nevertheless, they waited in tense silence, listening to the footsteps crossing the hall and ascending the staircase.

'It is not Aldeborough.' Frances stood perfectly still, praying that she was wrong, that the door would open and she would see his well-loved face, his fierce eyes, his smile that could turn her knees to water.

Watkins entered.

'Miss Vowchurch has called, your ladyship,' he addressed Frances with a bland face. 'She apologises for this untimely visit, but asks for a moment of your time.'

'What can the woman want at this hour?' demanded Aunt May. 'You had better show her up, Watkins.'

Miss Penelope Vowchurch was shown into the room, elegantly attired as always, as if it were the most natural thing in the world to demand admittance to one's hostess before she had arisen from the breakfast table.

'Miss Vowchurch.' However reluctant Frances felt, she extended her hand in greeting.

'Forgive me. I realise that this is not…that is, I did not wish…but I had to come.' Her audience stared at her. On closer inspection her face was pale and strained, her eyes troubled and the shadows beneath them suggesting that she had slept little.

'What is it?'

'The duel. You must stop it!' Her usual calm voice was agitated, as if breathing was not easy.

'So you were right to worry, Frances,' Lady Cotherstone gripped the edge of the table, her aged hands curled like claws. 'And who is my nephew engaged to fight, Miss Vowchurch?'

'Charles Hanwell. Can we not do something to prevent it?'

Frances could make no sensible reply, her blood running cold at the confirmation of her fears. It was left to Aunt May to answer, which she did. But nothing could disguise the anxiety in her taut lips, or in the harsh lines engraved beside her mouth. Her wrinkled face suddenly showed all of her years.

'We can hardly stop it, Miss Vowchurch. If you are correct in your assumption, it was this morning and will be well and truly over by now. What can have possessed the boy to put himself in danger this way?' Aunt May raised her hands to cover her face for one long moment—then drew in a deep breath to regain her composure. 'But tell me—' she fixed Miss Vowchurch with a bleak stare '—I am interested to know how you came by the information. I imagine that it is not common knowledge.'

'I…I heard a rumour,' Miss Vowchurch stammered.

'But even if it is true, what I don't understand is why you are here? What is it to you?'

To their concerted amazement, Penelope's voice broke on a sob and she hurriedly searched for a handkerchief to wipe away the tears that spilled from her eyes. It took a few moments, but then her words, uttered on impulse, with no thought for her audience, reflected a mind in turmoil.

'I cannot think. I have hardly slept—I know I should not say this but…I love him. He was going to marry me before it all went wrong—before he married *you*.' Her glance at Frances was full of barely suppressed anger. 'I would never want Charles to kill him. How could that be my intention? I cannot bear the thought of… We must stop them meeting at all costs.' Tears continue to fall from her beautiful eyes and she wept in genuine distress.

Frances looked at her, horror tinged with regret. She understood all too well the pain of loving where it was not returned. But Penelope's words chilled her to the marrow.

'It seems to me, Miss Vowchurch, that you know more about this duel than mere rumour,' Aunt May persisted. 'Have you spoken to Charles Hanwell about this?'

'No, no, of course not,' she denied, now flustered, dabbing again at her tear-drenched eyes with her handkerchief and trying for a brave smile. 'Forgive me, I am overwrought…'

The door opened again, this time to admit, with a magnificently silencing effect, the Dowager Lady Aldeborough.

Lady Aldeborough, viewing the assembled company with disdain and Aunt May with intense dislike, took control of the situation through ingrained habit.

'There seems to be quite a gathering in my breakfast parlour. Penelope, my dear, what brings you here? I am delighted to see you, of course, and I am sure there is a good reason. Where is Aldeborough?'

'Fighting a duel, we believe.' There was none of the customary malicious humour in Lady Cotherstone's clipped tones.

'A duel? Never! The Marquis of Aldeborough would never be involved in something so outrageous and inappropriate to his consequence. What can you be thinking of to spread such an inaccurate story? Now, dear Penelope, perhaps you will tell me why you are here.'

The sound of the front door slamming brought the conversation to a halt for the second time that morning. Frances felt that she would explode with inner tension if she had to stand and wait, so she picked up her skirts and ran from the room to the head of the stairs where she leaned over the banister to survey the hall below. There, handing his gloves and hat to Watkins, was Matthew.

'Matthew!' She ran down the stairs, heart full of dread, beating rapidly within her muslin bodice.

'Where's Hugh? Was it a duel? Is he hurt? Dead?' She grasped his sleeve and shook it urgently. 'Please don't keep me in suspense.'

Matthew gently released his sleeve from her clutching fingers and took her hands.

'It is over, Frances. Don't take on so! He is not dead or hurt to any real degree. There now—there is no need to cry.'

'Thank God!' The blood drained from her heart, leaving her sick with relief, but she brushed the trace of tears from her cheeks with her hand. 'Oh, Matthew! You have no idea… Where is he? Is he still at the stables?'

'Well…no. I came back alone after delivering Ambrose to his lodgings. Hugh will be here shortly…I expect.'

Frances raised her head, her glance sharp, picking up an element of uncertainty in Matthew's voice. 'But where is he?'

A further hesitation. 'He has gone to see Miss Vowchurch. He said that it was imperative that he see her immediately.' Matthew frowned.

'To see Penelope?'

'Yes.' He was startled by the stricken look on her face. 'I do not think there is anything here to worry you, dear Frances.' But the frown belied his reassurance.

'Did…did he say why?'

'No…just that he had to see her.'

'Penelope!' she whispered. It was like a nightmare, her worst fears realised, following so rapidly after that first torrent of relief and joy. 'But Penelope is here.'

'Oh, well. I expect he'll come on here when he fails to see her in Grosvenor Square.' He watched Frances closely, the distress that imprinted her pale features. 'I don't expect it means anything.'

Her fears swirled through her brain. So Aldeborough did return Penelope's regard after all. How much he must love her to go straight to her from the duel. How much he must need to tell her of his safety. And she loves him. Frances cringed inwardly as the final realisation that Hugh would never love her took hold of her emotions. She could not pretend any longer that his attentions at night were anything more than those demanded by a casual affection and duty. The cravings of her heart would never be answered.

'Are you quite well, Frances?' Matthew touched her hand in concern.

It brought her back to the present. It was time for action, not for mindless despair, and she forced her weary brain into making some rapid decisions. She could not simply wait here, could not face Aldeborough, knowing how much he wanted Penelope, could not watch their emotional reunion after the threat of death and separation. But she could do something to halt the threats from Viscount Torrington. She could, and must, do something immediately. And it would give her the solitude she needed to allow her heart to recover...if it ever could. She grasped Matthew's arm again, making him wince in surprise.

'Matthew,' she demanded forcefully. 'Will you help me?'

'Of course. Anything in my power.'

'I want the travelling coach. And Benson. It is imperative that I leave now, this minute.'

'What? Where are you going?'

'The Priory.'

'All the way to Yorkshire? Damnation, Frances, you cannot do that!'

'Yes, I can. And it is vital that I do.'

'No. Wait until Hugh gets back. Talk to him about it, that's the best thing. There is no need for you to run away. I'm sure Hugh would never—'

'I am not running away! You do not understand and I have

no time to explain. I must go now. Will you order Benson to harness the horses?'

'I must not let you go alone.' He rubbed his hand over his face, eyeing her uncertainly. 'Are you sure about this?'

'More sure than anything in the world.'

'Then I had better go with you. Aldeborough would never forgive me if anything happened to you.'

'There is no need, I assure you.'

'You have no choice.' Frances almost smiled, despite her anguish, at Matthew's masterful tone, so similar to that of his brother. 'If you go, I go with you.'

'Very well, I do not have the time to argue. As soon as possible. I will pack a bandbox. And I would be grateful if you did not tell anyone.' With which she turned to run up the stairs, leaving Matthew, somewhat bemused, to wonder what more the day could hold and what his brother would say to him when he found out.

An hour later Aldeborough let himself in at his own front door. His visit to the Vowchurch establishment had failed in its objective, but yielded the information that Miss Vowchurch would be awaiting him in Cavendish Square.

But first he must see Frances and put her mind at rest. The need to see her was overwhelming, merely to touch her soft cheek with his fingertips and see her sapphire eyes smile into his.

'Where will I find her ladyship, Watkins?'

'She is not at home, my lord.'

'What? Are you sure? But I thought… When did she leave?'

'Her ladyship left about half an hour ago. In the travelling coach.'

A cold finger of fear began to trace its path down his spine. Before he could find words to enquire further, the door opened behind him and Matthew entered at speed, dressed in caped greatcoat and top boots as if for travel and with a distinctly harassed air.

'Hugh! Thank God you have arrived. I tried to stop her, but she gave me the slip. I'm sure she meant to all the time. I'm damned sorry.'

'What has she done?' His left-handed grasp on his brother's arm was not gentle. 'Tell me!'

'Gone!'

'But where? For God's sake, Matthew, tell me what you know!' His first thought, which froze his blood, was that she had left him, fled from their marriage. He ran his hand through his hair, regardless of appearances, with fingers that were not quite steady. What in heaven's name had he done to force her into such rapid flight? But then sanity reasserted itself. He might not know why she had gone, but surely there was only one place she would go.

'The Priory,' Matthew confirmed, regaining his wits as he caught his breath. 'She said it was urgent and was…upset. Perhaps I should warn you, Hugh…I told her you had gone to see Miss Vowchurch.'

'What did you say exactly?'

The Marquis had become very still. He saw the question in Matthew's eyes. The uncertainty.

'Matthew! Surely you did not believe…but it seems that you did!' He struck his brother's arm lightly with his gloves. 'Did you really believe that I could be engaged in a liaison with Penelope Vowchurch?' Aldeborough groaned, but managed a wry smile at his brother's downcast demeanour. 'And now Frances probably believes it too!' He grasped Matthew's shoulder. 'I have to stop her, but first there is some unfinished business here which cannot wait. At least Benson will have the sense to put up at the White Hart at Hitchin. I'll find her there. You can come with me, for your sins.'

'To the Priory? But…you don't want me with you, do you? Besides, I had planned to—'

'You can drive my chestnuts in the curricle. My arm is too sore!'

'I will go and get them ready!'

* * *

'Aldeborough! At last!'

'Hugh, where has Frances gone?' asked Juliet. 'Matthew knows, but refuses to say.'

'She has probably left you, Aldeborough.' The Dowager's tone spoke of smug complacency. 'I knew no good would come of that marriage, but you were never willing to take my advice. How you could have allowed yourself to enter into an alliance with—'

'I think we need an explanation, dear boy,' Lady Cotherstone broke in quietly.

'I agree. But you should know that Frances has not left me.' He bowed ironically towards the Dowager. 'I know where I shall find her and I know, in some part, why she has gone. As for the rest of the explanation, I do not believe that I am the best person here to give it. It surprises me that you are visiting so early, Miss Vowchurch.'

She sat, the picture of griefstricken loveliness. 'I came be-cause…because…' Her breath caught a little. 'I cannot say.'

'As you are aware, I have just fought a duel.' Aldeborough's smile was icy, his grey eyes arctic. 'You will be de-lighted to know, Miss Vowchurch, that Charles is safe, in good health, if a little battered. Although I doubt he will be fit to show his face in polite society for some little time.'

'There, Penelope, it is just as we told you.' Juliet reached across to clasp her hand in comfort. 'There was no need to be so distressed.'

'I do not think Miss Vowchurch deserves your sympathy, Juliet. In fact, she deserves our condemnation, is that not so?'

'I do not know what you are implying.' Penelope suddenly rose to her feet, her pretty hands fluttering in agitation before she deliberately clasped them, to hide her nerves.

'I am afraid that Charles has been more than a little out-spoken. I went to see you before coming here, but it looks like our discussion must be had in public. He did not wish to take all the blame for the violence against my wife on himself, you see. I believe, surprising as it might seem, there was an understanding between you.'

'It is a lie. I have no connection with Charles Hanwell.'

She remained composed, but found it impossible to raise her eyes.

'I am afraid, Miss Vowchurch, that Charles made certain allegations.' The Marquis watched her intently. 'They were spoken in public and will become items of speculation.'

'No.' A faint trace of panic was now discernible in that one word.

'It would suit your plans very well if I were free to marry again, wouldn't it? And Frances stood in the way. But it would definitely *not* be to your advantage for me to die in a duel. Charles was not the most reliable of accomplices, was he? His interests were not quite as specific as yours. He was quite prepared to see both myself and my wife dead, rather than Frances alone, if it meant that he would inherit enough money to restore the fortunes of the Hanwell family.'

'I do not understand you.' Penelope's face drained of all colour as she faced the truth. 'I love you—have always loved you. And yet you have destroyed all my hopes and dreams— you have destroyed my life!'

'No.' Aldeborough's voice was cold, but perhaps not without a touch of compassion. 'You have destroyed your own. By pinning your hopes on something that could never be. And allowing yourself to be drawn into a callous plot of greed and hypocrisy.'

'No!' Penelope turned on Aldeborough a face now ravaged by tears and anger. 'It was *your* fault. You should have told me that you would not marry me. Instead you said nothing, letting me go on hoping that time would heal your sorrow and that you would find me an acceptable wife.'

Aldeborough's whole body stiffened as he drew in an uneven breath. 'Yes,' he admitted quietly, accepting the accusation, 'some of the blame is mine. I allowed Richard's death to touch me too closely.' Every word was wrung out of him. 'If I had not felt the guilt of his accident, if I had not closed my heart and mind to his death, I would have been more open with you. And because of that I did you, and Frances, greater harm than I could ever have realised. But nothing can excuse your desire to hurt Frances.'

Miss Vowchurch looked round the circle of faces, registering anger, pity, disbelief, disgust. Without a word she turned on her heel and, with what dignity she could muster, walked to the door. There she halted, turning back to look at Aldeborough, stretching out one hand in hopeless supplication. 'I would have loved you. I would have been a good wife to you.' She left the silent room, her footsteps receding into the hall.

Aunt May rose to her feet as if intending to go after her.

'No.' Aldeborough put out a hand to stop her. 'Let her go. She has failed and it is over now.'

'Very well. If that is your wish.' Instead, she walked over to her nephew's rigid figure to place a comforting hand on his arm. 'Now, all you have to do is find Frances and convince her to return. It may not be an easy task, my boy, if she thought you went to Penelope first.'

'Do you think I do not know that?'

Chapter Fifteen

The newly lit fire in the private parlour of the White Hart in Hitchin, although still more smoke than flame, was beginning to develop a comforting glow and warm the room, but Frances was too restless to sit and appreciate its soothing presence. Exhaustion made her light headed, but nervous energy kept her on the move, prowling from chair to settle, window seat to fireplace. She could not contemplate sleep and she had done no justice to the meal, the remains of which still littered the table.

She had not wished to halt her journey but had bowed to the dictates of common sense. Benson, Aldeborough's coachman of many years standing and thus a man of authority in his lordship's household, had assured her in bald terms that the horses needed a rest, even if her ladyship didn't, and that they should put up at the White Hart where they would be sure of good food and accommodation. Some inns were definitely not clean or respectable. And Aldeborough would dismiss him on the spot, Benson thought privately, if he allowed any harm to come to her ladyship. Some rum goings-on amongst the Quality, travelling alone with only a slip of a maid! But it was his job to look after the Marchioness, especially when her husband was unaware of her intentions, so look after her he would!

By reason of her title, and the fact that the Marquis was

well known to them from previous visits, Frances had been provided with a comfortable parlour and separate bedchamber with a smaller room for her maid. But her tired mind could not rest. It was imperative that she see her uncle. She must bring a halt to the series of events that threatened Aldeborough. And if she must sacrifice her inheritance, then so be it. Relief flooded through her as she remembered that at least Aldeborough was alive after the duel which he had been forced into. She could not contemplate the alternative. He had escaped the duel unharmed, but in the hours of enforced idleness in the coach, when her thoughts turned again and again to the same anxieties, she found that her relief was short-lived, to be replaced by despair that brought tears to gather on her lashes and spill down her cheeks. He must love Penelope Vowchurch so very much to go to her straight from the duel. It was more important to him to tell her of his safety and relieve her anxieties than to inform his wife. And Penelope had been so distraught. Frances was forced to conclude that she had entirely misread that lady's cold reserve. But she could not bear to remain in Cavendish Square to witness their reunion and happiness together. It was far better for everyone if she retire to the Priory and so allow Aldeborough some freedom. Her decision gave her no pleasure but it had to be done. But first she must undo the complications brought about by her marriage.

The White Hart was noisy with so much coming and going of carriages outside her window that Frances doubted if she would sleep at all. There were raised voices and footsteps echoing in the corridors as newly arrived travellers were shown to their rooms. Suddenly, her door was flung open.

'I'm sorry.' She turned towards the door. 'This is a private parlour—' The words died on her lips.

On the threshold stood Aldeborough.

'Good evening, my lord,' she managed for the benefit of the landlord who had ushered his new guest into the room and still hovered in the doorway. Her voice trembled with nerves, but she faced her husband bravely.

He said nothing, merely advanced into the room. He

stripped off his gloves and greatcoat and cast them on to a chair with barely confined fury. His eyes glinted with temper. Frances found herself taking refuge behind a high-backed chair at the head of the table, gripping the wood with fingers that were white to the bone. She had not expected him to follow her. Or at least, not so rapidly.

'Do you wish for some refreshment? Something to eat? I'm sure—'

He closed the door firmly on the speculative gaze of the landlord and turned to face her.

'No. I do not want anything to eat or drink. What I want, Madame Wife, is to know exactly what you think you are doing.'

'I am going to the Priory.'

'I realise that. But, in God's name, why? And without a word to anyone.'

'I told Matthew.'

'So I should be thankful for small mercies.' His tone was bitterly sarcastic, overlying the banked anger. 'But you didn't tell me!'

'I did not want to disturb you.'

'Disturb?' If she had meant to ignite the flames she had certainly succeeded. He took a few hasty paces around the room and came to rest, head bent, hands spread on the scarred oak of the table before him, flinching as he inadvertently exerted too much pressure on his wounded arm.

'I have just spent one of the worst twenty-four hours in my existence. I have fought a duel with your misbegotten cousin Charles, when against my better judgement I did *not* kill him. I arrive home to be informed by my mother that you have left me, without a word, taking my travelling coach, horses and Benson as well. You can imagine how much my mother enjoyed breaking the bad news! I have had to explain to her that—never mind, I'll not go into that. I have had to suffer Matthew driving me in my curricle for the best part of five hours, so I am covered with dust and my shoulder hurts like the devil.' He paused, but only to draw breath.

'There was no reason that I can see for you to follow me!' Frances interrupted when she could.

'Of course not! It would have been quite acceptable for me to allow my wife to drive around the country on her own. I have been out of my mind with worry the whole journey. And then, instead of finding you dead in a ditch, here you are, comfortably ensconced at the White Hart! At least Benson had the sense to put up here, otherwise I would be searching the whole country for you. No, my dear wife, of course I am not disturbed.'

'Well, there's no need to shout at me.'

'I am not shouting. I am being most calm and reasonable in the circumstances. It's worse than campaigning in the Peninsula. At least I did not have a wife to worry about there. The minute my back is turned you are involved in some harebrained scheme. You deserve that I should wring your neck.' He took another deep breath and glared at her. 'And don't stand there behind that chair as if I were going to thrash you. I cannot bear it.'

'That's not fair!'

'I don't feel fair!'

The door behind Aldeborough opened to admit Matthew, similarly covered with dust and unaware of the rapidly gathering storm.

'I have told the ostlers—'

'Go away, Matthew.'

'Consider me gone.' He retreated, a searching glance at Aldeborough's face and a flicker of compassion towards Frances. The Marquis locked the door behind him.

'Now tell me, Frances—what was so urgent that you needed to run off to the Priory at a moment's notice? And I would be grateful if you told me the truth.' He flung himself into one of the chairs before the fire, one booted foot resting on the fender. For the first time Frances could see the underlying fatigue and the lines of strain around his mouth. Her heart went out to him. She longed to put her arms around him and stroke away the tension. But this was not the time and she kept her distance, stoking her anger against him for her own protection.

'Very well. You won't like it, but I could think of nothing else and I won't change my mind. No matter what you say. Or do. I had to see my uncle. And it seemed to me that I could not wait if I was to ensure that your life was safe.'

His head snapped up, his eyes suddenly keen, impaling her on a fierce stare. He realised that she looked as tired and strained as he felt. And there was another emotion shading her eyes which he could not guess at. She held his stare with her own level gaze.

'My uncle blamed you for robbing him of my money,' she continued in a perfectly calm voice. 'You know that. You wouldn't discuss the highwaymen with me, but it was not robbery. It was to be cold-blooded murder. If you were dead, my uncle would be able to regain control of me and the inheritance. He would arrange the marriage with Charles which he had always anticipated.

'The plan did not succeed. Perhaps he thought it too dangerous to try murder again. So he tried blackmail instead. Charles kidnapped me to hold me to ransom. And you would have had to pay dearly for my release. Whatever the method, my uncle would get his money.'

'Did Charles tell you that?'

'Yes—well, he did not deny it when I accused him of blackmail. But that didn't work either. So what's next? What's to stop him trying again? He forced you into a duel where you might have been shot. I cannot live my life in constant fear that you will be killed or injured. I could not bear it if you were dead. So I thought if I went to see my uncle and offered him the money he so desires, then you would be safe. My inheritance is not worth your life,' she finished simply. 'That is why I left.'

It was all suddenly very clear. Aldeborough rubbed his hands over his face, the anger ebbing from his body, leaving him cold and empty. She had worked it all out. And been prepared to make a magnificent gesture. It was difficult to accept the glory of it. But the premise was wrong.

He rose to his feet, strode to the sideboard and poured two glasses of brandy. One of them he passed to Frances, relieved that, although she eyed him warily, she did not flinch. He tossed back the brandy and studied the empty glass for a moment.

'Frances,' he said, his voice low and controlled, his face expressionless, 'you humble me. Are you really saying that you would hand over your mother's inheritance to your uncle? How can I be worth such a sacrifice?'

'I will do it. You cannot stop me.'

'You are a lady of great resolution and I admire you more than you can ever imagine—but I have a confession to make.'

'Oh, Hugh. I know!' She put out a hand impulsively as if to touch his sleeve, but then drew it back to cover her lips. 'Indeed, it does not matter.' Tears began to slip slowly down her cheeks. It came to him that he had never seen her cry before, not once since the night that she had put her hand in his and trusted him with her life.

'You know? But how? Did Aunt May tell you?'

She shook her head. 'Matthew. When he came back to Cavendish Square from the duel.'

'But Matthew does not know!'

She brushed away her tears. 'He told me that you had gone straight to her from the duel. But she was in Cavendish Square all the time. She does love you, Hugh. Truly. She was in such distress and wanted to know what we could do to stop the duel. It was always meant that she should be your bride and she wants you. If you divorce me, then you can marry her and you can be happy. I do understand.' Tears fell more quickly and she could not stop them.

He took a deep breath. 'Oh, God! This is a mess, Frances.'

'I know.'

'No. You don't. Where the devil do I start to unravel it?' He looked at her. His heart broke as she valiantly fought to conquer her tears. 'Come here.'

'No,' she whispered and stepped back.

'Then I must come to you. I feel a need to kiss you.'

'I had rather you didn't.'

'I thought you liked me to kiss you.'

'Yes. I do. But it will make things worse, not better.'

'Very well. But I will not promise for ever.' Ignoring her reluctance, he took her hand and pulled her to the chair that he had just vacated.

'Sit there and listen. It seems I have a lot of explaining to do.'

'You don't have to—'

He framed her face with his hands and kissed her forcefully on the mouth to silence her. It had the desired effect. Frances closed her eyes to try to conquer the longing that surged within her. If only he could love her as he did Penelope. If only…

'Now listen—' his smile lit the fires in her blood that she had tried so hard to quench '—you were right to think that Torrington blamed me. And the highwaymen were paid to kill me and release you from the marriage. But things changed. What you did not realise was that *you* became the target for your uncle's plans rather than me. Perhaps he thought that you would be an easier objective.'

'Me? But why? How could my death have been of any value?' She shuddered. 'I cannot believe that we are discussing this in cold blood, that my uncle could actually have a hand in my death.'

Aldeborough took the other chair opposite to Frances, leaning forward to study his clasped hands. His face was grave as he contemplated the pain he must cause her, against all his instincts, and the destruction of any lingering belief she might have retained in her family. Finally he looked up and committed himself.

'Hedges did not tell you all the clauses in your mother's will. I asked him not to. It may have been wrong of me, but my only excuse is that I wished to spare you any further fear or anxiety. I thought I could safeguard you and preserve your peace of mind. You once told me that it was the one good thing that had come out of our marriage. I would not wilfully choose to destroy it.' He smiled wryly.

'Your inheritance stands, as you are aware. But it is dependent on one eventuality. If you die or fail to have children before the age of twenty-five, then the money will revert to the care of your father—and hence, in this case, to Viscount Torrington, your legal guardian on your father's death.'

Frances stared at him, eyebrows raised as her mind quickly assimilated the facts. 'So it would be to my uncle's advantage if *either* of us were dead.'

'Yes. If I am dead, you are free. If you die…well… But I have to be fair, Frances. I think your uncle would not oppose the scheming, but I don't think he was behind it at any stage.'

'Charles?'

'If he could not have you in marriage, then…I'm sure you see. I'm sorry. Did you like him very much, Frances?'

'No… Yes! It is simply that he is my cousin, you understand. He was the only one who ever showed me any passing kindness at Torrington Hall. I must have been very gullible.'

'Or very lonely.'

'Perhaps.' She thought for a moment. 'So the highwaymen? Was that to kill you or me?'

'Oh, I think you were right to begin with. That was to remove me from the scene. But Charles's attempted kidnap—that was not to be blackmail, Frances. He did not intend to ever release you. I think you would have conveniently disappeared and your body found in one of the seamier streets of London—it would be easy enough to achieve and blame it on a common thief.'

'I cannot believe that he could be guilty of something as terrible as that. Do such things really happen?'

'I am afraid so. And there's something else I should tell you.'

'So many secrets.' She sighed.

'The accident at the Priory when Beeswing fell—it wasn't the bridge. The mare's wound was caused by a pistol shot. Selby had his suspicions and Kington found the bullet buried in the wooden balustrade. I have no proof that Charles was behind it, but I have no doubts.'

'Charles? Charles tried to kill me?'

He did not need to answer. She was silent as she weighed his words.

'I see. Why did you not tell me all of this?

'You had spent your life in fear of your family. I know that the scars on your back are a testament to it. As my wife, at least you seemed happier, less haunted. How could I inflict such fear on you again?'

Frances could find no words. The facts were so clear, the implications so obvious. And he had tried to shield her—out of kindness, out of compassion. She should be grateful, but her heart cried out for more from him than he could give. She stared unseeingly at the brandy still clasped in her hands, determined to stay calm, to respond to him with composure. He deserved that much from her at least.

'Does the threat still exist?' she asked. 'Will Charles still scheme and plan until he has achieved his ends?'

'No. I believe not. Charles was distressingly outspoken after the duel,' Aldeborough explained with wry humour. 'He condemned himself with his own words, and unwisely, with a little prompting from me, before witnesses. I think it unlikely that we will see Charles in London again—he will have become *persona non grata*, if I know the grapevine round the clubs. With Masters as his second, nothing will be sacred! If there is any suggestion of harm to either of us in the future, he will be declared guilty out of hand! You can put your mind at rest.'

'Did you wound him? I could almost wish you had.'

'No. I deliberately fired to miss. But he damned well hit me—I didn't think he had the skill. Now, don't fuss!' He put out his hand as Frances sprang to her feet, spilling brandy heedlessly on to the flounces of her gown, a look of horror on her face.

'But Matthew said you were unharmed. I didn't know. Let me look.'

'There is no need. A flesh wound—nothing to be concerned about. Matthew's driving over the ruts of the Great North Road caused me far more damage.' He took hold of her hands and removed the brandy glass, putting it out of harm's way. He looked down into her eyes, dark with swirling emotions, holding them captive. 'Before I left Cavendish Square, Aunt May gave me some advice, which for once I agree with. She spoke the truth.'

He began to slide his hands up her arms, to pull her close, unable to resist her soft lips, the sadness and hurt in her eyes. His anger had completely dissipated. All he wished to do was comfort and soothe, to hold her close. But she pulled back, resisting the clasp of his fingers.

'Please don't.'

'My God, Frances. I didn't think that you found me so distasteful!'

'Distasteful?' She laughed bitterly. 'I love you. I love you and I envy Penelope from the bottom of my heart.' She stopped, aghast at what she had said. 'Forgive me. It was not my intention to burden you with that. If you could forget I ever said it—'

'Penelope!'

'Yes. So, you see, it is easier for me if you don't touch me just yet. Until I can accept things with more equanimity.'

'Well, it's not easier for me, so you will have to forgive my selfishness.' He tightened his grasp and pulled her forcefully into his arms. 'Just rest there a moment. Don't fight it. You cannot imagine how long I have waited to hear you say that you love me.' Frances found she had no choice but to obey. She stood within his embrace, letting him hold her, his cheek resting against her hair. Oh, how she wanted to remain like this forever. She did not have the strength to pull away. Silence fell around them, enfolding them, shutting out the world. But she knew that it was impossible.

Eventually he released his embrace, but only to take hold of her hands and hold them firmly against his chest.

'Do you feel that, Frances Rosalind? My heart beats for you. It took me a long time, far too long, to realise it.' He smiled ruefully. 'I love you. I do not love Penelope. I do not wish to marry her. I refuse to divorce you, I refuse to allow you to escape from me to the Priory, or any other of the mad schemes you might be contemplating. Chance gave you to me and you are mine, body and soul, and I will not let you go. I told you that I would never permit you to escape once before, but that was merely pride and arrogance. Now it is different. I love you. You have turned my life upside down and I would not have it any other way. Now, what do you have to say?'

She found herself unable to say anything. With a groan he bent his head and captured her mouth with his own. His lips were gentle, persuasive but with a hint of possession and she melted into his embrace, her doubts overcome by those few words. *I love you.* And by the promises made by the caress of his lips and his hands.

At some point, still touching, they moved to the cushioned settle by the fire where she remained within the protection of his encircling arms. He found he was reluctant to let her go.

'Why did you not tell me this before?' Her head rested comfortably on his shoulder, her hands still clasped in his.

'I did.'

'Never. I would hardly forget it.'

'You fell asleep in my arms,' he said. 'I knew you would not remember.'

'But why did you need to go straight from the duel to Penelope? If you don't love her, why did you need to go there? And you must know that she loves you.'

'No. She wants marriage. Status. Wealth. She had always expected to be Marchioness of Aldeborough. With Richard gone, she saw me as the next step to fulfilling her ambition. And I was too preoccupied to make it clear to her that it never was a possibility. I went to see her because of something Charles said when I had…after the duel. He was not alone in his plans, it seems.'

'Never Penelope!'

'Think about it, Frances. Who would see an advantage in your death other than Charles? I would be free to marry again. Hers was not the initiative, although she certainly encouraged Charles. But it was not in her plan to have me killed or shot in a duel. That is why she was so distressed when she came to Cavendish Square to try to prevent us meeting.'

Her face paled. 'To be hated so much.'

'No. You simply stood in the way of her ambition. She wanted Richard—she wanted me. I don't think she hates you any more than she loves me.'

'And I thought you loved her. I know you sometimes want me and you have always shown me kindness but you have never pretended that you loved me. Penelope always seemed so suitable.'

'She is not the wife I would choose. Yes, she is beautiful and sophisticated. Her education is excellent.' He grinned. 'But what would I talk to her about? How I will improve the estate? Horse breeding? We would bore each other to death in a day. Can you see her talking to Kington about roof repairs? In fact, I doubt that she would even consent to live at the Priory.

'But that is not the main thing. I promised that I would give you the protection of my name because it was necessary after I had become the means of your escape from Torrington Hall.' The light from the candles cast shadows on his face, which made him suddenly look unbearably weary. 'But instead of protection I brought you danger and the threat of death and a degree of unhappiness that caused you to flee from me. I was thoughtless and inconsiderate. I did not intend my marriage to change my life in any way—you would give me an heir and that is all I would expect or ask from you.' His face was stern and he forgot to drawl. 'I hope you can forgive me. I also promised that I would allow you the freedom to live your own life. Will that be enough for you? You say that you love me, but are you sure? I seem to have little to recommend me.' He ran his fingers through his hair, in his habitual gesture when under stress, wincing at his inadvertent use of his right arm, and waited impatiently for her reply.

He was amazed to see her lips begin to curve into a smile of pure pleasure and delight and raised his eyebrows in query.

'You are far too honourable, my lord. I am used to a more demanding, possessive husband! I think Aunt May would say that the duel has addled your wits as well as putting a bullet through your arm!'

'What are you saying?'

'I know why you offered to marry me, you did not trick me. I know that it was a marriage of utmost convenience for both of us. But you have shown me care and compassion when my mind refused to accept that any man was capable of that.'

She took a step forward and stood before him, reaching up to kiss him on his stern, unsmiling mouth.

'I love you, Hugh. I need you. I don't want freedom. I don't want to go my own way. I am yours and want nothing more than that. Touch me,' she pleaded. 'Make me believe that the dangers are over and that we can be together.'

His hands moved to her shoulders, still holding her away from him so that he could search her face.

'I want you as my wife, Frances, in every way a man can want a woman. Will you let me show you how much I love you? I very much want to make love to you.'

They still stood, separated by space and the tide of events that had finally swept them to this moment, this time for decisions. Their eyes spoke of all the doubts, uncertainties and pain of the past. Then Frances, on a little laugh, forced the issue by taking the final step to lift her arms around his neck and press her body against his. With a groan he wrapped his arms around her, holding her as if he would never release her, covering her mouth with his, first gently and then angling his head to deepen his kiss, making his thorough possession of her a reality. Her response was immediate and more than he could hope for, as he felt her slight frame shudder within his embrace. Her lips parted under his assault, enticing his tongue as it traced the outline of her lips, inviting it to plunder the soft depths.

At last he raised his head, but the two remained lost in the depths of each other's eyes, dark with intense desire, and the beat of their hearts, one against the other.

Chapter Sixteen

The sun was beginning to dip towards the horizon, casting a soft light over the stone-flagged terrace at the Priory where Frances was sitting. The golden stone of the old house glowed and gave off the subtle warmth that it had absorbed during the day. But it was still only early in May and she would soon have to retreat to the comfort of the library where she knew she would find a welcoming fire.

They had chosen to continue Frances's flight to the Priory, leaving Matthew to return to London, and had arrived the previous day, tired but with an indefinable sense of relief. On the journey Aldeborough had enfolded her in his love, assiduously attentive to her every need, reassuring her with the touch of a hand or the possessive arrogance in his eyes as they rested on her, but there was still a tension between them that troubled Frances. She could guess at the problem, but knew that he must work through it in his own way. So she remained silent and as well as her love she gave him the space he needed.

But she was not without hope because, on awakening that morning, she had found, awaiting her on her dressing table, a gift. A delicate miniature of a golden rose, painted on ivory, petals gleaming softly, new leaves sweetly curled. Created by the hand of an expert, without doubt. Beside it was a rosebud—a miracle that he had found one so early in the year—

newly picked with the dew still damp, its cream petals just beginning to unfurl. And beneath the floral offerings was a folded sheet of paper.

Frances flushed with pleasure at the memory. The miniature now stood in pride of place beside her bed, a permanent reminder of their homecoming to the Priory. The rose was pinned at her bosom where its petals glowed in the warmth of the sun. And the folded sheet... Well, she had carried it all day against her heart. She opened it, smoothed the creases with gentle fingers and felt her heart bound with absolute joy.

For he had written her a poem. A love poem, no less. Her eyes travelled over the words, deeply etched on the cream paper in Aldebrough's firm script, and now equally etched in Frances's own heart.

> Take thou this rose, O Rose,
> Since Love's own flower it is,
> And by that fragile rose
> Thy Lover captive is.
> Look on this rose, O Rose,
> And looking, smile on me,
> For with thy laughter's ring
> Thy slave I'll gladly be.
> Smell thou this rose, O Rose
> And know thyself as sweet,
> Your perfume holds me vassal,
> Adoring at thy feet.
> O Rose, this painted rose
> Draws not the complete whole.
> For he who paints the flower
> Paints not its fragrant soul.

The whole, as she read again the final line, was dedicated *To Frances Rosalind: My Own Incomparable Rose*.

She pressed her lips to the paper as she refolded it and tucked it away. How could he have known? How could he have chosen such tender words that would soothe her heart and yet cause it to ache with love?

She sighed a little and turned her mind back to the prospect of restocking one of the flower beds with spring bulbs for the following year, until her attention became concentrated on a grey kitten, attempting unsuccessfully to deter it from pouncing on the fringe of the Kashmir shawl draped around her shoulders. She laughed and picked up the ball of fur and claw as it changed its attack to the end of her blue satin sash. But she looked up immediately as she heard footsteps on the gravel path from the sunken garden.

Aldeborough, casual in shirt sleeves, followed by two energetic gun dogs, strode up the steps at the end of the terrace. The low sun behind him cast his features in shadow and outlined his body with a rim of gold. She watched him as he stopped to lean over the balustrade to exchange some final word with Kington, who laughed and raised a hand in acknowledgement of some comment. The Marquis looked windswept and dishevelled from an afternoon spent in the stables; his handsome face and graceful long-limbed body, which she now knew so well, still had the power to make her catch her breath. Her heart jolted a little as he turned his head to look at her, before it resumed its steady beat. He approached and stood before her, his expression enigmatic, his thoughts quite unreadable. Nor did his first words give her any indication. But she noted the frown between his brows and a flash of some intense longing in his eyes before he banished it and smiled down at her and her companion.

'Hugh. Come and sit with me,' she invited.

'What's this?' He sat beside her on the stone bench and lifted the kitten from her lap. It broke into a miniature purr as his fingers found the sensitive spot between its ears.

'A present. I went to the stables to see Beeswing and Selby presented me with this, I think to get rid of it from under his feet. It has very lively tendencies!'

'I can see that your sash has suffered. What will you do with it?' He fended off one of the inquisitive dogs with a booted foot.

'Keep it, of course. It might be a good mouser and I think the kitchens could do with one.'

'Only if the mice are very small.' He placed the kitten on the seat between them where it instantly curled up and fell asleep in the manner of small animals.

In spite of the humour, his dark brows drew together again in frowning contemplation and his mouth was stern. She made a decision, already half-formed, and took a deep breath.

'Hugh—tell me what troubles you.'

'Why, nothing. What could there be?' But his answer was a shade too casual and he did not look at her.

'He is still here, is that not true? He still stands between us.'

Now Aldeborough turned his head to meet her eyes for a long moment. She saw there uncertainty and an element of difficult grief. It pleased her that he did not pretend to misunderstand her.

Abruptly he stood up. 'Come and walk with me.'

He drew her to his side, her hand tucked through his arm as if to reassure himself of her presence, and led her along the terrace, through the old arches and pillars of the ruined priory to the iron gate that allowed them private access to the churchyard, to the church where she had been married when she knew so little of this man at her side. Long shadows were already being cast across the soft grass and a chill breeze began to stir her hair and rustle the new leaves on the beech trees. Frances shivered, whether with cold or tension she was unsure, and pulled her shawl more firmly round her shoulders. They walked in silence, since she knew exactly where he was leading her, only stopping when they reached the cluster of gravestones marking the earthly remains of past Laffords.

For the most part grey and weather worn, covered with moss and lichen, the words of love and loss indecipherable, they occupied the area of the old monastic graveyard enclosed by ancient walls, shaded by mature oaks and yew. Aldeborough's father and grandparents, generations of them back into the dimness of history when the house was first conceived. But Aldeborough drew her to a halt beside a new gravestone, startlingly unworn, the name and appropriate wording fresh and deeply incised.

Richard.

Richard, the brave, the carefree and heedless. The laughing, adventurous companion of childhood. And, unless she could achieve a miracle, Richard the divider, the destroyer.

Frances deliberately moved from her husband's side to stand opposite, the well-tended green mound of Richard's grave between them, a symbol of division.

'You have to end it, Hugh. You must lay his ghost or it will eat away at you—and us.'

'I know. I accept that.' It was as if he had been waiting for this moment, to unburden his bitter legacy to someone who would accept and not judge too harshly. He rested his hand on the stone. 'I accepted the guilt of his death because it seemed wrong, such a terrible waste, that someone so full of life as Richard should die so wantonly. How could he possibly die because of a chance accident? There had to be some blame—and there was no one other to shoulder it. And because the responsibilities came with the guilt, I made the inheritance of the title and the estate into a burden it should never have been. I resented having to give up my own life, one I loved, one I had chosen against opposition from my father, to take on a lifestyle that should never have been mine.' He hesitated before continuing in a flat tone, 'I was embittered and angry—and I allowed my anger to do more harm than you know.'

'Drinking and gaming? Letitia Winters?'

He grimaced, acknowledging the truth. 'Among other things.'

'Then tell me,' she stated calmly, 'so that there will be no more secrets between us.'

His body was tense. She saw anger there still and bitter self-mockery and wanted nothing more than to move towards him to take him into her arms to reassure him of her love, but he needed the catharsis of facing Richard and the repercussions of his brother's death. His voice was low but steady and his eyes never left hers, both a plea for understanding and a challenge.

'The drinking and the gaming you are well aware of—who should know better? And Letitia.' He sighed. 'She gave me comfort at a time when I allowed myself to become deluged in self-pity and hatred. I was not a heroic figure. I took you to the Priory that night because I was too drunk to consider your plight. I should not have allowed your honour to be compromised as I did. I married you for my own advantage— because I felt some pride in my family name and had no wish to drag it through public scandal. I neglected you, I left you without protection, knowing that you might be in danger, giving Charles the opportunity to abduct you—if he had murdered you your blood would have been on my hands as much as Richard's because I knew you were vulnerable. But I did not take enough care with you. I went to Newmarket, God help me, and left you alone in London. And I should have ended the situation between me and Penelope from the beginning, instead of ignoring it in the belief that it was not important. It was selfish in the extreme and it encouraged Penelope to believe that her position as my wife was desirable and attainable, regardless of the means. Whatever you might say, whatever arguments I might make for my actions or lack of them, I put your life in danger. I deserve your condemnation, Frances. Certainly not your love.'

She bowed her head, hands clasped tightly, to study the intricate carvings before her and the words that committed Richard to God's saving grace.

'Very well. I accept what you say. But I believe that I must redress the balance. You say that you neglected me. I do not see it like that. You gave me a family, status, wealth, luxury—you might take that for granted, but I cannot for I had none of it. You did not have to marry me. What was I? A nobody, hardly worthy of your consideration. You could have sent me back to my uncle with an explanation of my foolishness and a word of apology and all would have been smoothed over. I had no reputation to lose and yet you chose to reinstate me in the eyes of the world. How should I not love you? You showed me compassion and gave me back my self-respect. I will never forget the night you touched my scars with such tenderness and pressed your lips to them as if they were symbols of beauty, not of degradation. You removed the ugliness and the shame that I carried with me when I could not bear that anyone should know. I think that was the moment I fell in love with you.'

'I remember. I remember the fear in your eyes. It will live with me forever.'

'Yes. You say that you could have protected me from Charles. You knew that he was driven by greed and despair—Penelope too. You cannot take the blame for that. How could you possibly have foreseen the outcome of your marriage to me? There are too many complicated strands woven together to be separated and I do not see that you are answerable for my cousin's sins.'

'You are too generous, Frances.' His lips were still compressed into a firm line.

'I am realistic. Hugh, I love you but I can not—will not—live my life with Richard standing between us. Do you really think he would have wanted that?'

'No.' His eyes fell to the stone beneath his hand. 'I am certain that he would have been the first to damn me for a fool.'

'Well, then.' She let the silence stretch between them again. She knew he had to come to his own salvation.

'I know what the remedy is.' He turned from her to look out over the rolling parkland and woods to where the village was half-hidden by a fold in the hillside. 'It is here. The estate. The money is available. It simply needs time and interest and investment. My father and Richard…well, they did not see it as a way of life, rather a method of financing a town house in London and a hunting lodge in Leicestershire. I would try to make improvements here. I would breed horses. You have seen for yourself how much needs to be done and how much can be achieved. I have come to realise that this is a project that needs my time and can bring me satisfaction—perhaps it is in my blood after all. And now I have the added responsibility of a wife to consider.' He turned back to look at her, demanding her honesty. 'Would you be willing to accept life here rather than in London?'

'What? No London Season?' There was mischief in the curve of her lips. 'That was the only reason I would consent to marry you!'

'I think we might stretch a point there.' His face remained grave, but she sensed a lightening of the atmosphere and saw an answering gleam in his eye.

She did not answer at once. And then, 'Would you be willing to accept life here rather than in the Army—and be content?'

For the first time since they entered the churchyard, a shadow of a smile touched his face. 'You are very astute. Yes, I can. Perhaps I should give in to overwhelming pressure and let Matthew go—if only to keep him out of Pall Mall gaming hells.'

She smiled in recognition of the gesture, but remained where she stood, still separated from him. She held her breath. Matthew's future might be settled, but hers was still in the balance.

She did not have to wait long. He held out his hand, the old dominance evident in his commanding gesture and fierce gaze, and she was compelled to put her own into it.

'Well, Madam Wife?'

'I will live here with you. The place touches my heart, from the night you first brought me here. Make it work, Hugh. Remove the neglect and make it live again.'

It was what he had been waiting to hear and he realised with a warmth that spread through his whole body that she had pushed him to make the commitment. He raised their clasped hands to his lips, kissing her fingers in a silent promise. The lingering peace and serenity of the long-dead Augustinians settled round them in benediction as he stepped across the grave to take her in his arms.

'I have been thinking.' As they retraced their steps towards the house, he drew her to a halt in the shelter of a richly carved doorway to place his hands on her shoulders and turn her towards him. When she looked at him quizzically, he bent his head to kiss her hair, her eyes and then pressed his lips to the palm of her hand with utmost tenderness before folding her fingers over to seal the caress.

'That was very nice, Hugh.' Her eyes sparkled with a sudden hint of mischief. 'Tell me, my love. Will you write more poems for me?'

'Ah. Well…only if you insist.' He grinned, bending his head to touch his lips to the rose at her breast. 'I have a confession to make, Frances Rosalind.'

'Really, my lord?' She was charmed by the unexpected touch of colour that softened his cheekbones. 'And what could that be?'

'I had a little help. From a medieval troubadour who just happened to cross my path… But his sentiments towards his lady are mine, and the words that he expressed mirror the thoughts in my heart.'

'Then I forgive you. How could I not?'

Their eyes met and held for a long moment in complete understanding, in a bond as potent as shimmering steel.

'And now, my lady, as I was saying before you so sadly interrupted, I have been thinking about your inheritance. If you remember, it is dependent on one eventuality.'

'And that is?' She smiled because his train of thought was as clear and glittering as faceted crystal.

'You have four years in which to carry my child. Otherwise the money goes into the pockets of your uncle.'

'Four years? Such a short time.' Her smile was a delight to him. 'You will have to persuade me.'

'I want you to carry my heir, my son,' he said fiercely, startling her with the intensity in his voice and the insistent pressure of his fingers on her shoulders. 'That is the only reason I married you, after all.' The expression in his eyes heated her blood and she read desire in their depths.

'That is not very persuasive. I think you can do better, my lord. Besides, I want a daughter to whom I can leave all my money. We now have a family tradition, you realise.'

'I knew you would be difficult, my lady.' His kiss was hot and possessive, leaving her in no doubt of his intentions. Her heart leapt in unity and her response was immediate.

'Well, then.'

He linked his fingers with hers and pulled her once more into his arms, to turn his face into her hair. This love was still too new, too bright for him to take for granted. A wave of sheer disbelief swept over him, that she could love him, that he could love her with such certainty. She saw it as she stepped back and rubbed at the crease between his brows with gentle fingers, as he often did with her.

'My love. My soul. I adore you. Do you love me, Frances Rosalind?'

'Yes,' she sighed with magnificent understatement.

'Tell me again so that I may believe it.'

'I love you. I give you my body, my heart and my soul freely and without condition. That is your inheritance.'

He touched her forehead with his lips, gently, almost reverently, in recognition of her gift.

* * * * *

Introducing...

nocturne

**a spine-tingling new line
from Silhouette Books.**

**These paranormal romances will
seduce you with dark, passionate tales
that stretch the boundaries of conflict,
desire, and life and death, weaving
a tapestry of sensual thrills and chills!**

Don't miss the first book...

UNFORGIVEN

by *USA TODAY* bestselling author

LINDSAY
McKENNA

*Launching October 2006,
wherever books are sold.*

**Introducing an exciting appearance
by legendary
New York Times bestselling author**

DIANA PALMER
HEARTBREAKER

He's the ultimate bachelor…
but he may have just met
the one woman to change his ways!

Join the drama in the story of a confirmed
bachelor, an amnesiac beauty and their
unexpected passionate romance.

**"Diana Palmer is a mesmerizing storyteller
who captures the essence of what
a romance should be."** —*Affaire de Coeur*

**Heartbreaker *is available from Silhouette Desire
in September 2006.***

eHARLEQUIN.com

The Ultimate Destination for Women's Fiction

Visit eHarlequin.com's Bookstore today for today's most popular books at great prices.

- An extensive selection of romance books by top authors!

- Choose our convenient "bill me" option. No credit card required.

- New releases, Themed Collections and hard-to-find backlist.

- A sneak peek at upcoming books.

- Check out book excerpts, book summaries and Reader Recommendations from other members and post your own too.

- Find out what everybody's reading in Bestsellers.

- Save BIG with everyday discounts and exclusive online offers!

- Our Category Legend will help you select reading that's exactly right for you!

- Visit our Bargain Outlet often for huge savings and special offers!

- Sweepstakes offers. Enter for your chance to win special prizes, autographed books and more.

Your purchases are 100% guaranteed—so shop online at www.eHarlequin.com today!

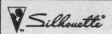